The Old Dominion
Or A Tale Of Virginia

by

G. P. R. James

The Old Dominion
Or A Tale Of Virginia
by G. P. R. James

ISBN: 978-93-65785-56-2

Published by

DOUBLE 9 BOOKS
2/13-B, Ansari Road
Daryaganj, New Delhi – 110002
info@double9books.com
www.double9books.com
Tel. 011-40042856

ABOUT THE AUTHOR

George Payne Rainsford James, a London-born novelist and historian, was born on August 9, 1799, and died on June 9, 1860. He served as the British Consul for a long time in a number of locations across the continent and in the United States. During the final years of William IV's reign, he was the honorary British Historiographer Royal. In 1799, George Payne Rainsford James was born in London's Hanover Square on St. George Street. His father was a doctor who had been in the navy and had fought alongside Benedict Arnold in the Battle of Groton Heights in America during the Revolutionary War. James went to the Putney school run by Reverend William Carmalt. He became passionate in learning new languages, such as Arabic, Persian, Greek, and Latin. When he was younger, he also studied medicine, but his preferences took him in a different way. His father, who had served in the navy himself, opposed his desire to enlist, which ultimately led to him being able to enlist in the army. James was injured in a minor battle after the Battle of Waterloo and remained in the army for a brief period of time during the Hundred Days as a lieutenant.

CONTENTS

INTRODUCTION

George Payne Rainsford James, Historiographer Royal to King William IV., was born in London in the first year of the nineteenth century, and died at Venice in 1860. His comparatively short life was exceptionally full and active. He was historian, politician and traveller, the reputed author of upwards of a hundred novels, the compiler and editor of nearly half as many volumes of letters, memoirs, and biographies, a poet and a pamphleteer, and, during the last ten years of his life, British Consul successively in Massachusetts, Norfolk (Virginia), and Venice. He was on terms of friendship with most of the eminent men of his day. Scott, on whose style he founded his own, encouraged him to persevere in his career as a novelist; Washington Irving admired him, and Walter Savage Landor composed an epitaph to his memory. He achieved the distinction of being twice burlesqued by Thackeray, and two columns are devoted to an account of him in the new "Dictionary of National Biography." Each generation follows its own gods, and G. P. R. James was, perhaps, too prolific an author to maintain the popularity which made him "in some ways the most successful novelist of his time." But his work bears selection and revival. It possesses the qualities of seriousness and interest; his best historical novels are faithful in setting and free in movement. His narrative is clear, his history conscientious, and his plots are well-conceived. English learning and literature are enriched by the work of this writer, who made vivid every epoch in the world's history by the charm of his romance.

Picking up a novel by the historical novelist G. P. R. James, with Virginia as subject and "The Old Dominion" for title, one inevitably expects a romance about Elizabethan adventures and noble savages, something after the manner of Fenimore Cooper, with an air of greater antiquity. What, then, is our surprise to find that the veteran romancer has given us a novel of recent history, with facetious sketches of Yankee oddities, a plot based on a legal *imbroglio*, and a painstaking study of that perennial problem, the negro question. "The Old Dominion" is, in fact, James's "American Notes" and "Martin Chuzzlewit," though the portraiture is altogether kindly, and the satire of the mildest kind. He has observed the life and manners of the country where he resided as British Consul with the same minute care as that which he lavishes on his historical studies. Without Dickens's virulent and entertaining comedy, the picture of life in Virginia in the thirties is probably far truer because of this scrupulous accuracy, and because of the moderation and patient endeavour to decide justly upon disputed points. Years before "Uncle Tom's Cabin," James gave the English public this thoughtful picture of slavery. He is not one-sided. He rather discloses at once the evils of slavery and the difficulties of emancipation in a purely imaginative way without pleading strongly for a remedy. He shows powerfully what a terrible retribution has been brought upon the land by those who introduced slavery. The negro's insane ferocity when freed from control, and the peril of a small white population at the mercy of a host of revolted slaves, are brought out in the history of the negro insurrection, which is traced from its origin in the preaching of McGrubber and the misguided brooding of Nat Turner, down to its repression. The hero and heroine and the love romance, with its profusion of obstacles to happiness, are the familiar ones, with a modern instead of a medi[ae]val environment. But the vivacity of the style is quite unusual. Mr. Byles is epigrammatic with his three distinctions between the North and the South. "In the South they fight duels whenever they can, have slaves for their servants, and grow tobacco and corn. In New England they never fight if they can help it, are slaves to their own servants, and make wooden clocks and wooden nutmegs." And our serious romancer even ventures on a broad joke quite frequently.

CHAPTER I

I wrote to you, my dear sister, from the pretty little town of Baltimore; and I hope you have received my letter. Although this so speedily follows it, my only motives for writing are, to occupy idle time, and to relieve your mind from apprehension regarding my safety during my passage through all the terrors of Chesapeake Bay: "that long and dreadful inlet," as you call it, "in which uncle Richard was shipwrecked twenty or thirty years ago." Believe me, all these dangers are imaginary. This Chesapeake Bay is a very calm, pleasant sheet of water, which may have its storms sometimes; but, sheltered from the full force of the ocean by what is called the eastern shore, has no terrors after passing the Atlantic. I have not even a single adventure to tell. Everything passed with provoking tranquillity; and I must needs eke out my letter by any little observations, borrowed from my journal, which I fancy may amuse you. I think I told you that I had engaged a passage to Norfolk in the schooner *Mary Anne*. I believe half the ships in the world are called "Mary Anne;" and, doubtless, it is a very safe sort of name. There is nothing to be said against it; and, indeed, my skipper assured me that he had never known a vessel of that name to be lost. However, if odours produce sympathies, the *Mary Anne* would soon find her way down amongst the fishes; for a more potent smell of herring never assailed my nose than when I entered the said vessel. I had not been on board previous to the hour of sailing, having taken my passage through our agent; and, certainly, I was somewhat disappointed at the accommodation presented, which had been previously depicted in very glowing colours, but proved somewhat cramped, and in no degree savoury. Always take a steam-boat when you can, my dear sister--for a short life and a merry one, is a good axiom at sea; and although steamers may rattle, and smoke, and shake, they generally carry you to your destination sooner, more pleasantly, and more safely too, than a sailing vessel. Well--we started from our wharf about half-past two o'clock on Tuesday afternoon; and I remained upon deck to take a last look at Baltimore, which I quitted with some regret. It is a smaller city than New York, but cleaner, neater, and, I should think, more healthy. Besides, I had met some very pleasant and kind people there; and civilities which would not affect one much in one's own country, touch one in a foreign land. When ties and old affections are left behind, courtesies and civilities are the best substitutes. The wind was quite favourable, the master assured me; and there was just enough of it to ripple the water, and make the ship go quietly on, without producing any rebellion of stomach or refractoriness of legs. I remained upon deck till it was quite dark, and more than one little star looked out with eager, twinkling eyes, as if it feared it should not have time enough to behold its own image in the waters before the sun rose and sent it to bed again. I then went below, and found the little cabin, round which our berths were placed, already tenanted by two gentlemen, who had never appeared upon the deck since I first reached it, and who were consuming time and brandy and water very nearly in silence. Whether they had been thus employed for the preceding six or seven hours, I know not; and how much of the spirit they had drunk it was impossible to discover, for they certainly were not tipsy, and the brandy itself was entombed in a vast bottle, called here a demijohn, so curiously concealed in wickerwork, that it is impossible for the keenest eyes to discover whether it is full or empty. Both were well dressed men, but very different in appearance from each other. I must venture upon some description, my dear sister, as our ideas of the Yankee race in England are very unlike the realities which we see before us in this country. I remember hearing a wealthy, respectable, foolish, ignorant woman, of a class such as frequently forces its way into society with us at home, deliberately ask an American, whom she knew to be such, whether all the natives of America were salmon-coloured. She had, doubtless, heard of red Indians; and, I suppose, with that brilliant confusion of ideas which trouble the brains of some ladies, had confounded our brethren on this side of the Atlantic, with the aborigines of the country. However, my two companions on the present occasion, though one was not of American or Anglo-Saxon race, had nothing of the Indian about them. One was a thin, spare, but well-formed man, about three and thirty years of age, who, from dress or appearance altogether, no one would have distinguished from an Englishman, had it not been for a certain jaunty, well satisfied, self-reliant air not altogether consistent with our staid and more sober character of thought. His face was by no means handsome, God knows. His eyes were somewhat protuberant, round, and sparkling; his nose was short, thickish, and a little tinged with red, which might have some affinity with the contents of the demijohn I have just mentioned. His upper lip was shaded by a thick, Austrian-cut moustache; his chin was prominent and decided; but his forehead was bold, high, and towering, and by far the finest feature of his face. The other seemed rather overdressed--certainly over dressed for a sea-voyage; but his face was actually much handsomer than that of his companion, and presented the peculiar character which marks, in almost every instance, Jewish descent; for he had large, almond shaped, dark eyes, an aquiline nose, a delicate mouth and chin, and a profusion of glossy black hair, floating in small, light curls about his head. His complexion was warm, but delicate; and, altogether, he was a very handsome man. But he wanted that air of Oriental calmness and dignity which you and I have often remarked in many members of his race. This I attribute greatly to the profession which I afterwards found he followed; the debasing tendencies of which I can conceive no man's spirit resisting. He had three diamond rings on one finger, and a large brilliant in the frill of his shirt; and, indeed, it seemed to me there was no part of his person on which he could stick such an ornament, that was not garnished by some precious stone. It was quite clear that no great cordiality existed between these two tenants of the cabin, although they were drinking out of the same demijohn, if not out of the same cup. As soon as I entered, the last-mentioned passenger asked me, in Virginian parlance, "to take a drink." I have learnt the habits of the country sufficiently to know that it is discourteous to refuse; and I was immediately provided with a tumbler and cold water, to which I added some of the brandy. When I had sipped a small quantity of the mixture, the first passenger I have mentioned broke out in a short, quick, merry laugh, and observed, in a quaint tone, that the skipper had failed to provide us with mint--a usual accessory to brandy and water in this country. With him I soon got into conversation, and found him a well read, liberally educated man of the world, with very free notions upon a great number of subjects, a taste for the arts, and a tolerable store of Greek and Latin. The other was more difficult to engage, and indeed the task seemed hopeless for some time; till, at length, the master of the vessel joined us, and then I found out that our friend with the diamond rings had points upon which he was accessible also. After helping himself pretty liberally to the brandy and water, the captain looked with a shrewd, good-humoured smile in the face of the over-dressed gentleman, saying--

"Well, Mr. Lewis, do you hope to do a good business this summer?"

"I don't know, captain," answered the other. "I want you to tell me a little bit of what's going on." Then, dropping his voice, he said in a sort of whisper which prevented my hearing the close of the sentence, "I hear they are going to sell up Mr.----"

"So they say," replied the captain, rather gravely, and with a sort of sigh. "I am very sorry for him, poor fellow. He was quite a gentleman; only too fond of those cursed cards. However, he has got a pretty stock in hand, and I guess they'll go high."

"Do you know what they are?" asked the other.

"I don't know them all," replied the master; "but there's some fifty of them; and five or six of them--Bill especially, and Anthony, are as good hands as ever worked in these parts."

"Well the market is not very high in Orleens," replied Mr. Lewis; "it's quite glutted, I hear; and fifty are hardly worth buying. Are there no more to be had about?"

"Why I hear Mr. Thornton wants to sell, up in Southampton county, not far from Jerusalem," was the captain's answer. "I can't tell what he's been about. He neither drinks nor gambles, nor fights cocks, nor anything; and yet he has contrived to muddle away all his money, and his plantation is mortgaged as high as it will go." The other paused upon this, and seemed to consider it with much satisfaction. In the meantime I had arrived at the conclusion that good Mr. Lewis was neither more nor less than a slave-dealer; and, taking but little interest in the subjects discussed, I walked up the companion-ladder to the deck again, to spend an hour or so beneath the stars, before I went to bed. The cabin was oppressively warm; the night sultry beyond description; and I felt sure that I could not sleep without inhaling some fresh air before I lay down. I was inclined to meditate upon many things with which it is no use troubling you, my dear sister, as they arose out of the conversation I had just heard, which deserved more calm consideration than I have yet had time to give them. I had hardly reached the deck, however, when I was joined by the first-mentioned of my fellow travellers, who, fixing at once, as usual, upon the most obvious topic, observed that it was a beautiful night. I agreed with him simply, and he then went on to say--

"It is much pleasanter up here than down below. The cabin is very hot, and that brute of a slave-dealer makes it still hotter."

"I have heard," I replied, "that you Virginian gentlemen hold these slave-dealers in great horror and contempt."

"First, let me tell you I am not a Virginian," responded he; "but I can answer as well as if I were. The slave-dealer is looked upon here, and all through the South, as a necessary nuisance. He is tolerated, and that is all; but there are very few cases in which that toleration is carried so far as to sit in the same room with him. At an ordinary, on board a ship, or in a stage coach, men are obliged to do it; and sometimes--for 'misery makes us acquainted with strange bed-fellows'--when a gentleman owes one of them a good round sum of money which he can't pay, he will not only put his legs under the mahogany with him, but drink with him across the table. *Hic et ubique*--it is the same thing. I have seen men drink with a money-lender in your country--which I presume is England--and I am quite certain that if a rattlesnake had a side pocket, and we could get in debt to him, and we should pull off our hats and be as civil to the reptile as possible." He ended with one of his sharp, short laughs; and, taking a cigar case out of his pocket, offered me a very delicious Havanah. The conversation went on much in the same style for some time; and at length the captain came up and joined us, telling us that Mr. Lewis had turned in.

"Well, that's satisfactory," replied my fellow passenger; "for though one must sometimes be in close companionship with a snake, one does not always like to hear him hissing. As soon as I am sure he's asleep, I'll go down and turn in too." By this time we had got so far into the bay that those beautiful sea anemonies, as they are called, or *medus[ae]*, were flashing past the ship in every direction, looking like the lamps which the Hindoo women are said to send floating on the Ganges. I made some observation upon them to my companion, and he replied somewhat in the words of Sir Henry Wotton:

"As if the heaven let fall
Its lesser stars upon the earth."

"But I think the wind is going to change, captain," resumed he. "Don't you see that haze over there?"

"I shouldn't wonder, Mr. Wheatley," answered the master of the vessel; "and if it does, it will blow pretty stiff." These hints determined me to go down once more to the cabin, and take possession of my berth, although the scene from the deck was very beautiful: the stars shining, still, bright, and clear above; the faint outline of the Virginian coast upon our right; the waters of the bay heaving gently under us, gemmed with phosphorescent light, and innumerable white sails gliding along in the same direction with ourselves, some near and some far off, but all, like the beautiful phantoms that pass by us on the wide sea of human life, deriving much of their charm from imagination and indistinctness. But the horror of sea-sickness--that most unimaginative and unpoetical of all maladies--made me anxious to get to sleep before it fixed its fangs upon me. Accordingly, I was soon in the little den allotted to me, which was certainly less comfortable, and not much more spacious, than a coffin. Some fatigue, however, and the late hour to which I had sat up at Mr. E----'s, on the preceding night, brought slumber to my eyes before the wind changed or the gale began to blow. I suspect we were tossed pretty well during the night; but nothing awoke me till day had long dawned. By this time the sea was tolerably calm again, but the breeze not quite so favourable as it had been before; and it was not till yesterday afternoon that we rounded Cape Charles, and entered what is called Hampton Roads. Thenceforward the wind was very fair, and we had no difficulty in making our way to this place. I cannot say that the scenery we passed was very beautiful; yet I do not think I was ever more charmed or struck by anything affecting merely the sight, than I was with the glorious sunset of that evening, as we sailed up the Elizabeth River. In the morning, some clouds had been in the sky; about midday they had thickened and grown darker; and the weatherwise predicted a storm. But, just as those who pretend to the most philosophical knowledge of human nature are generally the most ignorant of men, so the weatherwise, I have remarked, are the most ignorant of the weather. Before three o'clock every cloud had vanished; floating vapour might be here and there, but it was so thin that the eye could not even discern its shadow on the blue, and it was not till the sun nearly touched the horizon that a thin, golden line, brighter than the rest, showed that there was something to catch and reflect the rays. On the right hand and the left, were piney points, with deep bays and indentations between, but with hardly a house visible; though now and then some blue smoke curled up from amongst the trees, near narrow creeks or little rivers opening their mouths into the wider stream, on which hardly a sail was seen to float, and where merely a canoe with a black man quietly dangling his line over the side, gave human vitality to the aspect of the waters. Beyond, towered up dense and lofty forests, massed in the shades of evening, with a sort of light haze resting upon them, and thus leaving a sort of mysterious flatness over the surface. You could see that they were green, yet the tint was curiously indefinite, approaching black in some places, and showing brighter colours in others; but beyond all, to the west, rose up the most gorgeous sky I ever beheld, of a burning fiery yellow towards the horizon, a broad orange glow above, and thence passing gradually into pink and purple, as the rays of the setting sun reached his zenith. To us, indeed, the sun was already set; for he was hidden by the trees and the gentle slopes of the land to the westward; but that he was not yet below the verge of earth, could be plainly perceived; for every here and there along the shores, where a deep creek or cove wandered up into the woods, his rays could be seen, as it were a path of light, reflected from the surface of the waters. At the mouth of two of these creeks, standing long-legged in the midst of the blaze, I perceived a party of storks or cranes, finding their evening meal on some shoal of the river. But the absence of all traces of civilized man; the glorious sunset; the dim woods; the calm, dull, unexpectant attitude of the storks; the width of the river; the sea-like motion of the waves; the solitary negro fishing from his canoe--all gave a strange, solemn, sublime aspect to the scene, and I could not help figuring to myself that such must have been the appearance of the country as it presented itself to the eyes of the first settlers here, who were amongst the earliest of those who visited the North American continent, when first their venturous barques approached these shores. What bold and hardy fellows they must have been! How unimpressible and resolute! I declare the sight of that sunset made me feel a kind of awe; and I do believe that, had I been amongst them, the solitude and the grandeur would have had a sort of sacredness in it to my mind, which would have induced me to turn the prow homeward, and leave the holiness of nature unprofaned. They were not such tempers, however; and some of the results of their persevering and dauntless spirit of adventure were soon visible in the houses and wharves of Norfolk, looking black and ragged upon the sky, with masts, and sails, and columns of smoke, and boats flitting across and across the river, and the steamboat which I had disdained, lying puffing out her hot breath, and singing no very melodious song. I must say that the external view of the city is much more pleasant than the internal. From the water, on whose bosom it seems to rest, the very ruggedness and irregularity of the outline--especially in the magnifying atmosphere of twilight--give it a picturesqueness, and even a grandeur, which the interior wofully belies. The streets are narrow, irregular, ill kept, and full of the most unpleasant odours. At every crossing you stumble over a dead dog or cat. The air, too, is redolent of stale and salted fish and tobacco; and the part of the town nearest to the river seems a happy compound of Wapping and Billingsgate, while the ear is regaled with violent peels of Negro laughter, mingled occasionally with all the riches of the Irish brogue.

"Negro laughter!" you may exclaim. Yes, my dear sister! Whatever you may think, these poor, unhappy people, as we are taught to believe them, laugh all day long with such merry and joyous peals, that it is impossible to believe that the iron of which we are told, is pressing very deeply into their souls. At all events, I am quite sure it does not affect their diaphragms. I think I shall establish it as a good comparison to say, "as merry as a negro slave." Even in their solitary moments, too, there seems to be no brooding discontent about them. They are talking continually to themselves, and their soliloquies seem full of fun--at least, if we may believe the merry laughs excited by what they themselves are saying. This morning, I followed down to the very extreme end of the town an old negro, who, though he was somewhat lame in one leg, seemed very agile and vigorous. There was something about the man that caught my fancy; for though he was very plainly dressed, in a sort of frieze jacket and a pair of blue linen trousers, he was very clean: his white wool looked respectable, and his black skin shone like ebony. His occupation, at the time, was the humble one of carrying a large dead pig upon his back. These people are a curious study to me, having seen so little of them, and having received but a one-sided view of their character and of their treatment. So I watched him along the way, keeping a little behind, and on one side of him. Some distance down the street, at a house with a little garden before it, a huge monkey, with a face horridly human, was sitting, chained to a tree, eating what seemed to me a potato. The negro stopped, with the pig still upon his back, and gazed thoughtfully at the monkey for a moment or two. The brute grinned and chattered at the man, and held up his doubled fist in rather a pugilistic attitude. The negro grinned, and said aloud--"Ah, massa Jacko, you damn like old folks!" And on he marched upon his way. I must explain to you that "old folks," in negro parlance, means, generally, the mother and father of the speaker. At the further part of the town, where a rough paling encircled a piece of ground intended to be built upon, my black friend stopped, and deliberately unshouldered his pig, setting him up on his hind feet against the boards. But he could not be without his joke, even at his mute companion. Indeed, this race seems to have a poetical way of animating everything. "Ah, massa piggy." he said, "I carried you long way; you look mighty stiff. I damn tired too. So we both rest ourselves." As we were now at the outskirts of the town, and as I was afraid of losing myself if I went further, I turned back to my inn, which is tolerably comfortable, although a poor looking place enough. It is called the Exchange Hotel; and there you had better write to me, as when I go onward, I shall request my very civil landlady to forward all letters to me by the speediest conveyance. You may ask why I do not go onward at once, and get through my business in the interior without delay; but the fact is I am waiting for letters from Mr. Griffith of New York, who, having seen me in England, can identify me here. He only can prove that I am the veritable Simon Pure, and make clear my title to the property which our good aunt has left me. I expected these letters in Baltimore; but, in regard to some of the institutions, I wanted to see and examine, especially that of slavery, Baltimore is neither fish, flesh, nor red herring. It is in a slaveholding State; but so close to the free States, that slavery there is little more than a name. It presented itself to my mind there in no other way than to make me wonder that the gentlemen and ladies of such a nice town were so fond of black servants, which you know is not generally the case in England. I therefore came on to Virginia, where the slave system is in full force, and directed the letters to follow me. As soon as they arrive, I shall proceed into Southampton County; and if it be possible to remain incog. in this most inquisitive of all countries, I shall quietly inspect Aunt Bab's lands and tenements, and make every necessary inquiry before I disclose who I am. What I shall do with the property, I do not know. It is not necessary to me. I have enough without; and may perhaps abandon it altogether. I hear you exclaim, my dear Kate, "You will of course emancipate the slaves!" And you will be horrified when I reply, "I do not know." But be assured I will do what, on mature reflection and personal observation, I judge to be the best for them. No motive of sordid interest will have any effect upon me, or could ever induce me to keep my fellow man in bondage. But I confess my preconceived opinions have been very much shaken by what I myself have seen, even during my short stay here, and by the comparisons which my mind has unconsciously instituted between the condition of the negro in the free states and in the slave-holding communities. In the former, he is decidedly a sad, gloomy, ay, an ill-treated man, subject to more of the painful restrictions of caste than I could have conceived possible. Here, he appears to be a cheerful, light-hearted, guileless, childlike creature, treated with perfect familiarity, and as far as I have seen, with kindness. Whether this be a reality or merely a semblance, I shall know hereafter; but, depend upon it, I will not act till I *do* know. I must close my letter, for my fellow passenger, Mr. Wheatley, has just come to call upon me, and I have surely written enough for one day. Write soon if you would have your letter reach me, as there is nothing more uncertain than the length or shortness of the stay of

Your affectionate Brother.

P.S.--This Mr. Wheatley, who has just left me, is certainly a very amusing man. I cannot tell much about his principles; and he seems to vent his scoffs and jests at everything. But he has a good deal of originality of thought, no bad conceit of himself, and some very strong and fixed opinions, springing rather, I suspect, from the suggestions of his own mind than from anything which has been instilled into him by others. He always seems to set out from the beginning of things; and then flies along his chain of deductions like an electric current, skipping a few links here and there, I doubt not, and getting on to another chain which leads him far away. But with men whom I may never meet again, I have got into a way of amusing myself with their characters, rather than combating their arguments. I was never born for an apostle; and I do not think, if I had the power of depriving men of their opinions or even of their prejudices, I should do much good to myself, or them, or society. Indeed, I have come to the conclusion, that the great bulk of men's prejudices is part of their property, which we have no right to take from them. We may tax them to a certain extent for the benefit of society, but we must prove that benefit before we make it our plea; and the rest we have no right to meddle with at all. The self-conceited desire to do so, is the origin of all fanaticism and of the host of evils to which it gives rise.

P.S. No. 2.--Eleven o'clock Friday night.--I have just made a funny sort of acquaintance with my friend the negro pig-carrier. In going out about two hours ago, I heard a loud dispute at the foot of the stairs, and found another fellow as black as himself abusing no other person than Mr. Zedekiah Jones; for such is his euphonious name. I did not stop to listen; but one vituperative epithet was applied to him by his opponent, which I never should have expected to hear addressed by one negro to another. "You're a damn'd black free nigger!" cried the little scrubby fellow who was contending with him.

"You're black as I am," retorted Zedekiah, "and nigger too. I could'nt help being free. Ole massa 'mancipate me whether I like or no." The accusation and excuse were strangely characteristic; and a few minutes ago old Zedekiah came up to my room to ask if I had any boots or shoes to clean. It seems he is a sort of supernumerary shoeblack, or porter of the house. I shall get something of his history from him to-morrow, for he appears to be a good kind of merry creature; but, it being late to-night, I satisfied myself with obtaining his name. No letter has come yet, so I shall have to stay here another day.

CHAPTER II

Another letter, my dear sister, and still from Norfolk. It was useless to set out without the expected epistles to identify me, in case of need; and they only arrived this morning. Then came the great and important question of how, and by what manner, I was to proceed to my journey's end. It was one which I gave no heed to till this morning--an old habit of mine, by the way; for I fear my mind is somewhat discursive, and rambles about important points, to amuse itself on the outskirts of the question. No stage was to be had to the point which I wished to reach--no steam-boat, because it is far inland--no blessed post-horses, for those much enduring animals are unknown in this country; and there were only two resources: what they call here a buggy--that is to say, a rumbling, generally ill conditioned vehicle, with either one or two half-starved nags, for the hire of which one is charged the most extortionate price--or the old-fashioned mode of locomotion on a horse's back. I determined upon the latter resource; but upon going to a livery stable in the neighbourhood of the inn, I saw a collection of animals so miserable and forlorn, that I doubted much whether any one of them would reach the end of the journey without falling to pieces. Moreover, my good friend, the proprietor, made considerable difficulty as to hiring them out for so long a journey, and gave me clearly to understand that he should consider he was doing me a great favour if he acceded at all. Not wishing to lay myself under an obligation to this very independent gentleman, I walked away, determined to fall back upon the buggy, and to get my new friend Mr. Wheatley, to undertake the negotiation for me; for I somewhat feared that my temper, though I believe a tolerably good one, might break down under similar discussions. On going back to the inn, in order to send him a note, and finding my worthy acquaintance, Zedekiah Jones, standing at the door, I inquired of him, casually, if there were no other place than the one to which I had been directed where I could hire a horse. He grinned, and shook his head; but remarked, that I could buy plenty of very good horses if I wanted one to purchase. He knew of two, he said, which had come into town two days before, fresh and well-conditioned, and a capital match.

"But I only want one, my good friend," I replied.

"What horse carry your baggage, den, massa?" asked the man, with his usual grin. This was a new view of the case, which I had not thought of.

"But if I buy, or hire, two horses," I said, "who is to ride the other, Master Zedekiah?"

"Old Zed ride t'other," answered the negro, chuckling as if he were going into convulsions; "best groom you ever have. All my life with horses till I break my leg, when that damn horse came down with me at Richmond races. My gorry! I'd be glad to get upon a horse's back again. Old Zed ride t'other, massa, and take care of both--and you too." And he exploded again right joyfully. To shorten my story, there was something so amusing in the man's merriment, and so straightforward and good-humoured in his way, that if I had ever had any starch or stiffness in my nature, it would have been all relaxed and melted out. Putting aside all question of oddity, or absurdity, I said to myself--

"I will buy the horses, and I'll hire old Zed, if the landlady is willing to part with him. Sterne hired La Fleur much after the same fashion, and for the same qualities. We'll march off together seeking adventures. I'll be Don Quixote, and he shall be Sancho Panza. Not a windmill have I seen in the country as yet; but, doubtless, we shall find something that will do quite as well." The whole business was soon settled. The landlady was charitably glad that old Zed had got a good place, for she said she employed the poor creature more from charity than anything else; and, after ordering him a decent suit of apparel, and buying two pairs of capacious saddle bags, we proceeded to the stable where the horses were to be seen. They were very handsome beasts, and seemed sound wind and limb; and though the price was very high, I concluded the bargain for them rapidly, which I imagine produced greater respect for my purse than for my person; and thus, my dear girl, I shall set out to-morrow, mounted and squired, though I have not yet got my lance or shield, nor the helmet of Mambrino. On my return to the inn, I found Mr. Wheatley waiting for me, and told him what I had done.

"Bravo!" he said; "true Virginian style. But have you got a large pair of plated spurs? otherwise you won't pass current. Never mind; I'll supply you. I bought half a dozen pair when I first came to this state, and they have served as my introduction to the best society ever since. But let me give you a hint or two before you go. There are a thousand chances to one that you may miss your way, unless your friend Zed has a very general knowledge of the country. Do not, however, let that trouble you. Wherever you see a house, and it is convenient to stop, pull down the fence, and ride straight at it. You will find a hearty welcome. The Virginians are the most hospitable people upon earth, and their houses have the faculty of stretching to an inconceivable extent. As for food, you will always find, if nothing else, good ham, fried chickens, eggs, and butter; often a capital bottle of wine; and though, in the towns, men may think they are conferring a favour upon you by selling you the merest trifle in which it is their business to deal, at an exorbitant price--in the country they will think you are conferring a favour by taking whatever they have to give for nothing. The fact is, this exaggerated tone of indifference and independence in the store-keepers is only assumed as a balm to their vanity, a little wounded at having to sell anything. Every man of them fancies himself to be a member of the first families in Virginia, and would fain have his horses and hounds, and his score or two of negroes. Not having them, he is anxious to make himself believe, and to persuade others, that he only buys and sells for his own amusement, and does not care ninepence whether people take his wares or not." I believe there is a great deal of truth in this view of the subject. Whether Mr. Wheatley has given me as correct a picture of the Virginian country gentlemen or not, remains to be proved; at all events his advice, in many respects, may be valuable, and he has added to it three or four letters which I think may be found of service.

"The squire, the parson, the lawyer, and the inn-keeper," he said, "are great people in their way. I know them all in the direction in which you tell me you are bending your steps."

"But, perhaps," said I---- Before I could conclude, he interrupted me with his peculiar, short, quick laugh--always broken off suddenly, as if it were cut through in the middle, saying--

"I understand; you may not wish to have any trumpets blown before you. You may like to go quietly about whatever business you have to do. I saw that your carpet bag had no name on it, and therefore, of course, I asked the captain who you were, whence you came, whither you were going, and everything about you, in the true Yankee spirit. My dear sir, there is no such thing as secresy in this country. Every man knows everybody else's business much better than his own. It is a great deal worse in the East, that is true; and I have known one of my fellow-countrymen pursue a silent and reserved traveller through two long days' journey--quite out of his way too--simply because he knew he should never have a moment's peace for the rest of his life if he did not find out all about him. At last, the unfortunate traveller was obliged to open out and tell him the whole story--true or false I do not know--merely to be quit of him. However, I will write the letters for you, and you can deliver them or not, as you like; but mind, I tell you fairly, you can't conceal yourself. In this part of the country, the negroes do all the work in the way of inquisitiveness, which we Yankees do with our own tongues. There is nothing ever hidden from a negro; and the moment he or she knows it, every person of the same colour knows it throughout the whole town, and from them it gets to the masters and mistresses. If ever a young gentleman kisses a young lady behind the door, you may be quite sure there is a black eye looking through a chink; and then it is, 'Lors a marcy, Miss Jemima! what do you tink? Massa John kiss Miss Jane behind de door.' Then Miss Jemima runs to Aunty Sal, and exclaims, 'Lors a marcy!' too, and Aunty Sal tells it to Mammy Kate, and Mammy Kate tells it to her dearly-beloved nursling, Miss Betty, who sends it round through all the kith and kin of the parties concerned. Do you see that black man walking along, who has just been talking to your friend Zed? He knows all about you at this present moment.

"Yes, I see him," answered I, "the man carrying the sucking pig, you mean?"

"Pardon me; that is not a sucking pig," answered Mr. Wheatley; "that is *helotice*, a possum--*anglice*, an opossum; no bad dish let me tell you, and one of which the negroes are very fond. But this is not the season for them. After the persimons are ripe, they get exceedingly fat and tender."

"And what are persimons?" I asked.

"A sort of wild fruit," he answered, "in shape somewhat like a plum, and in taste like an apricot, of which the opossum is exceedingly fond. But suffer not yourself to be deceived by the wags up the country; for the Virginians are exceedingly fond of practical jokes. Now the persimon may look perfectly ripe and tempting to the eye; but till it is touched by the frost, soot and vinegar are honey and Falernian to it. Neither, if you have an abhorrence, as I have, of middle-aged pigs, suffer yourself to be tempted to eat an animal they call here a shoat--a name I am convinced they have invented to cover the abomination they are offering you. However, give me pen and ink, and I will write these letters for you. I would give you more good advice, but every one must buy his own experience in some degree, and the best council I can give you, as to all men in a strange country, is, 'keep your eyes open, and do as you see others do.'" I thought this very good advice; for what I might call the technicalities of any society are soon learned, and the pedantries of society are not worth learning. In Russia, every man, from the prince to the peasant, eats with his knife. In England, to do so is almost a social crime; and yet, where in reality is the misdemeanor? Nothing can be really and essentially vulgar that is not disgusting or offensive to others. The best-bred Turk eats with his fingers; but he takes care to wash his hands before he begins and after he has ended. Perhaps he is really more cleanly than the man who eats with a fork when he does not know whether it has been washed or not. However, my friend sat down and wrote the letters for me; and, in the meantime, Master Zed came in already dressed in his new apparel. I had not waited to see his choice of habiliments, but had restricted the shopkeeper--storekeeper, I should have said, God bless the mark! there are no shopkeepers here--to a certain amount; and unquestionably my new man's appearance somewhat startled me. He had got on a plum-coloured frock or tunic coat, with a velvet collar almost red; a pair of Windsor gray--I might almost say light blue pantaloons; a decidedly bright blue cravat; and a shirt-collar so high, so prominent, so extensive in every direction, that I could not but fear that the poor man's round ball of a head would some day disappear in it, white wool and all. He seemed, however, perfectly satisfied with the effect; and I could see him cast sundry glances at a tall looking-glass between the windows, which reflected an image such as is rarely seen upon this globe. True, if he were happy, I had no reason to be discontented; and happy he evidently was, poor man, though I fancy some shirts and stockings had been sacrificed, out of the amount of his equipment, to the splendour of the coat, the cravat, and the pantaloons. Not the least did he presume upon his finery; but, with a most deferential air, inquired what time I should be ready to start on the following morning, humbly suggesting that my horses' fore-feet would be better if shoed and pared, especially at some parts of the road not being of the best, and blacksmiths' shops being few and far between, it would be wise to set out all right, with a nail or two and a hammer in one of the saddlebags. Zed's precautions seemed to be not amiss; and this indication of care and forethought appeared a good augury; so I gave him some money to buy what he wanted, and dismissed him.

"They are good creatures," said Mr. Wheatley, looking up from his letter, "capable of strong affections and strong attachments; but child-like, and requiring constant supervision and care. Now this very man, who has been so thoughtful on a matter in regard to which right notions have been drummed into him by long habit, would make the most egregious, the most absurd, and sometimes the most distressing blunders in regard to things out of his routine. There are two propensities, however, of which the race is rarely ever free--to pilfer and to lie. The pilfering is usually confined to petty articles; and it would really seem as if they reasoned with themselves upon the matter, judging that what they take will please and benefit them more than the loss will pain or injure you. The lie, too, has its bounds and restrictions; it is like the lie of a child, issuing from fear or from the wish of giving pleasure or amusement."

"May not both habits," I said, "be naturally traced to the positions in which they are established? Having no property themselves, not even *in* themselves, may not their pilfering be a just retribution upon those who are depriving them of all? and may not the lie from fear, or from the purpose of pleasing, be traced to an institution which deprives them of that manly dignity which knows not fear and scorns deception?" Mr. Wheatley's short, quick laugh broke in upon me again. "I think not," he said: "you must see more of them before you can judge. Then perhaps you may be of opinion that the pilfering is a mere proclivity of their vanity or their small appetites. What they take is generally a bright-coloured ribbon, or a bit of lace, or a spoonful out of a pot of sweatmeats, or a glass out of a brandy bottle. You can teach a dog to abstain from taking anything till it is given to him; but you can't teach them, do what you will. There is no race upon the face of the earth who should more frequently repeat the prayer 'Lead us not into temptation;' for there is no race so little capable of withstanding it. Then as to the lying, it is mere childishness. First, they have what your authors call a 'diabetes' of talk. Truth is a great deal too limited for them; they must speak about something. And when the lie proceeds from fear it is nine times out of ten, unreasonable fear: they are afraid of being blamed--of not being thought quick and ready at an answer, and consequently, when any question is asked them, rather than seem ignorant, they fabricate a falsehood. If anything very important were at stake, a thousand to one they would tell the truth. But upon these matters you must satisfy yourself; for of all the rusty, rickety, breakable commodities in this world, second-hand opinions are the worst; and yet nine men out of ten supply themselves at brokers' shops, when they could get them fresh and strong from the manufactory." Thus saving, he set to the letters again; and after they were concluded, gave me a very cordial invitation to his house on my return, and left me, adding, "If you stay long, perhaps we may meet were you are going; for I have some business up there, which should have been attended to a month ago, at the county capital city, which rejoices in the name of Jerusalem, although. Got wot, it is less like Jerusalem than Carthage. Has it never struck you, how magnificently ridiculous the names of our towns are in this country? Mount Ida, about as high as my hand--Rome, descended from its seven hills into the midst of a swamp--Syracuse, a couple of hundred miles from the sea--and Jerusalem in a ham-producing district, with nothing but swine all around it, spite of Moses and all the prophets. In fact, the United States have been like a father with too many children, so hard up for Christian names as to be obliged to give them the most un-Christian names he could get." One more short laugh, and he was gone. And now, my dear sister, to-morrow morning at six, I start upon my journey to the interior; but do not let your timid little imagination conjure up images of danger and difficulty, which, take my word for it, have no foundation but in your fancy. Though of course, as society here is not so regulated as in Great Britain, seeing that a couple of centuries can never do for any country what ten centuries can do, the people are perfectly civilized, I can assure you--quite tame, upon my word. There are no longer any terrible Indians with tomahawks and scalping-knives; nor even ferocious backwoodsmen (at least about this part of the country) whose daily occupation is to gouge, or bore, or shoot down their adversaries. They are, as far as I have seen or heard, a good-humoured, jovial, kind-hearted race, somewhat hot and peppery it is true; but preserving many of those qualities intact which we, in our crowds and thoroughfares, have lost or impaired. In short, they have more character about them: the stamp is not worn off the shilling; but, above all, they are especially hospitable. Doubt not, therefore, that that hospitality will be extended to so engaging and agreeable a young gentleman as your affectionate brother.

CHAPTER III

Richmond, 10*th October*, 1851.

My Dear Sister,--First let me tell you I am safe and well; which assurance, I trust, will reach you before the news of all that has been taking place here can arrive in England. Some of the scenes I have gone through have been full of danger and horror, and have produced upon my mind, my character, and my fate great and important effects; as, indeed, must always be the case when we are subjected to sudden and unforeseen trials. It is impossible, in the scope of a letter, to give you anything like a clear account of all that has occurred; but whenever I have had an opportunity I have carefully made up my journal, as I promised our friend J----, when I left England, to do for his especial benefit. That journal, of course, contains merely notes and heads; and so many events, and scenes, and conversations remain merely upon memory that I must write it all over again, adding things every here and there which are necessary for a clear comprehension of the whole, which would otherwise in all probability pass away in a few short years. I know you will read them with interest, and so will J----. I shall therefore send the whole story of my last two or three months' adventures to you in detached fragments, and you will forward them to him when you have read them. In the meantime do not put much faith in newspaper accounts; for many of the statements I have seen myself are exaggerated, and many, very many, fall far below the reality. Indeed I do not know that I myself shall be able to bring home to your mind some of the sights that I have witnessed and the scenes through which I have passed; I am sure I could not do so were I to suffer the first impressions to pass away. But, thank God, it is all over; and although several of those whom I highly esteemed have left this world by a tragical and bloody death, those who are dearest to me have escaped almost miraculously. I see you smile, dear sister, at that expression--"those who are dearest to me." Smile away, for I cannot but hope that they will soon be dear to you also. Very likely I shall bring over the last portion of my journal myself, and we may read it together by the old fire-side, with many miles of the dark Atlantic rolling between us and the scenes I have attempted to depict. My faithful Zed will come with me; so have a comfortable room in the hall ready for one to whom I owe my life, and who has suffered many things in the service of your affectionate brother.

The above letter, which, together with the two that preceded it, have been given merely as introductory to the following history, caused a good deal of curiosity and even agitation in the mind of the lady who received it, and in that of the friend who is mentioned under the name of Mr. J----. They were much nearer to each other than the writer imagined when he wrote, and they were never after separated; but each felt a deep interest in the fate of the wanderer over the Atlantic, and looked in the newspapers in vain for the events to which he referred. Englishmen at that time took much less heed of events occurring in the United States of America than they do at present, and English newspapers rarely mentioned matters of merely local interest occurring in any of the several states. At length, however, at the end of about a fortnight or three weeks, came a large package, in the form of a letter; and every arrival of a mail-packet brought one or two more, which were perused with deep feelings by the sister and the sister's husband, and are now given to the public, *verbatim et literatim,* as they were written.

CHAPTER IV

On the 19th June, 1831, I set out from the city of Norfolk about seven o'clock in the morning; my departure had been fixed at six: but who ever sets out at the hour at which he has determined? Nobody, certainly, in Virginia, where time and punctuality seem to be, in the opinion of all men, very impracticable abstractions, little worth the attention of reasonable men. First of all, Zed was too late in bringing up the horses, and he had at least a hundred good excuses for the delay. Next, we had forgotten, in buying the saddle-bags, to buy any straps to fix them to the saddles. Then, no stores--or shops, as we call them, were yet open to supply the deficiency. And again, no pack-thread was to be found to supersede the need of straps. Finally, all the gentlemen of the inn with whom I had formed acquaintance, and who happened to be up, must needs shake hands and drink a mint-julep with me before I departed. It seemed the good ancient custom of the stirrup-cup, and I was fain to lump my companions altogether, and take one deep draught to their health ere I rode on. It was a glorious morning; the sun had not yet heated the air, and the wind blew from the north-west. After crossing the river we journeyed very comfortably for between two and three hours. Zed, radiant as Ph[oe]bus, was proud of new clothes, a new master, and a new horse; and to say truth, rode very well, although not very gracefully. Indeed, his broken leg, which had been set somewhat crooked, apparently enabled him to grasp his beast with greater vigour, making a sort of hoop round the animal's body, which would have been very difficult to shake off. We made the best of our way while it was cool; but between nine and ten we began to have indications of what the weather intended to do with us. They may say what they like of Calcutta, Jamaica, and the African coast; but I am sure that Norfolk, in the summer season, is the hottest place upon the surface of the earth. I began to feel the perspiration dropping from under my hat; and the roads seemed full of ruts and irregularities which I had not perceived before. Suddenly, my horse put his feet into a deep gutter, and made an awful stumble, but did not come down.

"Ah, massa," cried Zed, who had been keeping nearly in a line with me, "you hold de middle of de road, or you get into tobacco-ruts."

"Tobacco-ruts!" I exclaimed, "what do you mean by tobacco-ruts? I see no tobacco, Zed." My new groom laughed aloud.

"Don't you know, massa," he cried, "people used to grow tobacco on this road? Take two cart-wheels and an axle, put tobacco between them, or round de axle, wid two coloured gentlemen to roll it on, and push for'ard all de way to Norfolk."

"They don't surely do so now, Zed?"

"Not very long ago," replied he. "I recoleck very well seeing hundreds of tons roll along here. Sometimes dere was a freshet. Den you would see--oh, gorry--a whole heap of wheels and tobacco, and de gentlemen all dancing and playing on de banjo on de bank. Oh, dose was merry times, massa; but dey all become so damn democratic now." I must here remark upon two points of the negro character. First, that they are exceedingly fond of expletives, and not very choice in their selection; and, secondly, that, to a man, as far as I have seen, they are exceedingly conservative, nay, aristocratical in their notions. I will not pause to inquire whether they have any very definite ideas upon the distinction of parties, or whether they attach any significance to the objurgations they use; but certain it is that they have an abhorrence for the name of democrat, and occasionally swear somewhat blasphemously without any special occasion. We were soon obliged to bring our horses to a walk; but we had made good speed over the first twenty miles of our journey. At the end of the next five, we had the happiness of seeing a house on the right-hand side of the road, which promised us rest and shelter from the hot sun till the coolness of evening might be expected. It was a long, low house of two stories--or rather one story and a half, for the second was only half as tall as the first--with a verandah or porch extending all along the front. Beneath the shade of this verandah, in a large arm-chair of plain maple wood, from which he seemed incapable of rising, sat an elderly man with white hair, leaden complexion, and a dull, heavy unprepossessing countenance. In girth he was enormous; and indeed his obesity seemed the effect of disease, for there was an unhealthy heaviness in his whole aspect which was painful to look upon. His dress was negligent; his waistcoat and his shirt were unbuttoned; he had not been shaved for many days; and his hat had fallen, by accident and negligence, into a variety of curious dents and twists, which left no vestige of its original shape. A long tobacco-pipe was in his mouth, from which he continued to inhale puffs of smoke, slowly and leisurely, without paying the slightest apparent attention to anything going on around him. He saw us dismount at the door in the most impassible mood in the world; and as all was still and silent about the house, I should have doubted whether it was a tavern or not, had I not seen a tall bare pole in front, and painted on the frieze of the porch,

Blackwater House. Andrew Gorbel

By this time I had learned that such symptoms indicated an inn; and while Zed led away the horses, Heaven knows where, I stepped up to the fat smoker, and asked where I could find the landlord.

"I'm the proprietor," answered he. And, without even asking if I wanted anything, continued puffing away at his pipe with the utmost indifference. The fact is, that the people of this country are too thinly scattered for anything like what we call attention and civility. There is no competition amongst them. They feel that other men are more dependent upon them than they upon other men, and they are determined to make those whom they supply with anything feel that it is so. This is a good deal the case in the cities, but ten times more so in remote country places, where the solitary inn has the power of laying every traveller under contribution, or inflicting upon him the penalty of a long and inexpedient ride. I have come to this conclusion from remarking that in spots where commerce is beginning to centre, and two or three taverns have been set up side by side, the landlords, yielding to circumstances, have put on as much civility, if not obsequiousness, as any in the old world. Nothing like competition, my dear friends. It is what bows down most men to the worship of the golden calf, but is very comfortable and convenient for travellers.

"Pray, sir, can I get any dinner here, to-day?"

"I dar say you can." Puff--puff--puff--not a word more.

"What's the dinner hour?"

"One o'clock, if the lads have come back." Puff--puff--puff.

"Can I get anything to drink? I am very thirsty."

"Just in there you'll find the whisky-bottle, on the shelf in the bar. There's water in the pitcher, I think." I was turning away, to satisfy my thirst, when my fat friend hallooed after me--

"Hie! Will you jist hand me that newspaper off the bench." With a smile I could not repress, I did what he required, observing, in somewhat of the country language,--

"You seem somewhat troubled about the limbs, Mr. Gorbel."

"No, not a bit," said he; "my limbs is as strong as ever. It's what's above 'em is the trouble; they have got too much to carry. It's all come on in these cussed last three years, owing to the dry weather and the weevil, I think." I walked away, rather inclined to conclude it was the drought of his own palate, rather than that of the weather, which had brought him into that condition; and, with such an example before my eyes, contented myself with the cold water, without troubling the whisky. About a quarter past one o'clock, till which time I amused myself as best I might, I espied two young men coming up a cross road, or rather lane, through the wood, and another walking leisurely along through a field of Indian corn. On approaching the house, they walked at once into what the old man had called the bar, and rushed at a large tin washbowl. One washed his face and hands, and another did the same. All wiped on the same towel hanging behind the door, and most of them combed their hair with a universal comb which lay on the window-seat. All this was done in profound silence; for in this country, as well as most others, hunger does not tend to loquacity. Before the three first had finished their unfastidious ablutions, another and another had entered, till the bar-room was fuller of human creatures than I had imagined the whole country for twenty miles round could present. As I had come thither, I had seen nothing but forest and swamp, with the exception of a small village here and there, and a scattered house or two near it. A group of negroes, indeed, once or twice was seen looking over a ragged fence; but nothing of white humanity had been visible except in the aforesaid villages. Now, however, there were at least twenty white men about me. In a moment after, a little tinkling hand-bell rang, a door leading out of the bar-room opened, and in rushed the crowd, jostling each other like a pack of hungry hounds, into a large, low dining-hall, where each seized upon a seat, and helped himself to what was before him. It did not seem to matter what it was; to save time was the great object; one man seized upon a dish of cabbage; another snatched some pork and beans; a third thrust his fork into a potato; and a fourth emptied a dish of pickles upon his plate. In the meantime, a black lad of about sixteen, end two mulatto girls, were going round from guest to guest, repeating some mysterious words in a very quick tone, which caused each of the gentlemen to thrust out his plate, loaded as it was, with a single word of reply. When the boy came to me, I discovered that the talismanic words were simply, "roast mutton; corn beef; boiled mutton; roast shoat; roast turkey; chicken pie!" Happily, I had been warned as to the nature of shoat; but out of the rest I contrived to make a very good dinner, which, though it occupied not more than ten minutes to complete, was so slow of accomplishment in comparison with the time the others allowed themselves, that I found myself at the end left alone with the rotund landlord, who had rolled into a chair at the head of the table, and had gone on eating pork and cabbage up to that moment in profound silence. When I first perceived him, he was making a sign with his thumb over his shoulder, to the black boy, who instantly disappeared into the bar-room, and returned with the bottle of whisky in his hand. Mine host nearly filled his tumbler, and then pointed to me, saying, in a husky voice--

"Will you take a drink?--Good old rye--capital stuff--twenty year old, that. Though, may be, you'd like a julep. But I don't go in for juleps--the mint's over-heating, 'specially when one's dined."

"I thought you Virginian gentlemen took all your liquor before dinner," I answered, helping myself to a small portion of the whisky, which was, indeed, excellent.

"Some do, and some don't," he said, rather shily. "For my own part, I only take a glass or two of apple-jack before dinner; but I always have my glass of whisky-and-water after;" and, he added, about a spoonful of water to the tumblerful of spirits. "You see I'm a great sufferer from the dispepsy--indeed, most of us are about here." I thought it was no wonder, if they all ate as I had seen the people at that table. I literally saw one man pile up his plate with the following articles, in the order I put them down:--About a pound of boiled pork; the same quantity of cabbage; two large spoonfuls of a sort of French beans; a whole plateful of raw, undressed cucumber, cut in slices; a quantity of pickles, and a slice of ham. All this was consumed, I recollect, in the space of five minutes. However, my worthy host seemed to become gayer and more communicative upon the strength of his dinner; and in the course of a long chat with him in the porch, I obtained a good deal of information in regard to all the families for many miles around. He told me he had lived there for thirty years; he had built himself two houses, and knew everybody in the neighbourhood--man, woman, and child; white, black, and yellow. Amongst the rest, he had been well acquainted with Aunt Bab; and from some facts he told me, I am inclined to feel glad that I came over here--not, perhaps, to enrich myself, but to spoil a very nefarious scheme for the appropriation of her property by others. Besides much other intelligence, I learned that the spot about which was congregated most of my hitherto unknown relatives, was still at a distance of some twenty-five to thirty miles; and, consequently, as soon as the sun had declined sufficiently to throw some shade upon the road, I looked eagerly about for my friend Zed, and directed him to bring out the horses. Not a little patience is needed all over the world in the minor affairs of life. I do believe they affect us more, and more permanently, than those of greater importance. We cut the diamond with dust, which we cannot even scratch with steel; and I am confident that many a man's spirit is worn away and brought down with petty cares and small annoyances, who would have struggled manfully against great evils. The kind of servitude, too, of this country is peculiarly abundant in such trifling discomforts, proceeding from the character of the different classes of people and their relations to each other. As far as I have seen, there is no order, no system, no regularity;--a total absence of that military discipline and punctuality which makes everything roll smoothly.

My friend Zed was full three-quarters of an hour before he had brought out the horses and got everything else ready. First, he had forgotten what they call here the hitching-reins, for tying the horses up to any fence or gate where it may be needful; then he had left in the stable my gun, which I had given him to carry; then he had got one of the girths twisted; and, in short, there were innumerable little things to set right which should never have gone wrong. The day was intensely hot, however--more so than any one out of Virginia can possibly conceive; and, though resolved to cut this sort of thing short at once, I could only speak a few words of remonstrance.

"Beg pardon, massa," said Zed. "Things not got accustomed to me yet; they'll all come right by-and-by." Trusting that it would be so, I rode on. The next five-and-twenty miles seemed the longest journey I had ever made. I will not attempt to describe it, for that is impossible. The air was suffocating. Not a breath of wind moved the trees or came along the road. The long unwatered dust rose up at every footfall of the horses; the poor beasts were in a lather, though going at a very easy trot, and I myself was in that condition which, though it may be healthy enough, is very ungentlemanly in its aspect. What would I not have given for the coldest breeze that ever blew across the Scottish moors!--What would I have given for a good heavy gray cloud!--What for a drenching shower! But none of these things were to be had; and I went on with a sort of desperation, knowing that unless I slept in one of the marshes, where the evening frogs were already beginning to croak, I had no place of refuge for several miles ahead. All this while, Zed looked as cool as a cucumber. It was really quite provoking to see the glossy black shining of his skin, and his crisp, white wool, while I was dropping from every pore, "and larding the lean earth as I rode along." But the good man seemed really to have compassion upon me; and, about half-past five o'clock, he pointed with his hand to the left, saying,

"You look tire, massa Richard. Dere's a house. Better go in and stop dere."

"But whose house is it, Zed?" I asked.

"Don't know, massa," answered Zed. Then, in pity of my ignorance, he added, "Nebber mind dat. They very glad to see you, whoever it be. All gentlemen do de same." I looked in the direction in which he pointed, and clearly enough could see the house of which he spoke. His suggestion came at a very opportune moment, for we had just got out of the forest and come upon a large space of open ground some thousand acres in extent, which seemed rich and well cultivated, and the sun, then declining in the west, threw his full beams upon us, almost blinding me. The house seemed inviting, too. It was a large, red, brick building, somewhat like an old English manor-house, with a number of sheds and stables and outhouses scattered irregularly around it, and a backing of copse, not forest, but apparently consisting of orchards and shrubberies. I could not resist it, and, turning to Zed, asked, "Where is the road?"

"Oh, pull down de fence," answered Zed, "and ride straight ahead." He was off his horse in a moment to perform the office he proposed; but the fence was not high; my horse took it easily, and Zed and his nag scrambled over the best way they could. The house was about half a mile from the road; and, not liking to ride over the grain, I had to thread my way through a somewhat narrow path, which made the distance greater. This path, however, led into a road, and that road to the bank of a very pretty stream, over which was a bridge of rather primitive construction. A gentle slope led from the little river to the front of the house, covered, if not exactly with turf, with green grass, shaded by fruit trees. The whole reminded me of Old England--dear, never-to=be-forgotten Old England! There was so much of a home-look about it that I felt sure of a welcome, and, throwing the reins to Zed, sprung off my horse and mounted the old stone steps to the door. I had no occasion to ring any bells--my coming had been espied. The door was open before I could stretch out my hand, and, besides the nice-looking negro who opened it, I could see two black girls going up a large oak staircase and looking over their shoulders.

"Walk in, sir," said the man; "massa very glad to see you." And, without more ceremony or inquiry, he opened a large door to the right of the hall. My only hope was now that I should find the master of the house alone, for I began to feel all the awkwardness of the proceeding. It was not to be so, however. The scene presented, as I entered the room, was very pleasant in the abstract, but not altogether so in the circumstances then existing. I had evidently come upon a little party of gentlemen just after dinner. The room was a fine, old-fashioned room, large and lofty, with the windows all open and the blinds all shut. In the centre was a mahogany table, large enough to seat ten or twelve people, though only four now surrounded it, and on that table were some dishes of preserves and early fruits, glasses and decanters, and some curious old articles of silver ware. The gentleman at the head of the table was a tall, dignified, hale-looking man, with hair nearly white, an aquiline nose, and rather heavy eyebrows. His dress was somewhat between morning and evening costume. He wore a narrow black handkerchief around his neck, and a snowy white shirt, with a collar cut a good deal back from the chin, and a small, neatly-plaited frill in front. His coat was black and swallow-tailed, but he had on leather breeches and top-boots. The upper part, with its white waistcoat, might have graced a lady's evening drawing-room; the lower part was quite fit for cover-side. On the right of him was a gentleman in black, with a very thick white neck-cloth, hair like spun silver, and a mild, benevolent face. On the other hand was a gentleman of rather odd attire and appearance, with his hair combed flat and far down upon his forehead, who, in expression, rather than in features, reminded me more strongly of a parrot than any human thing I ever saw. A good-humoured, jolly-looking, fat fellow, about ten years younger than the rest, with a blue coat and bright gilt buttons, sat a little lower down, and completed the party. I would have given all Aunt Bab's fortune to be out of the house again. I am not by any means habitually shy; but there are moments when a cloud of shyness will come over me, and then, I believe, I am as stiff as a poker. I was soon, however, set at my ease. The master of the house arose (be was six feet three at least), and with an air of the utmost cordiality and urbanity, came forward to meet me, holding out his hand.

"Very glad to see you, sir," he said. "Pray take a seat. Will, put some glasses for this gentleman." (This was addressed to the servant.) "We have had a very hot day--singularly hot for this early time of year. That is Madeira; that is claret. But I dare say you stand in need of other refreshment. Let me order you some dinner." All this was said with an air of unceremonious ease and kindness which broke down all restraint; and I answered with a slight laugh:--

"Three minutes ago, my dear sir, I would have given a great deal to be out of your house again; but now, I am very glad I believed the report I have received of the hospitality of Virginian gentlemen. I must apologize first for appearing here in this traveller's guise, and next for appearing here at all. The truth is, I have ridden a long way, and, not accustomed to such tremendous heat, felt quite exhausted by it. Moreover, I knew not my road very well, or where I might find accommodation for the night."

"Where but here?" said my host, with a frank laugh. "I understand it all, my dear sir; make no further explanations. These things occur to us every day, and very gratifying they are; for, besides breaking a little the quiet routine of our country circle, they occasionally introduce us to pleasant acquaintances which sometimes ripen into friendships." Just as he spoke, who should put his head into the door but Master Zed, asking, unceremoniously, "Where shall I put de saddle-bags, Massa Richard?"

"Ask for Will, uncle, and tell him to show you the blue room," said my host. Then turning to me with a somewhat puzzled air, as if the familiarity of my servant prompted the question, he observed, "You are not a Virginian, I think?"

"No, sir," I answered; "I am an Englishman, come to wander for a month or two through the Old Dominion."

"Sir, you are most welcome here," responded my new friend. "My name is Thornton--Henry Thornton. This is my reverend friend Mr. Alsiger. This, Mr. Hubbard; and this, Mr. Byles--familiarly known amongst us as 'bold Billy Byles;' for a bolder man at a fence, a swamp, or a cane-brake, is not to be found between this and Charleston." This was said with a good-humoured laugh, and a nod to the gentleman in the blue coat and gilt buttons, who, for his part, shook hands heartily with me, and filled my glass full of claret. But nobody asked my name; and I was glad to find that this remnant of old chivalrous courtesy still prevailed in hospitable Virginia. After a pause of a few moments, such as is naturally produced when conversation has been interrupted, and has not had time to resume its course, Mr. Thornton observed:--

"I am always glad to meet an English gentleman, for my mother's brother married a lady from that country, who died not long ago; and the dearest, best, most charming old woman she was that ever the world saw."

"She was indeed," echoed the clergyman, from the other side. A smile, though it might be somewhat of a grave one, came up in my face, to find that I had so unexpectedly dropped in amongst dear Aunt Bab's connections. The quick eye of my host caught sight of the smile directly, and he readily drew his own conclusions; for he gave it me back again with a very slight inclination of the head, saying, *sotto voce*----

"Ah, ha!" None of the rest took any notice; and the wine continued to circulate round the table, until, suddenly, I heard from another room the tones of a piano, apparently very well played.

"Bessy thinks we are too long at our wine, and that is the way the gipsy calls us," said Mr. Thornton. "But we won't let her saucy tricks interrupt us. Fill your glasses, gentlemen. I will give you a toast. Here's eternal peace and good-will between old England and old Virginia; and may the kindred streams which flow in the veins of both never warm to anything but mutual friendship." All drank the toast with apparent alacrity and good feeling; and, although I am quite sure, from what I have seen and heard in this country, that a great many Americans remember with sore and irritable feelings, not only the war of the revolution, but the last war; and others who, for the purpose of pandering to the worst feelings of the basest of the population, affect enmity towards England; yet the majority of the wise and well-thinking would fain cultivate a good understanding between two countries, each of which bestows benefits upon and receives benefits from the other; ay and many, who have not forgotten all kindred ties, still look upon Great Britain as the birthplace of their race. Remembering, at length, after a very pleasant hour, that it was the custom in this country for a stranger to take the lead in departing from any scene of festivity. I rose, and proposed to retire to my room, saying:--

"I am not in fit guise to join any party of ladies, Mr. Thornton; but, if you will permit me, I will change my dress, and join you presently where those sweet strains are pouring forth."

"Let me show you the way," he said, taking a candle from the table; "and remember this is a place perfectly without ceremony. If you feel too much fatigued to-night for society, we shall expect to see you to-morrow at breakfast. If not, there is the room where you will find us assembled till ten o'clock this evening." And he pointed to a door on the other side of the hall, which was shut, notwithstanding the heat of the night. He now guided me up the stairs to a large, handsome room on the first floor, where I found everything that could be required for comfort, or even luxury; and, setting down the candle, for it was now twilight, he was about to leave me, still without asking my name. I stopped him, however; and a slight explanation ensued, which, notwithstanding my previous determination, I found myself bound to afford to one who had received me with such courteous hospitality. But I abstained from disclosing my name. He did not suffer me to go on long. "Say no more," he replied; "say no more. Your secret, if it be one, is safe with me. I dare say you have your reasons for remaining *incog.*; and, to tell you the truth, I am both glad you are come, and glad you are come quickly; for you have a good deal to hear and see about this place, and, perhaps, a little to do, which may require some thought as to the mode of doing it. My domestics will look to your general wants; and your own servants, I dare say, will take care of your more particular requirements." Thus saying he left me; and I sat down to think of the events of the day, before I went below to join what I could not but hear was a gay party.

CHAPTER V

It was by this time dark enough to make candles needful in the room; yet upon the western sky, as I gazed at it from the window, were still traced one or two lines of ruby light, with other lines which, probably, in the day, would have seemed but faint streaks of mist, now changed into a leaden blue by the approaching night. The principal features of the landscape also were still visible, though all the minor objects were lost. A glistening river reflected the colour of the western sky like a stream of blood; the undulating slopes of the land sometimes caught, on the summits, a touch of light, but were generally dark and grey; the distant trees in one or two places let through between their holes a glimpse of the fervid sunset sky; and high above were stars beginning to look out, eager for the departure of him who made them veil their glory. Nearer, far nearer, however, were little stars of earth. From under every bush, and amongst the branches of every fruit tree, dancing, skimming, now suddenly appearing, now suddenly eclipsed, were the fire-flies, those beautiful, most beautiful insects. I had seen many in Italy, coming out in clouds from the willows by the way-side, in the neighbourhood of Mantua and Modena. There, they looked like little sparks of fire, red in colour, whirling and bursting forth in clouds; but these in Virginia were larger, calmer, of a softer and more beautiful light, sometimes yellow like the moon, sometimes even of a bluish tinge, but exceedingly bright, and comparable to nothing I know of but small shooting stars. A spirit of calm enjoyment came over me after my hot and dusty ride, which I was in no haste to cast off; and I know not how long I should have gazed and pondered, but to the music of the piano were soon added the tones of a voice singing; and, resolving to improve the time to the utmost, I rose to search for my saddle-bags, and to ring for my good friend Zed. The room, I have said, contained everything requisite for comfort; but there was one exception. No such thing as a bell was to be seen. As if my step, however, awoke attendance, I had hardly reached the table when the door opened, and a neat little black boy in a white jacket presented himself, carrying in his hand a pair of slippers and a night cap. He asked, with the usual grin, if he could do anything for me; and, without waiting for a reply, pounced at once upon the saddle-bags, began untrussing them, and distributed their contents very skilfully in a chest of drawers. He was evidently well taught, though he could not refrain--what negro boy of fourteen could?--from examining curiously many of the unknown articles which he brought forth, and especially one of Palmer's neat little roll dressing-cases, which seemed to puzzle him amazingly. It was too much for human nature; and at length he turned, and simply asked me what it was. As I opened it to his eyes, he burst into a joyous peal of laughter, and, I could clearly perceive, would fain have been fingering the razors and other articles; but I dismissed him and told him to send my servant up. After dressing myself, and giving some directions to Zed, I walked down stairs again, looked in at the dining-room door to insure that I should find some known faces in the other room; and then crossing to the door which Mr. Thornton had pointed out, I entered with as much quiet dignity as a man of seven-and-twenty can assume. Instantly a blaze of light and a blaze of cheerful faces met my eyes. Mr. Thornton himself and the three other gentlemen whom I had seen before were there; but, besides these, the company included an elderly lady with silver hair and a very white cap, half a dozen fair-haired, bright-eyed girls of various ages from thirteen to twenty, two little boys, and a young man of about one-and-twenty. There was moreover in that room a young lady, very different in appearance from any of the rest, with jet black hair, dark eyes, and a fair skin, which nevertheless showed the *brunette* in its tint. She was small in every respect: her form, her feet, her hands were all miniatures; and, though exceedingly delicate and symmetrical, the whole had an aspect of insignificance, if I may so call it, at the first sight. She was tastefully and even elegantly dressed; though there was something a little fantastic in a bunch of wild leaves which she had entwined in her hair. As I entered, she was moving from the piano; and I naturally concluded she was the goddess of the song I had heard. She drew back, however, to the further side of the room when she saw me; and Mr. Thornton, rising, put his hand gently under my arm and led me forward to the old lady whom he named as Mrs. Thornton.

"These are my daughters," he added, waving his hand around the blue-eyed, fair-haired group. "This, my cousin, Mr. Dudley," introducing the young gentleman. "These two, my boys; and this, my saucy niece, Bessy. Nay, Bessy, come forth and don't affect what you never felt in your life, namely, shyness."

"Nay, my dear uncle," she answered, "I am not the least shy; but it was necessary to give you time to introduce all the generations of Adam, and to let this gentleman receive them into his cogitations. You did not tell me his name, however." This was a point which Mr. Thornton and I had not settled; but he answered, at once, with a shrewd twinkle of the eye,--

"Mr. Howard, my dear--Mr. Richard Howard. You are cousins, of course; for the Davenports, being related to all the best blood of England, must count cousinship with the Howards, beyond doubt. So make much of him, Bessy--make much of him." While her uncle had been speaking, Miss Davenport had surveyed me from head to foot, with an air which I must not call impudent nor even assured, but with a certain degree of saucy fun in the expression of her countenance, which I cannot say was altogether agreeable to me. I hate *piquante* women, and would a great deal rather that a woman had no wit at all, than that her wit should trench upon her womanly qualities. A strong-minded woman is worse; for then the feminine characteristics are almost obliterated--though you are sure to find out the woman somewhere; but the next bad thing to that is the *piquante* woman, whose wit overbears her tenderness. Still I was a little doubtful whether this was altogether the case with the fair lady before me; for, as soon as I perceived the way she scanned me,--and, being apparently rather short-sighted, she even put up a double eye-glass, to look at me more accurately,--I fixed my eyes quietly on her face, seeking to read something therein while she was examining me. The moment she detected me in so doing, the glass was removed, the eye-lids dropped, and a slight rosy colour came up in her cheeks, like day-dawn purpling the pale East. The next moment she said, as if in reply to her uncle's last words--

"My cousin is very welcome, then, to Virginia, Uncle Henry. God be praised, his name is Richard; for we have had Roberts enough in our race to extinguish any family under the sun."

"And pray what have the Roberts done to be so slandered, Bessy?" asked the elderly gentleman who had been introduced to me as Mr. Hubbard, walking across the room and addressing her in a tone of fatherly kindness.

"What have they *not* done?" interrogated Miss Davenport, with a gay laugh, "from Robert the Norman, and Robert the rhymer downwards. The records of horse-stealing and petty larceny are full of Roberts. Why in a book Uncle Henry lent me the other day, I counted at least twenty of them who had been convicted of one offence or another, to say nothing of a near relation of mine who would have cheated me out of everything I had in the world, if my uncle here would have let him."

"You forget my name is Robert, too?" replied Mr. Hubbard.

"Ah, my dear friend," she answered, laying her hand gently on his arm, "you are the exception, you know, which proves the general rule."

"And you are the greatest little hypocrite that ever lived," replied Mr. Hubbard, with a kindly smile. "Ay, I know you, Bessy. You cannot cheat me." Her face grew crimson; but she answered as briskly as ever:--

"All men think they know women's characters, but they know nothing at all about them; and how should an old bachelor know anything of woman? You had a great deal better marry me, and I will soon show you how well you understand me. We are not within the prohibited degrees, I think, cousin Hubbard, are we? Your great grandmother was my great grandmother's fifteenth cousin on the mother's side, if I recollect rightly; so the doors of the church are open to us, I fancy. But I will look in the prayer-book and see when I get up stairs, and tell you all about it to-morrow, and ask you to fix the day. But, my dear uncle, 'tis very sultry. Let us go into the porch." She was passing through us towards the drawing-room, when I detained her for a moment, to ask if she would not let me hear more distinctly the sweet voice I had heard singing at a distance. She looked up in my face with a quiet smile, saying,--

"I could answer you from the Bible, if I liked; but I will only reply--distance gives softness to everything, Mr. Howard. I will not dispel the illusion."

"How from the Bible?" I asked.

"Nay, nay," she replied; "I must not let my light, idle spirits carry me away into profanity. Sometimes, you know, the words of books we are much accustomed to read, come very aptly to the purpose, though very much out of reason. All I meant to say, that, while I was playing and singing, none of you gentlemen would come in; and now the opera is over I cannot do any more to-night; unless you all like to stand up and have a dance, and then I'll play for you until my fingers ache." Thus saying, she made her way to the door, and went out into the porch of the house. One by one most of the others followed; and I could see the sweet scene lying before the house, with the moonlight resting on the dewy grass, and the fire-flies flashing along the lawn. Even old Mrs. Thornton took her work in her hand, and followed the rest; and I was moving in the same direction, when Mr. Thornton stopped me, saying,--

"I want to talk to you a little." Then, lowering his voice, he added: "It is better that we should have a short conversation to-night upon points which, if I understand rightly, may considerably affect the matter in hand. I may be mistaken in the conclusions I have come to. As far as I have gone, I can have done no harm; but, as my friend Byles there would say, 'A hound that gets on a false scent, may be easily driven back at the beginning; but, if he runs on long, Heaven only knows where he will go to.'"

"I thank you for the opportunity, Mr. Thornton," I replied. "I want advice--I may want assistance; and, above all things, I want what the French would call *la carte du pays*."

"You shall have it as far as I can give it," said Mr. Thornton. "Just follow me into my little room, and we will have a clear understanding before we sleep." He opened a door at the other side of the parlour, and led the way across a stone hall, where we passed two or three negroes, all apparently as joyous and merry as they could be; but I was too much occupied with thoughts of my own to take the notice of them which I should have taken a day or two before. Consideration had been forced upon me rapidly. I was obliged to come to a conclusion much sooner than I had expected; and the question was, whether I was to place full confidence in my accidental host--to tell him all about myself and my own plans, or only to tell him as much as I could not conceal without ungentlemanly insincerity. His manner, his appearance, his language, were all those of a high-bred gentleman; his establishment was apparently that of a wealthy man; and there was a comfortable, home-like respectability about everything, that induced one to argue thus:--

"A man who has led such a life as this up to his age, is not likely to fall from it or to be subject to degrading and ruinous vices." But the conversation which I had heard between the master of the schooner and the slave-trader, as I came down the Chesapeake, did not connect the name of Thornton with very favourable memories. Before I could make up my mind exactly how to act, we were in the little book-room or library he had mentioned: and he courteously motioned me to a well-stuffed easy chair, while he took another on the opposite side of the table. For a moment an awkward pause ensued; and he then said,--

"Do not let me appear obtrusive or inquisitive; but I think I have the pleasure of speaking to Sir Richard Conway?" I bowed my head, replying,--

"The same, Mr. Thornton. From what has fallen from you, I imagine that we are no very distant connections, although it is by the merest accident I stopped at your house."

"My dear sir," he rejoined, "you have fallen into the midst of relations. Almost every one you saw around you is more or less connected with you, by blood or marriage. My uncle married your aunt; consequently we are first cousins, in law at least; all my children are in the next degree to you. Mr. Hubbard is as nearly connected. Mr. Alsiger stands in the same relationship, and our pretty little Bessy is your second cousin by blood." He paused, and thought for a moment, and then added, in a very grave tone,--

"So far this is all very satisfactory---that you should have come here in the first instance--that you should have come *incog.*--and that I should have divined all about it by a certain resemblance that you bear to an old picture at your aunt's house. But much must be thought of, Sir Richard--much must be told--many plans must be arranged. We must make a late sitting of it tonight, that you may have time to sleep over the matter, and take what steps you think fit to-morrow, not without deliberation. But, hark! There is a horse trotting up to the house." Walking to the door, he opened it, calling to one of the negroes, and saying--"C[ae]sar, tell Mr. Hubbard I hope he is not going home to-night. He is in the porch. Say I want to see him, to have some conversation with him." Then, turning to me, he added--"His advice may be very useful to us; he was once one of the most eminent counsel in Virginia; but his voice has become feeble; and he quitted the bar in consequence, I believe, of a rude judge saying to him--'Speak out, Mr. Hubbard! Neither judge nor jury can hear you.' He answered quietly, 'The ears of justice are somewhat deaf in Virginia.' But he never appeared at the bar again. His advice, however, is always excellent, for it's law and it's honesty. I would not advise a rogue to consult him; but he is the best adviser for a man of honour." He had hardly concluded the last sentence, when the servant to whom he had called opened the door, and said, in much better English than the negroes usually employ,--

"A gentleman, come on horseback, wants to speak with you, sir."

"Show him in," said Mr. Thornton promptly; but then added, "What sort of a man is he, C[ae]sar?"

"Very smart gentleman, sir," answered Caesar, with a slight snigger, if I may use such an expression. "Too smart; has got a good horse though."

"Well, show him in," repeated Mr. Thornton. The moment after, who should be ushered into the room but my fellow-traveller, Mr. Lewis himself, as much bedizened with rings and diamonds as ever. Mr. Thornton arose from his seat as the other entered, surveyed him quietly, and then remained standing. What it was in his air and manner I do not know; but I came to the conclusion merely from his look, that he comprehended in a moment the character of his visitor, and I watched the little scene that ensued with no slight interest.

"Mr. Thornton, I presume?" said Mr. Lewis, with a sweet soft air.

"The same, sir," replied Mr. Thornton, bowing. "In what way can I serve you?"

"Why, I have a little business to speak upon with you, Mr. Thornton," replied Mr. Lewis, with a side glance at me, whose full face he could not discern, as I sat with my back partly towards the door by which he had entered. "But perhaps we had better be private."

"As far as I am concerned," answered Mr. Thornton, "I do not know that there is anything I should not desire to be said in the presence of this gentleman; and if the business refers to anybody else, I always prefer that the communication should be made in writing, that I may think over my reply. Pray be seated," he added; and Mr. Lewis took a seat.

"Oh, if you, Mr. Thornton, don't mind, I don't," replied the other. "The matter is a very simple one--a mere matter of business. In short, I heard a few days ago that you had a lot of niggers for sale--some fifty or sixty; and though the lot is but a small one, I thought I would just step in and ask, as I was going up the country. No man can afford to give a better price than I can. I am known to treat well all I buy; and I just judged you might think it better to sell them to me, than to bring them to the hammer." A bright red spot had come up in Mr. Thornton's cheek; a deep furrow gathered between his eyebrows; his eye flashed; he set his teeth hard; and I thought there was some very violent answer coming. But instead of that, he remained perfectly silent for at least a minute, beating the ground with his foot.

"Pray where do you come from, sir?" he asked, at length, in a perfectly quiet tone.

"I live in Baltimore," answered Mr. Lewis; "but I do my principal business in New Orleans. I dare say we can make a trade, Mr. Thornton, for I deal as liberal as any man." Again Mr. Thornton remained silent, looking at the carpet. Then turning suddenly upon the other, he said, in a loud, stern voice,--

"You make a great mistake, sir. Let me tell you, no Virginian gentleman sells his servants, except in one of two cases. He is either bankrupt himself, or the servant whom he sells is too bad for him to keep. There is not one servant I have whom I would part with to you or any man, so long as he serves me faithfully, and I have the means to give him food. God grant it may never be otherwise!" Mr. Lewis turned a little white; but he stammered forth, in what seemed to be a somewhat impudent tone,--

"No offence, sir, I hope--no offence. I was informed positively----"

"I know, sir--I comprehend," interrupted Mr. Thornton, waving his hand. "You have been labouring under a mistake, which excuses your proposal. My name is Henry Thornton, sir. The person you wished to see is William Thornton, a distant relation of mine. There have been some painful mistakes already." Mr. Lewis still kept his seat, nowise abashed, though somewhat cowed; and, after biting his nether lip for a moment, he asked,--

"Pray, how far is it to Mr. William Thornton's?"

"About fifteen miles," answered my host drily.

"Lord bless my soul!" cried the trader, "what shall I do? My horse is dead tired; and I do not know the way." Mr. Thornton sat mute for a moment or two; and there was evidently a struggle within him. The old feelings of hospitality triumphed in a degree, however. "All the rooms in my house," he said, at length, "will, I believe, be occupied to-night; but there is one at the overseer's at your service. I will call a servant to show you the way." Approaching the door, he again called C[ae]sar, saying,--

"Conduct that gentleman to Mr. Jones's, and beg him to supply him with supper and what accommodation he may want." Then, with a very stiff bow, he saw Mr. Lewis depart, and closed the door after him.

"A slave-dealer never slept in this house since it was built," he said, in a somewhat apologetic tone, as soon as the man was gone. "I should almost be afraid of its catching fire, if he remained in it all night." He then broke into a laugh, partly gay and partly sarcastic, as it seemed to me; and, after musing for a moment, he observed,--

"This is strange--very strange, that he should have come here this night of all others in the week; but I am sorry now I dismissed him so rapidly. We have already got one good hint from him, Sir Richard, and perhaps might get more--though I do not much like fish that breed in muddy waters."

"I really do not understand you, Mr. Thornton," I answered. "This good man came down in the boat with me from Baltimore to Norfolk; and I heard some conversation going on between him and the master of the vessel, about the probable sale of a Mr. Thornton's slaves."

"And very likely thought _I_ was the Mr. Thornton," said my host, with a quiet smile. "Nay, make no excuse; it was a very natural mistake. But the case is this--Mr. William Thornton is my first cousin, with a hitch in the consanguinity which had almost made me, like an Irishman, call him my first cousin once removed. His father and my father were half-brothers; but his father was the elder by two or three years. They were both brothers of Colonel Thornton, who married your excellent aunt, Bab. Now, Colonel Thornton was as good a man as ever lived; but, having been a gay, dashing soldier, he had maintained in his household that sort of fine old Virginian economy which has brought so many of our best families to ruin. He was very nearly on the brink thereof when he married your aunt. Her fortune served, in some degree, to patch up his; her wise economy did the rest, without his ever perceiving that his native hospitality slackened in the least degree; so that, at the end of twenty years, he found himself, to his great surprise, a rich man, with an unencumbered estate. They had no children, unfortunately; and, very naturally, at his death, he left all he had to her who had saved it for him. Now we come to your part of the matter. Your aunt survived her husband twelve or fourteen years; and though she had not seen her own land, or any of her relations, except Mrs. Davenport and one other, for well nigh half a century, her heart naturally turned, on her death-bed, to those whose blood flowed in her own veins; and, as we all understood, she left her property to you."

"I have the will with me, duly authenticated," I replied.

"That is all right," rejoined Mr. Thornton; "but you were written to more than two years ago, and never answered."

"I beg your pardon," I replied. "I *did* answer as soon as I got the letters. I was then in India with my regiment, so that neither of them reached me for several months; but the first I received I answered at once, and the second very shortly after I received it, requesting further information as to the nature and extent of the property, and what steps were necessary to make it secure."

"Two letters!" ejaculated Mr. Thornton, thoughtfully. "I only know of one having been written to you. Do you remember the signatures?"

"I have them both up stairs," I answered. "One, I now remember, was signed 'Hubbard,' and advised my coming over immediately. The second was, I think, signed 'Robert Thornton, Attorney-at-law,' who desired I would send him out a power of attorney to act for me."

"This man's son!" exclaimed Mr. Thornton. "We never heard of that, and never received any answer to the first letter--perhaps it was intercepted. However, Mr. William Thornton almost immediately took out letters of administration to Colonel Thornton's property, as his next of kin--although your aunt had so long enjoyed undisputed possession. He has since, with the aid of this hopeful son of his, been fencing himself in with all sorts of legal forms and quibbles--has got possession of the negroes, let the old house and plantation, and is now, we understand, moving the legislature to escheat the property and grant it to him; the heirs being, as he declares, aliens."

"But does your law sanction such doings?" I asked.

"It sanctions a good many things that it should not sanction," replied Mr. Thornton; "and these matters of escheat and administration are so loosely managed here, that the property of persons dying without relations actually on the spot is an object of speculation and a means of livelihood to half the rogues in the state. Thank God, my dear young friend, you are here at last; for it is not too late yet to stop this iniquitous affair, though he has sold all the cattle and all the horses, which is a dead loss, I suppose."

"But can he not be made accountable?" I inquired. Mr. Thornton smiled.

"There are two sorts of banks," he answered, "from one of which you can draw money, from the other nothing but pebblestones. Now, Mr. William Thornton's bank is of the latter quality. The court required security, it is true, when they granted the letters of administration, but took men who are more deeply bankrupt than himself. That is the way we manage things in Virginia, especially when the people who are really interested do not appear to take care of their own property."

"But, my dear sir," I replied, "it was impossible. I was in India with my regiment. As some battles were coming on--expected every day--it was impossible either to ask for leave of absence or to sell out, until the war was at an end. As soon as that occurred, I *did* sell out; for the climate did not agree with me. I got bilious, and home-sick, and moody; disliked pillaus, abominated rice, and could not bear curry; was thoroughly disgusted with pale ale and claret, and thought Allahabad's sun the most unpleasant gentleman that ever rode the sky. Besides, I did not know what my aunt had left me. It might have been nothing but an old farthingale, for aught I knew to the contrary." Mr. Thornton laughed at the description of my disgust with India, but grew serious again directly, saying, "I beg your pardon. It is a very richly embroidered farthingale, I can assure you; as fine a plantation as any in Virginia, worth at least, under good management, from twelve to fifteen thousand dollars a year; a nice old house, somewhat like this; a good deal of scattered property; and about fifty negroes. The rest she emancipated; but these preferred to remain in their old condition, being accustomed to no other, and feeling that they wanted somebody to take care of them. Poor creatures! I dare say they are sorry enough now; but they had no notion into whose hands they are going to fall." His words made me muse for a moment. I then said, "Still, Mr. Thornton, I do not see how the words of that man Lewis, who was here just now, gave us any serviceable hint."

"Why don't you perceive?" he answered; "these fifty negroes, whom William Thornton wishes to sell, are the very fifty which your aunt left. He has not half a dozen of his own. He dare not bring these to the hammer, for fear of somebody opposing him; but if he gets rid of them by private sale, and sends them to New Orleans, we may whistle as long as we will, without getting either the servants or the money back again. But we had better consult Hubbard. Have you any objection to my telling him who you are? He will see the necessity of secrecy as well as we do."

"Not in the slightest degree," I answered. Mr. Thornton now rose and left the room. In two minutes he returned, bringing with him Mr. Hubbard, who seemed somewhat impatient of mood, saying, as he passed the door, "But really, Henry, I must get home. Positively I cannot stay to-night. I have got an attack of sciatica coming on. I feel it quite plainly; and nobody can nurse me like old Betty, you know." Mr. Thornton thrust him down into a chair, however, saying, "Rest your sciatica there, and let me introduce you to your cousin and mine, Sir Richard Conway." Mr. Hubbard rubbed the spectacles he had in his hand with the tail of his coat, put them on his nose, and gazed at me.

"Sir Richard Conway!" he exclaimed. "God bless my soul! I thought you were an older man. Well, I am very happy to see you, however; though you should either have come over sooner or answered my letter." All the explanations had now to be given anew; but he took my excuses in very good part, and plunged at once into an ocean of family affairs and points of law, which made him totally forget his sciatica and his desire to return home. The discussion was long; but it was highly beneficial and necessary. A definite course of action was laid out, to be commenced on the following morning; and at about half-past nine o'clock we arose from our conference, with the satisfaction of knowing that we were in a fair way of frustrating as iniquitous a scheme as was ever devised. I walked at once out towards the porch, where I heard music and singing going on of a simple kind, but of no very inferior quality, and I imagined that my fair connection, Bessy Davenport, had been prevailed upon to grant to others what she had refused to me. I was mistaken, however; she was leaning against one of the pillars, looking up at the moon. The music proceeded from a negro boy, sixteen or seventeen years of age, who was seated on one of the steps of the porch, cheek-by-jowl with one of Mr. Thornton's younger daughters, and playing on an instrument called a banjo--a sort of circular-bodied guitar, the strings of which he struck with the most extraordinary rapidity and skill, while he accompanied the sounds thus produced with the notes of a rich mellow voice, singing a wild negro song about--

"The shocking of the corn."

He was near the end of it when I came up, and I would willingly have encored it; but he changed at once to a very merry air; and a group of young people of the same complexion as himself, who had been standing round resting, I presumed, commenced dancing on the lawn with a right good will. They threw themselves into strange and grotesque, but sometimes picturesque and not ungraceful attitudes; and their whirling dark figures, the bright moonlight, and the flashing of the fireflies, actually amongst their feet, formed a scene I shall not easily forget. We stood gazing until the clock struck ten, little or no conversation going on meanwhile; but then Bessy Davenport and Louisa Thornton, my host's eldest daughter, came towards the door near which I stood. The former held out her hand frankly, saying.--

"Good night, Cousin Howard. We are all early birds here. May quiet dreams attend you; and if you ask me civilly, tomorrow, I will sing you 'Old Virginia,' or something equally classical." Thus ended my first evening on a Virginia plantation. In my own room, I ruminated on it all for half an hour, with sober pleasure. There had been something to amuse, something to interest, but nothing to excite or to disturb; and the mind could rest upon the memories of that day without one agitating sensation. I was a little fatigued with my hot ride, however, and at length I lay down on as soft a bed as I had ever met with, and my eyes closed quietly.

CHAPTER VI

I woke early in the morning, after having passed the night in dreamless slumber. Not a memory of the day's doings--not a vague shadow of thoughts, or words, or deeds--flitted across the chasm of sleep. When I opened my eyes, however, the daylight--faint and unconfirmed--was streaming in at the windows; and, for half an hour or more, I enjoyed one of those pleasant, idle lapses of existence which we so rarely have leisure to indulge, when life, like a river between its cataracts and rapids, rests unruffled by thought or action, without a ripple to mark that it is flowing on; and with nothing reflected from its tranquil surface but the faint, glistening images of the quiet things which surround it. I saw a patch of the blue sky through the window, and a soft white cloud float slowly across. I looked at the large, brass-topped andirons in the wide fireplace, and contemplated the lions' heads which adorned them. I made a human face out of the sleeve of my coat, as it hung over the back of a chair, with a large nose and a heavy eyebrow; and it looked so sleepy, that I had almost dropped into slumber again, out of mere sympathy, when suddenly the door of the room opened, and in came a nice-looking black boy, with a clean white jacket and apron, and a tray with several well-filled glasses upon it. He walked composedly up to my bedside, and presented the tray.

"What is this, my friend?" I said, taking one of the glasses, which appeared full of a clear brownish liquid, some lumps of ice and some fresh green herbs.

"The mint juleps, sir," replied the boy, waiting for me to drink, in order to take the glass away.

"The mint juleps!" I thought. "I wonder if it is one of the laws of the land that every one must drink a mint julep before he rises." However, I tasted the beverage, and it was delicious and most refreshing, at least for the time. The coolness imparted by the ice effectually screened the palate from all the hotter things which it contained; and it was not till afterwards that I found it would be advisable not to drink brandy with mint steeped in it so early in the morning. Hardly had the little *limonadier* gone, when my friend Zed appeared, and, while he was engaged with great skill and assiduity in putting all my dressing things to wrongs with true negro officiousness, he opened his morning budget of gossip by telling me that we could not have arrived at a better time, for there was soon to be a great camp-meeting in the immediate neighbourhood, where some very godly men were to hold forth. I had long wished to see one of these curious assemblages, and I accordingly took care to inform myself of the day and place where the exercises were to be held. Zed then proceeded, while I dressed, to tell me the whole politics of the family, with the business-like manner and volubility of a Spanish barber. From him I thus learned that Mr. Byles--or bold Billy Byles--was a suitor for the hand of Louisa, Mr. Thornton's eldest daughter, but that it was the general opinion of the kitchen and adjacent domains that he would not succeed in his suit, for that young Mr. Whitehead, the Presbyterian minister, came often to see Miss *Lou* in the morning, and was a very gentle, engaging young man. Master Harry, he said, my cousin's eldest boy, was a wild young dog, showing the true Virginian fondness for horse-flesh and fire-arms, having broken the knees of one of his father's best steeds, and burst two guns already, besides setting fire to the stables by exploding a percussion-cap with a hammer. How long he would have gone on I know not, had my dressing not been brought to an end; when, telling him to be within call after breakfast, I went down to the lower floor. I found the drawing-room--or parlour as they call it here--vacant, and sauntered out into the porch, where the first thing I saw was Mr. Lewis, walking his horse quietly along the road from the overseer's house towards the highway. The next instant I perceived one of the servants start out upon him, like a spider from the corner of his web upon an entangled blue-bottle, and hand him a paper. I knew well enough what sort of document it was, namely, a caveat against the sale or purchase of any of the slaves of good Aunt Bab, signed by Mr. Thornton as agent, and Mr. Hubbard as attorney of Sir Richard Conway, under a power which had been drawn up the night before. This power had been rapidly and informally executed, and probably was invalid; but my presence rendered it unnecessary, except inasmuch as it enabled me to remain incognito for some time longer, and watch the proceedings of the conspirators. I must remark, it was not dated, and was merely alluded to in the caveat, so that no immediate indication of my visit to Virginia was afforded by that document. Mr. Lewis had just passed on his way, after reading the paper with feelings which of course I could not divine, when, from the other side, I saw approaching a pretty little female figure, dressed in a peculiar style, or rather in a medley of a great number of styles and fashions, outraging all of them in some respects. She had no bonnet on, but merely a parasol over her head; the length of her dress, instead of being of that extensive flow which has succeeded the short petticoats of a few years ago, was brief enough to show an exceedingly pretty foot and ankle, but it was so conspicuously full as to put me in mind of the costume of some of the Swiss cantons. Her shoes had minute buckles in them instead of being sandalled in modern style; and her hair, instead of being propped up to a towering height with a scaffolding of tortoise-shell, lay flat, and was gathered into a knot behind, in the antique Greek mode. As soon as her parasol was turned a little aside, I perceived it was Miss Davenport; and though she came quietly on, with her eyes bent upon the path, apparently unconscious that I was in the porch, I was, I am afraid, unjust to her, and imagined that there was a good deal of coquetry in both dress and manner. She had puzzled me the night before--she puzzled me still. There was something of frankness, something of archness, which was not displeasing; but something also of daring, of independence, of wilfulness, which I did not like. Pretty she certainly was, nay, beautiful; for the more one examined the small features and delicate form, the more symmetry and the more grace were apparent. But I never was one of those who can fall in love with pictures, or statues, or even marionettes. Pygmalion's statue might have remained ivory to the great conflagration, before I would have sighed or prayed it into life; and as for actresses, I always feel a green curtain falling between me and them, even before the end of the play. It seemed that morning as if some peculiar demon had seized upon me, and made me resolve, for my sins, to see what really was in Bessy Davenport--to tease her, to worry her, and to bring out the latent soul. I went forward to meet her; and, as soon as she really saw me, her whole aspect and manner changed. A gay, light, half-sarcastic smile played upon her lip, her eyes sparkled, and, holding out her hand, she said,--

"Good morning, cousin; I hope your aristocratic head has been able to repose quietly in this democratic community." I might feel a little staggered by this easy salutation. It was rather like a small masked battery opening upon one when marching gaily up to an attack; but I rallied my forces at once, and replied, "As well as if all the coronets that ever were lined with ermine had rested beside me on the pillow. Democracy is not a catching disease, I should imagine, from all I have seen of it. But may I ask how *you* slept? I trust without any painful visions of slaughtered swains and disconsolate lovers, or any twinges of remorse for all the woes you have and will inflict upon mankind."

"None, in truth," she answered at once. "Do you know I once killed a rattlesnake?--yes, with my own hand; and when I saw the shining reptile lie dead before me, I remembered he had given honourable warning before he sprang, and then I might feel a little regret that I had struck him so hastily with the butt of my riding-whip. But man is a very different sort of reptile: he gives no warning, and is far more venomous." A strange sort of painful feeling was produced in my mind by her words. I asked myself, "Can this young girl, apparently not twenty, have already tasted of that bitter cup which man so often holds to woman's lip?" The shadow of the thought must have crossed my face, for I was roused from my half-reverie by a clear, gay laugh. "Now I will show you," she said, "how women can divine. I am no love-lorn maiden, pining for some faithless swain--no man-hater from personal experience of man's unworthiness. I never saw the man yet, and never shall, who could raise my pulse one beat to hear his coming or his going step. But let me do justice to both sides. No man ever said to me in a sweet maudlin tone, 'Bessy, will you marry me?' nor even, to my face, declared I was the most charming of my sex, or anything of that kind. But I judge men from what I have seen of their conduct towards others; and I believe them to be the most thoroughly selfish class of beings--at least as far as women are concerned--that God ever created."

"And when it becomes your case to listen and have sweet words spoken," I replied, "you will think you and the speaker are two bright exceptions." She coloured a little, and looked almost angry, saying, "Never! I will never give any one the opportunity; for I go very much with the old saying, 'no *gentleman* was ever refused by a *lady*.' I mean, no man who is really a gentleman would propose to a lady who had not given him such encouragement as would preclude her, if really a lady, from refusing him if he did propose."

"Then you would have a lady," I said, "give a man encouragement before she knows whether he really loves her or not. Or you would have her advance step by step with him, like two armies in battle-array, watching each other's movements, and each taking care that the other did not get the slightest advantage; sure to get upon some slippery ground before they have done, my dear young lady!" Her face was now glowing like a rose, and she answered quite impatiently, "Pshaw! you know what I mean; and every man of common tact will, in his heart, admit that I am right."

"In neither one or the other of the two cases," I replied.

"What two cases?" she asked.

"Two assertions, I should have called them," answered I; "the one you just now made, and the preceding one, that men are entirely selfish in all that concerns women. I have seen cases in which no selfish motive could be discerned in the beginning, in the course, or in the end of such matters; and, being a good deal older than you are, I have had more means of judging."

"Why, how old are you?" she asked abruptly.

"Seven-and-twenty," I answered.

"I thought so!" she cried, with a joyous laugh; "but you look a good deal older."

"Indeed!" I answered, perhaps a little mortified; "but what makes you seem to rejoice that I am seven-and-twenty only?"

"Excuse me," she replied, dropping a low curtsy. "I might say, because that makes you just a fit age for myself, or a hundred other civil things. But I would rather say nothing, Sir Richard."

"Sir Richard!" I exclaimed. "How came you to give me that name, Miss Davenport?"

"Because you are just seven-and-twenty; and because there is 'Richard Conway' printed in white letters upon the black trunks you left at Norfolk," she replied, with an air of funny malice, adding, "at least so your servant told the cook, and the cook told my maid, and my maid told me, dear cousin; and so there's my 'how.'"

"Good heaven, this babbling is very provoking!" I exclaimed, greatly annoyed; "it may spoil all our plans."

"No fear," she answered; "we are so surrounded by woods and wilds that the secret will keep till next Sunday at least; for the negroes will not see those of any other plantation till then."

"And *you* will tell no one?" I inquired.

"Honour!" she replied, in a tone of mock solemnity.

"If you do," I said, laughing. "I will tell your uncle, whom I see coming up there, that you and I have been standing this quarter of an hour at the edge of the porch, talking of love all the time."

"Love!" she cried, "what is that? I declare such an antediluvian monster has never been once mentioned between us till you brought it this minute out of the blue mud of your own imagination."

"A very savoury figure," I answered. "But as to love, if we have not been talking about it, notwithstanding all circumlocutions, we have been thinking about it."

"Not a bit," she replied. "We have been talking, and thinking too, of the most opposite things--of the very antipodes of love. Courtship and marriage, if you like; but what has love to do with them, cousin?" And she fixed her full dark eyes upon my face, with a look of the most perfect simplicity--assumed, of course, but very well put on. I felt somewhat revengeful, and I almost longed to try if I could not make the boasting little beauty know something of the power she scoffed at. But just then Mr. Thornton came up, and began jesting with his fair relation upon her morning reveries beside the stream.

"I saw you, Bessy," he said; "and if I had met with Mr. Howard, I should have sent him down to try if he could not break up your visions."

"I dare say he would have succeeded," she answered; "for he has been amusing me here with some of the driest subjects in the world."

"Of what kind, little hypocrite?" asked Mr. Thornton.

"Arithmetic--arithmetic," she replied gaily. "As, for example, how many ganders' heads are required to make one goose's. But, here comes Mr. Hubbard slowly down stairs; and there is Mr. Alsiger's back at the end of the passage; so I had better go in to get breakfast ready, for Lou won't be down this hour." And away she ran, casting her parasol into a cane seat in the hall. Mr. Thornton paused, and fell into a reverie for a moment or two, which he concluded by saying, as if to himself,--

"The poets are wrong." I knew not what he meant, of course; and whether those few words directed his and my thoughts, or not, I cannot tell; but at breakfast we got into a discussion of poets and poetry.

"It is wonderful," Mr. Thornton observed, after a few other remarks upon the subject, "that with all the superabundant energies which this country possesses, and all the imagination which she expends upon other themes, we have, as yet, produced no very remarkable poet." I ventured to say that I did not think it wonderful; and, of course, there was a call for my reasons.

"In the first place," I replied, "the energies of the people have other objects, and those principally material. In the next place, the imaginative faculty finds other occupation."

"How so, how so?" asked Mr. Hubbard.

"In orations, speeches, declamations," I answered, and then continued, with a smile, "perhaps I might add, in finding causes for offence in the acts of other nations; and without offence, let me say, Mr. Alsiger, in religious exercises which perhaps touch the fancy rather than inform the heart."

"Too true, too true!" said the good clergyman, with a sigh.

"Then again," I continued, "poetry is generally the offspring of leisure. Now, there is--at least it seems so to me--no such thing as leisure in America, and----"

"Excuse me," interrupted Mr. Thornton, laughing; "we have plenty of leisure in Virginia, if we did but know what to do with it. But you were going to add something."

"I was merely going to remark, as a matter of history, that poetry rarely flourishes in republics. Monarchies are its congenial soil. It is a flower that requires a hot-house."

"Oh, heresy, heresy!" cried Bessy Davenport. "What! can such noble and inspiring things as freedom and independence have no power to awaken great thoughts, or even to clothe them in immortal verse?"

"Your pardon, fair lady," I answered; "but you are assuming the premises. Freedom and independence, I would contend, can exist as well--nay, better--in a well-ordered monarchy than in any republic. The tyranny of a number--or of a majority, if you please,--is always more terrible than the tyranny of an individual--the tyranny of public opinion, more potent than the rule of a monarch, and more likely to be wrong. But all that is beside the question. I merely spoke of an historical fact. With an exception here and there, you find no very remarkable poets under republics: many under monarchs."

"I have never considered the facts," said Mr. Hubbard; "but let us test it, my dear sir; and to begin with the beginning, there is Homer. It is very true he lived under a whole host of kings, if there is any faith at all to be placed in the tales regarding him; but what say you to the whole batch of Athenian poets?"

"That they lived under archons, which were tantamount to kings," I answered. "And then, again, Pindar; he could not even endure the sort of mitigated republicanism of Greece, but fled to the court of a tyrant. Virgil, Horace--every great Roman poet, in short--flourished about the time of the emperors. In England, Gower, Chaucer, Shakespeare, all lived, and wrote, under monarchs; and it has even seemed to me that the greater the despotism, the better the poet."

"But Milton! Milton!" cried Mr. Alsiger; "he was a republican in heart and spirit."

"But he never wrote a line of poetry," I answered, "under the Long Parliament, or at least very few. Not much did he write under the tyranny of Cromwell; and all his best compositions date from the reign of one or the other of the Charleses."

"But Dante," said Mr. Thornton; "I cannot indeed, discuss his merits with you; for I have well nigh forgotten all the Italian I knew thirty years ago. He, however, lived under a republic."

"He is an exception," I replied; "although I can hardly look upon the constitution of Florence, at that time, as a republican form of government. It was rather oligarchical; and even then, shadows of an emperor and a pope overhung it. But Ariosto, Tasso, Boccaccio, and all the rest of the Italian poets were the mere creatures of courts. The same is the case with France, although she never had but two poets; and the same with Germany."

"May it not be," asked Mr. Hubbard, "that monarchies, up to the present day, have been much more frequent than republics?"

"Perhaps so," I answered; "yet it is very strange that we find no poet of mark actually springing from a pure republic. Where is the Swiss poet? although every accessory of country, history, climate, and natural phenomena seems to render the very air redolent of poetry." Bessy Davenport sprang up from the table, shaking her head at me, with a laugh, and saying,--

"I abominate your theory. You are worse than an abolitionist; and if you preach such doctrines here, we will have you tried for high treason." As soon as she was gone, and Mr. Alsiger had trotted home on his pony, which was brought up shortly afterwards, Mr. Hubbard, Mr. Thornton, and myself fell into secret conclave, and debated what was next to be done.

"I think," said my host, "the best thing we can do, before the day becomes too hot, will be to ride over to Beavors, take a look at the plantation, see the house, which is vacant just now, and, after having got some dinner at the little village hard by, return in the evening by my worthy and respected cousin's house, just to let him know that we have an eye upon his motions. I dare say some of the girls will accompany us on horseback; and their presence will make our visitation of the old place less formal and less business-like. There are two or three things worth seeing by the way; and we may as well spend the day after this fashion as any other."

"You will find no dinner there that you can eat," said Mr. Hubbard.

"Leave that to me--leave that to me," returned Mr. Thornton, with a nod of his head. "I will cater for you; and if you do not like so long a ride, you can come in the carriage."

"Perhaps that will be better," said Mr. Hubbard; "and, I suppose, it would be as well to have me with you, in case of your needing legal advice." Thus was it soon settled; and while Mr. Thornton went to order horses and carriages, and a great many things besides, I mounted to my own room to make some change in my dress, and to give my good friend Zed a hearty scolding for babbling about my affairs in a strange house. I might as well have left it alone; for though he promised and vowed all manner of things, and assured me, with many a grin, that he had not an idea he was doing any harm in what he had said, I have since found that the propensity to gossip is too strong in the negro composition to be curbed by any reasoning or by any fear. Indeed, I am inclined to believe it is part and parcel of the original sin; for certainly, if Eve had not got gossiping with the serpent, she would not have made such a fool of herself as she did.

CHAPTER VII

When I came down from my room, I found Miss Thornton and Miss Davenport already in riding costume, Mr. Byles preparing to accompany us, and Mrs. Thornton and Mr. Hubbard settling that they would drive over in the carriage, *tête-à-tête*; while before the door were a number of horses of various descriptions, some bearing ladies' saddles, and some equipped for men. Behind the train was a good large, roomy vehicle, of a very comfortable but old-fashioned form, into which sundry servants of various hues were placing those baskets and packages by the agency of which, I doubted not, Mr. Thornton intended to insure a comfortable dinner wherever we might stop. Having seated the ladies, the gentlemen were soon in the saddle; and away we went at full speed, as if there had been a fox before us, across the little bridge, and up the road towards the highway. As long as we had anything like green herbs beneath our feet, this was all very well; but when we came upon the public road, the dust soon compelled us to slacken our pace and proceed more leisurely. The party fell speedily into what I suppose was its natural arrangement: Mr. Byles riding beside Miss Thornton; I accompanying her fair cousin; and Mr. Thornton himself falling behind to give some directions to his eldest boy, who accompanied us on a beautiful dark chestnut pony--which, by the way, had an awkward habit of throwing out her hoofs at anything which might come behind her, and was consequently quite as well in the rear. Miss Davenport, as we went, was as gay as a lark; and, in the spirit of light badinage with which she had begun the day, contrived to tease me very heartily all the way that we went. I found that she was exceedingly well read, especially in modern history, and she managed to twist and turn a great many of the acts and deeds of Old England in such a manner as more than once to put me on the defensive somewhat warmly; and then she would laugh till her eyes almost ran over, and declare that Englishmen never could bear to hear a word said against their country. Positively, I was not certain, in the end, whether I did not hate her mortally. On the whole, however, I was not sorry to hear what Americans really thought of many of our doings; and I doubted not in the least that Miss Davenport's views were but the reflex of those most generally entertained. In them there was much of prejudice undoubtedly; many of her facts were wrong; many of the inferences unjust; and, almost always, the motives were, I may say, ridiculously distorted. Purposes and objects which never entered into the head of any one Briton from the Land's End to John O'Groat's House, were ascribed to the whole nation as coolly and positively as if they were demonstrated certainties. Still, her free-spoken comments gave me an insight into the feelings with which a great part of the American people regard my countrymen, and which is politely concealed from us in ordinary society. The scenery through which we passed was rather flat and monotonous, and the forest in general shut out all distant prospects. Nothing of any very great interest struck me by the way, except, indeed, the profusion and beautiful variety of the wild flowers, still in bloom, and the occasional gush of some delicious odour from the woods as we rode along. Birds of gorgeous plumage, too, were flitting amongst the trees; but, oh! how I longed for the delightful spring sounds of England--the voice of the thrush, the blackbird, and the lark. I would have given all the gay feathers of the birds in sight for even one song of the robin. There was a bird, indeed, which did, now and then, utter one or two solitary notes, as if he would fain have sung if he had known how; and Miss Davenport praised his voice as if he had been a nightingale.

"You do not call that singing?" I said; and when I tried to give her some idea of the music of our woods, she declared it was all prejudice, and that I was determined not to like anything in America. I had an account to settle with her, however, and I resolved not to lose any opportunity. Shortly after, a small bird of rather graceful form flew from one branch of a tree to another, mewing like a cat as it went, and I quietly asked her if that was a singing bird also.

"Pshaw!" she cried; and, touched for once, struck her horse with the whip, and dashed on towards a gate, at which the two who had preceded us had already arrived.

"Soberly, soberly, Bessy!" ejaculated Mr. Thornton from behind. "Don't set off like a mad thing."

"As soberly as I can," replied Miss Davenport, laughing; "but this man provokes me--he is so intensely English."

"Thank God!" I ejaculated as I passed on.

"For what?" asked the gay girl, half laughing, half pouting.

"First for being intensely English," I replied; "and, secondly, for having provoked you. It was exactly what I wished; for, to say the truth, Miss Davenport, I thought it was high time I should have my turn."

"Then I shall sulk," she said. And not a word more did she speak till, passing barns and stables, and sundry other outbuildings, the uses and purposes of which I cannot pretend to describe, we arrived at the door of a large, square, red brick house, much like, in some respects, that of Mr. Thornton himself. Before the bell could be rung, a neat-looking black woman appeared, and told us that the family (that is to say, the family who had hired the plantation) were in Richmond; but upon our object being explained, she very civilly told us to come in, and that we were quite welcome to look over the house and premises as much as ever we pleased.

"I shall stay here with Hal, and wait until the carriage comes up," said Mr. Thornton; "but you can go in and look around. Show him the portraits in the dining-room, Bessy." Miss Davenport made no answer; but Louisa Thornton and her swain had already entered; and while she followed them, I followed her, almost mechanically. Mr. Byles man[oe]uvred like a general, and contrived to lead his fair companion exactly in the opposite direction to that in which we were going; but Miss Davenport, in obedience to her uncle's commands, took her way at once to the dining-room, which we entered by the third door on the left. She said nothing, but looked quite grave, while I opened the closed shutters, and let in the daylight. It seemed to me that she was carrying on her sulky humour seriously; and, returning from the window, I held out my hand to her, saying--

"Let us make peace." She started; but gave me her hand, answering,--

"You are mistaken, cousin, I think. You cannot suppose that I am so silly as to turn jest into earnest--at least I hope not. But I cannot be gay here. This place is full of memories to me. In it all the earlier part of my life was spent, under the care of that dear and wise old lady." And she pointed with her hand to one of two pictures which hung over the large mantelpiece.

"They are very happy memories, it is true," she continued; "yet, my dear cousin, it strikes me that memory has the effect of moonlight, softening the harsher things of life, and saddening the brighter." The heart of Bessy Davenport was speaking now. I had got the key, and I never lost it again.

"It is very true," I answered gravely. "My own early years were very happy ones. I love the spots where they passed; I like to dwell upon their memories, but it is with a sort of mournful pleasure. Man, with his eager aspirations for new things, never loves to lose aught of that which he has once possessed; and often, when I sit by the fireside with my sister, in the old hall, she and I fall into reveries, longing both of us, I know, to give back tangible life and human energy to those who once sat there with us, and substance and reality to the spectres of remembrance. But, indeed, I knew not that this had been your early home; otherwise I do not think I should have let you come here with us."

"Oh, yes," she answered; "I am very fond of spending long hours here. My mother died when I was four years old; my father died before her. There was some dispute about my property; my cousin Robert tried hard to cheat me out of everything; and this was judged the best home for me during my early youth. A happier home it could not have been; for dear Aunt Bab would never send me to school, but taught me almost everything herself that she could teach, and said she was determined to make an English lady of me. You know that is impossible," she added, with one of her light smiles; "the rebel blood is too strong in me for that."

"And who is that gentleman?" I asked, pointing to the other picture which hung over the mantel, and which represented a fine-looking old man in a blue uniform.

"Oh, that is Colonel Thornton," she replied. "They are both fine pictures; the one by Copley, the other by Stuart. But there is a third you should look at, by some English artist, I do not know whom." And she turned towards the opposite wall. There, to my surprise, I beheld a perfect and masterly copy of the portrait of my own father which hangs up in our hall. As I gazed at it, I just caught Miss Davenport's eyes turning from the picture to my own face; and the next moment she said, "Should I have needed anything but that picture, Sir Richard, to tell me who you really are?" I felt something rising in my eyes, as I gazed here, in a foreign land, at the features which I had so often stood to contemplate in my own home, and remembered that picture was a pledge of early affection between brother and sister which had existed unbroken to the end of life. I quietly drew Miss Davenport's arm through my own and turned away out of the room. She said nothing for some minutes, but seemed unconsciously to take her way up the stairs where we could hear the voices of Miss Thornton and Mr. Byles, apparently in very gay conversation. At the first landing she stopped, however, saying, "And so you have a sister? I am very glad of it. Having a sister humanizes a man, and gives him something to think about besides himself."

"I have, indeed, a very dear and very beautiful sister," I replied. "But do you not think, Miss Davenport, that having a wife might humanize a man as well as having a sister?"

"Ah!" she cried, looking up with one of her gay smiles again, "are you a married man, then, Sir Richard?"

"No," I answered, "I am not so happy. But pray answer my question?"

"And is your sister married?" she asked.

"No, indeed," I replied; "but she is six years younger than I am. And now answer my question, as I have answered yours."

"No, no," she responded, "not now. My answer would have to be a saucy one, and I cannot make such here."

"Well, then, perhaps, I may ask it somewhere else," I said, laughing. What force she attributed to my words I knew not, but she quietly slipped her arm out of mine, and ran up the other flight of steps. As we reached the top, we heard, through the window, at the end of the long corridor which we had now reached, the sound of carriage-wheels below, and, looking out, we saw Mr. Hubbard handing Mrs. Thornton from the carriage, while Mr. Thornton was giving various directions to the servants.

"I fear my aunt will make herself ill with this jaunt," said Miss Davenport, evidently a little desirous of changing the conversation. "She is in very delicate health. Does it not strike you, Sir Richard, that American ladies are very weakly creatures, compared with Englishwomen? I must make an exception in my own favour; for Aunt Bab used to make me walk five or six miles a day, or ride, or skip, or take one sort of violent exercise or another during half of my time. In everything else I was quite a spoiled child; but in this she was inexorable, and I am reaping the benefit of it now."

"I have, indeed, remarked," I said, "that the ladies of this country are not so strong as those of Europe; but I cannot help thinking that the climate is more enervating."

"Not a bit of it," she cried; "that is one of your prejudices again, I am sure. We get feeble and delicate because we take no exercise, and live altogether in a sort of artificial manner. It is worse in the South than in the North a great deal, because here, with the multitude of servants we have, a southern girl hardly learns the use of her feet or her hands. The only time for exercising the first is at a ball, and the second when she plays on the piano. She gets up in the morning, and sits down in an armchair, and says, 'Julia, bring me my slippers; Susannah, comb my hair;' and so the whole day goes on. Climate has nothing to do with it. It is want of free air and proper exercise; bad hours, and all that sort of thing. We are up here, uncle," she continued speaking to Mr. Thornton, who was calling to know where we were; and in a moment after, the whole party were reassembled. We then walked over the house, visited the stables and outbuildings, and made a tour through the negro cabins, which lay at a little distance behind. The condition, mode of life, and treatment of the negro population in the country, were of course subjects of great interest to me, and as these were the first rural slaves I had seen, I asked a good many questions, in which Mr. Thornton aided and joined me. All the people seemed happy and contented--at least there was nothing to show the contrary; yet, in one or two cases--amongst some of the younger men especially--I imagined I perceived a sort of reserve--a holding back of their thoughts, as if they were either unwilling or afraid to speak out boldly. I called Mr. Thornton's attention to this fact, as we turned back towards the house; and he replied,--

"It is very possible that such is the case, especially here. The family who have hired the plantation are not Virginians, as I hardly need tell you; for such a thing as a gentleman hiring another plantation in Virginia is hardly known. Mr. Stringer is a northern man, who has bought some property near, which he is getting into order, and on which he is building a house in the modern style. He has not been long enough in the South to understand our ways; and they say his negroes are treated rather hardly, as is frequently the case with northern men, when they first come here. The general prejudice is, that they make the harshest masters; but I believe the cause of their exacting too much is, that they do not understand the character of the negro, nor his capabilities; that they expect from him more than he can perform either physically or intellectually. Indeed, how can they understand all the peculiarities of these poor people as well as we can, who have been brought up amongst them--played with them in our childhood, and grown with them from youth to manhood? The best way for you to form an accurate judgment on these subjects will be, to set out in the morning early, and take a walk alone through my plantation, or any of those in the neighbourhood: talk with the people in the fields or in the cottages; tell them you are an Englishman, and want to know something about them. No man amongst us has anything to conceal, I believe, Mr. Howard; and perhaps you may satisfy yourself that a great deal of unjust prejudice has been excited in regard to the condition of the negroes."

"But still I cannot help thinking this slavery is a very great evil, Mr. Thornton," I replied.

"Perhaps so," he said, thoughtfully; "yet it is one which exists. It is not of our making; and I can see no escape from it either with benefit to the poor people themselves, safety to the state, or justice to the master. I could discuss this question a long while with you, and may do so some day. In the meantime, examine and judge for yourself; and we can then talk of it more fairly. But it is a subject, depend upon it, which has many aspects; and no man who has not examined it under all, is competent to reason upon it. Abstract propositions have very little bearing upon complicated facts." I knew there was a great deal of truth in what he said. Such an institution (if it deserves that name), when it has lasted several centuries, and, in fact, grown with the growth and strengthened with the strength of a state, must have carried its roots very deep--too deep, indeed, for any wise man to attempt to eradicate it without great precaution. The case of the serfs in Europe, in ancient times, was very different. There was no outward mark of distinction upon them: they were of the same races, the same classes of intellect, the same capabilities, the same characteristics--as their lords. It was there, class-servage; here, it is race-servage; and the distinction is a very important one. Nevertheless, I was not convinced that such a thing as slavery should exist anywhere, or in any circumstances. But to deal fairly with the question, I resolved to do what Mr. Thornton suggested: to examine accurately; and I doubted not that I should have as good an opportunity of doing so as any Englishman ever had--perhaps better. As we walked on towards the house, I perceived that the eyes of my host and Mr. Hubbard were frequently turned towards the sky, especially about the south-west, and I saw, in that direction, two or three lines of leaden-looking clouds coming up over the trees.

"It is going to rain, my dear," said Mrs. Thornton; "had we not better have the carriage up, and get home?"

"If a storm be coming, it would catch you long ere you could get there," replied her husband. "There is a drop or two already, upon my word. Well, 'let it come down,' as Banquo's murderer says. We can but dine here, while it goes on. It will be but a thunder-burst. Here, Harry, run and tell Dick and Jupiter to bring all the things out of the carriage, into the dining-room. We will take the house by *storm*; and, in the first place, I will go and summon good old Aunt Jenny to surrender at discretion. Doubtless, as the garrison is but small, she will make no great resistance." Thus saying, he ran into the house. All the rest followed, and we found Mr. Thornton and a stout elderly mulatto cook or housekeeper, in the dining-room, fully agreed upon terms, and, by their united strength, pulling out the dining-tables to a sufficient length to accommodate the number of our party. To my surprise, the good yellow woman, after courtesying respectfully to Mrs. Thornton, kissed Bessy Davenport warmly; and, may I confess it?--there was something in the universal love which she seemed to inspire wherever she came, which gave me a little inclination to fall in love with her too, notwithstanding the state of semi-warfare wherewith our acquaintance had commenced.

CHAPTER VIII

Everything except poetry is pleasant when improvised; and our dinner that day was an example. In less than a quarter of an hour we had on the table excellent cold ham and roast fowls, eggs in a variety of forms, and several bottles of good wine. Fried chickens followed; and though the rain now poured down in torrents such as I have never seen elsewhere,--no, not in the far East; though the thunder roared and the lightning blazed, some times in three or four streaks at once, we were as gay a party as ever gathered round a social board. Bessy Davenport had recovered her spirits; Louisa Thornton seemed resolved to laugh the thunder down; Mr. Hubbard was full of quaint humour, and only now and then expressed a hope that "it would not end in a drizzle," as he must positively be at home before dark; and even Mrs. Thornton, though she now and then put her hands before her eyes, when the lightning was very vivid, congratulated herself at having a house over her head during the storm, and evidently felt the sort of comfort which is most forcibly brought home to us when we distinctly see the perils or discomforts from which we are sheltered for the time. Gradually the thunder abated; its roaring voice grew fainter, and followed not so close upon the blaze; but the rain still pattered down, making a sort of rushing sound upon the gravel before the house, when, suddenly, young Harry Thornton started up, exclaiming,--

"Hark! They are bringing up the carriage, I think."

"Nonsense!" said Mr. Thornton, keeping his seat. "That cannot be, my son." But by this time both Harry and bold Billy Byles were at the windows; and the next instant the latter exclaimed, thrown out of all softer sayings by his surprise,--

"By jingo! here is Mr. Stringer and all his family, with two carriages, eight horses, and an ox team. I should not wonder if there was a freshet down at the bridge." Mr. Thornton did look a little abashed at being caught revelling in another man's house during his absence, and that a northern man too; but he recovered himself in a moment, saying--"Keep your seats, ladies and gentlemen, keep your seats. I will warrant your welcome, and we have not yet begun our strawberries and cream." His exhortations were vain, however, upon the greater part those present; and finding that he could not restore order to the feast, Mr. Thornton rose with the rest; but, instead of going to witness the debarkation of Mr. Stringer's family from the window, he sought an umbrella and went down the steps to hand Mrs. Stringer out of the carriage. What passed between him and the master of the house I did not hear; but I saw the latter laugh and shake him by the hand; and, a moment after, he re-entered the dining-room, having on his arm a lady about three-and-thirty years of age, who looked scared and somewhat aghast, but, I think, rather from the effects of storm through which she had passed than from the scene presented by her own dining-room, for the sight of which she had probably been prepared as she came from the carriage to the house. Three young boys, from seven to ten years of age, followed close upon their mother's steps; and at last, after a short pause, appeared Mr. Stringer, in whom, now without his hat, I instantly recognized a gentleman whom I had met at dinner in New York.

"Farewell to my incognito!" I thought; but Mr. Stringer's first attention was paid to Mrs. Thornton, and then to Miss Davenport, who seemed an especial favourite both with himself and his wife; and I had time to remark, ere he noticed me, a singular-looking man by whom Mr. Stringer was followed. He could not have measured less than six feet two inches in height, while, from shoulder to shoulder, I do not think the extent was more than a foot. His whole frame was about an equal width; only his legs, pack them together how you would, must still have remained more bulky than his body. His arms were thin, and his hands long and bony; but his face, though exceedingly ugly, and not improved by the ill-cut, long sandy hair which thatched his head, or the rawish white skin that covered it, was highly intelligent, with a quick, eager, grey eye, which ran over every thing and every person in the room in a moment. The dress of this apparition was of no particular date, and had nothing very remarkable in form. I only remarked that it was all of black, not very new, and that the white cravat rolled round his neck and tied in a bow, with two little ends like a young pig's ears, might have been whiter and, perhaps, cleaner. While I was making my mental observations upon this gentleman, who still stood near the door without saying a word to any one, Mr. Stringer's eyes turned upon me, and the expected explosion took place.

"Why, Sir Richard Conway!" he exclaimed, "this is an unexpected pleasure. Nevertheless, welcome to Virginia, and especially to my house. My dear, allow me to introduce Sir Richard Conway." While my introduction to Mrs. Stringer was taking place, I know not what bursts of surprise and wonder were going on amongst the rest of the party. All I do know is, that Bessy Davenport was laughing heartily, and feeling, I fancy, a little conceited at being the only one who had discovered my secret. Mrs. Stringer was peculiarly civil and condescending; and I do believe, if

I had been a *real live* lord,--a thing less frequently found in this country than mammoths and mastodons,--she could not have been more gratified to find me in her house. In the meantime, the rain continued to pour down without showing the slightest disposition to restrain itself; and the party from the carriage gave us a fearful account of the ravages committed by the freshet, which had carried away the bridge, as Mr. Byles had suspected. The wine on the table, the strawberries and cream, and the remnants of the dinner of which we had partaken, however, proved a very serviceable refreshment to Mr. Stringer and his battered party; so that our intrusion was rather a benefit than otherwise to the worthy gentleman, whose letter, announcing his proximate arrival, had, it seemed,--with a facility for getting lost nowhere more common to letters than in Virginia,--tarried by the way till its writer got the start of it. Mrs. Stringer indeed was a little fidgety about well-aired beds and sundry household arrangements; nevertheless, we all made ourselves very comfortable for the next hour, while waiting for the rain to pass away. As, however, it remained obdurate, Mr. Thornton rose to depart; and then commenced, on the part of our host, very pressing entreaties that we would all remain the night; and an exceedingly well-devised plan for accommodating so large a party, was explained to us by Mrs. Stringer on the spur of the moment. Mr. Thornton, however, declared he was obliged to return home; his wife was equally resolute, as well as all those who had come in the carriage; whilst those who had travelled on horseback declared to a man they did not mind a little rain. Our host and hostess were particularly pressing that at least Miss Davenport and myself would stay; and Mrs. Stringer reminded Bessy that she had extracted a promise of a long visit from her. Bessy, however, was determined to go; and go we did, in as unpleasant an afternoon as ever I remember. It was the will of God, however, that we should not go far. As to galloping, that was out of the question; for the rain had sunk into the earth, and the horses' hoofs were buried in mud at every step. Mrs. Thornton insisted upon taking her daughter into the carriage, and leaving the horse to be led by one of the negro boys. Billy Byles, deprived of his companion, set off across the country as fast as the state of the fields would permit. Mr. Thornton and his son affectionately hung about the coach, which was in danger of being overturned more than once; and, at length, the former suggested to his niece, that she and I should ride on, by a narrow road (which he designated, and with which she seemed well acquainted), both in order to get out of the rain as soon as possible, and to send some oxen from the plantation, to drag the carriage through the ford. Away we went, then, laughing and jesting; for all Bessy's light spirits had returned, and the rain seemed only to have brought them into flower; but the road was abominably bad, and our progress necessarily slow. The way lay principally through the woods, and every here and there we came upon a drier spot where we could have a canter; till, at length, I perceived, by my old topographic habits, that we must be approaching a little river or stream, which we had passed in the morning. Suddenly we came upon it; but Bessy pulled up her horse for a moment; and certainly the scene before us was not of a character to invite further advance. The banks were very steep, and the descent of the road to the edge of the water nearly precipitous. Beyond flowed the stream which a few hours previously had rolled on clear enough, but with hardly sufficient water in it to cover a horse's fetlocks. Now it rushed along between its deep banks, a turbid, rapid torrent. It must have risen five or six feet during those few hours; and although the surface was still tolerably smooth, owing to the want of rocks or other obstructions of that kind, every here and there was a whirling eddy,--a dimple, as it were, in the face of the stream, which showed with what force and rapidity it was going.

"This is not agreeable," said Bessy Davenport; "the river seems resolved to bar our way; but let us try, at all events." And she began to descend towards the brink.

"It is madness to attempt it," I exclaimed: "no horse can swim that current, Miss Davenport. For heaven's sake, stop." But Bessy could no longer stop. The ground was of a reddish clay, now thoroughly soaked with the rain; the descent some thirty feet, and, as I have said, precipitous; and though, when she tried to check him, her poor pony made an attempt to resist the impetus his first start had given him, by throwing himself on his haunches, his feet slipped in the mire; and down he slid with increasing rapidity to the very brink of the water. There he made one more violent effort to stop himself; but it was worse than in vain. A part of the bank gave way under him; and over he rolled with his mistress into the river. There are times when all thought abandons us, and when instinct--a much surer guide--comes to our aid. But instinct has no memories; and I only know what I did by the result. I must have sprung from my horse, dashed down the steep and slippery bank, and plunged into the water, before I was aware of what I was doing. It was the work of a moment. Still I had nearly been too late, and should have been so, but for one slight accident. The stream had risen so high that the branches of the trees and shrubs in many places now dipped in the water; and one of them, catching Bessy Davenport's riding-habit, kept her for an instant or two from being swept down the stream. That brief interruption was long enough, however; for the moment I got my eyes above the water, I saw something wavering about near the bank, looking more like a mass of water-weed than a human being. I struck at once towards the object, not doubting what it was; and I remember, at the same moment, hearing a wild, shrill neigh, as her horse raised his head above the current, and was swept past us. I am a very strong swimmer; the tide aided; and in three strokes I was by the poor girl's side. The moment after, her head and shoulders were raised on my left arm; and, though at first she made an effort to grasp me with her hands, yet, with admirable self-command, she desisted as soon as I spoke; and I contrived to draw her to the bank and catch hold of some of the shrubs. The next three or four minutes--for really I know not how long it was--proved more terrible than all that went before. They were only like the struggles of some hideous dream. The tree I grasped gave way under our weight, and rolled into the stream; but I caught another as we were falling back,--along, stiff, snake-like vine-stem (they grow here wild to the most enormous size), and it held firm. But the steep and slippery bank afforded no footing, and back I slipped every time I attempted to ascend. I was nearly in despair; but despair sometimes lends energy and suggests means. The only way was to use the vine-stem as a sort of cable, and to pull myself up by it; but the difficulty was to do so with one hand; for my left arm bore a burden I would not have parted from but with life. However, I dug my feet into the bank; and though, this time, I got sufficient hold to support me, I knew that if I relaxed my grasp for an instant, she and I must both fall back into the river. I almost fancied at one time, indeed, it would be best to try the river again, and see if I could not support her to some easier landing-place; but before I did so, I turned and looked at her. Her eyes were open and fixed upon my face.

"Can you hold the vine for a moment?" I said; "for a single moment, till I run my hand further up?"

"I will try," she answered, and grasped the stem with both her hands. By a violent effort, I reached over, and caught the frail thing that supported us some two or three feet above, without relaxing my hold of Bessy herself, and then drew her up, till her feet were completely above the water.

"Now, if we can reach that old tree," I said, "round which this vine has been twining, you are safe." The greater danger was now indeed past; and what between her efforts and mine,--though every step had its peril, and I feared each instant that the vine-stem would give way under our repeated efforts to ascend,--we at length reached the stump of the old tree, which was still rooted firmly in the ground. There I seated her, with her back against the trunk, and felt fully repaid for all my day's work, when I parted the wet hair from her beautiful forehead with my own hands, and twisted it up behind her ears. Bessy said nothing; but held down her head and wept; and I easily understood that there was One to be thanked in silence, even before myself. I gave her time to recover herself a little; but as soon as she began to look up again, I said, in a gay tone,--

"And now, my dear Bessy, I have got to carry you back to Beavors. Thank Heaven, you are very light, and we are not likely to meet many people; for you having lost your hat and I mine, and both having acquired a remarkable portion of mud upon our garments, we are not the most respectable-looking couple that ever journeyed through the world together."

"For heaven's sake, do not jest at present, Richard," she answered. "You men cannot feel these things as we women do. I do not believe I shall ever jest again, when I think of the danger I have brought upon myself, and into which I have drawn you. But where is your horse? Mine, poor fellow, is drowned, of course. Poor Ned! I am very sorry for him; but from the way in which he fell, he must be drowned."

"Very lucky for you he *did* fall that way, my dear cousin," I replied; "otherwise he would probably have struck you with his hoof, and you would have been killed. Where my horse is, may be another question. I left him at the top of the bank; for you were in such a hurry, my dear girl, that there was no time to tie him up; and I had much ado to catch you, as it was."

"He has gone home, I dare say," replied Bessy; "but perhaps you had better see."

"First, I must carry you up to the road," replied I. But for a time she would not consent, saying she could climb very well. Her riding-habit, however, caught her at every step, and at length she was obliged to let me do as I pleased, till I safely landed her upon the road, within sight of the spot where our unfortunate adventure commenced. There stood the horse, almost precisely where I left him, though in a very different attitude; his head was bent down, his neck and muzzle stretched out almost in a straight line from his shoulders towards the water, and his eyes fixed eagerly upon the current, as, red and turbid, it rushed by. It seemed to me as if, with that strange sort of intelligence which characterizes the dog, the horse, and the elephant, he was waiting for our return, and watching eagerly to see us reappear by the same way we went.

"Now," I said, "we can get back more easily; for I dare say, with your country education, you can contrive to ride upon a somewhat unusual saddle, and I will walk by your side to prevent your slipping off."

"I could ride him without any saddle at all," said Bessy, with a smile. The horse was soon caught, and she placed upon his back. The clouds were now beginning to break; patches of blue were visible here and there, and the rain had almost ceased. I could have wished, indeed, that it had not turned fine quite so soon,--that it had continued even to drizzle a little; for there was something strangely out of harmony with our draggled and miserable appearance in the bright sunshine which soon burst forth. It seemed to make us look more ridiculous than ever. But it had one good effect; for it brought some of the negroes out into the fields, and we had an opportunity of sending some teams of oxen to assist Mr. Thornton and his party across the ford, and to give him information of all that had occurred to us. We coupled the tale, however, with the assurance that Miss Davenport and myself were quite safe, and that all we wanted were dry clothes to enable us to pass the night comfortably at Beavors. When we reached that place, as misfortune would have it, the whole family of Mr. Stringer, including the tall gaunt man in black, were standing under the porch, gazing forth upon the country refreshed by the shower; and every sort of exclamation of wonder and commiseration burst forth upon us when we presented ourselves, wet, bedabbled with mud, and with total loss of head-gear.

"Why, my pretty young lady," exclaimed Mr. Stringer, unable to refrain from a smile, "I hardly knew you when I first saw you coming in such an awkward condition."

"It is very lucky that you do see me at all," replied Bessy; "for if it hadn't been for my cousin here, who nearly lost his life to save mine, I should have been twenty miles down the Nansemond river by this time."

"Come in, come in, my dear Bessy," said Mrs. Stringer, "and do not stand talking in your wet clothes. You can tell us all about it afterwards." And with motherly care she took her fair young friend away into the house; while Mr. Stringer himself conducted me to a room upstairs, and offered me all the resources of his own wardrobe. As he was about five inches shorter than myself, and at least two inches less in width across the shoulders, the selection was somewhat difficult. I contrived to get into a loose morning gown, however; and, with a happy thought,--unhappily frustrated of effect,--Mr. Stringer sent a servant to ask the loan of a pair of pantaloons from the Reverend Mr. McGrubber, which I found was the name of his lanky friend in black. A moment after, the negro returned, with a grin which showed his white teeth from ear to ear, saying, "Massa McGrubber's compliments, but he can't. Him's only got one pair, and them's on." The laugh which followed, from Mr. Stringer and myself, did me fully as much good as the glass of mulled wine which my worthy host insisted upon my swallowing. As there was no other resource, I determined to go to bed till my own clothes could be dried and cleansed, or till some fresh apparel was brought over from the plantation of Mr. Thornton; and what between a little fatigue, the sultry weather, and the mulled wine, I fell sound asleep soon after Mr. Stringer left me, and began dreaming of Bessy Davenport.

CHAPTER IX

I was awakened out of one of the sweetest dreams in the world--though, unlike most story-tellers, I will not tell you all about it--by some one coming into my room with a light. I never was more astonished in my life. It seemed to me I had not been asleep ten minutes; and yet the sun, who had a full couple of hours' course when I lay down, had now gone to bed too, and all without was darkness. Another testimony to the fact of my long sleep, was the face of my good old friend Zed, who came grinning up with a pair of bags over his arm, and a note from Mr. Thornton; showing that our friends had arrived safely at home, had received our messages, and had sent us over the wherewithal to make ourselves comfortable, or, at all events, cleanly. Mr. Thornton's note treated our adventure more lightly than he probably would have done, had he been aware of the full extent of danger; but he recommended me strongly to accept Mr. Stringer's invitation to stay at his house for a day or two, saying,--

"You will be much nearer the scene of action; and, if I am not mistaken, affairs will be brought to a crisis sooner than we expected by the discovery of your being actually in the country. I will be over with you early to-morrow; and, if possible, will bring Hubbard with me. We can then begin the campaign in real earnest, should it be necessary." Having read this epistle and undergone a number of exclamations mingled with laughter, from Old Zed, I proceeded as rapidly as possible to dress myself, and descended to the parlour, which I found vacant of all but a negro servant, engaged in arranging tables and chairs, which possibly had not been found in apple-pie order by Mrs. Stringer on her return. The man informed me, however, that his master and mistress were dressing for dinner, which, to say sooth, I was not sorry to hear; for though I had eaten one good dinner already, I had somehow contrived in the intervening time to recover an appetite. The first of the party who appeared in the room was the fair companion of my perils, with all traces of the mishaps of the day obliterated from her appearance, though she was perhaps a little paler than usual. She gave me her tiny little hand at once, saying,--

"I am glad to find you alone, Sir Richard; for I really have not had time to thank you; and I fear you must think me very ungrateful."

"I shall indeed think you so," I answered, "if you ever give me such a formal name again. Call me Richard--Cousin Richard--anything of that kind you like; but never use that cold word Sir any more."

"Ay, then you are not such a terrible aristocrat after all," said Bessy, with one of her bright smiles.

"As much as ever," I answered; "though I suspect not half so much as you are at heart. But, without a jest, Bessy, it is impossible for me, after all we have gone through together, to be anything to you but Richard Conway, or you to be anything to me but Bessy Davenport. Sometimes in a life, five minutes are equal to five years; and by such measure must we calculate in the length of our acquaintance an hour or two out of this day. Is it a bargain?"

"Yes, Richard," she answered, giving me her hand again. "I pledge myself to it." I was just putting the seal upon the compact, with my lips upon that little hand, when the door opened, and in stalked the Rev. Mr. McGrubber. There is a sort of man in every part of the world, who is always in the place where he is not wanted. He is to be pitied rather than blamed, I do believe; for I am convinced it is a sort of idiosyncrasy which is even recognizable in his external appearance, just as particular temperaments can be discovered by the complexion. The moment I set eyes upon McGrubber, I could have sworn he would always be in the way; and so he was. I have said "in he stalked;" but it is impossible to describe by any words his peculiar sort of locomotion. It was more like that of a snake standing on its tail, than anything else. His long lean body seemed to go first, and then to drag the legs after it with an effort that was painful to behold. Whether he saw what I was about when he entered, or not, I did not know; and, to tell the truth, did not much care, although I thought I detected that peculiar sort of twinkle in his small grey eyes, which I have perceived in those of curious people, when they fancy they have made some pleasant little discovery. Bessy coloured a little, and seemed somewhat annoyed; so, to break the awkwardness of the whole business, I turned briskly to Mr. McGrubber, saying, "It has become quite a fine evening again, sir."

"I guess it has," replied the worthy minister, sticking his hands into his coat pockets, and spreading the flaps out like a pigeon's tail behind him. "It is warm too. I guess, miss, those bugs that come flying in at the window will knock the candles out, unless somebody does something to stop them."

"Very probably, sir," replied Bessy Davenport. "Suppose you try. You are more accustomed, I believe, to keeping peoples' lights burning than I am."

"Profanely speaking, nay," answered Mr. McGrubber, who, I should explain to you English people, meant by "bugs" all the tribe of moths and flying insects which literally load the evening air in a southern climate; and he was going on to tell us what lights he professed to keep burning; but before he could favour us with more of his conversation, Mr. and Mrs. Stringer appeared, the latter making many apologies for being late. She had found everything in disorder, she said, and had really had a great deal to do. Mr. Stringer for his part exclaimed that they kept up the custom of dining late, even in the country, as he found it much more convenient on all accounts; and Mr. McGrubber, who I found was the tutor of the young Stringers, favoured us with a discourse upon the iniquity 'of late hours, which he seasoned with a good number of texts from Scripture, uttered in a very nasal tone. I cannot say that I was much edified by his remarks, which had a good deal of fanatical impertinence in them; and I wondered how Mr. Stringer could tolerate such an inmate in his family; for he himself, though evidently a weak man, was well bred and well educated, and there was something atrociously presuming both in Mr. McGrubber's manner and in his conversation. It was not that he thought himself as good as anybody else; for that would be very easily tolerated, especially in an American, who, whatever may be his qualities of mind, heart, or position, always looks upon himself as on a par with the best man that ever was born. But that which makes the assumption of perfect equality tolerable, renders the assumption of superiority intolerable; and it was evident that Mr. McGrubber thought himself vastly better than anybody else, and wished every one to understand it. Yet he had not only eloquence of a peculiar sort, but considerable powers of mind, very much misapplied. His reasonings, though full of sophistry, were answered with more trouble than they deserved; for he would twist and turn like an eel. Fanaticism resembles *the one book* which venders an opponent in argument so dangerous. It is the all-absorbing thought which converts everything around into pabulum for itself. He had read everything upon the two or three subjects with which he cared to deal; he had armed himself with all the weapons of his party, and provided himself with shields and places of retreat against any opponent too strong for him; yet, though he evidently thought conviction defeat, it was not entirely from vanity he strove. Fanaticism on any subject is, I believe, a mixture of passion and self-conceit; and he certainly was not without the former, as after events convinced me. To all these peculiar traits he added an insatiable curiosity, which he had no reserve in trying to gratify. During dinner he asked me at least a hundred impertinent questions about myself, my family, my object in visiting America, my profession, my age, my fortune--some put in the form of guesses, some with most straightforward impudence; and when, in the end, I told him I did not think myself called upon to gratify the unreasonable curiosity of every stranger as to my private affairs, he answered,--

"Waal, I guess you're right in that; but I should think you did not come over here without some particular business, and any citizen of this republic may just ask what that business is." Mr. Stringer and Bessy burst into a laugh, and Mrs. Stringer looked considerably annoyed. Laughter often does more than argument; and Mr. McGrubber was effectually silenced for the remainder of the evening. Indeed, shortly after the dessert was put upon the table, the worthy gentleman, who drank no wine and hated everybody that did, rose unceremoniously, and left the room; nor did he make his appearance again that night. I know few things more pleasant than when, with a feeling of security upon one, after a perilous and eventful day, we sit down with our fellow-adventurers to chat quietly over the various incidents which excited our feelings and stimulated, perhaps, many a passion at the time, but which have now all the calm of memory about them. Nothing could be more tranquil or charming than the two hours which now succeeded. We talked over all that had happened; we recalled not only events, but thoughts and feelings; and brief lapses would often occur in the conversation when (I know not what Bessy Davenport was doing) I was scrutinizing, though not too closely, certain sensations or emotions of my own heart, a little anxious to know what they all meant, yet unwilling to examine them too closely, lest I should stop them in their play. Once I asked myself if I was falling in love with Bessy Davenport--with her whom I did not know the morning before, and of whom I could not have said, that very morning, whether I liked or disliked her. But just then, waking out of a reverie of her own, she suddenly raised her eyes, quiet and thoughtful, but full of light, to my face, and I concluded that my question was a very foolish question indeed, which I would never put to my own heart again, but leave that inscrutable inner man to speak for himself when he thought proper. As our eyes met, a slight colour came up in her cheek, but she rose quietly, saying,--

"Now I will sing you one song, and then I will go to bed, only praying that I may not dream of being drowned all night. What shall it be, Cousin Richard?" I was incapable of deciding, not knowing what she sang; and so, taking a seat at the piano, she chose for herself a little, quiet, simple Italian air, such as the peasants sing in the Abruzzi, which never find their way into operas, but have more real melody in them than half the opera airs in the world. Then, starting up, she wished us all "Good night," and left us. We separated within a few minutes after; for Mr. and Mrs. Stringer were fatigued with their day's expedition, and I gladly went to my room with the intention of meditating over many things. I was disappointed, however; for there was my good friend Zed, ready to pour upon me a whole budget of news, in his somewhat incoherent but voluble way. First and foremost was the account of Mr. Thornton's journey home. How the carriage had stuck in the ford, but had been got out quite safe; how Master Hal had been thrown by his pony into a pool of mud, and come out as red as an "Ingin." Then, what consternation they were all in when the news arrived of the accident which had befallen us; and then, how, just as he was coming away with my clothes, Miss Bessy's horse, with the saddle quite turned round under his belly, had come trotting and neighing up to the house. This last piece of information was very gratifying to me, for I knew Bessy mourned for her good steed; and whatever interested her was beginning to interest me also. It was never discovered, I may remark, how the poor brute got out of the river; but it is supposed he drifted down to a spot some two miles below, where the eastern bank became flat, and, landing there, found his way home. Zed, I found, judged the accident which had brought me back to Beavors a very lucky one, inasmuch as the great camp-meeting he had mentioned was to be held within a mile or two of the house. "Ah! massa," he cried, "such meeting as you hear there you never see. Gorr a mighty! I shouldn't wonder if you were converted yourself."

"What makes you judge, Zed, that I am not converted already?" I asked. The poor fellow grinned, and did not seem to know what to reply, finding himself on the horns of a dilemma. So his only course was to sigh and shake his head, as if he thought me in a very perilous condition of mind. I have remarked, however, that negroes, when they become puzzled with any question, are very dexterous in carrying the conversation off to something else; and so Zed now favoured me with a long catalogue of the preachers who were to hold forth upon this occasion, naming, amongst the rest, Mr. McGrubber, by whom I certainly did not expect to be either converted or very much edified. Two or three other names were mentioned, however, which I had heard spoken of with respect; and I resolved to go, at all events, to witness such a spectacle, at least once in my life, as a camp-meeting must present. Let me use a school-boy phrase and say, I determined to go "for the fun of the thing." I slept very well in the earlier part of the night; but I can never sleep more than a certain time during the twenty-four hours, and, consequently, with the first ray of daylight, my eyes were open. I felt strongly inclined to lie still and meditate; but as I never indulge such things, where the meditation is sure to be fruitless, I rose, dressed myself, and went downstairs. The house was still shut up, and nobody was stirring; but, to my surprise, I found two negroes asleep on the benches in the hall; and I afterwards discovered that it was a very common custom of domestic servants, even where good beds were provided for them, to lie down upon any bench or set of chairs they could find, and sleep out the night there, without covering or pillow. The door of the house, too, was unlocked; and, indeed, very little precaution of any kind seemed taken in this country against intruders. One would think this was an evidence of an innocent and virtuous population, were not the inference contradicted by the long and terrible list of crimes and offences which every newspaper shows each day. For want, then, of any better solution of this enigma of carelessness, I could only set it down to the account of that utter indifference to life and security which is so observable throughout the whole land. Taking up a stick which I saw in the hall, I walked out, very careless as to what course I followed, and proceeded, I dare say, two miles, without seeing a living soul. It was by this time five o'clock, yet nobody was in the fields--a clear proof that the negroes are not so much overworked, in Virginia at least, as has been generally reported. The morning air was fresh and balmy, rather cool than otherwise, with no indications of the heat which was to follow the higher rising of the sun. The whole fields, and especially the edges of the woods, were gemmed with beautiful flowers; and it had a strange and curious effect to see shrubs, and trees, and plants which we in England look upon as rare and delicate, blooming wild and uncultivated all around. Innumerable birds and beasts--ay, and even reptiles--were fluttering, running, or gliding in different directions; and it was clearly an hour at which the presence of man did not warn inferior animals to seek the shelter of the thicket or the brake. I cannot say that the aspect of the country was very picturesque. It was a flat, alluvial plain, through which the rivers and streams had easily worn deep channels, as they poured on towards the sea; and it was only on the banks of these that anything like landscape beauty was to be seen. The one I reached that morning, which was the limit of my walk, much resembled that which had nearly made a supper of Bessy Davenport and me the day before. I know not even now, whether it was the same or not. During the warm night, the water left by the rain had either evaporated into the air or had been sucked up by the light and penetrable soil. Everything had become dry, except where the river, evidently greatly fallen since the preceding evening, wended quietly on its way, no longer hurried by the mass of waters pressed within its narrow banks. By the side of the stream sat a negro, fishing, and as this was the first human being I had seen since I set out, I thought I might as well go down and talk with him. When I came near, I perceived he was one of the finest-formed men I had ever beheld, tall and powerful, with very little of the usual deformity of his race. He had, indeed, the thick lips, the nose flattened,--though not very much,--and the woolly hair of his race; but there was no bowed shins or large hands and feet; yet, as far as I could judge from his colour, he was of unmixed African blood. He did not condescend to lift his head when I came near, but continued his occupation, still gazing upon the glistening but somewhat turbid water.

"Have you had good sport?" asked I.

"I have caught no fish," he answered abruptly; and then turning round for the first time, he looked to see who was the interrogator.

"Is not the water too muddy still?" I inquired, somewhat struck by the man's manner and tone.

"Those who would catch large fish must fish in troubled waters," answered he gravely, casting in his line again. "I shall catch when the appointed time comes. Nothing happens, master, but at its appointed time, whether it be great or small." I confess I was not a little surprised at such a reply from such a man. I had heard of negroes who displayed as great natural powers of mind as men of the white races, but I never yet had met with one. In all whom I had seen there was a certain lack of intellect. Quick comprehension there might be--often rapid combination, cunning seeming to supply the place of reasoning powers; but it was more like the comprehension, the cunning of a child, exercised only upon the objects near at hand, without the power of generalization or remote deduction. In fact, this man's words afforded the first attempt at any thing like a grasp of a wide and comprehensive idea which I had ever met with in his race, and they excited my curiosity greatly.

"I agree perfectly with you," I answered. "I am a full believer in a special Providence; yet it would seem but a small and undignified exercise of that Divine power, to make you catch a fish at one moment more than another."

"What is small, and what is great, to God Almighty?" asked the man, still keeping his eyes on the stream. "He made the emmet as well as the biggest of beasts; he made the grain of sand an well as the mountain. How can you tell, master, how small events may affect great ones? My catching a fish, now or then, may, by giving food and comfort to a family, allay their discontent; and, putting off its outbreak, induce them to go on in quiet, till some further relief comes--in its due season also. Does not the Bible tell us that not a sparrow falls to the ground unnoticed? Everything is by God's will--everything is in God's time. What is small? What is great to Him? In a universe everything has its proper place, every event its proper moment; and the derangement of the least would destroy the order of the whole. My time, too, will come for whatever I have to do; and I am ready to do God's will, whatever it may be." I never was more astonished in my life than by this man's discourse. I had heard Hindoos many a time speak in a somewhat similar way; but they are proverbially a thoughtful, speculative, I may almost say a metaphysical race; but to hear such words from a poor despised negro--from one of a class to whom the higher ranges of thought seem forbidden, as well by capability as by education--was very strange. While he had been speaking he had only turned his face to me once; and when he ceased, I mused for a minute or two, not jumping at a conclusion at once, but asking myself, first, whether he had learned all this from some one else, like a parrot. Rejecting that suspicion speedily, as contradicted by his whole tone and manner, I next considered whether it was likely or unlikely that every faculty of the mind would be equally developed. Grasp of intellect, logical power, he certainly possessed; but a good many (perhaps) subordinate qualities and faculties are requisite to make such gifts available for man's conduct, either towards his fellow man or towards his God. I had nearly come to the conclusion that it was almost certain he must possess them, when suddenly a laugh--the unmeaning, almost idiotic laugh of the negro race--broke from his lips, followed by--

"Ah, master, I've caught you!" And I saw him pulling a large fish towards the shore. It seemed that this was all he wanted. He showed it to me with a sort of child-like triumph; and then, throwing away the pole with which he had been fishing, and rolling up his line, he walked some way by my side, as I took my path homeward. I was anxious to know more of this man, and tried to put him upon some of those tracks which I thought might bring forth the peculiarities of his mind. He seemed a little shy, however, in answering my inquiries, and in following any train of thought which was placed before him. This was natural enough in one of an enslaved race, in whose bosoms there must always be some feeling of wrong and oppression, so long as there is vanity in the human heart. However kindly they may be treated--however incapable they may be of taking care of, directing, and providing for themselves, they will always feel an uncongeniality--a want of sympathy with the dominant race, and shrink into themselves, more or less, when brought into communication with their masters. My companion gave me his name--Nathaniel Turner--and told me where he lived, which was not far distant; but only once was I able to bring from him a spark of that intellectual fire which he had previously displayed, and which, even now, was half smothered by that cunning which is common to savages and children. In stating that I was an Englishman, I alluded to our having emancipated our slaves in the West-India islands, and I could see a sort of eager light break forth from his eyes; but it was quenched the next moment, as if he still entertained some doubts and suspicions.

"Well, master," he said, "I can't tell whether you are right or wrong in freeing the slaves. I suppose you did it because you thought you had no right to make them slaves at first. But if you did think so, there was a great deal more to be done than merely to give them back their liberty. You had taken a great deal more from them than freedom; you had taken from them their country, their home, their habits; and, I think, you were bound either to restore to them all the things of their former state, or to take good care of them, and fit them for the state into which you had brought them. However, I am a poor, foolish man, and know nothing about these things. I have been a slave all my life, and I have had very good masters. I doubt not it will all be brought right in the end; and, perhaps, we niggers are placed in the situation proper for us. At all events, it is God's will, and so we ought to be content. Now, it's possible, this fish, here in my hand, would rather have been some great shark, or some beast, or some bird, or even, perhaps, a man; but God willed it otherwise: if not, he would never have been hanging on my hook. But should the pot say to the hand that fashioned it, 'Why madest thou me so?' I was born of a different colour from you and your friends; and that difference of colour is a great difference in this world. Content is everything, good master; and I am very well content as I am--*so long as it is God's will I should be so.*" The last words were spoken after a pause, and with a good deal of emphasis; and, anxious to know more of his thoughts and feelings, I replied,--

"Ay, but the difficulty is, in the complication of this world's affairs, to discover what is God's will, and what is man's."

"Whatever is, is God's will," he answered; and then added, in a slow tone, "His will will always be revealed in due time. If man cannot see clearly, God will give him eyes; and when his time comes, all must be accomplished. There is no standing against the hand of God; and let no man imagine that His judgment is not right." By this time we had arrived at a spot about a mile from Beavors, and I could perceive, walking along the edge of a wood enclosed with a snake fence, a figure which something within me told me at once was Bessy Davenport, come forth to take her usual morning's walk. She was advancing directly towards us; and, on seeing her, I left my sable companion, and proceeded to join her.

"Why, who have you been talking to?" she asked, as I came up. "It looks like Nat Turner."

"No other," I answered. "Do you know anything of him?"

"Oh, yes," she exclaimed; "he is a very extraordinary man indeed, and lives not far off, at Mr. Travis's, the next plantation. All the negroes look upon him as a sort of prophet, and certainly his powers of mind are so superior to those of slaves in general, that they may well do so. No one knows who taught him to read; and, if asked, he says no one taught him--it came to him of itself. Of course, that is nonsense; but, undoubtedly, he is a very extraordinary man, and his manners and language are far above his race."

"That I clearly perceived," I answered; "yet I could see a good many negro traits--at least I thought so. I should much like to see more of him. What is his general character?"

"Excellent," she replied. "He is, I have heard, a kind, good creature; but most austere and self-denying; eats very little, drinks nothing but water; and does not associate much with the other negroes, though he has a very great influence over them when he pleases to exert it. But he is quiet and inoffensive; and, therefore, his influence is beneficial rather than otherwise. In his hours of leisure he may be seen reading at the door of his cabin, while the others are dancing and singing, and, indeed, his conduct might be an example to many a white man I wot of."

"Should such a man be kept in slavery, Bessy?" I asked, with a sigh.

"You must not put such questions to me, Cousin Richard," she answered. "All we women in Virginia are, more or less, abolitionists, except when we encounter some of the northern fanatics, and then we stand upon the defensive, telling them they have no right to meddle with us. Indeed, one half of the State is in favour of emancipation; and I should not wonder if an Act for that purpose were to pass next year; though, heaven knows what we should do with the poor creatures if we did free them, for nine out of ten are quite incapable of taking care of, or providing for, themselves. I suppose we should have to become the slaves in their place, and work for them, for, assuredly, no negro will work for himself or any one else if he can help it--no, cousin, not even the paragon Nat Turner. He has, indeed, as you say, a good number of the African traits, and seems to have, as it were, two characters, one full of power and capability, and the other feeble and not to be cultivated--at least so Mr. Travis says. He is, moreover, marvellously superstitious--a believer in all sorts of signs and portents. You should go and see him in his cabin, Richard; he would take it as a great compliment."

"I will, some day," I answered. "But now, whither are you bending your steps?"

"Wherever fancy leads, and the air is freshest," answered Bessy.

"Then take my arm, and let us seek it," I rejoined.

"No, no," she replied, laughing; "you do not know our ways. No young lady takes a man's arm without being engaged to him."

"Then take mine," I said, in the same gay tone. She looked suddenly up in my face, and, seeing that I was smiling, she said, in the words of the song she had sung the night before, "*Tu mi burli*. But indeed it is against our customs."

"Very prudish customs, indeed, dear Bessy," I answered. She instantly passed her arm through mine, saying, "There! you shall not call *me* prudish, at least. I abhor a prude. Coquette I dare say you have called me in your heart a hundred times already; but you are wrong there, too, cousin mine. Having resolved, long ago, never to marry, I make use of my independence, and say what I like to any one; but that is all. I care not one straw for admiration, or anything of the kind."

"Are you then the woman whose resolutions can never be changed?" I asked.

"The woman!" she exclaimed, with a toss of the head. "Do you mean to imply that every woman is weak and irresolute?"

"Not at all," I answered. "That does not follow, dear cousin. A woman would show herself more weak by keeping a resolution founded upon mistaken grounds, than by breaking it. You are not so weak as to keep your resolution if you have good cause for casting it away."

"As what?" she asked. "What cause can I ever have?"

"Love," I answered. "If you found a man who loved you sincerely, and whom you could love in return, you would break it to-morrow, and do well." Bessy turned a little red, and then a little pale, and cast down her bright eyes. In order to change the conversation, I made some observations upon the extreme beauty of the wild flowers; but it was with difficulty I called her mind back from the train of thought it was pursuing.

"I think I shall go home," she said, at length; "for these people breakfast early, in order to let their boys have the full advantage of sweet Mr. McGrubber's conversation during the day. Good lack, good lack, Cousin Richard! but this love and marriage which we were talking of just now are strange things in their way. Who would ever have thought that extraordinary McGrubber could have found any woman upon the face of the earth to marry him? And yet he did; and a sweet, pretty little creature I am told she was. She is dead now, happily for her. It was what the old women call a happy release. I am sure I should have thought so if I had been his wife. So now to return to our subject, let me say that, when I see such wonderful things happening as sane women marrying McGrubbers, no woman may be confident of what may happen to herself, and, therefore, I cannot positively say that I will not break my resolution; but, if I do, 'twill not be with my own consent."

"You are a little paradox altogether, Bessy," I said.

"Then don't try to find me out," she answered, "for you never can do it."

"I have done it already," replied I, with a significant nod of my head.

"Then, pray, tell me all about it," she cried; "for I really know nothing of the subject myself."

"I will tell you all about it some day, Bessy," I answered; "that I promise you; but I think I had better not begin such a long discourse at present, for I see something very lank and very black coming this way, and, if I mistake not, its name is McGrubber."

"Oh, then, for heaven's sake, let us get out of his way," said Bessy, after having gazed for a moment in the direction in which I had been looking. "It is, it is, the great McGrubber. Let us turn into the wood, here. A path leads round in a way in which no human greyhound, if he had legs three times as long, could catch us." Thus saying, she led me along rapidly, till we were fairly into the wood, and then burst out into one of her clear, merry laughs at the idea of having baffled poor McGrubber. That he had seen us I was perfectly certain, and that, in the peculiar sort of charity which I attributed to him, he would not assign the best motive to our getting out of his way, I thought very probable; but, of course, I had too much discretion even to suggest to Bessy, that if her merely walking arm-in-arm with me was likely to be construed into an engagement between us, our flying into the woods from the presence of a parson was likely to be more misconstrued still. Bessy, however, had a bold, free way of settling all these things for herself, and, generally, I must say, she settled them very well. As we went, she pointed out to me all the various intricacies of the path we were pursuing, which was, indeed, quite labyrinthine, and she chatted with me on many subjects, quite different from those which had gone before. When we arrived at the house, we found Mrs. Stringer busying herself about the breakfast-table, and Bessy, running up to her, told her at once, in one of her gayest veins, how we had seen Mr. McGrubber coming towards us, and how we had doubled upon him into the wood, and passed him, unseen, within a hundred yards.

"Just as I have seen a fox do before the hounds," cried Bessy. "If I could but have drawn him after us, it would have been the greatest sport in the world. Cousin Richard and I would have led him through every swamp, and bush, and cane-break we could find."

"Oh no! you mad-cap," said Mrs. Stringer, "I am sure Sir Richard would never have been so unkind to the poor man. He is a bore, it is true; but there is no harm in him, I sincerely believe."

"I am not so sure of that," answered Bessy. "A man who thinks he understands everybody else's business better than themselves, becomes a very dangerous person when he makes a mistake."

"What is a bore?" asked Mr. McGrubber, entering the room just at this moment, after having evidently been listening in the hall. Mrs. Stringer, who had used the word, grew very red, and looked confused; but Bessy turned upon him at once, and answered in an ordinary tone, as if she were quoting from a dictionary,--

"Bore--A person who impertinently intrudes upon people who do not want him, and then keeps grinding them till he nearly bores a hole through them. That's in Johnson, is it not, Cousin Richard?" Her quiet look, the man's air of stolid bewilderment, and Mrs. Stringer's confusion, were, I must confess, too much for me; and I laughed till I cried.

"What is he laughing at?" asked Mr. McGrubber, in a solemn tone; "I see no cause for such levity." This was too much for both Bessy and Mrs. Stringer; and when Mr. Stringer entered, a minute after, he found us all three laughing as hard as we could laugh, and Mr. McGrubber standing, tall and stately, in the midst, a pillar of indignant solemnity. Breakfast was not yet over, when Mr. Thornton arrived on horseback, and I perceived at once that he was a good deal excited; but he refrained from all business matters till the party rose, inquiring into our adventures of the evening before, and giving a somewhat amusing account of the journey of the carriage home.

"I was very glad, to tell you the truth, Bessy," he said, "that our good cousin here was not with us. It would have been a grand triumph for an Englishman to see our roads in such a state after a shower; on one side holes six feet deep, in which a whole wheel would disappear at once, and, on the other, stumps and bumps of all shapes and dimensions."

"I dare say their roads are just as bad," said Bessy Davenport; "only they have not such good, honest showers as we have in Virginia, although I believe it always rains in England. Doesn't it, Cousin Richard?"

"Oh, yes," I answered, smiling; "but then it only rains marabout feathers, our climate is so soft and gentle."

"And you are wrong, Bessy, about the roads," added Mr. Thornton; "for there can be no doubt that the roads in Europe, especially in England, are admirable, while ours are a disgrace to a country so prosperous and so far advanced in every other kind of civilization."

"Well, you need not have admitted it to an Englishman, my dear uncle," said Bessy, laughing; "for my part, I am resolved never to admit to any of these proud Islanders that they surpass us in anything whatever. They are quite conceited enough without our encouraging their vanity."

"You show your hand, fair lady," I replied; "and henceforth I shall know the game you are playing. I shall never contradict you any more."

"Oh, don't say that, my dear cousin, I beseech you!" cried Bessy. "Without contradiction, what should I be worth? and what would you do yourself?" I believe the devil was in me, for I drew close to her, and replied to her question in a whisper,--

"I would try to get you to go to England with, me, and judge for yourself, dear Bessy." It was certainly neither a moment nor a mode for making a declaration; and I had not the slightest intention of so doing; but the words were uttered before I knew what I was about; and that, though spoken in a jesting tone, they had some significance for her mind, was very evident by Bessy's countenance, for she coloured like a rose, and quitted the room. Mrs. Stringer followed; and, as soon as they were gone, Mr. Thornton exclaimed,--

"Now, Sir Richard, mount your horse, and ride over with me to Jerusalem directly. Hubbard has promised to meet us there; and we must open the campaign at once. We have bold and daring men to deal with: and this morning early, I learned that, notwithstanding our caveat, all your poor aunt's servants were sold last night to that cursed dealer, with his gold chains and trinkets. We will cut him off though, Hubbard is to bring the sheriff with him; a warrant shall be issued immediately, and they shall not quit Virginia if my name is Thornton."

"I will order my horse directly," I answered.

"I beg your pardon for taking the liberty," said Mr. Thornton; "but I ordered it as I came up. It must be now at the door." In a few minutes, we were mounted; and by that sort of electric telegraph of gossip which seems to run through and around every Virginia country house, the whole family and servants had apparently gained information of what we were about, and were collected in and around the porch to see us depart. I heard one dark fellow say to another, as they stood about the horses, in answer to some question,--

"A going to stop Miss Bab's servants being sold to Orleens, to be sure."

"God bless 'em, Massa Thornton never let that," replied the other; "they stop 'em!" Even Bessy Davenport was there; and, after seeming to hesitate for a moment, she came up to the side of my horse just as I had mounted, and said in a low tone,--

"Had you not better take pistols with you, Cousin Richard? These men are often very violent and lawless."

"No, no," I answered, holding up my riding whip, which had a very heavy iron head, cast in the form of an eagle; "I can give a good account of two or three with this; and I should not like to show that I meditated violence myself." Bending down my head as I spoke, I added, in a whisper,--"Forgive me, Bessy; I did not intend to trouble or annoy you by what I said this morning. I may not be so conceited and self-confident as you think all Englishmen are." She looked up frankly in my face, and, notwithstanding all the people round her, held out her hand to me. I pressed it in mine for a moment, and then galloped away. At the gate leading into the main road, we saw Billy Byles coming up from the right, mounted on a very handsome horse, which showed a little more blood than bone, and Mr. Thornton instantly hallooed him up.

"Come along, Byles," he cried, "come along with us; you are just the sort of man we want. We are going hunting."

"Hunting!" echoed bold Billy; "hunting what, in Heaven's name?"

"A nigger-driver and his master," answered Mr. Thornton. "Lewis, the trader, bought, last night, all Aunt Bab's servants, notwithstanding our caveat against it; and we must catch him ere he gets to the state-line, or we may have trouble."

"Tally ho!" cried Billy Byles. "We'll give him a chase. You ride on. I'll rouse the country as we go, and join you in five minutes. There's Toliver, and Turner, and Sam Hicks, and Whitehead and his son, all close to the road, men always ready for action; and these fellows will show fight, depend upon it. Stop at the cross road just on this side of Jerusalem."

"No, no," said Mr. Thornton; "come to old Snead's hotel. You will find us there before the house. We shall get information there, and a warrant."

"Oh, warrants! Damn warrants!" responded Billy Byles, "I am always my own warrant. But go on; I'll come, and not keep you." On we went accordingly at a rapid pace, minding neither dust nor mud, both of which were to be had on the road, as it undulated up and down; and in about three-quarters of an hour, we had reached the town or village of Jerusalem, as the capital seat of the county of Southampton is called. I fancy it is always an active, bustling little place; but there was evidently an unusual excitement in it at the time; and as we rode up towards the inn, I saw my good friend, Mr. Hubbard, standing by his pony, and another gentleman on horseback, close to him, who, Mr. Thornton informed me, was the sheriff. I have since seen several specimens of the same kind in Virginia; and shall only therefore say, he was a very tall, lanky man, with a good carriage and a line countenance, with tremendously long limbs, and not a superfluous ounce of flesh or fat upon any of them. Could I suppose him to have been once a beast transformed by some beneficent fairy into a man, I should say he must formerly have been a full-blooded Irish stag-hound; and his horse was of the same character, all bone and sinew, but a remarkably fine animal. He was equipped as if for the chase, with a pair of long boots which came up almost to his hips; and he had a little hat stuck upon the top of his grey hair, which a very slight change would have turned into a jockey cap. As soon as he saw us, he dashed very unceremoniously through the little crowd towards us; and we learned from him (after a brief introduction between him and me, from Mr. Thornton) that the warrant against Mr. Lewis was already in the hands of a constable, who was saddling his horse; and that information had been obtained of the course of the trader and his party, they having passed through Jerusalem about an hour and a half before.

"Young Thornton is with him," added the sheriff, addressing my companion, "and you know what sort of a fellow he is; so we are likely to have a fight for it, and had better go prepared."

"Let us start off at once," said Mr. Thornton. "As he has got so far ahead, he may get across the state-line, where your writ won't run." By this time Mr. Hubbard had joined us, and being informed that Billy Byles was raising recruits, advised us to remain till he came up, if he did not tarry too long, and then entered upon some legal question with the sheriff as to the nature, power, and extent of the warrant issued--matters which I did not very clearly comprehend.

"Oh, yes, my good friend," replied Mr. Hubbard, to some question of the sheriff. "A slave being clearly a chattel, notwithstanding the Act of 1799, you can proceed just in the same manner as for the recovery of any other chattel stolen or abstracted. The abductors can be indicted, and a warrant against them can be issued to prevent their removal of the chattel from the jurisdiction of the State. Besides, in the case of Moosa *versus* Allain, Judge Martin's judgment clearly shows that a slave himself is entitled to the aid of a magistrate, to prevent him from being illegally removed from the State." There was something very harsh to my ears, as an Englishman, to hear even mild Mr. Hubbard talking of a human being as a chattel; and as I could be of no use in the discussion, I listened no longer. I thought, however, if I could get a knowledge of the country, I might employ any military science I possessed in preventing the escape of our adversary. A printed map could not be obtained; but as some two or three dozen persons had already surrounded us, I contrived to get hold of a pen-and-ink drawing of all the roads round about, and a torrent of information as to marshes, ditches, brakes, and *bad places*. In the meantime, sundry horses were brought out saddled, and sundry gentlemen began to mount; and before all was ready, bold Billy Byles and three other gentlemen rode up, with the gay and excited air of men bound for some exceedingly joyful enterprise.

"Now then," cried Mr. Byles, "let's be off. I hear they have taken right across for the old Nottoway encampment; but as they are going in waggons, we shall catch them soon enough." I looked at my pen-and-ink map, and saw marked down on one spot, "Indian Village." Two roads led towards it, one a distinct broad way, and the other seemingly a narrow but more direct path.

"Is this road passable?" I asked, of a young man standing near, and pointing to the map. He could tell me nothing about it; but another said,--

"I came along it this morning. It is wettish down there by the bars; but if you keep your horses' heads well up, you'll get through, I reckon. There's a little bit of a jog there to the left, which is not down on the plan, and if you take that, you'll come right down on the palisade on t'other side. There you can see by the waggon tracks, whether they have gone on or not, for that rain last night must have washed it pretty clean." By this time, all were prepared to set out except Mr. Hubbard, who preferred to wait our return in Jerusalem; and we made altogether a party of some fifteen horse. As we rode out of the town, I pointed out on the map, to the sheriff, the roads I have alluded to, and proposed that he and Mr. Thornton, with the main body of the party, should follow the wider road, while I and Billy Byles, with one or two others, should take the narrower path, and endeavour to cut Mr. Lewis's party off.

"No bad plan," said the sheriff, with a nod of his head; "but, will you have force enough?"

"I understand they have got several fellows with them--three Irishmen and a Dutchman, besides others."

"Give me two other stout men besides Mr. Byles," said I, "and I will undertake to keep them at a stand till you come up."

"A soldier?" asked the sheriff, laconically. I nodded my head.

"Well, go along then," he said; "there's your way up there; then the first to the right; but then mind the jog of the road to the left, about seven miles on. But Byles knows all about it; he knows the country right well. Here's their trail--these waggon ruts, freshly made and sharp at the edges. You can easily judge by these whether they have gone on; and if they have got beyond the camp, you had better stay there till we come. There will be nothing for it then but to ride them straight down as hard as we can go." The matter was soon explained to Mr. Byles, who was ready for anything; and after he, on his best judgment, had selected two stout fellows to accompany us, we set off at as fast a pace as we could well go, till we reached the month of the very narrow path which we had to pursue. Nor did we much slacken our speed there; although, to say the truth, it was rather a perilous undertaking to ride along it with such velocity; for the boughs swung across in many directions, whisking one's eyes, or one's knees, or one's head, every two or three hundred yards.

"Now we are coming near the bad place by the bar," said Billy Byles. "Keep a short rein and ease them up as you go through." And on he went, into what seemed to me neither more nor less than a morass. His horse made a terrible flounder at the first plunge, but was up again in a moment; and on we all went, stumbling, and sinking, and rolling, but scrambling on still, till we reached the other side of the *bad place*, and were once more upon firm ground. The next three or four miles were much more open, the road passing through a low sort of brushwood, with scattered scrubby trees, and a good deal of short grass between. We took advantage of it to the uttermost, and entered the thicker wood again after a gallop of some twenty minutes.

"I think we must have distanced them," said Billy Byles, slackening his speed a little; "the waggons cannot go more than three miles an hour at their very best, and we have not let the grass grow under us." On we went, however, at a very quick trot; and, at the end of three miles further, Mr. Byles said in a low tone,--

"We are coming near now. We shall soon know what we are about." At the same moment, I heard a sound, proceeding, apparently, from some spot not more than a couple of hundred yards on our left. It was a low sort of whining, complaining noise, something like a door turning on rusty hinges; and I said,--

"Hark! what is that?"

"An ungreased waggon wheel," replied Billy Byles. "We have caught them, for a hundred dollars." The next instant we heard somebody in the same direction whistling "Kate of Coleraine;" and Billy remarked,--

"That is that ruffian, Matthew Leary. He is always in any dirty job. He would sell his own father if anybody would buy him. Now then, let us push on and turn sharp to the left, when we get upon the main road, spreading out so that we shall head them and they can't pass." We rode on accordingly, and in two minutes more, we entered a good, wide, sandy road, from which we had only been separated for the last mile by an acute angle of the wood.

CHAPTER X

The sight which now presented itself, as we wheeled to the left, was not without its interest to one who had never seen such a thing before. The road, as I have said, was broad, and bordered on each side by thick wood, probably part of the primeval forest; but it was straight, and at the distance of about a third of a mile I could see an open space, only encumbered by what seemed to me a sort of ruinous stockade; in fact, the remains of an ancient Indian settlement of the Nottoway tribe. Between us and the stockade was a curious sort of cavalcade, the head of the line not being more than a hundred yards from us. It consisted principally of four-wheeled carts or waggons, apparently hired from farmers, and drawn by horses of various degrees of fatness and size. The waggons were, I think, five in number; and each was loaded as full as it could hold with families of poor negroes, in every attitude of grief and dejection. They sat on a little straw, thrown down in the bottom of the vehicle; and some, especially among the women, had their heads bent down on their knees as they sat, whilst others gazed around with a vacant, listless look of despair. Several children were amongst them; and, in fact, almost every age, from the white-headed old man to the infant at the breast; for Mr. Lewis, as he afterwards expressed himself, liked to buy a whole lot at once, and not to separate people. Each waggon had its driver on foot, all white men, and I think most of them Irishmen; but at the head of the procession came three very well-mounted men, the centre figure being that of Mr. Lewis himself, as gaudily dressed as usual.

"That's young Thornton on the right," said Billy Byles to me, in a low tone, "Robert Thornton, the d--d rascally attorney who makes so much mischief in the place; and that's Matthew Leary over on the other side; but who the devil that is in the middle, I don't know."

"That's Lewis the trader," I answered; "I came in the boat with him."

"Oh, ho!" ejaculated Mr. Byles. "Now let's ride slowly on, and have a chat with them, to give the others time to come up. Keep spread out, so that none of them can pass; and let me manage it, Sir Richard, for we may as well begin quietly, so that when the fight comes we may have help near at hand, for you see, all mustered, they are two to one." We accordingly moved slowly forward, and were soon close to the advancing party.

"Good morning, Mr. Thornton," said Billy Byles, in a cheerful tone. "You must have been out early to have got so far from your place by this time."

"So must you, Mr. Byles," replied Thornton, who, to say the truth, was a tall, stout, good-looking man, from whose appearance I certainly should never have divined his character. "*You* seem to have ridden hard too; your horse is all in a sweat." By this time, seeing their leaders stop to converse, the drivers of the waggons had brought them to a halt; while Mr. Lewis had noticed me with a somewhat shy inclination of the head, as if he suspected at once that something was not all right; and Mr. Leary began to talk in a low tone to one of the two men who accompanied us.

"We have been hunting," said Billy Byles, in answer to Robert Thornton's last observation.

"Hunting!" exclaimed the other; "hunting on the first of June!"

"Ay, ay, I know it is out of season; but you see I wanted to give our English friend here a sight of some sports such as he does not have in his own country. Have you seen anything of the rest of our party? for we have cut across, hoping to join them about here."

"No," answered Thornton; "we have seen nobody since we started, neither man nor beast. Now, Mr. Byles, I must wish you good morning, for I have business on hand."

"So I see," retorted Billy Byles, not moving out of the way a step. "A nice lot of negroes, upon my word. Why, hang it, there's old Lydia, who was Mrs. Bab Thornton's woman!"

"Perhaps so," said Thornton, impatiently; "but I must get on. Come along, boys!"

"Stop, stop, Thornton!" exclaimed Billy Byles. "I have got something to say to you in private--a little hint which may be serviceable to you."

"Say it out then," returned Thornton, with a flush upon his cheek. "I don't care a cuss about secrets; and I'm in a hurry."

"Why, then, the fact is," said Billy Byles, "that a warrant is out against you and one Lewis, together with other parties, for certain offences which I dare say you know better than I do. And you will not be allowed to go on, depend upon it."

"And who the devil will stop me?" demanded Mr. Thornton, with his face turning very red, and the veins of his temples swelling up.

"In the first place, I will," answered Billy Byles; "and if we are not enough here, there will be plenty more up in a minute, who will stop you quite effectually."

"*You* will stop me, will you?" cried Thornton, putting his hand in his pocket and setting his teeth hard. "Where's your warrant, sir,--where's your warrant?" At the same time Mr. Lewis, who had turned rather white, looked back to the drivers of the waggons, exclaiming, "Come up, come up, my men, and move these gentlemen's horses out of the way!"

"I'll mow them," cried Mr. Robert Thornton, drawing a brace of small pistols out of his pocket. "If you have a warrant, Mr. Byles, produce it; if not, stand out of my way, or by I'll shoot you as dead as mutton. Here's one for you, and one for your John Bull accomplice. Curse me, if I had him by myself half an hour, if I would not give him such a whipping, for the love I bear his country, as would send him back howling." He paused for a minute, to see if his braggadocio would have any effect; but Billy Byles continued right before him, and I only smiled, taking care, however, to grasp my heavy-headed riding-whip by the middle, in case he should proceed to any act of violence. At the same time the men from the waggons began to come up. Mr. Leary brandished a stout stick which he carried, and I thought I heard a noise of trotting horses not far off. The next minute the click of Thornton's pistol-lock was audible; and, with one glance to see that it was properly capped, he raised it right in the direction of my bold friend.

"Dammee, fire if you dare!" cried Billy Byles. But I saw that no time was to be lost; and the head of my hunting-whip descended upon Mr. Thornton's knuckles with such a blow as to make him instantly relax his hold; and down went the pistol to the ground, going off amongst the horses' feet, but hurting no one. In the meantime Mr. Leary had engaged in a struggle with one of the stout farmers who had accompanied us, and both having been pulled from their horses, were rolling over and over on the ground together. Mr. Lewis was still beckoning to the men behind to come up; but they seemed very little inclined to obey, and moved but slowly towards the spot where hard blows were going. Thornton, with the other pistol in his hand, had now turned upon me; but Mr. Byles, spurring his horse upon him, caught him by the collar, and threw him back; and the other farmer, riding up, pulled him off his horse and wrenched the pistol fairly out of his grasp. At the same time, the sheriff and his party began to appear from behind the old stockade, and there was soon a sufficient force on the field to render further resistance unavailable. When they saw Mr. Henry Thornton's face in the approaching party, the negroes, who had sat seemingly stupefied in the waggons, not comprehending what was going on, rose up and gave a cheer, mingled with a loud and joyful laugh, and the sheriff riding round, exclaimed, "Who fired that shot?"

"It was Bob Thornton's pistol," said Billy Byles; "but I think Sir Richard's gentle rap of the knuckles made it go off, before he would have dared to fire it himself."

"That's a lie," said Bob Thornton. "If he had not knocked it out of my hand, the ball would have been through your heart, you purse-proud jackass. But I will bring him to account for it. He struck me. You saw him, Mr. Lewis--you saw him, Leary; and the d--ned English cur shall smart for it. You all saw him strike me." My patience was exhausted, and I jumped off my horse, saying, "If you want more witnesses, sir, you shall have them." And at the same time, I laid the whip two or three times pretty severely over his shoulders. I believe he would have sprung at my throat like a tiger; but the constable coming up, took him by the collar and presented his warrant. There was a strong mixture of the lawyer and the bully in Robert Thornton's nature; and the sight of the legal instrument, duly signed and sealed, in an instant drew his attention in another direction.

"This warrant is worth nothing," he said, turning to the constable, after having run his eye over the document; "and if you arrest me upon this, I shall have an action for false imprisonment against you."

"I think you will find yourself mistaken," said the sheriff, with a smile. "It was drawn by Mr. Hubbard, and he does not often make mistakes."

"Oh! oh! old Hubbard again!" cried the other. "Some day, I shall have to knock that old fool's brains out, I'm afraid."

"Ay, they have stood in your way more than once, Bob," said Mr. Henry Thornton.

"Well, we will bail this, of course," said the other, without taking any notice of what his relation had said.

"That must be done at Jerusalem," said the sheriff; "so you had better mount your horse, and come along, sir."

"Wait one moment," said Robert, looking at me. "I want a word or two with this gentleman first."

"No violence, gentlemen, no violence," said the sheriff.

"Oh, no violence in the world," answered Robert Thornton; "only I wish to know who my new acquaintance is." Thus saying, he walked a little aside, beckoning me to follow; but Billy Byles, who seemed to have a thorough knowledge of the gentleman, whispered as I went--

"Don't be provoked to challenge him by anything he can say. He wants the choice of weapons, and he'll choose something you're not accustomed to." The hint was a good one; and I really felt much obliged to him for it, as the people in this part of the world not unfrequently settle affairs of honour in various wild and unaccustomed ways, which would have strangely shocked old Brantome, and which, assuredly, were not anticipated in his book on duels. As soon as we had got a little distance from the rest, out of ear-shot, but not out of sight, Mr. Robert Thornton made me a low bow, as if about to begin a very polite conversation, and said--

"In the first place, sir, I wish to inquire the name of a gentleman with whom my acquaintance has commenced so auspiciously--his name, state, quality, and degree.

"I will satisfy you immediately," I replied. "My name is Sir Richard Conway; my state, an English gentleman visiting Virginia; my quality, a baronet of Great Britain; and my degree, a major upon half-pay of the regiment of dragoons."

"Well, then, Sir Richard Conway, baronet, major, &c., I look upon you as a d--d blackguard and scoundrel." And he stared me straight in the face.

"My dear sir," I answered, with a calm smile, "I have had the honour of horse-whipping you already in the presence of several other people. I do not think it necessary to repeat it, as you can't easily take the past horse-whipping off; but if it will be any gratification to you, I will do it."

"Well, sir, for a soldier, you seem cursed hard to take an insult," he answered with a sneer.

"Not at all," replied I. "I have insulted you publicly, and on purpose. Your bad opinion of me I consider as no insult, but rather a compliment--at all events, till you have wiped out the horse-whipping you have received. And now, if you have nothing else to say, I shall wish you good morning."

"Stay, stay!" he cried, with his face very much flushed; "you must give me satisfaction for this."

"Very good," I answered. "I am quite at your service, wherever you please to name. You had better send some friend to my friend, Mr. Byles, and they will, together, arrange the preliminaries. I am myself staying at the house of Mr. Stringer, called Beavors, and shall remain there for a week. After that, I shall most likely be at Mr. Henry Thornton's; but Mr. Byles, I presume, will be found at his own house, and you must communicate with him." Thus saying, I made him a bow and left him, not at all sorry, I must confess, to have thrown the onus of the challenge upon him; for the idea of bowie-knives in a dark room, or blunderbusses in a saw-pit, does not at all meet my notions of the code of honour. We then mounted our horses, and after some little difficulty in the arrangements, Mr. Lewis and Mr. Robert Thornton being looked upon as prisoners (though not under personal restraint), pursued our way back to Jerusalem; the sheriff leading the party, and several other gentlemen following the waggons which contained the negroes, to prevent the possibility of any of the persons concerned escaping, as many doubts were entertained whether Mr. Lewis might not take the first opportunity of dashing away for the State-line. Various conversations, of course, took place; and I soon found an opportunity of communicating to Mr. Byles what had passed between Mr. Robert Thornton and myself, and of requesting him to act as my friend upon the occasion.

"Certainly, certainly," he answered; "you managed it capitally. Now let me hear your views as to the time, place, mode, and weapon. I can lend you the best rifle in the world."

"Excuse me," I answered; "pistols are the weapons we always use in England; and I certainly should prefer them. As to the place, you must appoint that for me, as I do not know the country. All the other arrangements I must leave to you; they are quite indifferent to me, except that I should like it over as soon as possible, for no business, especially business of this kind, should be long delayed."

"But have you got pistols with you?" he asked.

"Nothing but a pair for the pocket," I answered; "but surely they can be obtained in the neighbourhood."

"No tools worth using," he replied; "but I know where to get them. That, however, may delay us for three or four days. Still, I doubt if that won't be too soon for him. He does not want courage when his blood is up; but it soon cools down, and then the lawyer comes over him again."

"We must not give it time to cool," I answered; "and I have a very good excuse for hurrying things on, as a stranger in the land, whose stay must necessarily be uncertain." Having arranged all that matter with Mr. Byles, I joined Mr. Henry Thornton, who was looking somewhat grave, but did not in any way refer to the personal altercation between his relation and myself. At Jerusalem, which we reached after a somewhat tiresome ride, we found Mr. Hubbard, and one or two magistrates. A long, legal discussion. ensued, first as to the validity of the writ, and next as to the amount of bail which was to be taken from Mr. Lewis and Mr. Thornton, who, I found, were charged with a conspiracy to defraud certain persons, amongst whom I was one. There is no need to enter into any of the details of these matters; suffice it, that Robert Thornton easily procured the necessary sureties, and that, after much difficulty, Mr. Lewis did the same. The great question, however, was in regard to the custody of good Aunt Bab's negroes, whom Mr. Robert Thornton very much wished to carry back to his father's plantation. The sheriff peremptorily interfered, however; and, notwithstanding some threats and many arguments, took possession of them himself, to hold them for the lawful owner. The greater portion of the day had been consumed by these proceedings, and the whole party were glad to separate and get to their several homes. I wended my way back to Mr. Stringer's, accompanied, as far as the gate on the high road, by Mr. Henry Thornton and bold Billy Byles. There they left me, and I pursued my way alone, revolving all the little incidents of the day. I am always sorry when I suffer anger to overcome me, and I regretted having struck the pitiful trickster, opposed to me, more than the one blow which was necessary to knock the pistol out of his hand. I felt a certain degree of self-reproach, and, perhaps, some lingering shadow of the kind remained upon my face. Under the porch of Mr. Stringer's house, when I arrived, were several members of the family, and Miss Davenport, reading or working in the shade. A thousand questions were poured upon me as to the course and end of our adventure; but none came from Bessy, though her look was raised to my face, and her eyes seemed to question mine.

"Was there any resistance?" asked Mr. Stringer.

"Very slight," I replied; "one worthy gentleman thought fit to draw a pistol but it was knocked out of his hand, and went off upon the ground."

"Robert Thornton, of course," said Bessy; "bully and knave combined." I nodded my head, and the conversation went on, till Mr. and Mrs. Stringer retired from the porch to prepare for dinner, calling their little boy, who was there, to accompany them. Bessy Davenport had contrived to get a knot in the silk she was working, and she remained for a minute or two longer. The first minute was passed in silence; but she twice looked up in my face, and then said, suddenly--

"Cousin Richard, there is something you have not told us. I see it in your face."

"I have told you really all about the pursuit and capture of these people," I replied, laughing. "You don't wish me, I hope, to relate all that occurred in regard to warrants, and bail, and custody of negroes; for really the worthy gentlemen's law-terms were beyond my comprehension." She shook her head somewhat sadly, saying--

"You are insincere, as all men are with all women."

"No, indeed, Bessy," I answered, taking the vacant seat by her side. "I have told you all that is necessary for you to know." She started up, breaking the silk thread in two between her fingers, and exclaimed,--

"Well, perhaps you have. But I do hope, Cousin Richard, that you are not going to risk a valuable life against one that should only be ended by the hangman. There, I wont hear any more about it now, whether you are going to speak sincerely or insincerely. I look upon these things very differently from many of the girls in this neighbourhood. I look upon the men who fight duels as great fools or great villains, and think there are but two cases in which a man is bound to fight: one, when he has *received* so great an injury, and the other when he has *inflicted* so great an injury, that it is impossible for him and his opponent to live upon the same earth together." Thus saying, she ran away and left me; and, at dinner, there was no trace upon her countenance or in her manner of the more serious thoughts and feelings which I knew were in her mind. She was, indeed, if anything, gayer than usual; and amused us during the greater part of the evening with singing the merriest negro songs she could select. Suddenly, however, she changed entirely the tone of her music, and poured forth one of the most melancholy and touching strains I ever heard, beautifully suited to her exquisitely sweet voice, which, even in her gayest and happiest moments, had an expression in it that made one feel a thrill, not of melancholy, but of something very nearly approaching it.

"Heigh ho!" she exclaimed, rising as soon as that song was over. "Now that I have made myself and all of you sad, I'll go to bed and sleep it off, as the drunkards do."

"Stay a moment," I said. "Remember, you promised to show me where my new acquaintance, Nat Turner, lives."

"Did I?" she answered. "I don't remember; but I'll do it, cousin; and, as you are curious in ebony, I'll introduce you to a stick of another tree; but a very curious one too--one of the best old men that ever lived, and one of the wisest also, although he is a pure African. There's something curious about Nat Turner, something mysterious, supernatural; but if ever there was a pure, gentle-minded Christian--an Israelite without guile--it is good uncle Jack."

"When shall it be, then?" I asked.

"Oh, after breakfast to-morrow," she answered. "Mrs. Stringer fancies that if I go out so early in the morning, the dews will give me a fever, though they have been falling on my head almost every day for one-and-twenty years--there's a confession, cousin Richard, don't I look like seventeen? I must make haste, dear Mrs. Stringer, or I shall lose my chance. Women are looked upon as old women at two-and-twenty. Dear me! What a deal to be done in one year--to find somebody to fall in love with--to get him to fall in love with me--to fall in love with him myself (that's the most difficult and longest task of them all)--to get married (but that's nothing; it can be done in half an hour)--and to get all my wedding clothes ready. But, good night, good night. I'll go and arrange it all with Julia while she is combing my hair; and I dare say I shall get through--with patience and perseverance."

CHAPTER XI

It was a beautiful morning, and the breakfast was over by eight o'clock, notwithstanding the tremendously long grace with which Mr. McGrubber thought fit to season it. There was some chance, therefore, of a cool walk, although I could not think Mrs. Stringer's plan a good one; for it seems to me that the early mornings and the late evenings are the only endurable periods in a Virginian summer. Bessy Davenport ran up stairs to get some covering for her head; and I stood in the porch waiting for her, ready for our visit to my mysterious negro, and to the no less remarkable personage to whom she had promised to introduce me. But a moment before she came down, who should appear but Billy Byles coming round from the stable where he had put up his horse.

"It is all arranged," he said, speaking in a low tone, and shaking me by the hand. "On Saturday morning at six, in Hunter's Wood."

"Why, that is three days still," I said, somewhat annoyed at the delay.

"We couldn't arrange it otherwise," he answered; "the pistols stuck in Bob Thornton's throat desperately. He did not care a d----n how he fought you for that matter--muskets and buckshot as lief as any other way; but he should have to send for pistols. I told him we were in the same predicament, but that pistols it must be; and so we fixed Saturday morning to give him time. You had better come over and dine with me on Friday, and take a bed at----" Just then appeared Bessy Davenport, and he stopped short; but I answered at once, as if he had concluded his sentence, "With a great deal of pleasure; at what hour do you dine?"

"Oh, at three, at three," answered Billy Byles. "I have not got into these people's bad habits yet."

"Indeed!" cried Bessy coming up. "I did not know that you ever let any bad habit pass you, Mr. Byles, without trying it on at least."

"You are a wicked little satirist, Miss Bessy," he answered; "but I know the cause of your malice: you are angry at my taking Sir Richard away from you to dine with me on Friday."

"If you don't do any worse with him than that, I don't care," said Bessy; "but I doubt you both, I tell you. Come, cousin Richard, let us go, or we shall have a warm walk back." And leaving Mr. Byles, we walked on towards the edge of the forest. For the first hundred yards or so Bessy walked on profoundly silent, with her eyes fixed upon the ground; but then she looked up, with a sigh and a sad shake of the head, saying, "It wont do, Richard." It were needless to deny that the interest displayed in my fate by such a lovely creature produced very sweet emotions; but still there was no possibility of making any reply to what she said without subjecting myself to questions which I could not answer sincerely; and therefore, affecting not to have heard her speak, I tried to lead her mind away in some other direction. Though I think she saw the object, she gave in to it quietly; and we walked on for about a mile, talking of various matters of mere passing interest. Our way lay through the woods; and I may notice here how much more of the land, especially in this state of Virginia, is uncultivated than we generally imagine in England. When we talk of a plantation, we think of a wide tract of country all smoothly laid out in maize, or tobacco, or cotton, or rice, and don't comprehend that perhaps two-thirds of that plantation will be forest, either the first or second growth. I must remark, too, that a good deal of the country, especially on the sea-board, has gone back to forest; the earlier colonists having been like prodigals newly come into a fortune, and exhausted their lands with unvarying crops, principally of tobacco. Thus, what was once, we have every reason to believe, very fertile soil, will now only bear pine or other trees of hardy habits. At length we came to a small open space between the wood through which we had passed and another beyond. It could not be more than a hundred and fifty yards wide, but extended on either hand as far as the eye could see, like a long avenue through the forest. The grass with which the ground was covered was very green and soft, being sheltered, I suppose, from the heat of the sun by the woods on either side, and fertilized by the moisture which trees invariably draw around them.

"This is a curious interval in the woods," I said, looking up and down. "I should almost be tempted to think a river once flowed down here."

"Oh, no," she answered; "they have a tradition in the country that it was caused by what they call here a *flaw* of wind, which broke clear through the forest, like a hemmed-in warrior cutting his way through his enemies. The trees that the blast overthrew have long since decayed; but the path that he made for himself still remains. Man boasts his mighty deeds; but when will king or conqueror leave such permanent traces of his footsteps as are here?"

"And yet, dear Bessy," I answered, "man can occasionally hew for himself ways more magnificent, more indelible than this. The forest around may be cut down, the roots rot away, the plough-share pass over where we stand, and not a trace be left. But the mighty human mind, when nobly and vigorously exerted, opens out, for everlasting ages, paths which millions follow every day, and which are never blotted out. He who sweeps away the prejudices of a race--he who opens out a wide and noble path for the human mind--he who leads an Exodus from any land of darkness to a land of light, performs a more powerful and more permanent work than the tempest--ay, and one more beneficent."

"True, true," she cried eagerly, "very true; but such thoughts set my little weak brain whirling. I should like to have been a man, and done some great deeds; but here I am, a mere Virginian girl, no stronger than a butterfly, and fit only for small thoughts and petty personal adventures. But, talking of adventures, I could make your hair stand on end, if I chose, by a tale of what happened in this wood, through which we are going. It has been called 'The Hunter Wood' ever since."

"And what is it?" I asked.

"No, no," she answered, "I won't tell you now; I should only frighten myself; and in ten minutes we shall be at Nat Turner's cottage, for this is the boundary of Mr. Travis's property. We will come back the other way, for the sun will then throw the shade more northerly, and that will bring us to the house where uncle Jack, as they call him, pays a visit every year."

"Is that the old man you spoke of yesterday?" I asked.

"Yes; and very old he is," she replied; "how old, nobody knows, exactly; but he must be more than ninety, for he was brought from the coast of Africa, they say, when a good big boy, more than eighty years ago, in one of the last slave ships that ever came to Virginia."

"He is a slave, then," I said.

"Oh no," she answered; "he is so very much loved and respected, that several people joined together, and purchased his freedom."

"He must, indeed, be an extraordinary man to create such feelings in his favour," I remarked.

"The most extraordinary thing of all, perhaps," added she, "is, that he has not the slightest touch of the negro pronunciation. I dare say, you must have remarked, cousin Richard, that none of them can ever learn to speak English properly; that there is always a sort of thickness, a difficulty, about their utterance; and some sounds they cannot form at all. But this old man speaks as good English as you do."

"That is, indeed, extraordinary," I answered; "for so universal is that difficulty of utterance which you mention in the African race, whatever language they are speaking, that I imagined it to proceed from a natural defect. I have heard they talk both French and Spanish in the same peculiar manner that they talk English."

"Hear this man talk in a dark room, and you would not know him from an American," said Bessy. But I had soon an opportunity of judging for myself, for, shortly after, we came in sight of two or three cabins, with a larger house peeping over the trees at some little distance. Approaching the hut, farthest from us, I knocked at the door, on my fair companion's suggestion. We had heard voices speaking within, and, on entering, we found the cabin tenanted by two negroes, who were seated at a small table, with a bowl of milk, and some bread made of Indian corn between them. The first was my friend, Nat Turner, and a powerful, though spare man he was. The other was fully as dark in complexion, and had probably once been as strong in form; but he was now an old man, with the wool upon his head as white as snow, and a good many wrinkles in his dingy skin. He was well dressed in black, with very white linen, and a white neck-cloth tied in what I may call clerical style. I should have judged him to have been a man of about seventy, and stout and hale for his age; but, nevertheless, this was Bessy Davenport's negro, Jack, and, I must say, there was something very reverent and prepossessing in his appearance as he rose and made us a respectful, but not servile, bow.

"Well, Mr. Turner," I said, "I promised to pay you a visit, and Miss Davenport has been kind enough to guide me; otherwise, as a stranger in the land, I might have missed my way."

"You are very welcome, sir," answered Nat. "Pray, Miss Bessy, take dis stool. Here is good uncle Jack, whom you know." Bessy held out her hand to uncle Jack, who shook it kindly; but he did not miss an opportunity of reproof, and looking sadly at Nat Turner, he shook his head, saying,

"Whom callest thou good? There is none good but one--that is God."

"Well, I meant good as this world goes," answered Nat Turner.

"There is so little difference between any two of us," replied the old man, "that no one has a right to claim or receive the title of good; far less to arrogate superiority over other brethren."

"That is an admirable text you have quoted, my friend," I said; "but do you know, I one time heard a man make it an argument against the divinity of our Saviour?"

"He was very much mistaken," answered uncle Jack, mildly. "The young man to whom he spoke had addressed him as a man, and called him 'Good master,' looking upon him as nothing but a man. Christ reproved him for calling any mere man good, and in so doing spoke of himself in his human character. That man must have been very hard pressed for an argument against a belief that was too powerful for him."

"The case of many a man, I fear," replied I; "but do not let us interrupt your breakfast, Mr. Turner," I continued, turning to Nat.

"It matters not to me when I eat or when I drink," answered Nat Turner, in what seemed to be a somewhat stilted tone. "The man who wishes to bring the body under the mind must not care about such things. I have often gone without food for three days."

"I should think that must require some practice and preparation," I observed, somewhat inclined to smile, "and unless it was done from necessity, I do not see the use of it."

"Nor I either," said uncle Jack; "food and drink were given to us for our natural support, and while we reverence God's blessings, by using them moderately, we should show our thankfulness for them, by using them as He wills."

"The use was very great," exclaimed Nat Turner, in a more excited tone than before; "and as for preparation, I have accustomed myself to abstinence from my childhood. I knew from my earliest years that I was born for great things. What placed that mark upon my forehead before my birth?" And he laid his finger upon a sort of scar on his brow resembling a cross. But before I could examine it accurately, he went on in the same tone--"Who taught me things which happened before I was born, and which were only known to my mother and my father? If it was God who did this, why did He do so but to show that He intended me to--to--do great things?" I looked round to uncle Jack, beginning to think that the man was going mad, and the old man, taking my glance as a question, answered,--

"All the people will tell you it is as he says, sir. But I think Nat lets his mind rest too much upon such things. I fear it may do him harm. He has plenty of strong, good sense, and if he will but continually seek God's grace, to use it right, he may, indeed, do great things amongst the poor people who surround him. But the quickest walker goes farthest wrong, when he does not take the right way, and I fear that may be Nat's case."

"No fear, no fear," cried the other. "God, who willed me to be what I am, will teach me to do what I have to do." Then, dropping his voice into an almost sepulchral tone, he added, "He will give me a sign--He has promised it." Uncle Jack shook his head very gravely, and Bessy Davenport, who had not yet spoken, remarked,--

"We are often inclined, Nat, to misunderstand signs. Take care that you don't apply to yourself signs that may be intended for the whole world. Don't you remember, when there was an eclipse a little while ago, you said it was a sign sent to you?"

"I don't know what you mean by an eclipse," answered the man, gloomily; "but I know there *was* a sign, and a terrible sign too. However," he continued, in a more cheerful tone, "every one must read such things by the lights he has got, and the Lord will not suffer those whom he favours to mistake. He will direct us," he added, with a sigh, and then seemed inclined to change the conversation. I tried to keep it in the same course, for I wanted to hear more of his views on such subjects; but, with a great deal of skill--I might almost say, cunning--he avoided it; and I purposely brought up the subject of freedom and slavery. The old preacher spoke upon it frankly and freely enough, and with a degree of liberality towards the masters, which greatly surprised me. He said that the great majority were excellent, good, and kind-hearted people, and that, if they were all such, his race would be much more happy under their management than they could be under their own.

"The great evil of slavery, sir," he continued, "is the possibility of any extent of ill-treatment. Where such a possibility exists, the thing will occur. It is true, I have no opportunity of comparing any other state of society with this; and for aught I know, there may be evils as great, or greater, in all others. I cannot remember my own country at all distinctly. Some vague, general notions I have about it; and, if they be correct, I was a great deal worse off there than I am here; but I cannot be sure whether these notions come from my own recollections, or from what I have read or heard. One thing, however, is certain, slavery has existed in all ages. The Hebrews had their bond servants, and they themselves were hewers of wood and drawers of water to the king of Egypt."

"Ay, but they rose and delivered themselves, and God helped and directed them," said Nat Turner, with a peculiar flash in his dark eye.

"He is a God of justice and strong to deliver," said a voice at the door, speaking in a very nasal tone; and turning round, to my surprise, I saw the lanky and extraordinary figure of the Rev. Mr. McGrubber. Nat Turner started forward, and shook him by the hand, and uncle Jack made him a formal, and, I thought, somewhat stiff bow. Bessy Davenport gave me a rueful and yet a merry glance; and, judging that we should not profit much by what was likely to follow, I prepared to take my departure. Nat

Turner, however, instantly began the conversation with his visitor, who was evidently an old acquaintance and friend, by calling upon him to tell uncle Jack all that he had been telling him the day before. "*You* will convince him, but I can't," cried the man; not heeding a cloud that came over Mr. McGrubber's brow, and a quick sign that he made to him to be silent. "His heart seems as hard as the nether millstone towards his own people."

"My heart is not hard, Nathaniel," answered uncle Jack; "but I love my own people too well to try and make them discontented with a situation from which they cannot escape, but which may be ameliorated, if they show themselves peaceable, quiet, and faithful. It is my duty to preach peace and good will, resignation to the will of God and dependence upon his mercy; and not to stimulate men's passions, either in a right or wrong cause, to conduct which may end, God only knows how." While the two negroes had been speaking, Mr. McGrubber had evidently been upon thorns; though, at the end of uncle Jack's reply, he had put on a look of meek and pious resignation.

"Far be it from me, brother," he said, "to stimulate men's passions or induce them to act in any violent and hasty manner. God forbid that I should bring poor people into trouble, or do anything, which is not pointed out by calm reason and religion. But we are told that we shall not spare to speak God's truth; and when I am asked what is right and what is wrong, must I not say what is right? Ay, if any poor soul demands of me, 'Has my fellow-man a right to keep me in bondage?' wouldst thou have me reply 'Yea' or 'Nay?' I preach the truth, brother; let the results be what they may. That is in God's hand, not mine." Uncle Jack shook his head, with a somewhat melancholy look; but merely said, "The Apostle teaches us to be obedient to the powers that are; and again, we are told that servants should obey their masters. He who teaches differently, I cannot look upon as speaking by the Holy Spirit, and I fear that evil will come of it." Thus saying, he left the cabin; and Bessy Davenport and I followed, after having taken leave of Nat Turner. I thought, as I walked away, that I heard the voice of Mr. McGrubber, raised loudly and harshly; and I doubted not that poor Nat was receiving a stout reproof for having betrayed to the ears of others the nature of the reverend gentleman's communications with himself. On the whole, my visit had a good deal disappointed me. My first interview with Nat Turner had impressed me with an idea that he was very much more superior to the rest of his race than I found him upon further acquaintance. That he was superior, there could be no doubt; but I thought I had discovered traits in him that day of almost all the peculiar weaknesses of tho African race. That he was cunning, superstitious, and conceited, was very clear; and there was something in the expression of his face and the glance of his eye which inclined me to believe that there might be a certain degree of ruthless cruelty and fierce passion within, though now concealed, if not subdued, by the command he had acquired over himself. In comparing the two negroes with each other, one thing was very remarkable. In uncle Jack you could not, as Miss Davenport had already indicated, trace the slightest vestige of the African pronunciation. What I may call Virginianisms he unquestionably had: there was a certain intonation and also a pronunciation of some letters and syllables which in England we do not consider English; for instance, he pronounced the word "to" as we should pronounce "toe;" but nothing at all negro could be detected in it. On the contrary, Nat Turner, though he had evidently a good command of language, and could express himself with great fluency and propriety, had that sort of thick and jerking utterance which characterizes the African race. Uncle Jack was walking on slowly before us, and Bessy and I soon overtook him; but the good old man seemed unwilling to enter any farther upon the subjects we had been discussing.

"Mr. McGrubber," he said, "was a very good man, he had no doubt; but he did not think a very discreet one." As to Nat Turner, he remarked, "It was grievous to him to see a man fitted for better things, delude himself by vain imaginations. I believe, Miss Bessy," he continued, looking with a smile at my fair companion, "half the faults of men and women arise from vanity. This poor youth Nat, if he did not believe himself far greater than he is, would be far better than he is. But he is a good young man, and means well to all, I do believe." Soon after, we left him, and went upon our way, discussing between ourselves the characters of those whom we had just left.

"I cannot help thinking," I said, "that Mr. McGrubber is a rather dangerous man in this part of the country."

"He is a very odious one," answered Bessy, in the true woman spirit; for ladies, my dear sister, you must acknowledge, place the agreeable qualities, in comparison with the more important ones, higher in estimation than men do.

"He must have been speaking," I continued, "of things he did not wish us to hear, and was evidently in a great fright when Nat Turner alluded to them."

"Oh, that was quite clear," answered Bessy. "Uncle Jack clearly intimated, I thought, that the man had been trying to instigate the slaves against their masters. He is an Abolitionist, we all know, and I have a great mind to talk to Mr. Stringer about it, but it may make mischief."

"Every man has a right to his own opinion, of course," I said; "but I can imagine nothing more unpardonable than for a foolish fanatic to come into a state, not his own, and attempt, in his vain self-conceit, to cause a violent change in the relations of the different classes of society without a consideration of all the consequences."

"The consequences would be frightful," exclaimed Bessy. "Were the slaves to get the mastery, imagination itself cannot picture what would be the result. They are so violent in their temper--their passions are so uncontrollable, that the very thought makes one shudder. Did you ever see a negro in a passion, cousin Richard? It is the most frightful thing you ever beheld. He looks, and acts, and speaks, and, I am sure, feels, more like a demon than a human creature. I recollect when I was living with dear Aunt Bab, there was a girl in the house who had taken a peculiar and sort of irrational fancy for one of the small ornaments on the mantelpiece. Twice she had been detected and stopped in attempting to purloin it; but, at length, one day it was gone. Nobody doubted who had got it, and my aunt ordered the girl's room to be searched. I was present, though quite a little thing, and I remember her quite well, standing in the middle of the room, silent and motionless, her eyes following the other servants as they made the examination, with an expression I shall never forget. For some time, they found nothing, and she was beginning to look quite triumphant; but, at length, the object of search was discovered hidden away in the most cunning manner--suspended, hi fact, by threads underneath the bed. The moment it was disclosed, she burst forth, not with any contrition, but with rage and fury, such as I never saw in another human being. She stamped, she raved, she cried, she poured forth words so fast that no one could understand them, and she ended by tearing her clothes to pieces like a mad thing."

"And what did my aunt do?" I asked.

"Just what might be expected of her," answered Bessy. "'Tis rather a sad story; but aunt Bab was not to blame. She looked at her very gravely, and said,--

"'Have you gone mad, Juno? You must remain here till you have recovered yourself, and are able to listen like a reasonable being, and I will then come and talk to you. Now it would be of no use.'

"She then left her, ordering her to be locked in. But we had not been gone five minutes, when one of the servants came running in to say, that Juno had jumped out of the window, and was dreadfully hurt. My aunt would not suffer me to see her, and all, I know further is, that she lingered for about five weeks, and then she died, and Aunt Bab wept very bitterly over the poor misguided creature, as she called her."

"It is a sad picture of human nature, indeed," I said, "and from what I see of the negro population I am inclined to attribute less power to education and more to race than I once did."

"The more you see of them, the more you will think so," answered Bessy. "Good education might, and I have no doubt does, produce a great deal of improvement; but as no cosmetic that ever was tried will make a black man white, so I don't believe any education will make his mind and character those of a white man. And yet, this good old preacher, uncle Jack, appears to be an extraordinary exception."

"It does not seem to me," I replied, "that that proves anything. The fair test might be, to take a certain number of children of different races, and educate them from the earliest period exactly upon the same system, and then judge of the race by the average number of each which you found capable, in a certain time, of arriving at an ascertained point of cultivation. Thus, if out of a hundred Anglo-Saxon children ten should reach the highest proposed point in ten years, and only one negro, we might conclude that the Anglo-Saxon race was far more susceptible of cultivation than that of the negro. But solitary instances prove nothing. And now, my dear Bessy, let us, for Heaven's sake, talk of some other subjects, for, otherwise, we shall both of us sink into philosophers--a degradation for which, I am sure, nature never intended us."

"I suspect you intend to be saucy, Richard," answered my fair companion; "but, in sober sadness, we have had a very grave and solemn walk of it--very different from yesterday's."

"And I like yesterday's style best," I said. But though we changed to lighter tones throughout the rest of the walk homeward, we came upon none of those exciting, perhaps I may say dangerous, topics, in which we had previously indulged. I believe the truth is, with every young man and every young woman while unconscious of danger--unconscious that there is near them what, in common gallantry, I must not call a precipice, but a great leap to be taken or not, at their pleasure, which, nevertheless, they may still chance to fall over unawares--they go on sporting up to the very edge of the bank, and then, when finding themselves so near it, they pause and look down with some degree of doubt, and draw a little back and avoid the brink, till resolution comes, and over they go. Thus our talk on the way homeward was very commonplace, and at about a hundred yards from the house, amongst the peach-trees, we met Mr. Stringer, and with him, to my surprise, my Norfolk friend, Mr. Wheatley.

CHAPTER XII

With his usual quick and jerking manner, Mr. Wheatley took off his hat to Miss Davenport; saluted me, made a somewhat indefinite joke about Adam and Eve in the orchard, and then laughed and suddenly stopped, as usual.

"This is an unexpected pleasure, Mr. Wheatley," I said; "for though you hinted you might be coming up to this part of the country, I did not anticipate meeting you in this very house."

"Oh, Stringer is an old friend of mine," he answered. "We are both Northern men, with Southern principles, as they call us, in the blessed region of Yankeedom--eh, Stringer? We read '*M[ae]cenas atavis edite regibus*' together, when we were good little boys, and very well behaved; and so, of course, I come to see him from time to time, '*sub tegmine fagi*,' which may be translated, I presume, under the shadow of his own fig-tree. But, to speak truth, Sir Richard, the proximate cause of my coming here first, instead of going on further, and taking my good friend on my return, was no other than yourself. Thus stands the case. Your good landlady at Norfolk was assailed by sundry rumours--coming, Heaven knows how--that you wanted, and were in dire necessity for, two large black portmanteaus, which you left under her care; and hearing I was going west, as she termed it, she presented a humble petition and remonstrance to me to bring them on my buggy; to which, of course, I condescended, knowing that wherever you had strayed, or in whatever direction you had gone, I should be sure to hear everything about you at each house on the road. Thus I learned that you had first gone to Mr. Thornton's; then, that you and a young lady," and he took off his hat and bowed to Miss Davenport, "had attempted, unsuccessfully, to drown yourselves in the river, and that then you had come on to Mr. Stringer's."

"You did not get the story about the drowning quite right, sir," said Bessy Davenport. "It was I who tried to drown myself, and my cousin wouldn't let me."

"It came all to the same thing in the end, madam, I presume," replied Mr. Wheatley, laughing. "He had been nearly drowned in saving you, I was told; and as his was a voluntary act, as well as yours, the foundation of the story was pretty correct."

"Mine was anything but a voluntary act," said Bessy Davenport; "for I know when I found my pony rolling into the water with me, I would have consented to have my head shaved and be sent to the penitentiary, to be off his back and on the dry land."

"Or to be married and settled in the country," said Mr. Wheatley, "which is worse. However, 'all's well that ends well,' as the old comedy says; and here you are, madam, alive and comfortable; and Sir Richard--I should not have mentioned his style of dignity, God bless the mark! unless I had found he had discovered himself, or been discovered before I came--Sir Richard in fully as good a state of preservation as when I had the pleasure of knowing him in Norfolk. You are aware, I dare say, Sir Richard, that in consequence of our admirable republican institutions, which cause us to ignore all that we knew before of the horrible aristocratic institutions of Europe, a baronet or a lord in the United States is exactly like a Japan cabinet, a Chinese pagoda, or any other outlandish curiosity. No one knows how it ought to stand, how it ought to be placed, what are its ends, objects, or purposes. Some people, indeed, look upon this aristocracy as a sort of idolatry; regard you as the god, Fi-fo-fum, of some distant and pagan nation. The old man of the inn, who has got a fat stomach, and has lost two sons, asked me if I had seen the baronet, just as if you were a piece of porcelain or some other curiosity which people go to see. But the idol is the best image, after all; for the poor people, not being travellers, imagine decidedly that you worship nobility in your country. 'Tis a peculiar prejudice, somewhat characteristic of our people. They can conceive no respect for anything not religious, and very little for anything that is. We in the north begin with want of reverence for our parents, and end with want of reverence for our God. Here, in the south, they have a few traditions; and where there is tradition there is some reverence. But amongst us New-Englanders, the bump of reverence is altogether wanting. Where it should be, there is nothing but an hiatus; and yet there is plenty of fanaticism amongst us. By the way, Stringer, they tell me there is going to be a camp-meeting to-night, in your neighbourhood. Are you going?"

"No," answered Mr. Stringer; "I do not like camp-meetings. I think they offer very serious and unprofitable interruptions to the ordinary affairs of life."

"That's manly, and a manlike view," observed Mr. Wheatley; "the ladies, doubtless, differ. Do you go, madam?"

"No," answered Bessy Davenport; "I went once, and I will never go again. I did not know before to what a pitch human nature could be debased."

"Well, I shall go," answered Mr. Wheatley; "I always do. I like to see that same human nature in all its phases. I look upon it as one of the most curiously-constructed and multilateral pieces of machinery that ever was invented, and every side different from the other. Besides, sometimes one gets a good deal of good out of a camp-meeting. I have once or twice heard as good a sermon there as I ever heard in my life--sermons that have quite touched me about the liver and diaphragm. Oh! I shall go, certainly! won't you go, Sir Richard?" I told him that such was my intention; and it was concluded that we should go together that night, after dinner, he assuring me that I should, at all events, both see and hear things worthy of my attention, which I might never have the opportunity of seeing again. We were to have a whole host of eloquent preachers; one half the population, black and white, was to be assembled, and a large collection had been made already for lamps and torches, to give additional light to the solemn scene. I could perceive, several times during the day, that both Mrs. Stringer and Bessy Davenport were half inclined to be of the party; but they could not make up their minds: and certainly I was very glad that they refrained, after I had seen all that was going on in the outskirts of the ground. About half-past six o'clock, Mr. Wheatley and I set out, under the guidance of my good friend Zedekiah, who was vastly impatient at our long delay.

"All the exercises will be over," he said, "and you will come in in de middle of de unction, without having de pot boiling."

"Never mind, Zed, never mind," said Mr. Wheatley, as we walked on; "we have got fire enough in ourselves to boil half a dozen pots." Our way lay through the woods, with a cultivated field here and there intervening; and, at length, we began to see lights twinkling through the trees, giving notice that we were approaching the place of meeting. It was a tall grove, which had either been long cleared of underwood, or had grown up naturally without such encumbrance. First, we fell upon a number of tents and huts, belonging to those whom I suppose are technically called outsiders; and I cannot say that the scenes displayed by the various lanterns which were scattered about impressed me with any strong idea of either the sobriety or the morality of that excellent class, whatever might be their views of religion. Farther on, we came upon a scene not without its interest, at least in a picturesque scene. Under the tall trees was stretched out a sort of platform of rough-sawn deal boards, along the front of which, a great number of lights were arranged, and upon which stood, in a row, some eight or nine preachers. With an interval between this platform and the congregation, were numbers of benches and chairs, on which were ranged, without any other light than that afforded by the lanterns in front, some three or four hundred women; while through the trees around I could distinguish a great number of other groups, with here and there a lantern or a lamp. I need not dwell upon all that ensued; both because most people must have seen descriptions of these meetings, and because, in our sober and unexcitable country, the mixture of profanity, enthusiasm, and passion--ay, passion, that must be the word--that was displayed could only produce feelings of mingled disgust and abhorrence. I have no doubt that some people were there, full of feelings of deep and sincere religion; but the calm conclusion of my mind is, that such meetings tend to anything but the increase of piety. I believe it would be better to visit the temple of Juggernaut, than to visit one of these camp-meetings. One or two little incidents, however, I must mention not as characteristic of the scene, but as bearing upon some of the persons whom I have already mentioned in connection with my own story. On running my eye along over the preachers, one of the first whom I beheld was my ungainly acquaintance Mr. McGrubber; and, to say truth, I did not expect to be very much edified by the discourse of the worthy divine. It is true, his long black gown covered up a number of the anomalies in his strange, gaunt figure, though his curiously-shaped head and very repulsive features still stood forth in their native ugliness. A step before him, actually addressing the congregation, was a stout, tall man, of a very benevolent countenance, to whom I had been before introduced as a Doctor Shepherd. His voice was fine and powerful; and, as it was raised to its very highest pitch, I caught the greater part of what he said, though I continued standing behind all the benches. The oratorical part of his sermon was, indeed, not very extensive, for there was a sort of chorus--if I may so call what was spoken by himself--which, like those of the Greek tragedies, occupied the greater part of the drama. This consisted of such sentences as, "Come to Jesus, my beloved brethren--come to the foot of the cross-- resist not the Holy Spirit. I hear the sighs and groans breaking from your hearts.--Come and drink of the living waters--come and taste of your sweet Saviour's love!" I heard, and I write these sentences, with pain; for there was a strange want of harmony between them and the scenes I had beheld going on around, which made me feel them to be almost blasphemous in the circumstances in which they were spoken. The rest of his oration, or sermon, consisted of a somewhat disjointed disquisition upon the rights of the black and white races, and the equality of all men, of whatever colour, in the sight of God, which I should have thought would be considered incendiary by the more violent upholders of slavery, many of whom were, assuredly, present. Nobody, however, expressed any disapprobation; but, on the contrary, several very pretty young women rushed forward to the foot of the platform, cast themselves on their knees before the preacher, and gave way to the emotions which he had excited in sighs and groans, and cries of "Oh Jesus! sweet Jesus!" The worthy preacher seemed to me to fondle them with even an excess of brotherly love; but, at length, he gave way to another minister, who was no other than my friend Mr. McGrubber.

"Let us go," said I to Mr. Wheatley. "I have had enough of this sort of thing."

"No, no; let us stay and hear this fellow," he answered. "This is one of their great guns, rammed up to the muzzle with grape and canister--to my mind, one of the most dangerous fellows in the Union." There was no roar of artillery, when Mr. McGrubber began. He commenced in a tone hardly raised above a whisper; and it is wonderful how dead was the silence which followed. Every one strained to hear his lightest word; and I must say that all my previous expectations were disappointed. The dull pedagogue of the house, and the boor of the dinner-table, was eloquent, really eloquent, on the platform; and I never heard a more shrewd and well-arranged argument against slavery than he contrived to interweave with his exhortations to faith, repentance, and reformation. It was all done apparently quite naturally; and the very quietness of his low but piercing tones seemed to enchain all attention. I can remember several fragments of his discourse.

"I call upon you, my brethren--I call upon you, the black as well as the white, the Jew likewise and the Gentile, to come to the foot of the cross and receive salvation. Why standest thou back, thou man of the dark skin? Why shrinkest thou from the presence of thy Redeemer? Is it because of the bonds upon thy hands? Is it because of the degradation which man, thy fellowman, has inflicted upon thee? Knowest thou not that he is the Saviour, the Liberator, the God to whom judgment belongs--who will avenge-- who will wipe the tears from the eyes of the oppressed, and pile coals of burning fire upon the head of the oppressor? Come to Jesus, thy Lord and thy Saviour. Thinkest thou that He regards the colour of thy skin? Has He not said,--

"'Though thy sins be as scarlet, I will make them as white as snow?'

"And shall he who can so wash the spirit, have regard to the hue of the flesh?" Again, after awhile, he said, "But perhaps they have persuaded thee, as they have tried to persuade me, that thou art no man--that thou hast no soul to be saved--that thou art as the beasts that perish. But yet we find by their own law, that in the third, or the fourth, or the fifth degree of white blood, thou becomest as the white man. Will they tell me at what particular hue or shade of colour the soul--the responsible, the immortal soul--enters into the breast that was before void and tenantless? Nay, nay! Feel, understand, that thou too, whatever be thy colour, art an heir of eternal life, a child of God, an object of the Saviour's love; that they may shackle thy hands and bruise thy feet in the stocks, and the iron may enter into thy soul; still, the God of Israel is thy God, of whom it is written, '*Vengeance is mine. I will repay, saith the Lord.*'" He subsequently took even a bolder strain; and, thrusting all religious topics aside, talked openly of slavery in its moral and political aspect. He did not at all conceal his opinions, nor temper his terms; but denounced the peculiar institution of the South, as alike degrading to master and man, as evil in itself and all its consequences. One of the most powerful parts of his discourse, as it struck me, was that in which he justified not only slaves themselves in attempting to escape from bondage, but all those who aided them in their efforts for that purpose. Breaking off in the midst of an argument, he suddenly began a sort of tale or apologue; he told how a white man, an American, a freeman, had been wrecked on the coast of Morocco; how he had been seized and exposed in the slave market; sold to the highest bidder; carried up into the country; sold again and again; till, at length, he found himself working in a garden in the neighbourhood of Tangiers. Then he painted in glowing terms the misery of the poor man's situation; how he had thirsted and panted and pined for liberty; how he had cast his eyes over the blue sea, and longed for his native land, and his friends, and his family; how the very luxuries of the climate and the kindness of his master were disgusting and abhorrent to him in his state of slavery. He then told us that a friendly Moor, in whom he had created an interest, determined to assist him in escaping. The two Europeans who were in the port had entered into the scheme, and that a thousand difficulties and dangers, on which I need not dwell, were encountered and overcome, till, at length, the fugitive was placed safely on board an American ship. "Were these men wrong?" he exclaimed. "Were these men criminal? Had he not a right to seek his liberty however he could find it? Did not the whole of these States ring with applause and admiration of those who enabled him to recover freedom, the best boon of life? Oh, perverted moral sense, which can in one instance laud to the skies the same conduct which in another, precisely similar, it dooms to the prison or the gallows?" While all this was going on, I felt some sort of apprehension as to the result, and I looked round from time to time to see what would be the impression upon the audience. The greater part of the listeners were white men, many of them slave owners, generally men of strong passions, but little subjected to control; and it would not at all have surprised me to see the preacher dragged from the platform and horsewhipped before the congregation. But I was mistaken; not a sound even of disapprobation met my ear. Some sighed, and some shook the head, but nobody attempted to interrupt the preacher. As soon as Mr. McGrubber had done, I turned away with Mr. Wheatley, and we bent our steps towards Beavors, keeping silence till we had got beyond the limits of the meeting.

"Well," said my companion at length, "what do you think of it all, Sir Richard? Moral, religious, and social, isn't it? Ha, ha, ha! We Americans are strange people, and take the oddest of all possible ways to arrive at our ends. We gather together a whole heap of men, women, and children, at night, in the midst of a forest--make two-thirds of them as drunk as possible--stimulate the passions of the others by every kind of exciting and enthusiastic discourse, and hug and fondle the young women, all for the purpose of promoting religion and morality."

"That part of the subject, I have long made up my mind upon," I replied, "from the description of others, and from what I have seen in fanatical meetings, where excitement was not carried to anything like the same pitch. But that which astonished me the most, was to hear so many men, in the very heart of a slave-holding state, preach doctrines perfectly adverse to its most cherished institutions, and to see such doctrines listened to, not only with patience, but with assent. I expected every moment to behold worthy Mr. McGrubber heartily pommelled for his pains."

"Oh, you are quite mistaken as to our state of feeling," said Mr. Wheatley, with one of his short laughs. "Virginia is well-nigh an abolition state. There is hardly a man here who would not emancipate all his slaves, if he could do so without utter ruin to himself and great danger to the State. Perhaps you are not aware that in the last session of our legislature, a bill for general emancipation was introduced, and lost, I think, only by one vote. Next session 'twill be carried, to a certainty, if my Northern friends will let it."

"I should think," I replied, "if the negroes hear many more such sermons as that of the Rev. Mr. McGrubber, they will take the matter into their own hands, and free themselves, with a vengeance."

"There is the danger," answered Mr. Wheatley, more gravely than was customary with him. "Not that an insurrection of the slaves could ever be successful in this country. You will never see a St. Domingo tragedy enacted here with any success. The whites are too strong and too much upon their guard. But what I apprehend is, that my fanatical friends of the North, not content with letting public opinion, which all tends towards emancipation, work its way quietly, will go a step too far, and either instigate the negroes to some sudden outbreak, which will be put down with some bloodshed, or else create a re-action in public sentiment, by their irritating diatribes. Men may be led who will not be driven; and, let me tell you, you can't drive a Virginian. You have seen to-night how much these people will bear quietly, when it takes the form of argument; but there can be no doubt, that such men as this McGrubber are even now circulating incendiary pamphlets amongst the slaves, which are read to little knots of them by any one who can read. In other instances, the same principles are spread by pictures and horrid bad prints--a sort of hieroglyphic abolitionism; and if this is carried too far, the tendency to emancipation will be extinguished at once, and every man will arm himself to resist to the death."

"It is a pity," I remarked, "that in all questions where there are two parties, each carries his argument beyond its legitimate limit. Passion enters in and exaggerates all things. Passion on the one side begets passion on the other; till, upon points where men were very nearly agreed, they break each other's heads, because they cannot fix the exact boundary of debate. How ridiculous that, when you admit Virginia has been within one vote of carrying emancipation, she should, as you say, be ready to retrace every step in that direction, simply because the North urges her a little too vehemently to follow it."

"Stop a minute," he answered; "that is not exactly a fair statement of the question. Each State has its reserved rights. It gives up to the federal government the decision of certain questions affecting the interests of the whole Union. Its domestic laws and institutions it reserves entirely for its own decision. The North--I am a Northern man you must remember--seeks to violate this compact, upon which the whole Union depends, and wages war--for it is a moral warfare--against the South, upon the institution of slavery. That institution is, in fact, the battleground. The South occupies it, and says,--'It is mine. You shall not drive me from it. It is true, I care very little for this debatable ground, and may hereafter, in my own good time, give it up as a thing not worth contending about; but I will not give it up to force; and on this ground I will fight you; for if you carry this aggression by my imbecility or indolence, no one can tell where you will attack me next. In regard to your abstract doctrines, you may be right or you may be wrong; but with regard to your interference with my domestic affairs, you are decidedly wrong; and that I will not tolerate.' In short, my good friend, whatever the North has done, and whatever the North may do, in this sense, only tends to rivet the chains on the hands of the negro more firmly than before. It may seem very absurd, but such is human nature; and although I admit that in many of the arguments used by the abolitionists, and even by this man, McGrubber, to-night, there is a great deal of force, yet their strength is changed to weakness when men become convinced, as every Southern man is, that they are used for political, factious, and partisan purposes. You cannot have a domestic police in such a union as this; and every man will whip his own children in his own house, when he thinks they deserve it."

"Although I judged it rash and most dangerous," I answered, "to preach such doctrines as we have heard to-night to a large crowd of negroes, yet I could not help thinking that many of Mr. Mc Grubber's arguments were exceedingly specious, if not cogent: that little apologue of his, for instance, of the white slave in Barbary and his liberation. It struck me as a very happy illustration of his views."'

"A cunning piece of rhetoric," answered my acute friend, "peculiarly illustrative of the rhetoric of fanatics. Do you not remark that whenever they have a point to carry, they employ a figure, and in that figure they pre-suppose a complete parity between two really dissimilar cases. Knock away the *petition principia*, and what do you find? Here he places a white man, always accustomed to freedom, and with all the intellectual qualities impliedly cultivated by a white man's education, with a white man's wants, wishes, habits, and feelings, exactly upon a par with a negro born upon a plantation, habituated from infancy to slavery, without a thought, a desire, or a notion beyond the state in which he was brought up, except such as may have been instilled into him by abolitionists. Is this fair to begin with? Is there a parity between the two cases? Then again, the white man in flying from the bonds which had been accidentally imposed upon him, returns to home, to his ancient habits, to the free use of faculties and endowments which are sure, if rightly employed, to lead to competence, if not to wealth, to independence, and to ease. The negro flying from his master, on the contrary, leaves family and friends, old habits and associations, food, care, and protection in sickness or old age, for a wide, unfriended, uncertain, future, where there is nothing probable but long-protracted labour, unbefriended sickness, unpitied decrepitude, and death on a dunghill. His nominal independence is shackled by the continual necessity of seeking food by labour; and his freedom becomes a curse instead of a blessing, in consequence of the prejudices of colour and caste. Is there any parity between these two cases? I declare I would a great deal rather be a slave to the hardest master I have ever seen in Virginia--and I have now been here many years--than I would be a free negro in an abolition state. But this was all rhetoric, mere rhetoric, the most cowardly and contemptible of all species of sophistry. Much better to say boldly, 'You have no right to reduce any man to slavery--you shall not do evil that good may come of it--the Declaration of Independence says, that all men are created equal; they are endowed by their Creator with certain inalienable rights; among these are life, liberty, and the pursuit of happiness. By holding any man in slavery, whatever be his colour, you violate this first great principle of the American constitution, you break the solemn pact upon which this union was founded, by which alone she claimed, maintained, and accomplished her independence of Great Britain.' Better to say this, and fight it out upon this ground, than go sneakingly to work to get petty advantages in Congress, or criminally strive to render the slaves discontented with their masters. I have come to the conclusion, my dear Sir Richard, that the abolitionists are the very worst enemies of the slaves themselves, who, after all, are but mere----" Here his ovation, which was much more grave and earnest than anything I had ever heard fall from his lips before, was brought to a close by a loud outcry, proceeding from a spot immediately in front of us. Cries for help, loud exclamations, and blows, seemed to be going on.

"Don't you do dat, Jack. Oh, you mean to murder me. Help! help! murder! I tell you notin' but de truth. Jim, I did not tink dat of you. Help! help! murder! What you knock my head so for?" I thought I recognized the voice of my good friend, Zed; and ran forward as fast as possible; but before, in the turnings of the wood, I could reach the scene, I heard another voice, which also seemed familiar, exclaiming in a loud, imperative tone--

"Let him alone! Fools, would you make an outbreak before the time? If you strike him again, I will dash your brains out. The man only says what he thinks true." As the last words were uttered, I came out upon that little track of open ground which I have before spoken of as close to the Hunter Wood. A small edge of the moon was peeping up above the trees; and some half dozen yards before me was a negro on the ground--no other than my friend Zed--with a second just raising a thick stick over his head. Close by was a tall, powerful man, whom I afterwards found to be Nat Turner, in the act of throwing furiously back, from the scene of conflict, a fourth gentleman of the same hue, who had apparently been bent upon the demolition of poor Zed. I sprang forward at once upon the man who was belabouring my good servant, took the descending blow upon my left arm--which I do believe it very nearly broke--and knocked him down at once. Zed sprang upon his feet and seized the fellow by the throat as he lay, while Mr. Wheatley stood by, laughing and exclaiming--

"Bravo, Sir Richard! a very pretty exhibition of the manly art, as you call it in England. You will know the hardness of a negro's head for the future; for you will find your knuckles all out, if I am not greatly mistaken."

"Let the man get up, Zed," I said, not very well pleased will my companion's untimely merriment, for I was smarting from the blow on the arm; and, to say the truth, my knuckles were cut as if I had struck a stone wall; "let the man get up, and if he wants to be knocked down again, he shall have it." No sooner was his throat free, however, than Zed's assailant sprang upon his feet, and took to his heels as fast as he could go. The other two followed at the same speedy pace, although Zed cried aloud,--

"You need not run, Mr. Turner; you are a good man, and come to help me first." However, none of them stayed; for it is rather a dangerous thing in these states for a negro to be any way mixed up with an affray in which a white man is struck. As we walked homeward towards Beavors, the cause of the conflict was explained to me and my white companion. It seems that Zed, just at the close of Mr. McGrubber's harangue, had taken his way back towards the house, accompanied by two men whom he called Jack and Jim. As they went, they commented, amusingly enough, I doubt not, upon all they had heard, passing Nat Turner, who followed them a step or two behind, but who seemed, Zed said, in a gloomy mood, and would neither speak to them nor join their party. Zed, it would appear, took up ground in direct opposition to his two swarthy companions. He had had some experience, when his leg was broken, of the condition of a sick and free negro, and he declared that freedom was the most miserable state in the world, and that Mr. McGrubber and all the Abolitionists were great fools or great rascals for wishing to force it upon the slaves. The dispute got hot and angry; they mutually began to call each other bad names; the slaves in general feel no good-will and a certain degree of contempt towards free negroes. From words they came to blows, and Zed was in the high-road to have his brains knocked out, when Nat Turner came up to occupy one of his assailants, while I delivered him from the other. There was no great significance in Master Zed's story, excepting so far as it showed that amongst some of the slaves, at least, there was a fierce and eager desire for freedom; but a few words had been spoken by Nat Turner just as I was approaching, which made me ponder and doubt. He had said--

"Fools! would you make an outbreak before the time?" I could come but to one conclusion, namely, that an outbreak of some kind was contemplated, and that a time was fixed for it. I knew not how soon it was to take place. I determined, however, to watch what was going on around, and, without putting my poor acquaintance, Nat Turner, in peril, to give Mr. Thornton a hint that I had reason to believe the existing calm was treacherous, and likely to be followed by a storm. In the meantime, Mr. Wheatley walked on by my side, laughing and talking in his light but pungent way; commenting, notwithstanding Zed's presence, upon the peculiarities of the negro race, and declaring that they were nothing but great babies, always ready to scratch, and fight, and whine upon the very slightest occasion. We found the whole party, with the exception of Mr. McGrubber, assembled in the drawing-room at Beavors. Bessy's lustrous eyes turned upon me eagerly, as she inquired,--

"Well, what do you think of it, Cousin Richard?"

"I think it a very disgusting exhibition," I replied; "and, though it may seem a very ungallant speech, all the time I was there, I was thanking Heaven that you were not there too."

"Just as well, just as well," said Mr. Stringer. "And now let us have a little claret sangaree, and go to bed, for it is waxing late."

CHAPTER XIII

These have been many days in my life which have been most tedious. The imaginative man can perhaps fill them up with his own fancies; but what little imagination I have--and it is certainly very small--must be excited by some external objects. Mine is a sort of lazy fancy, which wants stirring up to activity. I can sit by the side of a dashing brook, and see it sparkling and foaming onward, and regard it as a little epitome of life, with its rapids and its shallows; its sunshine and its shade; its quiet lapses and its turbulent activity. I can see in its different aspects the hopes and fears, the joys and sorrows of existence. I can even watch the root-frequenting trout coming soberly forth into mid-stream, like some money-getting recluse, issuing forth into the current of speculation, to be angled for by man or the devil; and I can endow the old gentleman with all the thoughts and feelings of humanity, wondering what he is calculating now, and asking myself in what stock he is about to embark his capital. But there are some days when there is nothing suggestive in external circumstances; and dull and wearily do the leaden wings of time flap on. Oh, the heavy hours I have passed in an Indian bungalow, hearing the rain drop, drop, drop for ever, without a book to solace the passing hour, without a sight or sound to waken the soul from a lethargy which is not sleep; and I have envied the impassibility of the good Hindoos, who, squatted in the neighbouring sheds, were pleasantly occupied in profound meditations concerning nothing. But of all the weary days I ever spent, the worst was that which succeeded the evening of the camp-meeting; and many circumstances tended to render it so. A sort of dead monotony seemed to have fallen over the whole family of Mr. Stringer. The boys, whose wicked activity and genial love of mischief might have afforded some amusement, were closely cooped up during the whole morning by Mr. McGrubber. Mr. Stringer himself was busy, supplying all deficiencies which a somewhat prolonged absence had left in the ordering and arrangement of his farm. Mrs. Stringer sat all day long embroidering, like a lady of the olden time. Bessy Davenport sat, solemn and demure as a nun, by her side, drawing patterns of collars and cuffs, as if she had been working for her daily bread in a Manchester manufactory. Yet, ever and anon, she looked up at my face with eyes which seemed to say, "Do you recollect, Cousin Richard, that you are going to fight a duel, and may very likely be killed, and leave me whom you love--you know you do--to mourn you all alone?" I asked her to go out and take a walk, but she declined, saying it was too warm. And then again Mr. Wheatley had ridden over to Jerusalem upon some business, promising to be back again that evening or the next day. There were not many books in Mr. Stringer's house, and I had brought none with me except one, wishing to make the world my book rather than my oyster. As a last resource, I went out and took a stroll by myself, and heartily wished the time was come for loading and firing; but there was nothing to amuse me--nothing to occupy my thoughts--and the day was sultry, but not scorching; a thin, white haze covered the face of heaven; the flowers most susceptible of atmospheric influence had half closed their petals, and everything seemed as weary about the world as I was. Air, I could find none; so, as a last resource, I sat myself down under a tree and began to meditate. I won't trouble you with what I thought about. I composed there a whole essay upon duelling, condemned it logically in principle and practice, thought every man who gave way to it a great fool, myself at the head of them, and rose up just as much determined to fight Mr. Robert Thornton as ever. The evening of that day passed a little more pleasantly. Mr. Wheatley returned, and enlivened us a good deal with his gay talk. Bessy sang us some very beautiful songs, and there seemed to me a deeper sentiment, a more tender expression in her tones, than I had ever heard before. Yet she did not talk very much to me. She seemed amused, nay, pleased, with Mr. Wheatley, and had I not known him to be a married man, I might have felt a little jealous. She got into corners with him, and talked in a low voice, and though she sometimes laughed and often smiled, there was a sort of earnestness about her manner which annoyed me a little. The morning of the next day passed very nearly in the same manner, only Mr. Wheatley was there all the time, and he, at least, kept up his share of the conversation. About Bessy Davenport, I remarked a good deal of what I may call flutter. She was now sad, silent, gloomy, abstracted; then gay-- almost wildly gay--but still with a saddened gaiety. I remarked that her eyes often turned to my face, and I thought I understood her better than the day before. At length, about half-past one o'clock, I rose, saying,--

"I must go, I think. I will change my dress. I have engaged to dine with Mr. Byles, Mrs. Stringer, and, in the hospitable Old Dominion, I suppose I must pass the night there; but I shall set out in the cool to-morrow morning, and meet you all at breakfast." I thought I heard a gasp from the other side of the table, and, turning round, I saw Bessy as pale as the spring moon.

"Good-bye, for the present, my sweet cousin," said I, holding out my hand. She gave me hers, as cold as that of a corpse, saying in a voice very low, but perfectly distinct,--

"Farewell, Richard--farewell!" Just at that moment, Mr. Wheatley exclaimed, "Going to dine with Mr. Byles! What, my old friend Billy Byles? Hang me, if I don't go with you. No one needs an invitation in Virginia, and you will give me a seat in your buggy, I dare say." This was rather unpleasant; but it could not be helped, and I only made one attempt to escape the unsought-for companionship: "I have no buggy with me," I said, laughing. "I go on horseback; but I'll take you up behind me if you like."

"Oh, no," answered he, "I have a double-seated drotsky here, and as pretty a pair of little tits as ever were driven. I will drive you over, and we will take your broken-headed man Zed behind, to look after the traps. Come, let us go and make ready." And he quitted the room. I followed, venturing but one more look at Bessy, and in about half an hour we were rolling rapidly along towards the house of Mr. Byles. After we had entered upon the high road, Mr. Wheatley turned towards me with a smile, saying, "Do you know why I come with you?"

"No, indeed," I answered, "unless it be to dine with your old friend Mr. Byles."

"No, indeed," returned Mr. Wheatley, with one of his short laughs; "I never saw bold Billy but twice in my life. I came to take care of you."

"You are really very considerate, Mr. Wheatley," I said drily.

"Very gallant, you mean," rejoined my companion. "You must know there is a young lady, with the most beautiful hair, and eyes, and teeth, and lips in the world, and the prettiest foot and ankle, and the most charming little hand, who has got it into her dear little head, that Sir Richard Conway is going to fight some giant or some windmill, and was diplomatizing with me all last night to see if I could not, or would not, tell her all about it, imagining that I had come up to be your second. Now as I was convinced she was in the right--ladies always are right in everything--and knowing that Billy Byles is not the safest man in the world to trust in such matters, I determined to go over with you to act as a sort of moderator."

"I am much obliged to you," I answered, a little mortified, "and much obliged to my sweet Cousin Bessy for the interest she takes in me. But I must say, my good friend, this is altogether a little irregular, according to our notions on the other side of the Atlantic; ladies there do not meddle with such matters, nor friends either, except when they are invited."

"Pray, my dear Sir Richard," interrogated Mr. Wheatley, "do not you, who are clearly a man of the world, fall into the great error of your countrymen, and fancy you can carry England about with you wherever you go? When you are in your own room, with nothing but your trunk, you can be as English as you please; but the moment you are brought in contact with Virginians, you must be Virginian to a certain extent. We manage these little affairs of honour quite differently here and in Great Britain. There, you are obliged to sneak about as if you were going to steal something, breathe no syllable of the matter to anybody, except the choice friend, and seek out some lonely spot on a common, where you can see for ten miles round, for fear you should be interrupted by the police. Now here, the constable of the township would load your pistols for you, and keep the ground clear. The first thing a man does when he is called out is to say to his wife, 'Mary, my dear, I am going to fight Jack Robertson to-morrow. I wish you would look that the lock of my rifle goes easy.' 'I'll look to that,' answers Mary; 'and I'll cut you up some patches. What time would you like the carriage, love? Don't ride on horseback; you know it always shakes your hand.'" I could not help laughing at this description, delivered with capital mimicry of the male and female voices in the colloquy; but I replied, "It would seem all ladies do not take it so quietly, from what you tell me of Miss Davenport."

"Oh, that's quite a different case," said Mr. Wheatley, with a merry glance of the eye. "She is not your wife yet, you know. She has no chance of being an interesting widow, whose husband was killed in a duel. But, joking apart, for I see you wince, Miss Davenport has cause to dislike duels. Her father was killed in a duel by a dear friend and near connection, all in consequence of a confounded mistake; and his death was followed by a long train of law-suits and misfortunes, quite sufficient to give her a horror of the pleasant little practice of being shot at without pay. By the way, I don't think she knows one-half of her own history, poor girl!" he added, in a meditative tone; "if she did, it might make some difference." His words, from the manner in which they were spoken, seemed to me to have more significance than appeared upon the surface; but I had other things to think of, and the next moment he rambled on in his usual way, saying,--

"Now don't be surprised, and don't show any irritation, if you find a dozen or two people on the ground, black and white. It is just as likely as not; and mind, if they chance to get in the line of fire, shoot a white man, and not a black. A white man's life here is worth nothing; a black man is worth from nine hundred to a thousand dollars. We are a commercial people, and always take a business-like view of these transactions. Pray when is this pigeon-shooting to come off?" He proceeded to ask a great number of questions, but I cut him short, saying, "You must excuse me, my good friend, for keeping up some of my Old English prejudices here, while you and I are alone together. From me you shall hear none of the particulars, though I dare say Mr. Byles will tell you all about it. With us, it is a matter of etiquette for a principal in such an affair to talk about it to no one but his second."

"Oh, very well," he answered; "perhaps you are right. In my part of the country, I mean the part where I was born, they carry matters further than even you do in England, for they won't let us fight at all, and send a man to the penitentiary for asking his friend to take a morning's walk with him. In fact, the three great distinctions between the North and South are these. In the South, they fight duels whenever they can; have slaves for their servants; and grow tobacco and cotton. In New England, they never fight if they can help it; are slaves to their own servants, and make wooden clocks and wooden nutmegs." Probably one could not have had a more serviceable or amusing companion, when going about a disagreeable piece of business, than Mr. Wheatley. There was a lightness, or, to use a vulgar expression, a devil-may-carishness about his conversation which imperceptibly led one away from serious views, even of a serious business; and when I got out of his carriage, at the door of Mr. Byles's house, I could have fired a pistol at an antagonist without half the hesitation and remorse which I should have felt an hour before. The house of Mr. Byles was very different from any gentleman's dwelling I had yet seen in Virginia, and was indeed an ornamented sort of cottage--the reality of that whereof we see many imitations in Great Britain. It was all upon one floor--unless indeed there were rooms for the servants upstairs, which I do not know--and parlours, dining-room, bedrooms, &c, stretched out in a confused sort of labyrinth, which I did not attempt to penetrate any further than I was led by others. An enormous swarm of little black boys, with one respectable elderly gentleman of the same colour, were all ready to receive us: and, by the way in which they climbed into Mr. Wheatley's carriage, seized upon all the loose articles it contained, and carried them off, Heaven knows whither, they put me in mind of the little hairy savages, which boarded the ship of Sinbad the sailor, during one of his marvellous voyages. None of them seemed to know anything about their master, however. It was a thing recognized and understood, that whoever came to the house was to make himself comfortable--that the house would contain any possible number, and that all that was in it was at the disposal of the guests. Mr. Wheatley had set about providing for himself as soon as we arrived; Zed had rushed away with my valise, where, and about what, I knew not; and I stood solitary for a moment or two, in the midst of a spacious, low-ceiled drawing-room, filled with as many nicknacks as would have bedizened the boudoir of a London lady. At length, a very neat little boy, of fourteen years of age, with his snowy white jacket and trousers and apron, contrasting magnificently with the jetty hue of his hands and face, came in and asked, with a grace quite oriental, whether I was the Honourable Sir Richard Conway.

"Honourable, I trust I am," I replied, "and my name is Richard Conway."

"Ah, then, here is your room, sir," answered the boy. And he led me into a very handsome bedroom, immediately out of the drawing-room, where I found every possible convenience that either London or Paris could supply. It seemed to have been the pleasure of Mr. Byles to accumulate under the roof of a very unpretending dwelling, the form and structure of which I suspect it would be impossible to describe, all the luxuries of a dozen different climates, and to enjoy them, and make his friends enjoy them, without those conventional restraints with which they are usually associated. Zed was already there, having arrived at my quarters by some undiscovered passages, and was busy in arranging all the toilette apparatus of Palmer and Savory, upon principles conceived by himself, partly indoctrinated by me. I threw myself into a chair, and, for a moment or two, gave myself up to meditation, thinking--"This afternoon all these appliances for luxury and comfort--to-morrow, perhaps, stretched upon that bed with a pistol-shot through my heart!" I am not much given to such considerations; but there are moments when they will force themselves upon me, and I end by exclaiming, "What a farce is life!" Starting up with this conviction upon me, as I knew it must be near the dinner-hour, I proceeded to change my dress, and get rid of the soil and dust which the roads, now thoroughly dry, had left upon me. Not twenty minutes after, my little black friend made his appearance again, with a tumbler full of a bright yellow liquid, upon a silver salver, saying,--

"Dinner will be ready in five minutes, sir."

"What is this, my friend!" I asked, taking up the tumbler.

"Apple-Jack, sir," replied the boy.

"And am I to drink this before dinner?"

"If you please, sir," he answered, in a decidedly affirmative tone. So I drank it, and found it by no means unpleasant. I suppose in these regions, where vast tracks of swamp and forest-ground still remain unreclaimed, spreading around a sort of miasma, such kind of stimulating drinks, which would kill us in the old world, are not without their use; and certainly they do not seem to produce the same stimulating effects that they would in Europe.

A minute or two after, Billy Byles himself entered without ceremony, and apologized for having been absent at his stables when I arrived.

"I have asked nobody to meet you," he said, "because I know your English prejudices upon these occasions; and I have given Bob Thornton a hint not to bring more than two or three friends, at the utmost, to the ground, to-morrow. I find Wheatley, of Norfolk, brought you over, and he is as good a man as any to have with us."

"I can assure you he came with no invitation of mine," I replied; "but hearing I was coming over to dine with you, he invited himself, and, of course, I could not refuse his company. As we came, I found that Miss Davenport's suspicions and his own knowledge of such affairs had made him aware that some *rencontre* was going to take place."

"All the better, all the better," answered Billy Byles; "and he is always so cool and self-possessed, that in case of difficulty he is ready to take the right ground in a moment. But now, let us go in to dinner." I followed him into the drawing-room, where we found Mr. Wheatley, and thence into an adjoining dining room. There, as nice and well-cooked a dinner as could be seen in any part of the world was set before us, seasoned with excellent wines, and my two companions drank pretty deep. But after all the meats had been removed, and fruits, &c., set upon the table, Mr. Byles interposed, saying,--

"Before we take anymore wine, we had better look at our tools and be certain that everything is right and in good working order. Then we will have a bowl of punch and a cigar, a game of piquette, if you like, and then to bed, for we are to be at the Hunter-wood to-morrow by five, and that is three miles off--Apollo, my good fellow"--to the black man, who was still in attendance--"fetch me the mahogany case which is on the table in my room, and bring an oil-cruet and a feather." The man soon returned with the pistol-case and the other things, and we set to work to examine the instruments of destruction. One screw wanted a little easing. A small portion of rust had gathered about the bore of one of the pistols, and had to be removed. The balls, of which there were a dozen ready cast, were all smooth and well pared, and fitted closely and accurately. The patches were nicely greased; the powder found not to leave a trace upon white paper; and everything, in short, brought into neat and exact order. My two companions set about the examination as amateurs; and I, who certainly knew, practically, more of the matter than any of them, and whose life might depend upon the result, thought I might just as well inform my mind upon the same subject as sit idly looking on. When all this was settled, a bowl of excellent punch was introduced, with some capital Havanah cigars. We talked of matters in no way connected with the business of the following morning; and the time slipped away without any piquette, till, on looking at my watch, I found it was ten o'clock. Then, telling Mr. Byles to have me called in ample time, I retired to bed. There are moments when thought, having done all its serviceable work, had better be dismissed altogether. It is a happy art-- and every man should strive to acquire it--to be able so to dismiss thought, when its results are arrived at, and it can be no longer serviceable. Resolving to consign the future to the future, I lay down and slept profoundly, till the negro boy appointed to attend upon me entered the room early on the following morning.

CHAPTER XIV

It was hardly daylight when my little black attendant brought a glass of mint-julep to my bed-side, and told me it was time to rise; and I had hardly refused the beverage, which I did not choose to take that morning, of all others, when Zed hobbled in with his white wool, and his face as polished as an ebony cabinet, all glowing with excitement. I understood quite well that he knew all about the business in hand, and he seemed to look upon himself as a sort of squire to a knight arming for the tilt-yard, eager and anxious for his master to do great deeds, and never for a moment doubting his success. The morning was a dull and cheerless one, though it was warm enough. The sky was covered; and a thin, white mist hung over the ground, not sufficient to hide objects, even at two or three hundred yards' distance, but sufficient to render them somewhat hazy and indistinct. In fact, it was a morning quite in harmony with the business I was about. However, I was soon dressed and in the drawing-room, where I found Billy Byles already up and waiting for me.

"I hope you have taken your mint-julep," he said; "it will steady your hand."

"Thank you," I answered; "my hand is quite steady enough, and I don't think brandy would make it any firmer."

"Well, come and take some breakfast, at all events," said my host; "never fight upon an empty stomach."

"I have been obliged to do so before now," I answered; "but I will take some breakfast if we have time; for, to say truth, I am very hungry."

"Oh, plenty of time, plenty of time," answered Mr. Byles. "I always like to be on the ground first, so I took care you should be called early enough. Wheatley will be here in a minute. I woke him myself, and the lazy dog said the great bore of fighting duels was the getting up in the mornings." We had not been five minutes at table when Mr. Wheatley appeared, just as gay and unconcerned as ever; and although I could not help feeling an impression of some heavy thing impending, I joined in the conversation as cheerfully as I could, feeling that it was of no use to think of what was coming, when it could not be avoided. It had been agreed that we should proceed to the ground in Mr. Wheatley's double-seated carriage; and about twenty minutes after we sat down to breakfast, it was announced that the vehicle was at the door. When I went out I found three or four negroes, beside Zed, surrounding the carriage. Mr. Wheatley and I took our seats in front: Billy Byles sprang into the hinder division: Zed scrambled in beside him, with the pistol-case under his arm, and away we went towards the place of encounter. The moment we started I could see two or three of the negro boys take to their heels and run on towards the woods as fast as their legs could carry them; and I could not but think of the speech of the poor old Scotch nobleman when going to be beheaded: "You need not run so fast, boys: there will be no fun till I come." Billy Byles acted as pilot, directing Mr. Wheatley how he was to drive; and I must say a rougher ride I never took in my life; for we went over fields without the slightest pretension to a road; fences we pulled down unceremoniously to let us pass; and I certainly did think more than once that the whole business would end in our getting our necks broken. I was afraid, too, that various evolutions and man[oe]uvres which we had to perform would make us late; and more than once I took out my watch to see how the time went.

"Plenty of time, plenty of time," said Billy Byles. "You see that wood there; well, that's the Hunter-wood, and we just cross the narrow part by the path into the savannah, and there we are." The wood was soon reached, and out we all got, for the carriage could go no further.

"Here, give me the pistols," said Mr. Byles; "you stay here by the horses: we shall be back in half an hour." And leading the way by a very narrow path, he speedily brought us to that long strip of open ground which I have before described, and which I had passed in pleasant talk with Bessy Davenport. We now struck it considerably higher up, however, and at no great distance from the high road to Jerusalem. But it had a much more melancholy aspect now than when I first saw it. The mist which I have mentioned rested more heavily in that narrow avenue; and the trees cut off all the rays of the sun, who was struggling, as he rose, to disperse the gray clouds that covered the sky. All was sombre and cheerless-looking, and Billy Byles laid down the pistol-case under a live oak-tree, and rubbed his hands as if it had been winter. I gazed up and down the long open strip, to see if my antagonist was apparent, and Mr. Byles exclaimed, in a congratulatory tone, "First on the field, you see, Sir Richard! but we have five minutes yet to spare. I won't open the case till they come, for this unpleasant mist may damp the tools."

"Rather bat-fowling work," said Mr. Wheatley. "Lucky you chose pistols, for I don't think one could see at rifle-range." Before the five minutes were over, a gig, with two men on horseback, appeared towards the high-road end of the savannah, halted there, and having tied the horses to the trees, came forward on foot towards the place where we were standing.

Before they came quite close, they paused again; and a somewhat sharp discussion seemed to go on between Mr. Robert Thornton, whom I could now distinguish, and one of his companions, for their gestures were exceedingly animated. They then approached, and Mr. Thornton saluted me by touching his hat, to which I returned a silent bow.

"Well, Sir Richard," he said, "for my own part, I don't see why you should not apologize even now, if you like it."

"I have no apology to make," I replied; "and, moreover, we came here, I think, to act, and not to talk." As I said this, I turned away and took a step or two up and down the meadow, leaving the gentlemen who had accompanied me and Mr. Thornton to make their arrangements as usual. They were all pretty well skilled and experienced in the business, I imagine; for the pistols were loaded and the ground measured out very rapidly. I was not sorry for this, as I had nothing to amuse myself with but watching some half-dozen black faces, peeping out from behind the trees at the end of the wood.

"Now, Sir Richard," said Mr. Byles, stepping up to me with a pistol in his hand, "you will have the goodness to stand here, where I have put down my glove. The words are, 'One, two, three, fire!' but you can fire any time after the word 'Three.'"

"Mind, you keep your arm to your side, and cover your angles," said Mr. Wheatley.

"I will take care," I answered, with a smile; "I am not quite inexperienced in such affairs."

"I suppose not, from the way you take it," he replied. And when they had placed me in a proper position, my two friends withdrew. I could see that my adversary, Mr. Robert Thornton, marched up to his ground with every appearance of boldness. I had been rather inclined, by his preceding conduct, to think that he was somewhat nervous; but no symptom of timidity was now apparent, except indeed a slight touch of swagger in his walk and manner. As he stood before me, I measured him deliberately with my eyes, and thought I had him very sure. He stood on a somewhat angular position, which I was sorry for, as I did not wish to injure him severely, or run the risk of killing him; though I certainly did intend to wound him so as to prevent him doing any more mischief for the present. There seemed to be some little talk between himself, his second, and another friend--about what I know not; and then the two gentlemen left him, and a moment after the words were given by Mr. Wheatley. A slight degree of hesitation, remorse, or what you will, made me reserve my shot till the word "Fire!" had been pronounced. My antagonist fired at the word "Three," but his ball went quite wild. I then raised my hand and fired, being perfectly certain of hitting him, I thought somewhere about the elbow. I fancied, too, that I saw him stagger a little, but he did not fall; and he exclaimed, loudly,--

"Give me another pistol!" Billy Byles and Mr. Wheatley both ran up to me with a fresh weapon, and while the former put it in my hands, the latter whispered,--

"Mind what you are about. He will aim better this time; you have grazed him, and his blood is up. Don't try to spare him, or you'll get killed yourself." It all passed in a moment, and they were gone back to their places before I well knew what had occurred. I continued, however, to eye my antagonist deliberately while the words were spoken, and I could see that he was scanning me in the same manner. This time we both fired together at the word "Three;" and, almost before I heard the report, I felt a smart blow upon the arm, which made me recoil a little with a sensation as if a piece of hot iron had been run into the flesh; but Robert Thornton fell back at once, amidst the long grass, and I lost sight of him. My two friends were up with me in a moment.

"You are wounded! you are wounded!" said Billy Byles, with friendly anxiety. "I saw you stagger; you must be wounded."

"But slightly," I replied; "take the pistol, and just get my handkerchief out of the pocket." I had learned a little of surgery in India, and saw, by the jerking of the stream of blood which was flowing from my arm, that some artery was cut. I therefore made my two friends fold the handkerchief and tie it tightly some way above the wound, by which means the bleeding was soon reduced in quantity, though it continued to ooze a little, though not sufficient to do any harm. I then turned my eyes to the spot where my opponent had stood. Three persons had now gathered round him, one of whom had raised Thornton's head and shoulders on his knee.

"You have done for him!" said Billy Byles; "he seems as dead as a mackerel."

"I hope not," I replied. "I did not intend it; but he stood awkwardly, and it was impossible to be sure of one's shot. I do hope he is not killed."

"Pooh, nonsense!" ejaculated Mr. Wheatley. "What did he come here for, but to kill you, or be killed himself? We had better make the best of our way to my buggy, and get home as soon as possible, for I suspect the ball is still in your arm, and we must send for the surgeon."

"I will see how he is, first," I answered; and walked quietly up to the spot where my antagonist lay. His friends were perfectly gentlemanly and polite; and the two who were standing up bowed civilly as I approached.

"I am afraid he is gone, Sir Richard," said one of them.

"I hope not," I replied, with a sensation I cannot describe. "I can assure you I did not intend it; I only sought to wound him."

"You did that at the first fire," answered the other. "See here--your second shot has gone through his chest." I now perceived that the blood was streaming from one wound in the fleshy part of the back, just below the shoulder-blade, and behind the right arm. This seemed of no great consequence; for it was clear it had not penetrated the chest; but there was another wound much more formidable in appearance, where the ball had entered the side, just in front of the arm, and had issued out at the other side a little further forward. That it had touched the lungs I could not doubt; but though I do not know much of anatomy, I felt sure that the heart must have escaped, notwithstanding the death-like paleness of his face, and the state of complete insensibility in which he lay. I knelt down, and put my fingers on his wrist; the pulse was very feeble, but still beating free, and I said,--

"Gentlemen, he is not dead, and I should hope will soon recover. If you would take my advice, you would try and restrain the bleeding as much as possible. Get him to the nearest house, and send for a surgeon immediately. The shaking of a carriage may produce great hemorrhage; but there are a number of negroes about who can carry him more easily."

"Hi, boys!" cried Billy Byles; "come here, come here!" And immediately at least a dozen black men and lads ran out from the woods towards the scene of action.

"You had better get home yourself, sir," said the gentleman who had before spoken to me; "for I see you also are wounded, and the blood is running off the tips of your fingers. One thing I will say, Sir Richard; a fairer fight I never beheld. You have behaved quite like a gentleman, and a man of honour, and a d----d good shot too." Seeing that I could be of no further service, I bowed and retired from the ground. As we walked along through the little path in the wood, it became a question where I was to go. Mr. Byles wanted me to return with him to his house; but Mr. Wheatley, more prudently, urged that I should go back at once to Mr. Stringer's. "It is nearer by a mile," he said; "and, besides, he will have plenty of women there to take care of him. He-nurses are always bad ones, my friend; and, moreover, there may be certain persons who may tease their little hearts to death, to know how he is going on, who would not venture to come to the house of a gay bachelor to see him." This latter argument was very conclusive in my own mind; but I made light of the wound, saying, "Oh, this is a mere nothing. I shall be well in a few days." Although, to say sooth, I felt very unpleasantly faint. We soon reached the carriage, which we found tied to a tree; for Zed, it appears, would not be debarred the pleasure of sharing in the day's sport. He came hobbling after us, the next instant, however; untied the horses, placed the pistol-case under the seat, and after fumbling for a minute in a corner, produced an old champagne-bottle, which he held out to me, saying,--

"Here, master, take a drop o' dis--good old rye; you look mighty white, and bleeding like piggie. My ole massa never go out to fight without taking some rye wid him in case of de worse." I took some of the whisky, which, to say the truth, was not altogether unnecessary, for I had lost a good deal of blood. Then, requesting my two companions to tie the handkerchief still tighter, I got into the carriage, and we drove off towards Mr. Stringer's.

CHAPTER XV

As we came in sight of Beavors, the fact arose suddenly to my remembrance that, although Mr. Stringer and his family themselves were not very early in their habits, Bessy Davenport was generally up and about shortly after daylight. In spite of all that I could do, I was covered with blood; my white summer trousers were soaked and dabbled; and there was no cloak or great coat in the carriage which I could throw over me to conceal the ghastly spectacle. I knew that whatever might be her feelings towards me, the sight would alarm and agitate her; and, turning my head towards Mr. Byles, inquired if we could not get into the house by some back way, which would enable me to reach my room unperceived, and remove the "bloody witness from my person."

"Oh, yes, master," answered Zed, taking the words out of Mr. Byles's mouth, and apparently divining instantly what was passing in my mind. "Master Wheatley drive round by the right hand road to the back. Then we go through the pantry-hall, and up the little back-staircase, which runs behind Miss Bessy's room. But she never use it; she always go down the great stairs. Then your room is just opposite, and you can slip in in a minute." Zed's plan seemed admirable, though it did not turn out as well as we expected. We reached the back of the house, indeed, unperceived, and entered what Zed called the pantry-hall. It is wonderful how often when we have laid a scheme for any purpose as perfectly as human calculation could arrange it, some little circumstance occurs which does not usually happen more than once in a year, and throws all our well-conceived arrangements wrong. The very moment after, leaning on Mr. Wheatley's arm, I had entered the pantry-hall by the one door, in came Bessy Davenport by the other, with a bunch of flowers in her hand, exclaiming, "Henry, Henry, give me a glass of water." The next instant her eyes fell upon me, and she turned deadly pale. Everything was forgotten in the agitation and terror of the moment--reserve, playfulness, coquetry, if you will, the presence of strangers. She dropped the flowers at once upon the floor, sprang forward, and threw her arm partly round me, as if to support me, exclaiming, "Oh, Richard, Richard! you are hurt! you are wounded! I knew it, I was sure of it. My heart told me it would be so." The best medicine that physician ever compounded could not have done me half so much good as her words and her look. "I am very little hurt indeed, Bessy," I answered. "A little blood makes a great show, and it all comes from my arm, which will be well, I dare say, in a couple of days."

"Only your arm, only your arm," she said. "Oh, Richard, do not deceive me."

"I do not indeed," I answered; "it is only my arm. Ask Mr. Wheatley."

"But you are so pale," she continued; "you may bleed to death. Henry, get a horse directly, and gallop over to Jerusalem, tell Doctor Christy to come here without a moment's delay. Say, Sir Richard Conway is badly wounded. Come to your room, Richard; I can stop the blood--I think, I hope. I am somewhat of a surgeon amongst the servants," she added, with a faint smile. "Come this way, for all the boys are in the hall." And she led me by a small staircase, which, passing at the back of her own room into which there was a door from the landing, opened by another door upon the main corridor. I was soon in my own room, and seated in the arm chair, with Mr. Byles, Mr. Wheatley, Zed, and Bessy around me. Nothing could persuade the beautiful girl to go. In spite of all we could say, she would see the wound herself, and treat it after her fashion, which, I must say, she did with considerable skill. My coat was taken off, the sleeves stripped up, and though I could see her give a shudder when the blood spouted forth, on the bandage being removed, she did not lose her firmness for a moment.

"Now tie it round tight again, tie it round tight again," she cried to Mr. Wheatley who had unfastened the bandage to remove my coat. "Zed, run into my room, and get two or three handkerchiefs. Juno will give them to you."

"Plenty of handkerchiefs here, Miss Bessy," said Zed, handing her some from my portmanteau; and, taking one of them, she folded it several times. Then placing it on the wound, she bound another tightly over, so as to act as a compress, and watched in deep silence for a minute or two to see if it would have the effect she wished. The blood oozed through after a time, but very slowly; and, with a sigh, as if of relief, she said,--

"That will do, Richard. It will not bleed much or long now; but you must sit quite quiet till the surgeon comes." I took her dear little hand in mine, and pressed my lips upon it; and not caring for the presence of others, she left it still in mine, gazing thoughtfully into my face. She was still in the same position, when Mr. Stringer entered the room, hurriedly, in his dressing-gown.

"What is the matter? What is the matter?" he exclaimed. "They tell me you are wounded, Sir Richard?" There were plenty to explain the matter, and each gave his own version of the affair; Mr. Wheatley, in his peculiar and pungent manner; Billy Byles, drily and in a few words; but Zed, with amplification and details, which I would fain have stopped, both on my own account and on account of one of the listeners. He seemed to consider it a point of honour that his master should not have come off worst in the encounter, and he took particular pleasure in dwelling upon the two wounds which Robert Thornton had received.

"Ah, yes, he hit him every time," said Zed; "and would have shot him through from side to side the first shot, only, I fancy, he did not want to kill him, Master Stringer. That is how he got his wound; for if he had just sent the ball through his head the first fire, he would not have been wounded at all."

"Then is the unfortunate man dead?" asked Bessy, in a low tone.

"No, no," I answered; "he is not dead, my dear cousin. I assure you, I did not intend to kill him; but he stood so, that it was almost impossible to prevent his injuring me without the risk of taking his own life. I think--I trust he may still recover." Bessy put her hands over her eyes, and sat silent; and I could not but remember what I had heard on the preceding day, that her father had fallen in an encounter of the same kind. Though Hope is a very persuasive angel, yet there is a certain little devil, lying hidden in some of the deep windings and turnings of the mind, which is always, with low-voiced cunning, suggesting something contrary to the flattering promises of the charmer. Even now he whispered,--

"Bessy finds a parity between the case of her father and that of this man. However she may dislike him--whatever may be her feelings towards me--some of her sympathies are enlisted on his side." I did not like the thought at all; but she sat quietly beside me, and did not seem to entertain the slightest thought of quitting the room.

"It strikes me," said Mr. Stringer, after a few unimportant inquiries, that there are altogether too many people here round a wounded man. Sir Richard does not seem to be losing much blood now, and some of us had better retire till the surgeon arrives, who, I find, has been sent for. Bessy--Miss Davenport--I think I must constitute you head nurse; for you know Mrs. Stringer's nerves are not equal to such scenes, and you have been brought up with more strength of character.

"I am as weak as a child," said Bessy, in a low tone; but then, instantly recovering herself, she added, in a gayer manner, "Well, I will undertake the task, and risk all sorts of ingratitude. You must not think me bold, Richard, if I come in and out at all times and seasons to see to my patient's progress--being my cousin too, I have a right. Your servant will stay with you, of course. Can't you have a bed, or a sofa, or something put up there for him,

Mr. Stringer? I am going away just now to take some hartshorn, or some mint-julep, or some rye-whisky, or something--what would you recommend, gentlemen?--I have just found out that I have got some nerves, and am not quite so much accustomed to scenes of blood and slaughter as you are." It struck me that there was the slightest possible touch of bitterness in what she said; but I found afterwards that I was mistaken. Strong emotions, even of the tenderest kind, sometimes have recourse to hard words, and even to light jests, to hide themselves not only from the eyes of others, but also from the sight of those who feel them. Bessy, Mr. Byles, and Mr. Stringer quitted the room, leaving me with Zed and Mr. Wheatley. The latter, with great tact and good sense, chatted so calmly and cheerfully that the time seemed very short till Dr. Christy, the surgeon, quietly, and almost silently, entered the room. He did not wear creaking shoes, that besetting sin of medical men. His manner was all very calm and composed, without the slightest haste or bustle in his aspect, although I could judge from the perspiration on his forehead that he had ridden hard. After a few minutes' conversation on subjects barely relevant to my situation, he proceeded to examine my arm.

"The ball is still in," he said; "your muscle is very firm, Sir Richard, or they had not put powder enough in the pistol. However, we shall easily extract it, for it lies perfectly straight." He put me to a good deal of pain, however, though not for more than a few seconds; and then dropped the bullet into a basin of water. I thought it was all over; but he must needs probe the wound again, and then, shaking his head, observed,--

"There is something more, I am sorry to say. We must not leave anything extraneous in the wound, for fear of bad consequences hereafter. A moment more, and it will be all over. Whatever it is, I know its exact position." He then had recourse to the forceps again, and, in an instant, brought up a small splinter of bone, not bigger than an ordinary iron tack.

"That is unfortunate," he said; "the ball has just touched the bone, which may delay your recovery for some days, and will require you to keep quiet and be very cautious. Otherwise, the wound might heal almost with the first intention."

"I think first intentions are always best, doctor," said Mr. Wheatley; "although they say second thoughts are. However, my friend must submit to fate, like the rest of us, and I presume there is nothing dangerous about the wound."

"Nothing whatever," answered the surgeon, "if he is but prudent. I think, Sir Richard," he continued, "from what I have heard of your conduct on the field, it will be a satisfaction for you to know that there is a prospect of your antagonist recovering. He was brought to town at once, and I and my partner saw him. One was merely a flesh wound; the other was one of those curious wounds that we sometimes see, which, going close to several vital organs, leaves them all untouched. An inch further back would have sent the ball through his heart; an inch higher up would have carried it through one of the great vessels of the lungs. Neither were touched; and, though he must suffer for a long time, I think, from various indications, he will recover. And now, if I might advise you, you will go to bed; keep yourself as quiet as possible, and do not rise till I see you to-morrow. I will send you a draught to insure you a good night's rest and keep down fever. But you had better have somebody in the room with you, lest, in tossing about, the compress should get deranged and hemorrhage return." Thus saying, he left me. But I cannot pretend that I followed his instructions to the letter. I had a notion that Bessy would return to see me, and, therefore, I determined to sit up till she came. Nor was I disappointed. The surgeon had not been gone ten minutes when she knocked at the door; and appeared to have quite recovered from the shock of the morning.

"I am determined," she said, "not to care for what people may think in England, although we independent American women are often shamefully afraid of English opinions; but I cannot think there can be anything wrong in attending upon a sick cousin.--Can there, Mr. Wheatley?"

"Not in the slightest degree," answered Mr. Wheatley. "It was a part of the old-time chivalry. Then every lady had a great number of cousins, and they all attended upon them when they were wounded, which was, I think, every other day." And he gave one of his short, low laughs. Nevertheless, Bessy stayed with me for a full half-hour; and I do not believe she would have gone then, if Mr. Wheatley, much to my annoyance, had not given her to understand that Dr. Christy had ordered me to go to bed directly. The rest of the day passed dully enough. Towards night, a good deal of pain and fever came on; and though that opiate produced some wild and uncomfortable sleep, I woke the next morning, feeling languid and exhausted. But I had suffered in the same manner from a previous wound; and when the surgeon returned, he said, I was going on as well as could be expected.

CHAPTER XVI

I do not wonder that the patriarchs lived to the good old age which they attained. I do not wonder that they counted by hundreds where we count by tens. Sparsely scattered over the face of the earth, with their flocks and their herds and their servants; living a frugal and a homely life; inheriting a constitution unbroken by many generations of vice, indulgence, and luxury; with constant but gentle activity of body, and rare and scanty excitement of mind--there was little in the whole course of their existence to wear down the frame and to impair the health. The sword was so seldom drawn--in short--only enough to keep it from rusting--that it did not fret the scabbard. With us, how different is the case! The pursuit of wealth, of pleasure, of fame; the constant exertion of mind and of body; the struggles of an overpacked population, each man like the cuckoo whose offspring tried to shoulder the other out of the nest; the wearing and fretting of continual disappointments; the musquito-bites of small cares; the everlasting thought for the morrow--all these things break us down and shorten life, "*Et corpore frangitur curis et laboribus.*" Nevertheless, in this troublesome and toilsome existence--troublesome and toilsome even to those whom fate and fortune have most favoured--come lapses, either of calm and pleasant tranquillity or of dull and heavy inactivity. Such was the case with me for several weeks. My wound would have healed, probably, at once, had it not been for the slight injury to the bone of the arm. That, however, produced a long train of unpleasant, though not dangerous, symptoms, for which there were no remedies but patience and perfect tranquillity. Anything like exercise was actually forbidden; and I found to my cost when, once or twice, I broke through the rule, that violent irritation and even inflammation followed. There was nothing for it but to submit quietly to a sort of life which was not at all congenial to my habits or my taste. But there were many mitigations to a state which would have been dull and wearisome enough in ordinary circumstances. I suffered very little as long as I was perfectly quiet. I was allowed to rise and go down to the drawing room with my arm in a sling; and I had constantly the society which was most delightful to me, with very little of that which might have annoyed or irritated me. Sometimes there was a little business to break monotony; sometimes a little cheerful society from without. But I had always Bessy Davenport near me; for, by some arrangement, made between her and Mrs. Stringer, she had agreed to stay at Beavors and keep her friend company, while Mr. Stringer, his boys, and the tutor, went up into the interior of Virginia to visit the natural bridge, Weir's cave, and the Peaks of Otter. Perhaps my situation had some share in deciding her to stay; at least, she said so; for Bessy had a habit of always putting the most open and straightforward construction upon her actions, depriving others of the power to insinuate motives by boldly avowing her own. One day, when Mrs. Stringer was saying how kind it was of her to stay with her during Mr. Stringer's absence, she answered laughing,--

"I should always be glad to stay with you, my dear friend, at any time when I could be of comfort or assistance to you; but you must not thank me on the present occasion; for the truth is, I am staying to nurse and amuse my cousin Richard there." And she did so, untiringly. I do not intend to enter into many details of the next month's events, if indeed events they could be called; but some must be slightly touched upon. The day after the duel, I had several visitors--Mr. Henry Thornton, Billy Byles, the sheriff of the county, and others. Mr. Thornton continued to come, two or three times every week, and once or twice brought Mr. Hubbard with him, when some little matters of business were talked of. Mr. Wheatley returned to Norfolk on the morning of the third day; and I should certainly have felt his loss much, had not Bessy Davenport been there. From Dr. Christy I heard every day of the progress of Robert Thornton, and glad indeed I was to find that the surgeon's favourable anticipations were likely to be verified. It is true the unfortunate man struggled for his life during nearly ten days; but from that time, his convalescence, though slow, was steady. It is true, that he was somewhat thrown back at one time by the decision of a court in regard to Aunt Bab's slaves. My claim was admitted; and though an appeal was taken, the slaves were placed in the hands of the sheriff, till the case could be finally decided.

"There can be no doubt whatever upon the question," said Mr. Hubbard, when he communicated the facts to me; "and the poor people, in the end, will be put at your disposal. But with regard to the landed property," he added, shaking his head, "we shall have more difficulty. They are trying to get it escheated, and I fear we shall not be able to prevent it. I think, nevertheless, I see a course of proceeding to frustrate their ultimate object of getting possession of it themselves, though we cannot place it absolutely in your hands."

"How is that, my dear sir?" I asked.

"Oh, a little legal fiction," he answered, "a little legal fiction; but you must let me mature my scheme, and then I will tell you all about it." I was well contented to let the question remain in abeyance; for, to say the truth,

I did not care how it was decided. Having fully as much as I wanted, and a surplus for any contingencies which might involve increased expenditure, I was not anxious for an augmentation of fortune, although I will confess that I felt no little desire to frustrate those land-sharks, always desirous of preying upon the inheritance of others, which swarm in the southern states of this union. It is quite extraordinary, how many, how voracious, and how dexterous they are. With the execution of these visits of courtesy or business, few events occurred to interrupt the perfect tranquillity of Beavors, especially after the departure of Mr. Stringer and his sons. One day was a complete pattern of the other, except that a little variation crept in as I improved in health. After a time, I was permitted by the doctor to take a short walk out in the cool of the morning, and another in the evening, with a strenuous recommendation not to carry exercise to the length of fatigue. I had learned to know exactly the sound of the opening of Bessy Davenport's door on the great corridor. Her maid always went in and out the back way; but she had seldom got on the veil which she usually wore over her head, nor raised her parasol from the seat in the hall, before I was at her side; and then we had a short dreamy walk in the shady parts of the plantation. which afforded some of the pleasantest moments I have yet known in life. It may seem very strange that we who, in the early part of our acquaintance, had talked a great deal of love and marriage, and the mistakes that are made in both, now seldom touched upon such topics at all. Nothing had been said, nothing had been done, to bind us in any shape to each other; and a certain tranquillity was in the minds of both, I am assured, which seemed as if all had been spoken and all was understood. We walked along, side by side. We conversed on various topics, some strange and new, at least to one of the parties--of Europe and its monuments--of customs, of scenes, of enjoyments, all different from those of the land in which we then were--nay, of a still older world in the far East, the cradle of the human race, where, as if for the purpose of preserving a connecting link between the past and the present, God had implanted in the mind of man a tenacious adherence to ancient habits, which gives us, to the present day, living pictures of those early times when His word was first revealed to a chosen nation separated from all other people, to preserve, amongst struggles and contentions, and errors and follies, the knowledge of the one true God. Then she would tell me strange tales of the aboriginal inhabitants of this vast continent; of the Indians, which, even in her young days, had been numerous in Virginia; and we would deviate together into some of the by-paths of thought, leading us afar into discussions of art and science, on the state of society, and what was good and what was bad in the present artificial condition of man. A great change appeared to have come over her, I knew not how or why. Her opinions seemed softened--perhaps I may call it weakened. At all events, they were put forward with less decision. A more calm, a less cutting spirit seemed to animate her; and she would often laugh gaily at her former harsh opinions upon some subjects, and say,--

"My dear Richard, I have all my life been acting on the defensive, and been obliged to show a bold front to the enemy; especially," she added, with a quiet smile, "when I feared there might be treachery in the garrison." Then we would walk home again, and take our early breakfast, often without the company of Mrs. Stringer, who was in delicate health; and if Werter fell in love with Charlotte cutting bread and butter, I might surely feel my love increased, when I saw those beautiful hands tending to all my wants, and cutting the food which I was still unable to cut for myself. She would trust nobody else to do it; and certainly she did it better than any one. Oh those little marks of kindness and tenderness! how they sink into the heart, and how peculiarly they are woman's! After breakfast, she would often read to me for an hour or more; and then we would sit side-by-side in the shady part of the house--for now the full heat of summer was upon us--speaking very little; but both feeling very deeply, I do believe. Our evening walk was shorter than that of the morning; for every one seemed to have a horror of the dews of sunset; but the after hours, till bed time, passed very pleasantly; for Bessy now had no coquetry about her singing, and her store seemed inexhaustible. Yet there were some songs which, though perhaps neither so rich in melody nor so scientific in composition, pleased me more than others; and I would have them over and over again. Perhaps it was that there seemed some fanciful relation between them and our mutual fate. One I remember especially:--

BESSY'S SONG

"I will not love," the maiden said.
"My breast is hard as steel;
No heart e'er loved but was betrayed--
Mine will not, shall not, feel."

Why droops the maid her sunny head?
Why swims her dewy eye?
What is there in that distant tread,
That makes her heart beat high?

"I will not wed," the maiden said;
"None ever me shall see,
Like captive in a triumph led,
A tyrant's slave to be."

Why decks the maid her glossy hair
With orange-blossoms bright?
Why binds she round her forehead fair
That veil of snowy white?

The fish may 'scape the fisher's net;
The deer, the hunter's dart;
The toils of love, more deeply set,
Are pitched in woman's heart.

She stands before the altar now--
Her heart, her hand are given;
Love's rosy hope is on her brow,
And in her breast lies heaven.

Thus passed the time; and day by day I grew better in health. The wound in my arm began to heal. I recovered strength, and even thought of some day mounting on horseback and taking a ride for exercise.

About this time, Mr. Hubbard and Mr. Henry Thornton came together to see me. I was sitting with Bessy in the drawing-room; but although the two gentlemen came on business, they did not seem to think her presence any impediment.

"My scheme is now pretty well matured, Sir Richard," said Mr. Hubbard; "and as I think it may be as well to take our measures at once, I wish to explain it to you. No alien can hold real estate in Virginia; and the real property of any person dying without heirs in this state is subject to escheat. The legislature can then grant the lands to whom it will; but this is always regulated by a certain vague sense of justice; and those who have been serviceable personal friends to, or nearly connected with, the deceased, can usually obtain the grant, if they apply in proper form and show good cause. You are an alien; and we do not suppose that the object of dear old Aunt Bab's property would induce you to become an American citizen, even if your declaration of such an intention would save it, which is doubtful. But we think that your conveyance, regularly drawn up, of your right, title, and interest in the property, to a person having as near a connection with the original American proprietor as yourself--indeed nearer, for your claim is peculiarly under your aunt's will--would be conclusive with the legislature against the intrigues of Mr. Robert Thornton and his father."

"Besides," remarked Mr. Henry Thornton, bluntly, "we have more influence with the legislature than he has by a great deal; and that is the principal thing in Virginia and everywhere else, my good friend Hubbard."

"Perhaps so," said Mr. Hubbard, quietly. "But let me explain the whole matter to Sir Richard fully. We do not propose that you should lose the property; but an honourable understanding can be entered into with the party to whom you assign, that he or she, as the case may be, holds it as in trust for you. Do you understand me?"

"Perfectly," I replied. "The assignment, I suppose, is in reality invalid, and only useful as giving a direction to the operations of the legislature." Mr. Hubbard nodded his head.

"But pray," I continued, for I had already arrived at my own conclusion, "have you fixed upon the person to whom the assignment should be made?"

"We know of no one who fulfils all the conditions," answered Mr. Hubbard, "except Miss Davenport. She is full niece to Colonel Thornton, half niece to Aunt Bab; and though the half blood does not inherit, it gives a good claim. Thus, in fact, she is nearer in every sense than Robert Thornton; and your assignment will, we think, remove every obstacle."

"Besides, she is a girl," observed Mr. Thornton; "and our Virginia legislature is very fond of girls." Bessy's face had been in a glow for several minutes, and I never saw her look more lovely.

"I do not understand this," she observed, with marked emphasis. "Richard, I will not take your property from you. Though it is the home of my youth, and I would buy it willingly if it were to be sold, it is yours, and I will not have it."

"Be quiet, my dear, be quiet," interposed Mr. Hubbard, with a kindly smile. "We only want him to give it to you to secure it for him. You can give it back to him again in various different ways, and a great number of valuable things to boot, if you like."

"Well, well," returned Bessy, laughing and sitting down, "if that is the case, manage it as you like. I would not have that Robert Thornton possess Beavors for anything I possess myself." It may easily be conceived that I consented readily; and as it was judged advisable that the assignment should be made before any active steps were taken towards the escheat,

Mr. Hubbard promised to bring me the deed next day. It is strange how dissimilar things connect themselves. This mere matter of business seemed to me to afford an opportunity for doing and saying that to Bessy Davenport to which my mind had been for some time made up. I was very little doubtful of what her reply would be. I was sure she was not a coquette at heart; and words and looks and acts had told me she was mine. When the two gentlemen were gone, I seated myself beside her, and put my arm over the back of her chair. It was nearly round her waist, but she did not shrink from it.

"Let us talk over this matter, Bessy," I said, quietly; "for there are two or three points which these friends of ours have not considered, as, indeed, how could they, for they know nothing about them----" But just at that moment Mrs. Stringer entered the room--I never heard of its happening otherwise in my life,--and the words, almost spoken, died away upon my lips.

CHAPTER XVII

Accident, circumstance, fate, fortune, luck, chance, or whatever it may be called, which rules the life of man, and keeps him on, or throws him off, the railroad of existence, is certainly, to all appearance, the most wayward, whimsical, unaccountable sort of power that human nature was ever subjected to. I made up my mind, disappointed in what seemed a fair opportunity, to come to a full explanation with Bessy Davenport on the following day. I was very confident I should easily find some happy moment, when we were alone together, to bring about this explanation easily; for of all hideous and detestable things to which man sometimes bows himself, formal declarations of love and proposals of marriage are the most abhorrent to my notions. I was disappointed in my expectations, however, by a dozen little incidents of the most trifling nature. In the morning, before breakfast, it rained; Bessy and the housemaid were both late; and the mulatto girl continued brushing carpets and tables, and dusting very ancient and curious Chinese cups and saucers, and opening and shutting windows, and rubbing knobs of doors, until it was breakfast time; and then Mrs. Stringer, for a marvel, came down herself to distribute the good things of life to her guests with her own hands. Before breakfast was over, Billy Byles appeared, congratulating me upon my recovery, which might be considered complete; and telling us that Mr. Hubbard and Mr. Thornton and Lucy, and perhaps one of the other girls, would be over in half-an-hour with a budget of news and some papers on business. We easily conceived his object in preceding them; and Bessy laughed at him a little, and told Mrs. Stringer she had better have dinner ready for a large party, as it was clear, from Mr. Byles's manner, that their friends were going to stay all day and he with them. So it proved; and, what between reading over and signing the deed of gift to Bessy Davenport, and a dozen other matters of no importance, I had not one single moment to speak a word to Bessy during the whole day. She knew not that I was somewhat fretting with impatience; and, full of life and spirit, and gay good humour, she gave way to everything that was proposed in the way of amusement. At length, towards evening, our friends departed; but Bessy and I were not left alone; and I knew that my object was hopeless for the rest of that day, as Bessy would retire when Mrs. Stringer did. The next day Mr. Stringer and his sons were to return; and I saw no resource but to make an opportunity, if I could not find one. We had just had some coffee, and I was asking Bessy to sing, when the man-servant, Henry, came in with a packet in his hand which he gave to Miss Davenport, saying,--

"Mr. Robert Thornton sends his compliments, Miss Bessy, and says he has found a number of old letters and papers of importance which belong to you, and therefore he has sent them to you."

"They can't be very valuable," said Bessy, "or he would not have sent them. Let us see what they are." And, sitting down at the table by the lamp, she opened the packet. Its contents seemed entirely to consist of letters, yellow with age, and somewhat stained with damp. They were all neatly folded, and docketed with what I supposed to be an abstract of the contents of each. The first two or three Bessy turned over carelessly, after looking at what was written on the back; but then she came to one which seemed to interest her more; and, opening it, she read it through with a straining eye. The next had still more effect; for I could see her give a start when she read the docket, and her hands trembled violently as she opened the paper. She had not read above ten lines, when, suddenly gathering all the papers together, she started up and ran out of the room. She was evidently terribly affected, how or why, of course I could not tell; but my uncertainty was soon removed by Mrs. Stringer, who had been sitting near her fair guest, and who, with a curiosity which cynics would say was natural to women, had taken a glance from time to time at the papers which lay before Miss Davenport.

"That hateful man, Robert Thornton," she said, "will never miss a chance of giving pain. Only think of his sending those letters to poor Bessy."

"I see they have grieved and agitated her," I replied; "but I do not know how."

"Oh, I took a little look from time to time," said Mrs. Stringer, with a laugh, "and I could see what was written on the backs, for it is all in a good, legal-like round-hand. The last one was marked, 'Statement of the death of General Davenport;' that was her father, you know, who was killed in a duel when she was quite a child." This explanation satisfied me. The occurrence passed as a piece of petty spite on the part of Robert Thornton; but neither I, nor Mrs. Stringer, nor Robert Thornton himself, fully knew how painful and terrible was the influence which that unfeeling act of his was to exercise upon the fate of Bessy Davenport and myself. He might guess it in part, but he could not know the whole. Somewhat more than an hour elapsed before Bessy returned. Her face was very pale, and she had evidently been weeping; but her manner at first was calm, and she sat down and took up some woman's work and employed herself listlessly. Poor girl! she had nobody to consult, nobody to confide in. Mrs. Stringer was not a person with whom she could trust the inmost secrets of her heart, and they were all involved at that moment. What an invaluable thing is a wise friend, at those times when the thoughts, and the feelings, and the passions (which work calmly and silently in the human heart so long as intellect and reason reign) are cast free from subjection by some of those strong emotions which shake the ruling power upon its throne, and each clamours loudly, like different parties in an excited crowd, drowning the voice of the others, and urging this course or that in the excited impulse of the moment. But Bessy had no such friend; or, at least, the only one she could have consulted securely, whether wise or not, was shut out from her counsels by emotions of which I then knew nothing. I tried, as best I could, quietly to cheer her. I strove to lead her mind away from subjects of painful thought; but conversation was evidently an effort to her, and at length she rose, saying to Mrs. Stringer,--

"I do not feel well, my dear madam. I think I will go to bed."

"I will go up with you, my dear," said Mrs. Stringer, "if Sir Richard will excuse me. Bed is the best place for either headache or heartache." Bessy moved towards the door, at first turning her eyes away from me, without wishing me good night; but the next instant she stopped suddenly, returned, and gave me her hand, saying,--

"Good night, Richard--good night." Her eyes filled with tears as she spoke, and she ran hastily out of the room. A vague, confused apprehension of, I know not what, look possession of my mind; her conduct seemed strange to me--stranger than could be explained by the interpretation which Mrs. Stringer had first put upon it. That she was sensitive, full of strong feeling, and, when moved, deeply moved, I was sure; and I could easily conceive that, reading the account of her father's violent death, even though it had occurred many years ago, and she had no personal recollection of him, might affect her greatly. Yet there seemed to me to be something more. I betook myself speedily to my room, and as I passed thither I heard Mrs. Stringer's voice in conversation with Bessy in the chamber opposite. Sleep did not visit me soon; nevertheless, I was awake almost by daylight, and dressed and down stairs before any one else was up in the house. It was a beautiful, clear day, and I doubted not, for habit is very potent, that Bessy would take her usual morning walk. The great door of the house, as usual, was unlocked, for few at that time thought of locking a door in Virginia, and, going out into the porch, I sat down to wait for her, who I now felt more than ever was inexpressibly dear to me. I saw the negroes go out to their work, the cattle driven towards the stream, the long shadows of the trees grow shorter, the sparkling dew dried up from the grass, but Bessy did not come, and I began to be really apprehensive lest the shock should have affected her health. I waited till I was summoned to breakfast, and then I found Mrs. Stringer alone. I was disappointed and agitated; but, concealing my feelings as much as I could, I inquired if she had seen Miss Davenport, and how she was.

"She won't come down just yet," answered Mrs. Stringer. "That horrid man has shaken her nerves desperately. He sent her a long and detailed account of her father's death, she says written to her aunt Barbara by the gentleman who was his second. He has filled her mind with dreadful thoughts, and she has hardly been able to sleep all night. I dare say, you having been wounded in a duel so lately, Sir Richard," she added, with a smile, "has given greater effect to the letter." I could not smile in return; and the morning passed away very heavily till shortly after noon, when Mr. Stringer and his sons returned. They had a great deal to tell of the marvels they had seen, and of the enjoyments of their tour, and I was congratulated warmly by my worthy host on my recovery. In the course of the afternoon, when the whole family were present, Bessy Davenport glided in, pale, and evidently suffering. To any not very watchful eye no difference would have been perceived in her conduct towards me; but to mine there was a very great difference indeed. She shook hands with me kindly, nay, warmly; but a deep sigh, almost like a gasp for breath, accompanied the simple mark of good will. During the evening her eyes never met mine; when I spoke to her, she answered without raising them, and I became exceedingly uneasy. What could be the cause of such a change? I had done nothing, I had said nothing, that could give her the slightest cause for offence. Could that wretched man have written something in the papers which he sent to poison her mind against me? I could not believe it; and yet, in the folly of agitated passion, I almost wished I had shot him dead on the spot when he had stood before me, instead of sparing his miserable life to be the bane of mine. I resolved, however, to have a clear and full explanation. Candour and straitforwardness are nowhere so necessary as in love. A moment or two after Bessy had retired for the night, I went up into my own room, telling one of the servants I met in the hall to send my servant up to me. I then sat down and wrote to Bessy, saying:--

"You cannot be ignorant, dearest Bessy, of my feelings towards you; and I have flattered myself--perhaps vainly, perhaps foolishly--that they were returned. Since last night great changes have come over me; your sadness has infinitely distressed me, and I would fain share your sorrow. But your manner towards me has agitated and alarmed me. I have in vain sought for an opportunity of speaking with you in private to-day. Do not deny it to me to-morrow.

"By all the many memories that are between us of the last two months, I adjure you deny me not this favour, nor leave me in uncertainty, which is terrible to me."

"There, go to Miss Davenport's door," I said, giving the note to Zed; "knock, and wait for an answer." Of course, his absence seemed long; but at length he returned, bringing me a few words written with a pencil on a little scrap of paper. They ran thus:--

"Dearest Richard,--You shall have what you desire. I will *find* an opportunity to-morrow; but do not try to force one. I grieve to have given you pain, and shall always grieve to do so."

Then came some words which had been carefully scratched out with the pencil. They seemed to me to have been--"But I *must* do it!" And then she went on:--

"It will probably be towards evening, when Mrs. Stringer will not let the boys go out. In the morning I shall not be down, for I am ill and wretched.

"Your affectionate cousin,

"Bessy Davenport."

There was matter both for pain and relief in Bessy's short note. Those sweet first words--"Dearest Richard"--gave me back at once to full hope and happiness. My love was not unreturned; her affection was not withdrawn from me. I was still dear to her--nay, *dearest*; and Bessy was too frank to write that which she did not mean. Yet what was I to infer from those mysterious words scratched out; if I read them rightly, they were--"But I *must* do it!" Do what? Give me pain? What earthly compulsion could force her to do so? She was free; her hand was at her own disposal. No one could dictate to her; no one could say, "You shall, or you shall not, wed him." Then came those last words, "I am ill and wretched." What could have rendered her so? Surely not a mere brief account of an event which, however painful, had happened twenty years ago to one of whom she had no remembrance. I was puzzled, and by no thought or reflection could I find any clue to the mystery.

"Well, to-morrow will give me a full explanation," I thought. Yet I continued well nigh half the night reading Bessy's note again and again, and trying in vain to draw from it some indication, however slight, of that which had affected her so deeply.

CHAPTER XVIII

I will not pause upon the passing of the following day, although its earlier part was, for me, full of that agitated, I might say painful, expectation which is often more difficult to endure than actual grief or disappointment. The only events of which I have a distinct recollection were delayed till evening. Bessy did not appear below till nearly ten o'clock in the morning. She was very pale, and greatly subdued in manner; and there was something in her eyes, whenever they turned towards me, which grieved and alarmed me. It was nothing unkind, nothing cold, nothing indifferent; but a sort of tender, beseeching look, as if she would have said: "Do not look so wretched, Richard. It wrings my heart to make you suffer, but I cannot help it." Those scratched-out words, "But I *must* do it," kept vibrating in my ears; and I would have given all I had in the world to hasten the moment of explanation. Mr. Stringer was in a fuss; he saw there was something wrong, and he knew not what; and, with very questionable tact, he gave a great deal of his company to two people who heartily wished him away. Mrs. Stringer was very quiet, but seemed to be omnipresent; and the boys thought their recent return to their home gave them a right to be exceedingly vociferous and troublesome. It was one of the most miserable days I ever passed in my life. In the evening, we all assembled in the porch; and, once or twice before she did so, I thought Bessy was going to rise; but she hesitated, and retained her seat. At length, however, she started up, saying, "Come, Richard, and take a little walk with me."

"My dear, it is very late," said Mrs. Stringer; "and you have not been well. The sun will soon set."

"Oh, a walk will do me good," answered Bessy, with a touch of the old spirit; "and we shall not be long; besides, my dear Mrs. Stringer, I want to speak with Richard in private." And she laughed, but not gaily; adding, "You know we have got a great deal of important business to transact. Did not Mr. Hubbard tell you that he had made over to me vast possessions--to have and to hold, &c. &c. &c.? Come, Richard, get me my veil out of the hall, and give me your arm, like a good knight and true." I went for the veil and cast it over her head. I gave her my arm, and felt her hand tremble violently as she took it. We walked down the steps in silence, across the grass-plot, through the little peach-orchard, into the field bordered by the wood through the devious paths of which we had wandered some time before to escape the companionship of the Rev. Mr. McGrubber. I was impatient; and as we entered the field, I said,--

"Now, Bessy----" But she cut me short, murmuring,--

"Not yet, Richard; not yet, dear Richard." We walked on, and entered a path in the wood; and at the end of about a hundred yards further, found a little open space, with one large old tree separated from the rest. The rays of the sinking sun found their way in here over the turf, and chequered the green with gold. Bessy paused here, near the foot of the tree, raised her eyes to my face with a look of solemn earnestness, and placed her hand in mine, uttering the one simple word,--

"Richard." We were both terribly agitated; and it seemed to me that she could hardly support herself. Therefore, before I said a word that could increase her emotion, I made her seat herself upon the mossy root, and placed myself beside her. What I had to say needed no long consideration.

"Bessy," I ejaculated, holding her hand in mine, "you must have seen my feelings towards you. You must have learned, long ere this, that I love you dearly--most dearly." She cast down her eyes, and a slight rosy colour came up into her cheek; but she answered slowly and firmly, "I have, Richard, I have some time ago; I have seen all, known all, just as well as if your tongue had spoken it."

"Then surely, dearest Bessy," responded I, "you could not have given me the encouragement you have, you could not have continued to make yourself all-in-all to me in this world, without resolving to make my love happy, and to be all-in-all to me through life."

"I did resolve it," answered Bessy, in a sad and solemn tone. "I cast all my former vain notions aside--all the idle, thoughtless, unreasonable determinations of a wild girl--and resolved to give you my hand whenever you should ask it."

"Then you are mine," I cried, pressing my lips on hers; "you are mine. I ask it now."

"Stay, stay, stay, Richard," she cried; "stay till you hear me out, if I have voice and heart to speak. An obstacle has arisen. An unforeseen, insurmountable obstacle. Alas, alas! I can never be your wife." And she burst into a violent flood of tears.

"But what is it?" I exclaimed. "There may be a thousand means of remedy left."

"None, none!" she answered. "It is connected with the irrevocable past. It never can be removed, changed, or modified. I might, it is true, become your wife; but I should find wretchedness instead of happiness; remorse instead of love; my misery would make you miserable; and in less than six months after I gave you my hand, the never-ceasing reproaches of my own conscience would bring Bessy Davenport to the grave."

"But what is it?" I cried. "For Heaven's sake, explain!"

"Do not ask me, Richard--do not ask me," she said; "at least not now. Have pity upon me, have compassion! I dare not dwell upon it. The truth came upon me with a crushing weight--the truth, which I never knew till two nights ago, fell upon my heart as if a mountain had been cast upon it, and it has left me very weak. Some time hence, when we are both calmer-- when we can look back upon this time as people who have been asleep look back upon sweet dreams that have faded away for ever--when the dreadful reality will serve but to strengthen and to tranquillize, though it may chill us--then I will write to you, Richard. Perhaps then you may be the happy husband of another, and can look upon Bessy Davenport as a sister, and compassionate the sorrows she has endured; then I will write to you, and tell you all." Grief and disappointment are the most selfish things upon earth--often the most unjust, the most unreasoning. No language can tell the anguish I had that moment endured, the irritating, fiery, maddening feeling of disappointment. It is my only excuse for the cruelty and unkindness of my next words. There was a struggle even to prevent myself from bursting forth in vehement and angry reproach; but the habit of self-restraint in some degree conquered, and my answer was apparently calm and cold, though all beneath was fiery excitement.

"Bessy," I said, bitterly, "may you be happy! Me you have rendered miserable for ever. I have loved you with the truth, and tenderness, and passion, and force of a first and only love; not as a boy loves, but as a man, once and for ever. And you talk to me as being the happy husband of another! Bessy, Bessy, you have never loved, or such a wild, impossible vision could never cross your brain!" She started on her feet like a fawn frightened from her ferny bed, and gazed at me with a look of agony I shall never forget.

"Oh, how have I deserved this?" she exclaimed. But then recovering herself, she took my hand in one of hers, and raising the other towards heaven, she said, in a low and earnest voice,--"May God above judge my heart, Richard; may He cease to bless, protect, and comfort me; may He never help me at the hour of need, support me in the hour of sorrow, save me in the hour of danger--if I have not loved you as well as woman ever loved man! What is it makes me miserable now--has broken my heart, crushed my spirit, enfeebled my body? Loved you!--Oh, God, how I have loved you!" And casting herself on my bosom, she pressed her lips again and again upon my cheek.

"Bessy, I am wrong, I am wrong," I said; "forgive me, dearest Bessy. Only confide in me--only put full trust and reliance upon me--let me not be sent blindfold to the sacrifice of every hope of happiness in life. Talk not to me of ever marrying another. I have never loved but once, and never can----"

"Hear me, Richard," interrupted she, more calmly and gently, putting back the arm I had cast around her. "You yourself shall be the arbiter of our destiny. You yourself shall condemn me, if you will, to death--to a death of remorse and self-reproach. I will be your wife, if you command me; but it must be some time hence. When we are both calmer, when we can both look with reasonable eyes upon our relative position to each other; when I can venture to let my mind rest upon the past, of which you are now as ignorant as I was a few days ago; when you can give due weight and have consideration to a woman's feelings, I will write to you, and leave you yourself to decide. You shall say to me in reply,--'Bessy, be mine, though death be the consequence;' or, 'Bessy, you are right. We must not attempt to pass the barrier which God has placed between us.' But mark me, Richard, and remember, should you view the matter as I do, and see that our marriage is impossible, Bessy Davenport will be to you as another sister. Never, never, so help me God, shall my hand be given to any other! I have loved you, when I thought I could never love any man; and for you I was ready to cast away every prejudice, every resolution of my life. My love is yours for ever; and I should as soon think of breaking a vow as of allowing one thought of another to cross my mind." A slight flush covered her face as she spoke; but strong emotions often bring their own calm with them, and she went on in a manner much more tranquil.

"And, Richard," she said, "I have gone perhaps beyond what maiden modesty would warrant. I have told--I have shown you--how I love you. But you will not, I think, misunderstand or blame me; first, because I am, as you know, a wild, untutored girl, accustomed to speak frankly whatever thought, or fancy, or feeling, crosses my brain or heart; and, secondly, because this is an occasion in which concealment would be wrong to me and wrong to you--when I must tell you how I love you in order that you may see how terrible is the sacrifice of that love to duty."

"I do not misunderstand you, dear Bessy," I answered; "I will try to be more calm, more reasonable. You have said that I shall be the arbiter. When will you give me the explanations which will enable me to be so rightly? At present I can conceive no cause, I can imagine no possible motive, why you should not be my wife; and I fondly hope and trust that when all is explained, I can remove every doubt and scruple from your mind. But I promise you, my beloved, that if I see a reasonable motive, a just and righteous cause, I will endeavour by no sophistry to persuade you against your better judgment. I will endeavour to think for Bessy Davenport as I would think for myself, were my mind free and without passion. But, dearest Bessy, make the time short; tell me when you will give the whole explanation."

"Oh, Richard," she answered, with a mournful shake of the head, "I would fain give time for both you and myself to think deliberately. I may be wrong in the view I take at present, and I am certain you would be wrong if you were to decide now. Well, well, within three months, I will write to you the whole, and enclose you the old letter which I received two nights ago. After you know all, you shall wait a fortnight, a full fortnight, before you decide, and then your decision shall be final. I will say not one word against it; you shall command, and I will obey."

"My commands shall not be very hard, Bessy," I answered; "for though you think so very ill of mankind, if I have the slightest knowledge of my own spirit, I would rather insure your happiness than mine. If we must live as brother and sister, without a dearer tie, so be it."

"Oh, thank you, thank you, Richard," she answered; "those words relieve my mind of a great weight. I see you will have consideration for me."

"I will, indeed," I replied. "But now tell me, beloved, how are we to pass the intermediate time?"

"I have determined," she said, "to go over to my uncle Henry's, and to remain there with him. I have already told my maid to have everything in readiness, and have written for my uncle to come for me to-morrow." She paused for a moment, and then added,--"But you will let me see you from time to time, will you not, Richard? There can be no harm in that. We are not parted by inclination, but by fate."

"Assuredly, I will come to see you often," I answered; "for till this is decided, you are still my own Bessy; and although I thought of returning speedily to England, I will not quit this land till our fate is fixed." She drew a deep sigh, as if there was some relief in the words I spoke, and then she said, suddenly,--

"Now let us go back, Richard. It is growing quite dark, and they will send somebody to see after us." I drew her arm through mine, and we walked slowly homeward, nearly in silence. We both thought that it was the last solitary walk we should take together for many a day, and the present had been a very eventful one. But, as usual with human calculations, our conclusions were all wrong. We had another walk to take ere long, and that more eventful still.

CHAPTER XIX

Bessy seated herself in the hall before entering the drawing-room, where we heard many voices and gay laughter going on.

"Go in, Richard, go in," she said, giving me her hand; "let me recover myself a little. I shall be better soon. The worst is over; I shall join you presently." I pressed my lips upon her hand, and went into the drawing-room. Though still anxious--though still grieved--I was not near so much agitated as she was. As she had said, the worst was over, and ever buoyant hope had risen up again speedily in my heart. She had promised to tell me all within the next three months; and I could not, I would not, believe that any barrier really existed between herself and me, which a little argument, a little persuasion, would not overcome. Woman's mind, I thought, more timid, more delicate than man's, magnified difficulties and dangers, and sometimes even *created* them where they did not exist.

"But there can be no obstacle between us," I said to myself, "which reason and love cannot overcome." In about ten minutes, Bessy joined the rest of the party, and was certainly more cheerful than she had been the night before. The evening passed heavily enough, however; and about half-past nine she retired to rest. Half an hour after, the whole party separated, and I proceeded to my own room, not to sleep, but to meditate. I was anxious to think of every possible obstacle which could lie between Bessy and myself; and, as we are often inclined to do, to lay out plans for removing that of which I had no means of ascertaining the weight or the nature. When I entered the room, I found the candles lighted, and Zed, in one corner, upon his knees, very busy over something lying on a chair. He did not hear me enter; and, while throwing off my coat and waistcoat, I asked him a little sharply,--

"What are you about there, Zed?"

"Only looking up your pistols, master," said Zed, raising his head.

"Why, you seem to be loading them," I exclaimed.

"Just loaded the little ones, master; will load the big ones in a minute."

"Stay, stay. Why are you loading them?" I demanded, "I don't want them loaded."

"Oh, always better to have pistols loaded in troublesome times, master," answered the man earnestly. "Better let me load them." There was something in his manner which struck me as strange: and I replied,--

"Come here, and speak to me." The man hobbled up to the chair where I was sitting, and I fixed my eyes inquiringly on his face.

"Do you know anything," I said sternly, "which makes you judge that it would be better for me to have my pistols loaded this night, after they have been so long unloaded?"

"No," replied the man firmly.

"I suspect you do," I rejoined; "and remember, if you *do* know of any evil about to take place, and do not inform me, you will be an accomplice."

"Master, I do not know anything," replied Zed; "but I do not like the looks of things. I will tell you all I do know, and will lay down my life for you, master, for you have been a very kind master to me. This evening I went out to take a walk all by myself; and, down in the wood out there, I saw a good number of coloured gentlemen together--more nor common-- and they were not talking loud and laughing, nor poking fun at each other; but they had all got their heads together and were whispering quite low; and Nat Turner was there, and Nelson, and Harry, and James, and several more who, at the time of the preaching, I overheard say very wild things. So I say to myself, 'I'll go home and load master's pistols--no knowing what may happen.'"

"Did you see any arms amongst them?" I inquired.

"No; they had no arms," he answered; "not even sticks; but they had a great big demi-john of some liquor."

"Most probably they were out upon some frolic," I suggested, entertaining some slight suspicion that my good friend Zed had not entirely forgotten the beating he had received in coming from the camp-meeting. "Give me that light jacket," I continued, "and then you can go, Zed. I have got a good deal to do before I can go to bed." The man did as I bade him, laying the small pistols he had loaded on the table, before he went; and I could hear his step descending, not as usual by the back staircase, but by the great stairs into the hall. There it seemed to stop, and I heard no further, but judged it not at all improbable that Zed had gone to Mr. Stringer's room to communicate his suspicions to that gentleman. I should have explained before, that the great hall ran straight through the middle of the house, dividing it into two equal parts, and being itself divided by a large thick door from what was called the pantry-hall. On entering from the front of the house, the first room on the left hand was the drawing-room, or parlour, as they call it here. Then came a little parlour used as breakfast-room, and then the dining-room. On the opposite side of the hall was, first, Mr. and Mrs. Stringer's bed-room, then a dressing-room; and then, facing the dining-room, another bed-room where the children slept. Mr. McGrubber slept at the top of the house in a room next to the school-room. My room was over that of Mr. and Mrs. Stringer; and Bessy's on the opposite side over the dining-room. Thus, when Zed went down the great staircase, though his tread was very heavy, I should lose the sound of his foot if he entered Mr. Stringer's room or the dressing-room. To say the truth, I did not attach much importance to his information or his fears; and, sitting down at the table, I leaned my head upon my hand and gave myself up to meditation.

"What could be the impediment," I asked myself, "to my union with Bessy Davenport, which seemed so formidable in her eyes?" I traced back the history of my family as far as I knew it. I dwelt upon all that I had ever heard even in my childhood's days, which could in any degree account for her scruples or her doubts. But I could find nothing. My mind was too much excited for sleep to approach my eyes; and, many a time, I went over and over the same ground, turning the question before me in every different direction, and only puzzling myself more and more. Hour passed by after hour; the dull chime of the hall clock sounded one and two; and I resolved at length to lie down to rest. Just, however, as I rose from my chair, I fancied I heard voices speaking in a low tone on the outside of the house; and, approaching the window, I looked out. There was nobody there, and I returned to the table. I had hardly reached it, when I heard distinctly a window raised. I paused to listen; and then came what seemed to me a faint, smothered cry. Snatching up the pistols from the table, I advanced towards the door; but before I could reach it, it was thrown open, and Zed appeared. He carried a large key in his hand, and his eyes seemed starting from his head.

"Run, master, run," he cried, "down the back staircase, out through the little hall into the wood. They are murdering all the white people down below!"

"How many are there?" I exclaimed.

"Oh, thirty or more," answered Zed; "but I have locked the door between the halls, so they can't get through. Run down the back staircase; run, master, quick quick!" Resistance was evidently in vain, and I rushed out of the room, but not to the top of the back staircase. Something dearer to me than my own life was to be protected; and, darting across, I threw open Bessy's door and went in, followed by Zed. For the last two or three nights, she had burnt a light in her room; and, while my faithful servant locked the door behind us, I hurried towards her bedside. She had started up at the first sound of our coming, and gazed at me with eyes full of terror and surprise.

"The house is attacked by revolted negroes, Bessy," I exclaimed. "They are murdering every one below. Come quick, come quick! I will protect you with my life." She sprang out of bed and was seeking for some clothes, but a piercing shriek rang up from the rooms below, and I caught her hand, saying, "For God's sake, come!"

"Run, missie, run," cried Zed, "down the back stairs, out into the wood. I will keep them here some time--I hear them coming up stairs--run, run!" Half carrying, half leading, I drew her to the door opening to the little staircase, making Zed a sign to follow; but he shook his head, and, just as I passed through the door with Bessy, I heard him say, "Won't hurt me. What's a poor black man's life worth?" I hurried Bessy down stairs as fast as possible, feeling tempted, I will admit, to lock the door behind us, for the key was in the lock on the outside, few persons thinking it worth while at that time in Virginia to take what seemed the unnecessary precaution of fastening their doors. But I thought of poor Zed, and I refrained. The pantry-hall was quite vacant and very dark, so that we had to feel our way through; but, as we passed, I heard voices speaking loudly above, and what seemed to me the blows of an axe upon a door. At length we reached the open air of the stable-yard, over which the sinking moon was throwing her pallid light. Before us, at the distance of some sixty or seventy yards, were two of the women servants flying in terror, and one of them dropped a cloak which was over her shoulders, made a snatch at it from the ground, but ran on without recovering it on seeing Bessy and myself issuing from the house, doubtless imagining us to be pursuers. I thought it no robbery to take up the cloak, and throw it over my fair companion.

"To the left, Richard, to the left," she said, "between the two buildings. It will lead us sooner to the wood." I hurried on as she directed, and soon entered a path amongst some tall open trees, with greensward beneath, which, at the end of five minutes, led us to the outskirt of the forest. We plunged in, and all was darkness round us, so that we were obliged to go more slowly; for though the path continued, it was frequently obstructed by obtruding trees.

"Your feet, dear Bessy," I said, in a whisper; "you have nothing to protect them."

"Yes I have," she answered, in the same tone, "my slippers were by the bedside." As she spoke, I heard steps advancing quickly upon the path behind us, at the further end of which was a little break of light, like one of those gaps which we sometimes see in a dark cloud, and I discerned the figure of a man, with what seemed a hatchet in his hand, coming rapidly up. Throwing my arm round Bessy, I drew her out of the path, and, taking one of the pistols out of my pocket, resolved to wait and see if the man would pass us, before I fired, first because I had no ammunition with me, and secondly because I feared the report might attract attention towards us.

"Dis way, dis way, they must be up here," cried a negro's voice. "Kill 'em all; kill 'em all!" I could faintly see him as he rushed forward, whirling the axe in his hand. I thought he would have passed us; but no: he caught a glimpse of something white in the wood, and stopped short.

"Still, Bessy, still!" I whispered, raising my arm, and aiming deliberately, as well as I could, by the faint light. He took a step forward towards us, and I obtained a clearer view of him. My finger pressed the trigger, and I only heard the ringing report of the pistol and the sound of a heavy fall. There was neither cry nor groan, and I suspect the ball had gone right through his head.

"Now, Bessy," I said, "the report may bring them hither quickly. Do you know any way that will lead us from the other side of this path?"

"Yes, yes," she answered; "I will show you. It will take us to what I call the labyrinth. We shall be safe there." We hurried on; and I thought she gave a little start as we came suddenly upon the body of a negro, lying partly on the path and partly in the bushes, with the axe he had carried thrown full ten feet from him, so that we passed between it and his corpse. She did not quail nor falter, but led me on to the mouth of a little side path, down which we went. With many a bend and many a turning, it led us, after more than a mile, into those low woods, intersected by many little by-ways, in which she and I had passed more than one hour of deep, though very varied, interest. We passed the open space overshadowed by the great old tree, under which she had told me how she loved me; but that she could never be my wife. The sinking moon shone upon the spot now as the sun had done then. We both remembered the emotions which had now been swallowed up in others; and while her right hand clasped my arm, her left was extended and lay gently upon mine. It seemed to say, "Don't you remember, Richard?" Still we hurried on, however, for I felt that we were yet too near the scene of slaughter to pause in safety there.

"Will not this lead us to the river, Bessy?" I asked.

"No; take to the left," she answered, "and we shall come to the house of Mr. Travis, where we shall be safe, I doubt not."

"I fear, Bessy, the insurrection is general," I replied. "Poor Zed gave me some intimation this evening; but I foolishly treated his warning with too little consideration. However, we must seek some place of shelter, though it will be necessary that we take every precaution to avoid falling into fresh danger. Can we not reach the town?"

"We shall have to pass close by the house," she answered. "It would be madness to attempt it to-night. The revolt can hardly be so general as you think." We walked quickly on for about two or three miles, still keeping within the shelter of the woods, though the path was crossed with roots, and in some places encumbered with briars. I felt Bessy's hand lean more and more heavily on my arm. Grief, anxiety, and terror had weakened her, and I became convinced that she could not go much further.

"What is the distance to Mr. Travis's house, now?" I asked.

"Perhaps three miles," she answered, with a sigh.

"Hadn't we better stop here and rest?" I said; "morning will soon arrive, and you cannot walk that distance at present, I am sure."

"A little further on there is an open space," she answered; "and I recollect there is a bank that used to be covered with wild flowers and soft grass, and we can sit down there and rest a little, for I am, I confess, very, very weary, dear Richard."

"Let me carry you," I said. But she would not suffer me, saying:--

"Your arm, your arm." At the end of about a quarter of an hour we came to the spot she had mentioned. It was indeed like a place made for lovers. The moon, though she was below the woods, still spread a soft light over the sky and the grassy bank; and the tall irregular trees around, waving their wide branches over it, were all distinct, though softened in the half light. I led her up the bank, and seated her where it seemed driest; then, taking my place by her side, I put my arm fondly round her. For a minute or two she spoke not, but she sighed deeply, and her head sank silently on my bosom. I was almost afraid she had fainted, but I soon perceived, by the soft breath upon my cheek, that such was not the case; and I said:--

"Now, dearest Bessy, take a short sleep; it will refresh you. I will roll up this jacket and make a pillow for you."

"No, no, I will rest here, with my head upon your shoulder," she answered. "I know, Richard, I can trust you as a brother." I would not touch her lips, but I pressed mine upon her brow. Then, wrapping the cloak tightly round her, without removing my arm from her waist, I leaned gently back against the bank, with her head still resting on my bosom. Then, drawing the undischarged pistol from my pocket, I threw my right arm over her also, ready to fire at the first approach of danger. I felt Bessy's heart beat against mine, but I was her brother. In two minutes she was asleep, utterly exhausted; and I kept watch while the last ray of moonlight faded from the sky. Very soon after, the first faint beams of morning began to spread up towards the zenith.

CHAPTER XX

It was a beautiful night and a beautiful morning, calm and sweet and peaceful; contrasting strangely and painfully with the dreadful scenes which had been enacted within the last few hours. In our flight from the house, and the long walk we had taken with real dangers on every side, and all those which imagination never fails to supply in moments of agitation and peril, I had had no time for thought. But now, as I rested here, with Bessy in my arms, and the tranquil change going on above from night to morning, the mind seemed hurried on with wild rapidity, as if by a runaway horse. Thought thrust upon thought; memories, expectations, fears, hopes, doubts, questions, all trod upon each other's heels; and before one had time to obtain full possession of the ground, it was gone, displaced by another. What a multitude of incidents had occurred since, a few months before, I had laughingly taken my departure from Norfolk, feeling life and the world to be great jests, and hardly believing in the reality of anything! What a multitude of incidents! I speak not of mere material facts, but of mind and heart facts. What new friends, what new enemies had arisen! What perils, what pains, what hopes, what happiness, what new objects, purposes, desires, had crowded upon me! What new thoughts had entered the brain, what new feelings had been born in the heart! It seemed almost a life-retrospect--like one of those pageants of past existence, which, I am told, sweep before the eyes of a drowning man in the last expiring blaze of consciousness. For some time, this great and strange impression--for it was more a general impression than a sequence of ideas--kept possession of my mind; but then I forced my thoughts away, and fixed them upon the more important facts of the present. What had become of Mr. Stringer and his family? Were they all dead, all slaughtered? What had become of poor Zed, who had so heroically risked his own life to secure to me and Bessy a few moments more for escape? Was it to be expected that, in the rage and excitement of the moment, the furious savages, drunk with blood and murder, would spare any one who opposed them, of whatever colour he might be? Then, again--how far had the insurrection spread? With the little information I possessed, it seemed to me that this revolt must have been long planned and deliberately arranged. I remembered the horrible massacres of St. Domingo; and how silently and secretly the first outbreak of that great and bloody insurrection had been arranged by the negroes--

how confidently, carelessly, and securely the planters had reposed on their own strength till their self-reliance was drowned in blood and flames. That such might be the case in the present instance was clear. Whether it was actually so or not, I had no means of judging; yet I could not help fearing that the insurrection had been very general. The negroes could have no particular motive for attacking the house of Mr. Stringer more than any other--indeed less; for there being more white men in it than in numbers of others in the neighbourhood, the assailants were likely to encounter more vigorous resistance. Mr. Stringer had given no special cause of offence; and in his house was staying one of the apostles of the abolition party. The more I thought of the whole, the more probable it seemed to me that the insurrection had been very general. I knew and had seen how rapidly and secretly the negroes communicate with each other--how unaccountably the most trifling piece of news would pass amongst them, from house to house, over a wide space; and, surely, I thought, in a case of such terrible importance as this, the same means of communication must have been brought into operation. Then came the terrible question--"If such is the case--if revolt and massacre are stalking abroad over the land, where shall I find shelter and safety for this dear girl?" I had no means of forming a sane opinion. My knowledge of the country was but scanty. I knew, generally, the direction in which the county-town, Jerusalem, lay; but I knew not how to reach it by the shortest and most secure road; and the only resolution I could form was, to lay all the conclusions I had arrived at before Bessy when she awoke, and trust to her better knowledge of the people and the district. While these reflections had been passing through my mind, the faint gray of the morning had brightened into a rosy glow, and the rising sun poured streams of light across the little open space in which we were. There she lay, dear girl, with her head still resting on my bosom, looking still more beautiful, it seemed to me, than ever. I had fancied that one great charm of her countenance was in her eyes; but now, veiled by the pale lids, with their long black fringes sweeping her cheek, those eyes could add nothing; yet, how lovely she looked. A soft glow was upon her cheek; and, indeed, the rosy light of morning coloured her whole face, while the slightly-parted lips showed the pearly teeth, and her bosom heaved gently and regularly with the breathing of calm and quiet sleep. I could have lain there and gazed at her for ever. For more than an hour after sunrise, it seemed as if fatigue, I might say utter exhaustion, had obliterated all trace of the dreadful scenes we had passed through, and the perilous situation in which we were. It was evident she dreamed not at all; but, at length, she moved a little. A broken word or two came from her lips.

"Oh, Richard!" she said, and then came something that was indistinct; then she spoke again more plainly. "Your father, you know it was your own father--do not, do not press me." Then she awoke with a start, and gazed around her wildly. She would have sprung up, but I still held her in my arms, saying,--

"Bessy, you forget." And, looking into my face for a moment, she seemed to recall the past with sensations which must have been strangely mingled. First came a look of terror; then a bright smile, and then her whole face and forehead were overspread with a burning blush, and she buried her eyes for a minute or two on my bosom. I tried to soothe and quiet her, and she was soon conversing with me, anxiously, but calmly, upon the circumstances in which we were placed.

"We had better, in the first instance," she said, "go on to the house of Mr. Travis. He is so good and excellent a man, so kind to his servants and to all the people around him, that he would be the last to be attacked. Then again, from the edge of the wood, we can see the house quite plainly; and if we perceive anything unusual, or that indicates danger, we need not go on."

"It is too far, however," I answered, "for you to go on without some refreshment, Bessy. If you will go a little further amongst the trees, so as to be hidden from the road, I will seek some wild fruits, such as I have seen growing round, and we will make our breakfast, like two hermits, here. I will not go beyond call." She had some little hesitation at letting me depart; but we found a place where she could conceal herself completely, and I went on my foraging expedition, which produced some supply, though not a very abundant one. Many of the wild fruits, of which, through this country, there is generally a large quantity, were now nearly over; still, in the shady places, I found some strawberries and raspberries unwithered, and two or three other kinds, looking like plums and cherries, which were fair enough to the eye, though whether they were edible or not I could not tell. I judged, however, that in her young days Bessy must have made acquaintance with them; and at the end of about a quarter of an hour, I went back with both my hands loaded. Some I found were bitter, some poisonous: but the rest served in some degree to refresh her; and, as we sat and took our humble fare, the strange situation in which we were placed seemed to present itself more strongly than ever to her eyes.

"I can hardly believe all this, Richard," she said. "It seems to me like a dream. Are we really living and waking on this earth? or are we the sport of some strange mad fancy?"

"The facts are too stern to be disbelieved, dearest girl," I answered. "Indeed, I almost dread to think how many dark and terrible realities there may be around us even now."

"And yet, amidst them all, Richard," said Bessy, with tears rising in her eyes--what sweet and beautiful things are eyes!--"how can I ever thank you, not alone for saving my life a second time, but for all the tenderness and brotherly delicacy you have shown me. When I spoke so ill of men, Richard, some months ago, I did not know there was, in the world, such a man as you." She wiped the drop of emotion from her cheek, and then added,--

"But what are these darker things you apprehend? Those we know are dark enough. I hardly dare to let my mind rest upon them." I explained to her, as well as I could, the reasons there might be to suppose that the insurrection of the slaves might have been general throughout all that part of Virginia, or even further; and I dwelt especially upon the difficulties which we might encounter in seeking some place of safety, hoping that her better knowledge of the country might enable her to suggest something, where I, in my ignorance, was at fault.

"I do not think the revolt can have been very general," she said. "St. Domingo, which you mention, was, I believe, in a very different condition from this State. The negroes were much more numerous there, and the white race were a feeble, inactive, colonial population. They had not the vigour and energy of the free citizens of a republic. You may smile, dear Richard; but you will see that, although this insurrection may have spread further than I imagined, and many terrible things may happen in the meantime, the gentlemen of Virginia will speedily unite and put it down with a strong hand. However, the only thing for us to do, seems to me to consist in obtaining some information as speedily as possible; and the place where we are most likely to find it is, I still think, at the house of Mr. Travis. We can reach it in an hour; and it is nearer than any other place. Let us go. I am quite ready now." We went on upon our way, conversing in very low tones, and keeping a watchful eye upon the path as far as we could see in advance; but all was peaceful and still around us. The air was soft and balmy; the only sounds were a few short notes from the birds amongst the trees; the only moving objects the butterflies flitting across; or, here and there, a squirrel darting from one side of the path to the other, and running chattering up the trees. How pleasant would that morning's walk have been, with one so much beloved, in other times and circumstances! At length, Bessy paused.

"We are not far from the house," she said. "That light at the end of the path is coming from the open ground of the plantation. We had better turn aside here, if we can find our way through the bushes, and see if we can discover anything before we approach." We soon found a place where we could pass; and, proceeding cautiously, reached the outer edge of the forest ground. The house was before us, not a hundred and fifty yards distant; and beyond it were some of the offices and several negro cabins. Not a human being was visible, however. The eye could range over the unfenced fields without a single labourer being seen. No grooms appeared about the stable; no women sitting at the cabin doors; no children playing about before them. The windows of Mr. Travis's house were all closed, and only the door in front was partly open.

"I do not like the appearance of things here, Bessy," I said. "Do you see?"

"Yes," she answered. And I could feel her hand tremble on my arm. "The place looks strangely desolate. Perhaps they have fled at the news of the revolt."

"It maybe so," I answered; "but I cannot take you there, Bessy, till I know more. Who can tell what may be in that house? Can you fire a pistol?"

"I dare say I can, Richard," she answered. "But why?"

"Because I will leave this with you," I replied, "and go forward and see what has occurred there. If I should not come back soon, the only thing for you to do will be to make the best of your way to Jerusalem, by the safest path you can think of. The gentlemen of the place will make that their rallying point, you may depend upon it."

"Oh, no, no, Richard," she cried: "if you go to death, I will go with you. Indeed, indeed, I cannot stay here alone. I should die of fear for myself and you. I was in terror all the time you were absent this morning." I saw that it was vain to reason with her; and making our way out of the wood, we came quietly to the open space cleared around the house. At the same moment, a large dog came round from the stable to the front door, raised his head, and began to howl. It was the most melancholy sound I ever heard; still it encouraged me to go on. As soon as the poor brute saw us, he ran forward, but without barking, or any sign of enmity; and, when he came up, licked my hand, as if he was glad to see a human being.

"We have an ally here, in case of need, Bessy," I said, and, mounting the steps, I pushed open the half-closed door. All was silent, and in the hall there was no sign of disarray or confusion. Hats and articles of clothing were hanging about as usual in the halls of country houses. Some fishing-rods stood in a corner, and a powder-flask and shot-pouch lay upon a chair. There were no guns, however, in a place where guns seemed once to have stood, and on the floor-cloth was the print of a naked foot stamped in some dark fluid; it seemed to me to be blood.

"They must have fled," said Bessy, who had not remarked the foot-print. "Everything seems quiet and in order."

"It may be so," I answered; "but I have many doubts." That mark on the floor-cloth, the half-open door, the windows closed--all created very terrible suspicions. With the pistol, which remained loaded still in my hand, I pushed open the door of a room on my left; it seemed to be the dining room, for there was a long mahogany table in the middle, with chairs ranged round it at a little distance. Here also was no sign of disorder, except, indeed, that there was a double-barrelled fowling-piece, still loaded and capped, lying across the table.

"This is very lucky," I said; "I shall take the liberty of appropriating this, which may serve to defend us in case of need, and may procure us food as we go along, Bessy, should we not be able to make our way to some town or village as soon as we could wish."

"Oh, Mr. Travis will easily forgive you," replied Bessy. "But let us make sure that there is nobody lurking in the house, for I think they must have left some of the coloured people behind them, otherwise the door would not have been open."

"Let me go first," I said, "and we will examine the rooms on this floor." Going out again into the hall, with the gun under my arm, I looked up the stairs and shouted,--

"Is there anybody in the house?" There was no answer; everything was still and silent. I then turned to the room opposite the dining room. It was a handsome drawing-room, neatly furnished, with books upon the table, one of them open. There was a door on the left-hand side of the room, opposite to the windows, and Bessy said,--

"That is probably Mr. and Mrs. Travis's bed-room."

"I will go in and see," I replied; "but first let me lock this door into the hall, that we may not be attacked from behind." Having done so, I moved over towards the other door, begging my fair companion to remain in the parlour while I reconnoitred; for I had a sort of presentiment that I should not go far without finding something which I would fain hide from her eyes. She followed me close, however, and I opened the door. The light was faint, for there were curtains over the windows; still I could see well enough to induce me instantly to put Bessy gently back with my left hand, saying,--

"Let me go in alone, my beloved. Here are sights not fit for you,"

"Have they not fled?" exclaimed Bessy, in a tone of alarm.

"Their spirits are fled," I answered sadly. "Their bodies are here." Entering the room, I partly closed the door, and then, undrawing the curtain, the whole terrible scene was full before me. Lying on the floor by the side of the bed, from which he had evidently started in haste, was Mr. Travis himself, with two terrible hatchet-wounds on the top of his head, one from which it seemed the weapon had glanced, and the other sinking deep into the skull. In the bed lay his wife, with her brains dashed out, and the pillow all soaked in blood. But, more horrible still, on the floor, near the foot of the bed, was a little cradle, and from it the wretches had dragged an infant not four months old, and killing it with blows of their axes, had cast it down near its father's feet. My blood ran cold. I have seen many a man fall in battle, I have passed over the field and gazed upon the slain, but I never saw any sight which so horrified me as this. When man is arrayed against man in deadly strife, the mind is prepared for scenes of death of every kind, and the hand clenching the sword or the musket, the scattered arms and broken weapons, have all that sort of harmony with the work of the fell destroyer, that they deprive it of part of its terrors. But here everything was in strange and terrible contrast. The peaceful aspect of domestic life was all around; the lightsome, gay parlour, with its open book; the instruments of music; the quiet, shaded bed-room; the little cradle with its light curtain of rosy silk--all added horror to the sight of violence and blood, and death. I could not stay to contemplate it, but left the room speedily, and closed the door. Bessy threw her arms round me, and hid her eyes and wept.

"This is but what we might expect to find, my love," I said. "But, dearest Bessy, we have other things to think of now than mourning for the dead. We shall be in perfect safety here for a time; for these blood-thirsty wretches will not return speedily to the scene of their barbarous deeds. I must find you some clothing and some food, for we cannot tell where we shall have to go, or how long it may be ere we find a place of safety."

"Food, Richard," cried Bessy; "I could take nothing now. I do not feel as if I should ever taste food with appetite again; and, indeed, I do not think we are so safe here as you believe. Doubtless these savages, as soon as they have made themselves masters of the country round, will return to plunder the houses. Nothing seems to have been touched here. We had better get back to the woods at once."

"They will not come soon," I answered. "In the daylight they must fight their way, and for some time they will have other things to think of than plunder. We will not stay long, however; but I must have food and clothing for you. I blessed God last night that it was so warm and dry; but another night it may not be so. And who can tell where we may have to lodge this very evening? You stay here, and lock both the doors; keep this pistol with you; I will go and seek for the different things we may need, and be back in a moment or two. I must have more arms if I can find any, and powder and ball, if they are to be had, though I doubt not these men have carried off the greater part of the weapons in the house. Let me be but well armed, and I shall not mind half-a-dozen of them. At all events, let me have the means, dear Bessy, of defending you in case of need." It was with evident reluctance she remained below; but I was afterwards very glad I had succeeded in persuading her, for, in the rooms above, I found two sweet girls, much of her own age, both murdered in the same barbarous manner. I took some of the clothes which I found in the bed-chambers to carry down to my dear companion. It seemed like plundering the dead; but that was no time for false delicacy. My search through the rest of the house was not quite so successful. Every gun, of which I afterwards found there had been many, had been removed by the atrocious murderers, except the one which I had found in the dining-room. In a small room behind, however, I discovered a brace of very beautiful pistols and a sword. These I took, as well as the powder-flask and shot-bag that were in the hall, the latter of which was half full of buckshot. The flask was nearly full of powder, and with these arms, if attacked, I thought I could make a very good defence. Of food, I could find none in a fit state to carry away, except a packet of biscuits; but these were something in our distressed condition; and I luckily discovered in the side-board drawer a hunting-flask containing some brandy. With all these various articles gathered together, I returned to Bessy, whom I found standing very nearly where I left her. Then, leaving her for a few moments to dress herself, I went to the half-open door and looked out. I had not been there a minute when, across the further end of the open space, three or four hundred yards distant, I saw a negro pass, with a gun upon his shoulder. I drew instantly back, but still continued from behind the door to watch the course he took. He did not look towards the house, however, but marched on with a sort of exulting step, as of one who had done great deeds. Perhaps it was prejudice, perhaps not; but I could not help thinking he was one of the murderers, rejoicing in the retribution he had inflicted upon those who had deprived him and his race of liberty. In a few minutes Bessy joined me, and I asked her where the path in the wood led to, in which I had seen the negro disappear.

"That is the way to Jerusalem," she answered--"at least one way. There is another path here at the back of the house, but they soon join."

"Then I fear we must not direct our course thither," I answered. "I have just seen an armed negro pass that way; and, I doubt not, he has others before him. Were he alone, he would be soon dealt with; but, in all probability, they have marched to make an attack upon the town." She seemed very much alarmed, and asked, in almost a despairing tone,--

"Then where shall we go, Richard? My uncle Henry's house lies up in the same direction. Good God! I hope *they* have not been attacked and murdered too."

"I hope not," I answered. I could express nothing except hope; and that, to say the truth, was but feeble. It was exceedingly difficult to determine on what to do. Every course presented dangers; and to remain where we were was, undoubtedly, very perilous. If the actual murderers did not return, other bands of revolted negroes would probably visit the houses that had been attacked, for the purpose of plunder. In the fields and woods we were likely, at some point, to meet with the insurgents; and it was evident, that when they murdered young girls and infants, they would spare no white person. Still the woods afforded more means of concealment, and a wider space; and I was just about to propose to Bessy to betake ourselves to their shelter, when she suggested that we might find horses in the stable, by which we could reach the high-road, and ride in any direction we might find reason to believe was open.

"At all events," she added, "we shall find some white people there to give assistance in case of need." I caught at the idea eagerly; but we were disappointed. The horses had all been taken away, and not a soul was left in any of the negro cabins. An anxious consultation followed; but the only course we could decide upon was to seek the cover of the woods again, to find out some quiet and concealed spot, and to wait there till the sun set; then, under the veil of night, to make our way, as well as we could, to the county town, where we believed all the gentlemen of the neighbourhood would rendezvous in sufficient force at least to keep the insurgents in check. We took the path at the back of the house, which, at all events, would carry us some distance on the way we intended to go, and walked on for about two miles, looking behind from time to time, and keeping a vigilant eye on the road before us, which, luckily, was very nearly straight.

"Bessy, dear love, you are tired," I said, as I felt her lean heavily on my arm. "Let us turn into the wood here, and rest a while. I neglected to load the arms I procured in the house, and I may as well do it now."

"I do not think Jerusalem can be more than four miles distant," she answered, "and I can go a little further, Richard; we had better get as near as we can. Besides, about three quarters of a mile on, this path joins the other, and we can better discover what is going on, if we conceal ourselves just between the two." We proceeded on our way for about half a mile further, when, suddenly, from some distance in front, came the rattling sound of musketry. It seemed but one straggling volley; but, the moment after, I thought I heard the sound of horses' feet at the gallop. Catching Bessy up in my arms, I carried her through the underwood, to a spot where I thought we could lie concealed. I set her gently down upon the turf, and, placing myself partly behind a tree, looked out towards the road. A minute had hardly passed when three negroes, on horse-back, rode by at full speed. I was strangely tempted to give them the two charges out of my gun, but the thought of Bessy restrained me, and I contented myself with listening eagerly to ascertain if others were flying along the road, which I knew must lie upon the right hand. In that direction I could hear no sounds, however; and, seating myself by the dear girl's side, I said,--

"Three of these villains have just passed right along the path which we came up. They must have had a brush with some of our friends near the town. This is hopeful, dear girl; for it shows that the gentlemen are rallying in force at Jerusalem, and if we can make our way thither to-night, we shall probably be safe."

"Then the negroes are defeated!" she exclaimed, clasping her hands with a look of thankfulness; "they are defeated and flying!"

"Nay," I answered, with a smile, "three are certainly running away; but I fear, dear Bessy, that is no indication of the result of the skirmish. Very few affairs of this kind take place without more than three running away, even of the victorious party. It will be better to stay here, and pursue our way after nightfall. We have shade and a soft turf, and plenty of wild flowers and singing-birds; and if we could but forget the terrible scenes we have just passed through, we might spend a few hours here pleasantly enough, even though I have nothing but biscuits to regale you with."

"I thought, Richard, we had no singing-birds in my country," said Bessy, with a touch of the old spirit in her tone, though greatly saddened.

"Oh, yes, you have, dearest," I. answered; "I have found one since, which I will still try to cage." Oh, the bright light that sometimes breaks through a dark cloud! Gloom, sorrow, fear had beset us during the whole of the preceding night and that eventful morning; but every step, every moment, had strengthened the bonds between Bessy's heart and mine as we went on together in the truest and most touching relation of woman to man--the protected and the protector. The agitation and the danger, too, lent the charm of contrast to the comparative calm and security with which we sat in that sequestered spot uncrossed by any path; and, as we partook of our scanty meal, with my arm supporting her waist, and her shoulder partly resting on my bosom, we both tasted a kind of happiness, only brightened by the gloom of all around, which is seldom vouchsafed to any in the course of this troublesome life.

CHAPTER XXI

Bessy and I had time enough to talk over many things; yet no word of love was spoken between us--no reference made to the subjects which had so completely engrossed us not eighteen hours before. She was completely in my power. I might have said what I pleased, exacted what promises I pleased; but I would not take so cruel an advantage of her position. There was something so trusting, too, so confiding, so utterly and entirely reliant in her own conduct, that I should never have forgiven myself in after years if I had shown the least want of generosity in deed, or word, or thought towards her in such a situation. Nor, indeed, was it at all necessary to say anything. Her head rested on my bosom; her beautiful eyes looked up confidingly in my face; her hand lay clasped in mine. What need of words to speak all that was in our hearts? As old Sterne truly says, "Talking of love is not making love;" and it was sufficient for us to feel that we did truly love each other. Two or three hours passed by, and they did not seem long. Everything was still and quiet around us. There was no further sound of musketry, no galloping of horse. Once or twice I left her for a few minutes to approach as near as was prudent to the one path or the other, which were here separated by a belt of wood not more than three hundred yards wide. But nothing could I discover. No sound met my ear; no moving object was to be seen as far as the trees would let my eye penetrate. I believe--I even then believed--that we might go on in safety. But, ever self-deceiving, human nature would not let me act upon the belief which was really in my heart. Those hours there with Bessy were so very, very sweet, that surely I may be forgiven for conjuring up imaginary dangers, and forcing myself to believe them real; and summoning prudence and discretion to second the voice of inclination. Dear Bessy, did you not give in to the self-delusion too? It was very warm in our little sheltered bower; for though the trees kept off the sunshine--the fierce Virginian sunshine--they deprived us of the breeze which we only knew to be blowing by the waving of the tops, and the whispering of the higher leaves as they jostled each other amid the bending boughs. Traces of fatigue were on Bessy's face; and I coaxed her to go to sleep, persuading her it would give her strength for our onward walk. It was very pleasant to watch her while she lay with closed eyes; and when I had been gazing upon her in the early morning, I could not make out what was the especial charm. There must be something, I think, in the aspect of peace and calm--not without life, but living, animated, perfect tranquillity, so harmonious to the latent hopes and expectations of immortality, when all shall be absorbed in the serene and deep sense of God's great goodness, that the contemplation of even a faint and inadequate image of such a state fills the bosom with strange and bewildered admiration. Bessy needed no great persuasion indeed, for her eyes were very heavy; and besides the omnipotent and ever watchful Eye, there was another loving wakefulness to watch over her. She leaned upon my shoulder, and her eyes closed. Then, suddenly, she opened them with a start--some memory of danger or of grief crossed the still waking fancy--and then the sweet eyes closed again, and she slept profoundly. I could have slumbered too in such dear proximity; for I also was somewhat weary, and felt less strong than was my wont. But I would not suffer an eye to close while there was danger near my treasure. An hour, perhaps an hour and a half, passed. I could not tell how the day had gone by, for I had forgotten to wind up my watch, and it had stopped; but I judged by the aspect of the sky that it must be near four o'clock. Sometimes I had gazed on Bessy as she lay, and thought to myself, how false a forger must nature be if the writing on that lovely face did not speak a noble, sweet, frank spirit below. Then I remembered an old picture in my father's house, of the Children in the Wood, nearly in the same attitude as we lay there, and as innocent of evil thoughts as we were. I smiled at the quaint comparison that wove itself in my mind between those babes and ourselves. At other times my eye roved round our little shady resting-place, and my ear was turned to catch any sound that might announce the approach of danger. Two pistols and the gun lay beside me, and the other two pistols in my pocket were in reach of my hand. To say sooth, I had some confidence both in my courage and my dexterity, and I doubted not that I could give a good account even of a numerous body of assailants. Yet all was so peaceful that there seemed to me no danger, and I fondly thought we should reach the county town that night and find security there. Peril, by custom, loses its fearfulness; and I could willingly have passed many a day with Bessy in those wild scenes, even with all their anxieties, had it not been for her sake. But I felt that she could not bear such excitement long; therefore I was anxious that it should all come to an end, even though the tediousness, and the dulness, and the oppressiveness of formal society were forced upon us, instead of the wild, genial freedom of the woods. About four, however, as my eye rested upon the ground before us towards the junction of the two paths, something seemed to arise through the low bushes at the foot of the trees, which rather puzzled me. At first, I thought it proceeded from the early mists of evening. It was like the blue hazy vapour which ascends from the ground at the close of a warm day; and it lingered and spread out among the shrubs and bushes without using above a foot or two from the ground. It speedily increased, however; and, from one particular spot, went up a bluish-white cloud, rolling in graceful sweeps up to the tree-tops, and spreading itself in ever-varying circles as it went. It was evident, at length, that some one had lighted a fire in the wood at no great distance. Now, indeed, there seemed cause for anxiety. The wind blew from us towards the spot whence the smoke arose, so that I could catch no sound of voices, even if any were speaking there. Still, that some persons were very near us was certain; and that they were a party of the revolted negroes was more than probable. Various considerations engaged my mind for several moments; but, on the whole, I thought it would be better to wake Bessy, and remove as quietly as possible to some more distant spot. What she had been dreaming of I know not, but it was evidently something alarming; for when I spoke to her and gently raised her head, she uttered a quick cry of fear. It was very low, but it was sufficient, as the wind then lay, to reach other ears than mine. I was explaining to her what I had seen and what I thought best to do, and pointing in the direction of the smoke, when I saw the bushes move, perhaps thirty paces in advance.

"Lie down!" I whispered, withdrawing my arm from around her body; "lie down, and keep quite still, whatever happens. There is somebody coming through the wood. I have the lives of six here beside me, and then I have the sword. I do not think they can be many; and if not, I am their master." Bessy obeyed without a word; but put her hand over her eyes, as if to shut out more completely the sights which she thought were to follow. I quietly raised the gun, which I had reloaded with buckshot, and, placing it to my shoulder, levelled it at the spot where I had seen the bushes move, resolved not to fire until I could fire effectually. A moment after, a branch was agitated somewhat nearer and more to the right; and my aim was instantly directed there. Again the same indication showed the person approaching nearer still, and I followed the waving boughs with the gun. At length, a dark face appeared, peeping through the leaves, not more than twelve yards distant; but, luckily, at the same moment, I perceived the gaudy colours of a printed handkerchief, such as is very commonly worn on the head by the negro women in that district. A minute after, a voice exclaimed,--

"Master, master, put down your gun. I not come to do you any harm. We run away like you." I dropped the point of the gun, but still kept it in my hand, watching eagerly the ground in advance, lest the woman should be followed by any of the murderous bands that were roving through the country. The bushes seemed all still, however; and, quietly and timidly, she came on, as if still fearful of the weapon in my hands. She was a girl of about eighteen or twenty years of age, and a dark mulatto; but well formed, and of a frank, good-humoured countenance.

"Ah, Miss Bessy," she cried, when she came within six or seven feet of us, "is that you? You must have had a hard time of it, I reckon. Oh dear! oh dear! that this should ever come to pass! Why, how did you ever come to get away? Those nigger-devils have killed every one at Mr. Stringer's, minister and all--him who preached to them so fine. I dare say he wish now he had not told 'em to kill their masters. He little thought he have his own head split with a hatchet." Bessy had risen, and gazed for a moment on the speaker, as if she did not recollect her, and the girl continued:--

"Why, don't you remember Minerva, who lived with Mr. Travis? Ah, they killed my poor master and missus, and even the poor little baby, Eddy; and never say one word to the women, but go about murdering in de night; and so we all go frightened and run away into de woods, for we did not know that our turn might not come next, for dey are all so furious; and Nat Turner say he is sent by de Lord to kill and to slay and to 'terminate all on whom he finds de mark. Now, who can tell whether she has got de mark or not? So five of us come away here, and all the rest have gone away, I do not know where, and taken de children wid dem." While she had been speaking, I had still kept my eyes upon the brushwood before me, and had satisfied myself that no one followed her; and Bessy, who had been somewhat bewildered at first, both by the news of the danger and by being suddenly woke from her sleep, now recognized the girl, and said,--

"I remember you now, Minerva. You were the child's nurse, were you not? I do not think you would betray us or injure us."

"I would not for my life, Miss Bessy," replied the girl. "I would die to help you, but would do nothing to hurt you." We Englishmen are not very fond of warm professions, for we rarely make them ourselves, and have no allowance for different customs, blood, and temper. Yet the girl's face looked frank and open; and I invited her to sit down beside us, wishing to extract any information she might possess. It was not much that she could give; for, as I think I have elsewhere remarked, there is not a perfect sympathy between the mulatto and the black race. The former are inclined to be somewhat conceited upon their approximation to their masters; the latter view the mulattoes with a certain degree of contempt and dislike as inheriting a portion of the blood of the slave-holder, without his power or intellect. They often intermarry, it is true; still this latent sort of aversion prevails; and you will always hear the negroes speak of the yellow man or the yellow woman with a cold and slighting tone. On the present occasion, it would seem, many of the mulattoes entertained some apprehension that the vengeance of the negroes would be extended to them on account of the white blood in their veins. This was especially the case amongst the mulatto women; and Minerva told us, she had only ventured to hold communication with some of the people of her own colour. From them she had learned that from thirty to forty white persons had been slaughtered during the preceding night; that being attacked totally unprepared, no resistance had been offered, and that the negroes in the morning, in considerable numbers (swelled doubtlessly by her imagination), and armed and mounted, had marched upon Jerusalem, intending to sack and burn the town. They had been met upon the road, however, at the distance of about a mile from where we then were, by a body of armed white men, who had fired upon and dispersed them. But she added, what was very important in our eyes, that they had since reassembled in greater force than ever, and had murdered a party of four white people whom they had met upon the road. She could not give us any of the particulars, for she had only heard them from a mulatto man, who had heard them from somebody else. We must all have had cause to know--sometimes to our cost--how dangerous it is to rely upon current rumours in times of peril and excitement. It seemed to me, too, that the girl was inclined to shirk some of my questions. I asked Bessy, therefore, in Italian, which she spoke very well, if the woman was to be relied upon.

"Oh, yes," she answered; "I have always heard her spoken of as a very good, honest girl, although, doubtless, she, like all the negroes, is inclined to magnify whatever she hears."

"Were the white men who you say were killed upon the road armed?" I asked, turning to the girl.

"Yes, that they were," she said; "for the gentleman told me there was a terrible fight. But all the white men were killed, nevertheless; de niggers were too many for them."

"Can you tell which way the black men went after that?" I inquired.

"No," she answered; "I know nottin' about dat; only dey did not come down here, or we should have heard de horses' feet.

"Three men passed by on horseback," I observed, "and the rest may have been on foot."

"Oh, no," she cried, "dey all got horses; dey take de horses, and de guns, and de gunpowder, wherever dey go. Dey took all ole master's horses after dey murdered dem all. Oh, I wish I knew who it were dat murder de baby, I would tear his heart out." And a look of fury came into her eyes, that could not well be feigned.

"Dat Nat Turner is de head of it all," she continued. "He tinks himself a prophet; but I tink him a devil; for who but a devil would murder poor innocent babes and young children?" Here our conversation paused for a moment or two; and then Bessy inquired the names of the other four women who were with her brown companion. She repeated them severally, and at the mention of one of them, I could see that Bessy's countenance fell.

"Why, how came you with *her*, Minerva?" she inquired. "I have heard she is a very bad woman."

"Ah, well, dat's true," answered the girl; "she *is* a bad woman, Miss Bessy, and beat her own children, and get drunk, and all dat; but then she was master's slave, and she is so nearly white dat all de niggers hate her, and Nat Turner once said he would kill her if she didn't mind. Dat was when she break her husband's head wid de stone bottle--so we could not refuse to take her wid us, for dey would kill her, certain sure." This seemed a very reasonable account of the matter; but we had no time to consider much farther, for while she was speaking, another mulatto woman, considerably older, whose approach I had not remarked, suddenly appeared in the brake before us, and Bessy started up with a look of pleasure, exclaiming--

"Ah, Jenny, is that you? I am very glad to see you."

"Ah, Miss Bessy, Miss Bessy!" cried the woman, taking her in her great fat arms, and giving her a kiss, while the tears ran over her cheeks. "Thank God you have, escaped! I thought that noble gentleman would take care of you. And when I went over the house--that terrible house--and all the corpusses lying about, and the poor boys with their brains dashed out, and that McGrubber at the top flight of the stairs, all hacked and hewed with the axes, and found your room empty, though the door was all broken to pieces, I did hope you had got away. Yet my heart failed me to think what would become of the dear child."

"This is the cook at Beavors, Richard," said Bessy; "she was dear aunt Bab's cook too."

"Oh, I remember I have seen her," I replied, "the day we went over and took possession of the house in Mr. Stringer's absence. Jenny, I am very glad to see you here. But did anything happen to make you quit the house after you had stayed so long?"

"Dear, yes, sir," answered the good woman. "I heard they were killing all the yellow people as well as the white, and I thought it better to get out of the way; though, afterwards, as I walked along, I called myself a great fool for my pains, and I don't believe the story now; I think it's all a lie. But as I passed by here, I saw smoke in the woods, and heard women's tongues, and that made me come up. But you must not think, Sir Richard, that all the black people are as bad as Nat Turner and his gang. Only two of all the men at Mr. Stringer's would join them, and I will take my oath that none of my dear old missus's servants would lift a hand against a white man after all you did, and got them out of the hands of the dealer, and had to fight and be wounded to prevent them being taken to Orl[ee]ns." I could not help smiling at the curious version she had got of my quarrel with Mr. Robert Thornton; but I found afterwards that the general notion of the poor people was, that their remaining in Virginia had entirely depended upon the result of my duel with that worthy gentleman. If he had killed me, they thought they would have all been sent away at once to a place of which they seemed to have a particular dread. But other considerations pressed strongly for attention; and, after musing for a moment, I said,--

"I fear that smoke may betray us to some of the wandering parties which may be about. What have they lighted a fire for, Minerva? They cannot want a fire on this hot day."

"Oh, but dey want something to eat," replied the girl; "and old Lou is roasting a rabbit she snared."

"Oh, there is no fear, Sir Richard," said Jenny. "They have all gone the other way; besides, they tell me a number of them ran away with buck-shot in their skins, and they'll be a long time before they come back again, I reckon. Why, the road all the way to Jerusalem 's quite clear now."

"I wish I could believe it so, Jenny," I answered; "for I want to take Miss Davenport there as soon as possible. But I understand there are some thirty or forty in the band; and though I would defend her to the last, I should soon be overpowered by such a number."

"Ay," answered Jenny, "there were sixty of them this morning--I counted them myself; but there are not so many now. They have begun to melt away, and there will soon not be twenty of them left together, unless there are others coming up that I don't know about. But you can soon satisfy yourself, Sir Richard; for if you just walk along, keeping in the inside of the woods, with the sun a little bit to your right, at the end of about half an hour you will come upon the high road; and if you see no trace of them between this and that, you may be sure that it's all clear. They won't venture on the high road in a hurry again; for the gentlemen are all assembling at the town, and are too many for them. I'll go with you, if you like, and show you the way. I'm not afraid. Indeed I should have gone to Jerusalem myself, only it's not pleasant for us poor creatures. The gentlemen take us up because we are black, and the niggers kill us, because they say we are yellow; so what are we to do?"

"Let us go on, Richard," said Bessy. "I do not think there will be much danger." A moment's thought, however, made me resolve, before I took her with me, to reconnoitre the country in front by myself. It was evident that Jenny's information, like that of the mulatto girl, Minerva, was merely upon hearsay; and I did not choose to risk the life of one very dear to me upon the strength of vague rumours. Besides, Bessy had now with her one on whom she could depend, and who, in some respects, might be more serviceable to her than even I could be. Jenny, in all probability, knew all the paths and by-roads in a country in which she had been born and brought up. She knew the customs and ways of the people, and could judge of their movements and their purposes much better than I could do. She was, moreover, a very stout, powerful woman, and did not seem to lack courage or decision; all very serviceable qualities of body and mind in the circumstances wherein we were placed.

"I will go on, dear Bessy," I said, "and see what I can discover for a mile or so in advance. I will return as soon as I have satisfied myself that the way is clear. In the meantime, you stay here with Jenny till I come back, unless you find some cause for apprehension. In case you are obliged to leave the place, tear up a handkerchief, or this paper, in which the biscuits were wrapped, and drop the pieces on the way. You had better keep these two pistols with you. The sound will reach me a long way, and would, I suspect, frighten these scoundrels more than the shot."

"Oh, give me one of them, Sir Richard," said Jenny; "I'll shoot 'em if they come here, and then break their skulls with the hammer like a cleaver."

"Here is a bigger one, Jenny," I said, giving one of the larger pistols I had found at Mr. Travis's. "You will protect your young mistress, I know, Jenny. Dearest Bessy, you are not afraid to stay till I come back?"

"No," she answered, faintly; and then added, "I would rather go with you, Richard; but I will not embarrass you, and perhaps you judge best; only

do not be long, dear Richard; for I shall be fearful for you till you return."
I took a step or two forward; but then my heart smote me for a piece of
selfish forgetfulness; and, returning, I inquired of Jenny whether she had
seen anything of my poor servant Zed.

"No, I have not, sir," replied the woman. "Poor old man, I don't think
they would hurt him: he was as black as any of them. Oh, he must certainly
be safe; for I should have found him somewhere lying about if they had
killed him. Besides, what should they kill him for?" I explained to her how
he had devoted himself to give Bessy and myself time to escape. But she
still retained the same opinion; asserting that he must have got away before
the door into Bessy's room from the corridor had been broken down. Thus
she forced me to be satisfied. I walked away again towards the south-west.

CHAPTER XXII

My progress was somewhat slower than I had anticipated; for, in many places, the bushes grew very thick, and tangled underwood sometimes prevented the possibility of advancing in a straight line. Occasionally, too, a piece of swampy ground retarded me sadly; but after having once caught sight of the wider part, or rather wood-road, on the right, I always returned to within a few yards of it whenever any impediment forced me to make a circuit, knowing that it must necessarily lead into the high-road to Jerusalem. I thus exposed myself, it is true, to some danger of being seen. But we are all, I suppose, curious creatures in one respect. Whatever may be said of man's selfishness, and by whatsoever strange cause a sort of transposition of self into another may be supposed to be brought about, certain it is that he who is the least careful, perhaps reckless, of his own life, becomes wonderfully cautious, and even timid, when one whom he loves is involved in the same peril with himself. I am fully of opinion, from the difference of my feelings that day, when Bessy was with me and when I was alone, that no military or naval man should have his wife with him in camp or on shipboard. I felt, as I walked on, as if I could have routed a whole troop of those insurgent negroes. I had a double-barrelled gun, well charged; a pistol and a sword; and I thought I could answer for the lives of four at least. Besides, the conviction grew upon me that these men would be easily disheartened. The murder of women and children, I thought, could be no very exhilarating remembrance; and whatever may be said of the courage of despair, I am certain that the man who fights with a rope round his neck is sure to fight ill. However, neither I nor they were put to the test upon the present occasion. All was quiet as I walked along; and athwart the path, wherever I caught sight of it, poured the calm beams of the declining sun, unchequered by the shadow of a living thing. Several times I was tempted to go back by the thought of Bessy, and the fear that some danger might approach her during my absence; still, I believed it better to make sure that the wood, up to the junction of the two roads, was clear, and I walked on. At length I came to a spot where, through an opening of the trees, I caught a glimpse of what seemed a sandy streak running along before me; and a moment after I heard a voice crying,--

"Hi, hi! haw, John, haw!" I hurried on with a glad heart, in the thought that I might find some farmer driving his team to the town. When I came within sight, however, I perceived it was only a negro carter, sitting on a barrel in front of a heavily-laden cart, and driving a team of oxen by his voice along the high-road to the county town. At first, I was tempted to send a message by him to the sheriff and magistrates; but, remembering the looseness which besets a negro's tongue, I judged he was more likely to tell it to the first person of his own colour whom he met, than to carry it to those for whom it was intended. He did not perceive me as I stood among the bushes, but went on, now urging his slow beasts on their way, now breaking forth into a beautiful negro song, called "The Shocking of the Corn." The easy indifference with which he went,--his apparent unconsciousness of any subject of agitation or alarm, was a great comfort to me. I argued, in the first place, that the high-road was clear of the enemy; and, in the second place, that the insurrection could not have spread very far; for had he been conscious of its existence, instead of sitting there on his barrel, with his chin bent almost down to his knees, he would have been gazing about in every direction with all the excitable curiosity of a negro. Satisfied that Bessy could proceed in safety towards Jerusalem, I turned upon my steps, and made my way slowly back towards the meeting of the paths. Though my mind was certainly much more at ease, yet I took care to cast my eyes round on every side as far as possible, seeking for any indication that could confirm or impair my sense of security. I met with nothing, however, till I came to a very narrow path, if path it could be called, along which a man might make his way on foot, but which seemed scarcely wide enough for any one to pass on horseback; and yet upon the green grass which covered it, I saw the print of several horses' hoofs. They might have been there when I passed before, but I had not remarked them; and this sight was the cause of fresh anxiety to me, as great as the sight of the savage's footprint to Robinson Crusoe on his desert island. The only thing to be done, however, was to hurry forward and rejoin Bessy as soon as possible. I listened for every sound as I went, but I heard nothing. There was no report of fire-arms, no scream or cry, except that of a blue jay as he flew from tree to tree. At length, I reached the junction of the roads, upon both of which I saw the marks of horses' hoofs. Whether they were fresh or not, I could not distinguish, for the ground was dry and sandy; and they might very well have been left, I thought, by horsemen who had passed in the morning. Pushing my way on through the bushes, I presently came to a little open space not more than a hundred and fifty yards from the angle where the two paths joined, and in the midst I perceived a spot covered with white ashes, and a sort of tripod of poles over it, something like those on which our gipsies swing their kettles. This was clearly the place where the mulatto women had been cooking; but all were now gone, and with a feeling of dread I cannot express, I saw the marks of horses' feet here also. After one hasty glance around, which afforded no indication to base any conclusion upon, I hurried on towards the spot where I had left the dear girl with the two women, and made my way straight to it, having taken care as I went to mark particular trees, so as to guide me on my way back. I came in sight of the little bank where it was first seen over the bushes in front. Could I be mistaken? Bessy was not there! Could I have missed the track, and come upon some spot in the mazes of the forest like that where I had left her? Vain hoping against hope! I broke through the bushes like some wild animal pursued by dogs. I came rapidly on the ground. There could be no more doubt or mistake. There were the fragments of the biscuits of which we had made our scanty meal; there the paper in which they had been wrapped; but not a living soul. Oh! how my heart sank! But what had become of her? They had not killed her there, that was clear; for no sign of a struggle was visible, and they were not likely to impede their course by dragging a corpse away with them. Yet I thought I saw upon the ground the traces of men's boots or shoes--large, broad footmarks, and several of them. I could not be very sure, for the ground was hard, and covered with dry grass. What I saw might have been the marks of my own feet, and I stood bewildered with feelings of dread and horror, such as I had never known in life before. I had heard of men losing their presence of mind in dangers and difficulties. I had never known it in my own case; but now my brain whirled. The thought of Bessy in the hands of those ruffians seemed to confound, almost to annihilate, every other thought; and I stood for more than one minute hesitating, undetermined, like a frightened girl. Reason returned, at length, however. The first thing was to discover some trace whither they had taken her, dead or alive. They must have come from the angles of the roads, that was clear, and probably had gone away by the other side. I examined the trees and bushes with anxious care, and in one part, where they were not very thick, some of the branches seemed bent back, and one twig I perceived was broken. A step or two farther on, a large old tree stood prominently forward, and on its rugged bark near the root was a small fragment of cotton stuff, in colour resembling that in which the woman Jenny had been dressed. This was the way they had dragged them, I concluded, and I went on with steps which seemed sadly slow to the impatience of my spirit. But I was too much alive to the necessity of watching the most minute circumstances, if I would discover any trace of Bessy, to hurry rashly on. At length I came to a place covered thickly with tender wild plants, about the height of my knee, and there I could clearly perceive, by the crushed stems and leaves, that a number of persons must have passed. But here, too, the troop seemed to have separated. The shrubs were beaten down to the left, but very much more to the right, and the party who had taken the latter course seemed to have bent their steps in a direction almost back again. After a moment's hesitation, I took the right-hand track, and found traces of the band for a considerable distance. At length they ceased, or, at all events, my eyes could detect them no longer. The party seemed, in fact, to have separated, each man pursuing a course by himself; and I stood anxious and confounded, not knowing which way to take. I cannot describe the pain of that moment; and now that it is all over, it is hardly possible to convey to you all the fears, the pangs, the anxieties, that pressed upon my mind and overloaded my heart. The scene of blood and horror which I had witnessed at the house of Mr. Travis, the blood dabbled bodies of the two lovely girls who had been torn from their beds and gashed to death with hatchet-wounds, the infant with its brains dashed out upon the floor, were all present to my mind at that moment, and all connected themselves with the thought of her I loved, and seemed only to illustrate the fate of Bessy Davenport! I felt as if I should go mad; but there was an eagerness, a fierceness, pervading the wild, tumultuous sensations within me--a spirit, good or evil, which seemed to cry eternally, "Find her! find her, dead or alive! and take vengeance on her murderers, if thine own life be the sacrifice!" I could not consider accurately, or scan earnestly, which was the way the larger or less bodies had taken; but after a moment of confused and doubtful pause, I plunged headlong amongst the bushes, forcing my way through the tangled laurels, as they are here called, till I came to a more open space, where older trees rose out of the turf with very little undergrowth. The struggle with the obstacles in my way certainly had not calmed me; but many a rapid thought had passed through my mind as I forced my path on, and I paused on the more open ground to try to compose and direct my thoughts. The sun was now hardly an hour above the horizon; his slanting beams passed in long stripes of light between the boughs of the old trees, and gilded the grass beneath them; and as I gazed round, I fancied I perceived that upon one somewhat various and circuitous track, every here and there, was a dark little spot of shadow, as if something had depressed the turf, and left an indentation which interrupted the long lines of light. It was a man's footmark, and eagerly I followed it for near a quarter of a mile. At the end of that distance, I know not what it was made me pause. I have heard of people, who, like some of the inferior animals, have a sense, a strange mysterious impression of the vicinity of some noxious creature--of a snake, a crocodile, a tiger. Such seemed, at that moment, the case with me. I felt as if something loathed and dreaded was near, and slackening my pace, and stepping noiselessly, I advanced through the trees into one of those little open brakes which were frequent in the forest. The moment I did so, my eyes fell upon a tall negro-man lying at the foot of an oak, with a musket by his side. As he lay, his face was turned a little away, and the boughs cast a deep shadow over him; but the sound of my footfall, light as it was, made him snatch up his gun, and start upon his feet in a moment;

and, with a strange feeling of satisfaction, I saw Nat Turner, the leader of revolt, before me. His musket and my gun were instantly levelled, and I heard the cock of the musket click; but the next instant, the sun shining full on my face, he recognized me, and exclaimed,--

"Hold hard, Englishman, hold hard! If you fire, you will never know what you want to know." The hope of finding Bessy was all powerful, and as he still held his musket at his shoulder, I exclaimed,--

"Ground your arms, then, and I will ground mine." He obeyed at once, trusting without hesitation to my honour. I dropped the gun from my shoulder, and we stood for a moment or two gazing upon each other, as if waiting to see who would speak the next word.

CHAPTER XXIII

"Well," I said at length, "what have you to tell me?"

"Sit down there," he said, in a calm and even commanding tone, "and speak low; for there are more ears near than yours and mine. I do not want to take you at a disadvantage. If we have to fight this thing out, let us fight it out together; though still I am better off than you are; for you love life, I hate it. You have hopes, I have none, but to do the work upon which I am sent, how much soever I detest it, and then to quit it for the grave." As he spoke, he seated himself where he had before been lying, putting his musket carelessly down beside him, as if he had no apprehension that I would take advantage of any negligence on his part. I was more careful; for what he had said of more ears being near than ours had roused suspicions; and placing my gun close to my hand as I seated myself, I drew the pistol from my pocket, and laid it within reach.

"There is no need of such care," he said, in a somewhat sarcastic tone;-
-"the first loud call, the first gun-report, will bring plenty of others hither."

"I have *your* life, at all events, at my command," I replied. "You cannot escape me; and I do not intend you shall, though my own life be lost the moment after." The man laughed till he showed all his white row of teeth.

"Why, then," demanded he, "should I tell you anything? But be not too sure, Englishman. I would fain spare your life. You are not one of our oppressors; you have never held a slave. Your countrymen, I hear, have set my countrymen free, wherever they were in bondage; and we have no quarrel with you."

"Then why," I exclaimed, thinking of the unhappy McGrubber, "did you kill a man who was the advocate of your emancipation, the bold denouncer of your masters? Why did you chop him to pieces with your axes, in Mr. Stringer's house?"

"Because he did it all for his own selfish purposes," answered Turner; "because he did it all for the political ends of himself, and his party, not for any love of us, or of freedom, or of justice. Do you think we are to be caught by such vain talk? Do you think we never hear from our brethren who have fled to those Northern states? Do you think they do not send us word that they are worse off there than they are here? That they are treated like dogs by the very men who pretended to be their friends? That they are excluded from their churches? That to ride in the same carriage with them is an abomination--to shake them by the hand--a defilement? Do you think that we know all these things and then--although all that these preachers and Abolitionists say is true, holy as the gospel, just as God himself--do you think, I ask, we give them thanks for what they say, when their acts do not accord with their words, and we know by their deeds that they despise and hate us, although they profess to regard us as brethren, and equal with themselves?"

"Well, well," I answered, "all these abstruse discussions are vain. I know nothing of your parties in this land; I have nothing to do with them. I act as I think right myself; and I try to keep my professions and my deeds upon a par----"

"And so you do," interrupted the man.

"The question now is," I continued, "what have you to tell me concerning Miss Davenport?"

"You shall hear presently," he answered. "Last night--a terrible night it was--and nothing but the will of God and His command sustained me in the dreadful work He had appointed me to do----"

"Forbear! forbear!" I cried, my blood boiling with indignation. "Do not blaspheme the name of the Lord, by giving His word as a sanction for the murder, the dark, silent assassination of innocent girls and babes."

"He sent me forth to destroy," said the man, in a gloomy but still a solemn tone. "He told me--He Himself, when, like him of old, I lay in a trance, but having my eyes open--when His visible presence was before me, and I heard His voice within my soul--He told me that Christ had laid down the yoke He had borne so long for me, and that I was to take it up--that Satan and the avenger were loosed, and that I was to go forth and destroy, sparing neither age nor sex of the oppressor. Even as He gave commands to the Israelites of old, so gave He commandment unto me, and the command was to destroy. I have obeyed it to the uttermost, although my heart often quivered when my hand struck firmly. Yet, when we had smitten root and branch in Stringer's house, last night, and I found that Bessy Davenport had escaped, I rejoiced, while all the others were furious, and I said, 'This is God's doing.' For she had been like an angel amongst the people--she had comforted, she had befriended us all. She had sat by my own mother on her death-bed, and had wiped the cold sweat from her brow, and held the cool drink to her lips, and spoke the words of comfort in her ears. She knew no difference between white and black then; and why should I know any difference now? Yet if I had found her, I would have killed her too, for it was God's command not to spare. But the Lord delivered her. It was His doing, and I was grateful."

"Well, well," I cried, somewhat impatiently, "come to the point. It matters little to me what were your motives; they will be judged by yourself and others. All that I know is that you and your companions have murdered in cold blood women and children who could not wrong you."

"Does not he who kills the serpent tread upon her eggs?" said the man, gloomily. "Do you suppose we would have another race of oppressors grow up when we could nip them in the bud? Even worldly policy would say 'No.' But what have I to do with worldly policy, when I Lave got God's command in my heart? Did He not tell me to destroy, to smite them hip and thigh, as soon as I saw the appointed sign in the heavens? When the sun was darkened at noon-day, I was to commence the work, and not to withdraw my hand until it was accomplished."

"Foolish man!" I exclaimed; "that was only an eclipse, a thing that returns continually at fixed and certain periods by the mere movements of the earth and the moon. But, without argument, what have you to tell me? Give me the information you promised about Miss Davenport." He mused for a moment with a very gloomy brow; and although I cannot of course tell exactly what were his thoughts, I believe that the idea of the sign in the heavens, on which he laid so much stress, being a mere natural phenomenon, gave him much discomfort. At length he murmured, as if speaking to himself,--

"An eclipse!--I have heard of such things. No, no; it was the sign--it was the sign. Well, well," he continued, turning his face to me; "I will tell you. Do you remember going out to walk with Bessy Davenport, and sitting with her under an old tree, and a long conversation you had with her, and how she wept and told you, though she loved you, she could never be your wife?--I was very near you then, though you did not know it."

"I did not, indeed," I replied. "But what of that?"

"Well," responded Turner, "I was sorry for you; for I am not without a heart, though you may think so. There was something said about a packet of old letters, and she would not tell you what they contained, though in them lay the bar between you and her. Well, when the men had dashed in the door, and we found that she was gone, the others ran about like mad things seeking for her; but I stood still in the room, and I saw a packet of old letters lie upon the table. I took it up. It is the only thing, I have ever taken, except horses and arms; for I do not rob or steal; but I said to myself--'If ever I see that young Englishman again, he shall see this, and know the truth. Every man has a right to know the truth regarding his own fate.' Here it is, you can take it." Without rising, he drew the papers from his pocket, and held them forth to me. I rose hastily, and incautiously approached him without my arms. He gave me the paper; but at the same moment some evil spirit seemed to come over him, for his eyes rolled wildly in his head, and he murmured in a low, guttural tone--

"Now I could kill you."

"Do not be too sure of that," I answered, retreating.

"Fear not, fear not," he cried. "It is gone. It is a temptation, but it is over. It is pleasant to see the red blood of our enemies, and when we have seen it, we like to see more, and it becomes a thirst; but it is over." I seated myself by my arms again, and put the papers in my pocket.

"As to this packet," I said, "I thank you for it, and will give it to Miss Davenport as soon as I find her. You mistake me, however, if you imagine I will read a word of it before I give it to her. No man of honour would do so, even if he knew his happiness for life depended on it. Now, therefore, tell me where she is? What have you and your people done with her? for I gather from your words that you have not injured her." He gazed at me for a moment with a fixed stare, and then asked--

"Do you not know where she is?"

"No," I answered; "but you must know; for you and your people passed over the very spot where I left her, not five hundred yards from this place." He was silent for a moment or two, and then answered coldly,--

"If you do not know, neither do I." There was something almost sneering in his tone; and starting up with my weapons in my hand, I exclaimed,--

"Turner, you are telling me a lie."

"A lie!" he cried fiercely, rising likewise; "a lie! and that to me, the destroying messenger of God, commissioned to bring down the high, and to raise up the lowly;--to me, who never told anything but truth in all my life!"

"Ay," I answered angrily, for I felt quite sure he was deceiving me. "You are telling me a lie; and if you do not instantly let me know what has become of Miss Davenport, I will send the charge of this gun through your heart." He gave a low whistle, and then a laugh; and I had hardly time to raise the gun to my shoulder, before three stout negroes were by his side, each with a musket in his hand. These were somewhat fearful odds; but there was no escape, and I made up my mind instantly. They might hit, or they might miss me; but I felt very sure that before I fell, I would have two of their lives. The right-hand barrel of my gun for Turner himself; the left-hand barrel for the man next to him: such was the calculation; and then, if I still survived, I had the sword and the pistol left. Long deliberation under such circumstances is neither possible nor necessary. Both hammers were up, my finger was on the trigger, murderers were before, and the next instant I should have fired at any risk, and at any odds. But just at that moment I heard a rushing, rustling sort of sound, close upon my right hand; and, afraid of being taken on the flank, I paused and turned my head a little to see who was coming. At the same moment, a tall, stalwart black man standing on the right of Nat Turner fired his musket, and I felt the ball go through my hair, and slightly graze my temple.

"That is one shot lost," I said to myself, drawing back towards the great tree, and so covering my right side. "He shall not have time to load again." But before I could discharge my gun, the space between me and my adversaries was occupied by two figures which I recognized, indeed, but not quite distinctly in the excitement of the moment and the somewhat waning light.

CHAPTER XXIV

"Hold, Nelson, hold!" cried Nat Turner, in a loud tone; "why do you fire before I give the word? By the Lord, you will bring them all upon us. Do you not know they are close at hand?" These words were spoken before the fresh actors had appeared upon the scene, and just as the man had pulled the trigger; but the next instant, an old negro, with a snow-white head, rushed in between me and the others, and holding wide his arms, exclaimed,--

"Forbear, madmen, forbear! Nathaniel, Nathaniel, wretched dupe of your own superstition, I command you, in the name of the Lord, to forbear! Fly, fly, while the means of escape are left you! Get you down to the coast and away--anywhere, by any means; for destruction is dogging you close, and the avenger of blood is behind you. Poor, misguided, self-sufficient creature, for whom the word of Jesus was not sufficient, escape for penitence and submission; and may God have mercy upon you for the bloody deeds you have done!" As he spoke, I more fully recognized the excellent black preacher, uncle Jack; but, at the same moment, the man who had come with him approached me, and pulled my arm; and, turning round, I saw my faithful Zed.

"Come away, master, come away," he said; "they not hurt him--they dare not hurt him. Come away. A great number of 'em scattered all about. Let us get to Dr. Blunt's as fast as we can."

"Here, take this pistol," I said, "and make sure of a good aim on that man to the extreme left. I will take care of the other two. I will not stir one step till I hear what they have done with Miss Davenport. Steady the pistol against that tree, and take care not to miss."

"Oh, Miss Bessy quite safe," cried Zed; "she gone to Dr. Blunt's too. Come away, master, come away, or we shall have more upon us." While these words had been spoken between him and me, more conversation had gone on, which I did not hear, between the good preacher and the revolted negroes. His words seemed to have some effect. When I looked round, their muskets were no longer raised; but a dull, gloomy look was about them, which augured not well, and I did not choose to leave the old man to their mercy; for I had remarked that they are hard and even cruel to each other when they have the power. Touching the preacher's arm, I said, aloud,--

"Come away, sir, come away. I could take two of these men's lives, perhaps more; for each barrel of this gun is loaded with large buck-shot, which would scatter and kill on either side; but I do not choose to do so. Go on with Zed; I will bring up the rear, and, if they press too close upon us, will fire right in their faces." While I was still speaking, two more of the armed insurgents came up, and gathered round Nat Turner, gesticulating and jabbering in a low tone. Taking advantage of their inactivity, we made our retreat through the bushes, keeping close together, Zed leading the way. From time to time I turned my head, looked round, and listened; but I could perceive no sign of anyone following me, for a hundred or a hundred and fifty yards. At length, however, I heard a rustling in the bushes behind, and I said,--

"Zed, they are pursuing us. Get into the broad path as soon as possible, where we may have a fair sight of them. Here, take this powder-flask and shot-bag. If I have occasion to fire both barrels, give me the pistol instantly; then take the gun and re-charge it as rapidly as possible. You will have time; for each shot will throw them into confusion."

"Oh, Sir Richard, forbear, if it be possible!" said the preacher.

"I will," I replied; "but it is necessary to be prepared, my good friend. If we are to die, let us sell our lives dearly. At all events, so to resolve is our best chance of safety; for even one man, who knows what he is about, can do much against an undisciplined rabble like that." Three minutes more brought us into the wide path, which looked cool and calm, and refreshing in the fading light; but a sound behind made me turn my head ere we had gone a hundred and fifty yards; and I saw the dark forms of the pursuers pouring out of the wood, now at least ten or twelve in number. I instantly raised my gun, and shouted,--

"Keep back, or I will fire upon you!" Courage and cowardice are very curious things. I have always remarked, as a general rule, to which there may be some exceptions, that those who show themselves fierce and sanguinary when there is slight or no resistance, are easily cowed by determination and a bold bearing. The very raising of the gun to my shoulder, though at too great a distance for buckshot to have been very efficacious, made the foremost man halt and recoil upon those behind; and two or three slipped in amongst the trees on either side of the path, to be out of the line of fire. On we hurried as soon as they were brought to a check; and though more than once I was obliged to face about,--for they continued to gain upon us on account of the old man's inability to walk fast,--yet the raising of the gun had always the same effect as at first. At length we began to see the brighter light streaming in at the end of the path from the open fields of the plantations of Mr. Travis and Dr. Blunt. Our pursuers were now within about seventy yards; and I hoped, as they saw us approach the cleared ground, they would cease to follow us, especially as their leader had not shown himself ill-disposed towards myself. But, on the contrary, when we were within twenty yards of the edge of the wood, they hastened their advance to a run, and one or two of them raised their muskets. It was no time for hesitation; and I fired the right-hand barrel straight in amongst them. It was a fair range, where the shot would scatter, but not lose much of its force; and I saw two of them instantly drop.

"O God!" cried the old creature, "that man should be forced so to shed man's blood!"

"Hurry on--hurry on!" I exclaimed. At the same moment two or three musket-shots came dropping round us, but without taking effect on any one; and in another minute we were on the open ground. Our situation was, perhaps, more dangerous than ever at this moment; for we were in a field of tall Indian corn, not yet gathered in; and had they possessed the habits and skill of the Indians, their numbers were sufficient to have surrounded us completely by creeping, unseen, through the long stalks. But, turning to observe their motions, I saw a number of them appear at the mouth of the path, pause and observe us for a minute or two, and then retreat into the wood, as if afraid of showing themselves in the open fields.

"Ay, ay," said Zed, "dey know the white men have been about them, and dey daren't come on. Dey would would have killed you long ago, master, if dey had not thought Colonel Halliday was near, and been afraid to make a noise of firing. I s'pose those fellows who came up last told them he had gone on; but how de deuce dey 'scaped him I don't know. Oh, dey won't come out; dey be afraid he too near still--dam cunning, dam cunning." Nevertheless, I continued to watch the edge of the wood from time to time, till we came to a wide stubble-field, where the view was clear on every side. Then, holding out my hand to Zed, I said,--

"Well, my good friend, I have now time to say I am heartily glad to see you safe and well. My mind has been much troubled about you since we last met."

"Oh, tank you, master, tank you," said Zed, taking my hand and shaking it quite friendly; "quite well, tank you; how you been all dis time?"

"As well as might be," I replied; "but I have a good many questions to ask you. First, however, tell me where we had better direct our steps to now?"

"Oh, Dr. Blunt's," answered the good man; "and de niggers all good and true. We shall be quite safe there. But what you want to know, master?"

"First," I said, "how you got out of that dreadful situation in which we left you at poor Mr. Stringer's." The man laughed; for people of his complexion are true disciples of Democritus, laughing at everything, however serious.

"Oh, I got out very well in the end, master," he said, "though I did think at one time I should have been killed. When first they came to the door, I made a noise in the room to make them think Miss Bessy was still there, for fear they should take it into their noddles to run round to the back staircase and cut you off. But when they began to hammer on the door with their hatchets, I went to the other door and listened, and hearing you open the outer door of the pantry-hall, I said to myself, 'They are safe!' Then I halloed out quite loud, 'She's not here, she's got away, up to some of the rooms at the top. I've come round the back way, but she's gone.' Then I told them to stop their hammering, and I would open the door for them. But they went on and crushed it in; and then those vagabonds, Hark and Will--they are the worst niggers of them all--got me by the throat, and asked me how I came in there? So I told them I came the back way; and then they vowed I had helped her away, and Hark lifted up his hatchet to split my skull. He would have found it a pretty hard one; for once de horse threw me down a bank thirty feet, and I fell on the top of my head among the stones. That did not break it, and I think it would have taken two or three good knocks to get inside. But just as Master Hark was going to try, Nat Turner came up, with a gun in his hand, and he caught the other gentleman's arm, and said, 'Let the man alone. The first man who sheds a drop of our own blood, I'll shoot him dead. Do you think if we get to killing each other, we shall ever get the better of the whites?' Then Hark said, 'That in that case, I must come along with them, and shed some white blood too;' and then I couldn't go back. But I told them I couldn't keep up with them all along of my game leg, which makes me hobble so; and then they said they would put me on a horse."

"And how did you get away in the end?" demanded I.

"Why, I thought at first they had trapped me," answered Zed; "but very soon they heard something stirring upstairs, and they all rushed up together to kill that long Yankee man, who preached to them at the meeting. Lord, how he did pray for his life, to be sure! And what a screech he gave when the first of them struck him! But while they were murdering the poor creature, I sneaked downstairs and opened the door between the two halls, for I had got the key with me, and locked it on the other side, and went away out behind the stables. I wouldn't go to the stables, master, for they were sure to go there themselves after the horses; but I got under a thick laurel-bush, and curled myself up, just like Mr. Stringer's large black, dog used to do in the porch----he! he! he! There I lay snug, and I heard them come to the stables and take out the horses, and turn over the hay and straw to see that there was nobody hidden there; and I heard Hark and Will laughing quite loud, and talking about the Yankee minister. One said, 'He has preached his last preaching;' and t'other said, 'He has screamed his last screaming too; and as he sees we have gone the way he taught us, he ought to be content.' And then they laughed again quite loud." My blood ran cold at the horrible levity which Zed depicted; but I could not help believing, from all I had seen myself, that his picture was a very true one; for there is a sanguinary mirth, as well as a sanguinary fierceness. Nothing like real earnestness of purpose and steadfast determination seemed to exist in any of the revolted negroes, excepting Nat Turner. In all the rest, everything was impulse--the impulse to slay, the impulse to laugh, the impulse to hack their victim with unnecessary wounds. Poor creatures! in their state of ignorance, and almost brutality, they seemed a combination of the child and the wild beast; with the levity and thoughtlessness of the one, and the strength of the other.

"I do believe," I said, after musing for a moment or two, "that this man, Nat Turner, is of a better disposition than the rest, and might, had his mind been well directed, have become a good and beneficent person." Zed shook his head, and responded,--

"Don't think so, master; he is dam cunning, that's all."

"Why he saved your life, Zed," I answered; "and at first he showed no inclination to injure me."

"Ay, ay," answered Zed, "that's all his cunning. He saved my life because he knew it would not do for black folks to kill black folks; and he would not fire at you because he knew that the white people were about, and he did not know how near they were. He would have shot you soon enough, if he had not been afraid of the report of the gun. Why, he was the very first to run up and kill McGrubber, although he always pretended to be great friends with him."

"I am hopeless of that man, sir," said uncle Jack, who had hitherto remained silent. "I had once great expectations in regard to him, and, perhaps, my opinion might not have changed, even in consequence of the revolt and the massacre of white men; for he has peculiar notions regarding himself, is extremely superstitious, and believes he has a right to shake off what he calls the yoke of the oppressor. But the man who can murder in cold blood young girls and innocent babes, is a villain beyond all hope. Here we are, however, approaching the house of Dr. Blunt.--Hold! Let us take care;

there is a man pointing a musket at us from the window. He thinks we are some of the insurgents."

"Keep back then," I said; "I will go forward. There is light enough for them to see me." And, advancing before the rest, I waved my hand, exclaiming,--

"Do not fire, do not fire. We are friends."

"Who are you? What are you?" cried a boy's voice; for I could now perceive that the musketeer could not be above thirteen or fourteen years of age. "Father, father," he added, calling to some one within the house, "here are three men coming, who declare they are friends."

"My name," I said, "is Sir Richard Conway, whom you may have heard of. One of the two men behind me is Uncle Jack, the preacher; the other, my own servant, who saved my life when the murderers attacked Mr. Stringer's house." By this time two or three other persons had appeared at different windows, and one of them exclaimed,--

"Oh, welcome, welcome, Sir Richard! We will open the door and let you in. We are here, as it were, in a beleaguered fortress, and shall be glad of your military experience and advice. Stay a minute and we will give you admission."

CHAPTER XXV

Bolts and bars, which, I should think, had not been used for many a long year before, were removed from the door of Doctor Blunt's house, apparently with some difficulty, for I heard a good deal of thumping within before I obtained admittance. I myself was gladly welcomed; but there was some hesitation about my companions;--not much, indeed, in the case of Uncle Jack, of whom the rumour had already spread, that he was endeavouring, even at the risk of his own life, to appease an insurrection which he knew to be hopeless, and which could only have a course of barbarous massacre, and end in the bloody tragedy of legal execution. My word given for Zed, and my assurance that he had saved my life in the massacre at Mr. Stringer's, succeeded at last in obtaining admission for him also; though much whispered discussion took place amongst some of the gentlemen at the door, of which I could hear some part.

"Why, we have four negroes already in the house," said one.

"Those two will make six, and there are but seven of us in all," added another.

"You have left out Sir Richard and the boy; and let me tell you the latter is as good as any of us," replied the first speaker. "But they only make nine; and what with six negroes in the house, and thirty or forty outside, we might have hard work of it."

"But if Sir Richard passes his word for the man," said a third, "we may be quite sure of him."

"I am quite willing to do that," I interposed; "he has saved my life at the peril of his own; and, whatever happens, I am sure he will be found on our side." At that moment a stout, broad-built, middle-aged man, with a somewhat stern countenance, appeared from some room, apparently at the back of the house, accompanied by no other than my friend Billy Byles. And myself, and the stranger, who was the owner of the plantation, were introduced to each other with the usual words:--

"Doctor Blunt, Sir Richard Conway."

"Sir Richard, I am glad to see you," said Doctor Blunt, in a courteous tone. Then turning to the others, he added, "Admit the man, admit the man. If Sir Richard pledges his word for him, he is quite sure. Now, Sir Richard, permit me to speak with you for a few minutes. You are in the British army, and have seen some service."

"Four or five campaigns," I replied; "and amongst people barbarous enough, though rather more civilized than these."

"Well, sir," continued the doctor, with a tone in which there was some pomposity and a little excitement, "you shall tell us what you think of our plan of defence. We are certain to be attacked to-night; for this is the only house in the neighbourhood which the villains have not assailed. They waited for greater numbers; for they knew that they would meet with resistance here. Pray come into the parlour with me, sir, and we will talk the matter over." I followed him, while Billy Byles remained a few moments to speak a few words with his old acquaintance Zed; and although I was most anxious to see Bessy, and to hear all that had befallen her since we parted, the doctor was so full of the perilous conjuncture which he apprehended, that, in common politeness, I was obliged to delay the inquiries I meditated.

"Now, Sir Richard," he said, closing the door; "you will see that we have two windows in this room facing the orchard, and two in the room similar to this on the opposite side of the hall. The back of the house we have barricaded; fastened up all the windows, put up all the shutters, and only left a little look-out as it were, where some one can be placed to give timely information if the enemy approaches on that side, which I do not believe to be likely. Our precautions, however, will give us time to prepare, in case the attack should take place there. Now that you are with us, we have nine men in all, including my son Simon, and we have plenty of arms and ammunition. I propose to place two men at each window, and to station one at the little look-out at the back, to insure us from attack on that side, and have in each room a negro on whom we can depend, to hand us fresh arms and ammunition." He entered into a good many more details, showing the means of communication from room to room, in case some advantage should be gained at any particular point, and seemed altogether to have a very tolerable notion of defending his premises against a superior body of assailants. He was very minute in his details, however, and I wished to heaven he would bring his long statements to an end; for, although I was by no means insensible to the necessity of preparation and forethought, I was thinking of Bessy Davenport all the time, and paid, I am afraid, little attention to various arrangements of which he thought a great deal, but which, to a man accustomed to such things, were mere matters of child's play.

"Now, Sir Richard," he said, in conclusion, "such are my arrangements. Have you any suggestions to make? I shall defer of course to your military knowledge and experience." I was quite sure he would defer with very great unwillingness, and that his plans must be touched with considerable delicacy. I therefore replied,--

"Your arrangements seem to me to be admirable, Doctor Blunt; and I do not see anything that requires alteration, unless, indeed, you should judge that it would be better to defend the floor above this. You have here very stout shutters and bars. You could place mattresses across the lower part of the windows, upstairs, so as to leave nothing but the heads of your defenders exposed. You are well aware, I know, that an aim upwards, by inexperienced marksmen, is never so certain as an aim down, or on a level. They are always sure to fire either too high or too low; and even if they were to get into the house, we should have the opportunity of firing upon them down the stairs, while we were pretty nearly under cover."

"Why, Sir Richard," he said, "I think myself, that, considering----" I saw he was getting up objections in his mind to any other plan than his own; but, luckily, he was given further time for reflection by the entrance of Billy Byles, bringing Zed with him.

"Zed tells me, Sir Richard," cried my good second, "that you have had a brush with these fellows yourself just now. Let us hear all about it. But first tell us what you think of our arrangements for giving the rascals a hammering if they come here."

"Oh, I think they are excellent," I replied. "I have not the slightest doubt we shall repulse them with great loss."

"I have been thinking," said Doctor Blunt, before Mr. Byles could reply, "and, indeed, Sir Richard judges so too, that it would be better to barricade these windows down below, and make our defence from above. What is your opinion, Byles? You see we should have greater command of the approaches; would be more under cover; and, even if they broke in, could better defend the staircase, when we were already at the top." I had not the slightest objection to his appropriating my view, so that he adopted it; and was very glad to hear Billy Byles approve highly of the arrangements.

"But let us hear, Sir Richard," he said, "what you think of the numbers of these people. Zed says they are about twenty."

"Oh, no," I answered; "his eyes magnify. I could count no more than twelve, and two of those I shot. Whether they are dangerously hurt I cannot tell; for my gun was only loaded with buckshot, and the distance must have been nearly sixty yards. They fell over at once, however, as if they had been pretty hard hit."

"You don't often miss your aim, I fancy," said Billy Byles, with a laugh, for he was just as gay and unconcerned as ever; "but if there are only ten or twelve of these fellows, we have no great cause for alarm, for we could lick them out of the field with our horsewhips."

"You must not *depend* upon their being in such petty numbers," I replied. "Doubtless, they will increase considerably as night comes on; for they were evidently afraid of showing themselves beyond the edge of the woods in daylight; and their plan will be to attack unexpectedly in the night, till they can muster a much larger force than they have at present."

"That is our great advantage," answered Billy Byles. "We are not afraid of showing ourselves in the daylight, and hunting them down wherever we can find them. When I was at Jerusalem three or four hours ago, the gentlemen mustered one hundred and fifty strong; and the dragoons were coming in very rapidly; while parties were spreading all over the country to clear the woods of these villains. I should not wonder if they did not come here at all."

"I differ with you," I replied, seizing what I considered a favourable opportunity to lead to the subject of which I most wished to speak. "I agree with Doctor Blunt in thinking they will attack this house certainly to-night, especially as they know there are so many ladies in it."

"Ladies! my dear Sir Richard," exclaimed Doctor Blunt; "there are no ladies here. The only one who was here I sent away this morning."

"Why, I heard that Miss Davenport was here," I exclaimed, with a degree of alarm which all must have perceived. Dr. Blunt gazed upon me, and Billy Byles turned his eyes from him to me with a look of doubt, and, I must say, of great apprehension also.

"Why, did she not escape from Mr. Stringer's with you?" exclaimed the latter at length. "We all heard so."

"She did," I answered; "but I left her for a short time in the wood, while I went to see if the road to Jerusalem was clear. When I came back she was gone, and I was told, shortly after, she was come hither."

"Poor Bessy!" ejaculated Billy Byles, in a tone of deep feeling; and I turned my eyes sternly upon Zed. I could see the old man was shaking in every limb; and the moment my look fell upon him, he dropped upon his knees.

"Pardon, master, pardon!" he cried. "I only told you so to get you away; because you would stop to fight with four men with muskets, and you nobody but yourself. What good could you do Miss Bessy, getting yourself killed?" I could not speak for a moment or two, and I shook violently, under exhaustion, anger, and the sudden and terrible disappointment I had met with. The man's words crushed out all my hopes, revived all my fears and anxieties--nay, almost drove me to despair. My thoughts were all in confusion; my brain seemed to whirl. Where was she? What had become of her? Was she in the hands of those terrible men? or was she wandering about in the woods, likely to perish, without any one to aid or help her? Or, if she had fled at the approach of the party I had seen, was she not sure to fall into the hands of some other band of murderers?

"You are ill, Sir Richard," said Billy Byles. "Get him a glass of brandy. I can easily conceive what you feel. I know if Lou had been left in such a situation, I should be just as bad. Zed, you rascal, you ought to be licked."

"Well, perhaps I ought, Master Byles," said Zed, still upon his knees; "but I did it for the best."

"Damn the best!" exclaimed Byles; "it is always the worst thing in the world."

"Oh, master, forgive me," cried Zed. "Either beat me or forgive me."

"Leave the room," I said with a gasp; for I felt I could hardly draw my breath. "I cannot, I will not, speak to you now."

"Here, take this brandy, Sir Richard," said Doctor Blunt, "and let us consider the matter more calmly. It may not be as bad as it seems at first. Where did you leave Miss Davenport?" I related, as briefly and as clearly as I could, all that had occurred after Bessy and I took shelter in the angle of the wood; and in doing so, in some degree recovered hope and confidence from the recollection that Bessy was not left alone, and that Zed had more than once declared that some one, whom he called Colonel Halliday, had passed that way with a party of white men.

"Come, come, this is not so bad," said Billy Byles, "if she had got old Jenny with her. That was worth a troop of horse; for she's a 'cute old girl, and knows what she's about quite well. Then, if Halliday passed that way, he has, most likely, taken them all with him to some place of safety."

"But this story may be as false as the other Zed told me," I replied.

"I don't think that," answered Billy Byles; "he had a reason for telling the one lie, and none for telling the other. But I'll soon know. Uncle Jack was with Master Zed, and he'll tell the truth, at all events." Thus saying, he left the room, and returned in a minute, saying,--

"It is quite true; Halliday was there with six or seven men. Uncle Jack saw him in the wood, and, depend upon it, he has taken Bessy away with him."

"I can hardly think she would go," I replied, "without taking some means to let me know she was safe."

"Oh, you cannot tell," said Billy Byles; "he might be in haste; and hurry her away. Halliday is a wild dog, and not to be contradicted by man or woman when he has got any notion in his head; but from your own account, you must be nearly starving, Sir Richard."

"God bless me! I beg your pardon; I never thought of that," said Dr. Blunt. "The stores of our garrison are not very sumptuous, but they can get you a slice of ham and some bread in a minute." The food was soon brought, and a bottle of most excellent Madeira; but I had scarcely eaten two mouthfuls, and drunk one glass of wine, when a boy's voice was heard calling loudly from above,--

"Father, fatter, the moon is just getting up, and I think I see the negroes gathering at the edge of the wood."

"Here, boys, pull in all these shutters," cried Dr. Blunt, "and make them as fast as possible; then each man take his station as he was told before, only at the upstairs windows instead of these. Move up the powder-flasks and the bullets. Don't hurry, Sir Richard, don't hurry; we shall have plenty of time."

"Less time for eating than for fighting and drinking, I suspect," said Billy Byles. "Here, Sir Richard, let me fill your tumbler. I'll take one for company. I say, Blunt, order half a dozen of this Madeira to the rooms upstairs. It is dry work fighting upon cold water."

"Ay, bold Billy Byles to the last," said Dr. Blunt; "but we'll have the wine up, and some brandy too; for some of our people may want a little of that kind of courage, though you don't, Byles."

"Father, father," cried the boy's voice again, "I can see them coming through the corn."

"How many are there?" shouted Dr. Blunt.

"Twenty or thirty, I should guess," replied the boy; "but I can't count them, they are so close together." While all this had been taking place, several men, some black, but mostly white, had been closing the windows and barricading them as well as they could; and as soon as I had drunk the wine which Mr. Byles had poured out for me, I made a little tour through the lower rooms to see that everything had been rendered as secure as possible. I then accompanied Dr. Blunt and the rest of the party to the floor above.

CHAPTER XXVI

While the men were dispersing themselves, some going into one room, some into another, I turned directly into the right-hand room in front, which I judged to be that from the window of which the boy had challenged me as I came towards the house. He was still there, with a gun in his hand, and there was a candle burning on the table.

"This is my son, Sir Richard," said the doctor, who accompanied me. Turning round from his post, the boy shook hands with me frankly. He was a fine-looking lad, with bright eyes, but he could not have been more than thirteen or fourteen years of age. Pointing with his hand, he said,--

"There they come, father; but they are mighty slow about it."

"You had better put out the lights on this floor, Dr. Blunt," I said.--"they will only serve to direct the enemy's fire, and lose us the advantage which the position of the moon gives. We are in shadow here; but you perceive we can see almost every pebble of the ground out there."

"To be sure! to be sure! Well thought of! Put out all the lights," said Doctor Blunt.

"Now, will you go round, doctor," I continued, "and see that every man has his ammunition close at hand? I wonder if these bullets will fit my gun."

"They are quite small," said the doctor, moving away; "you had better put two or three in." When he was gone, I approached the window at which the boy was still standing, and leaning out, took a general survey of the moonlight scene which presented itself before the house. It was one which, at other times, or on any ordinary occasion, would have presented no single point of interest. The ground was very nearly flat, slightly undulating, indeed, towards the eastward, with a small lawn or field in front of the house, and an orchard of what seemed peach and plum trees, at about a hundred and fifty yards' distance. Sweeping all round the horizon, was a dense belt of forest-ground, dark in the shadowy moonlight, like evening clouds upon the edge of the sky, and the space within this barrier of wood was lighted up by the full, clear beams of the rising planet. It was one of those nights which, on this continent, are peculiarly beautiful; when the moon drowns, in her own effulgence, all the stars immediately round herself, but leaves the rest of the sky full of bright luminaries, which, large and full, seem to vie the one with the other in aiding her to make up for the absence of the sun. Fields which had been cultivated, and from most of which the crops had been reaped, to the extent of five or six hundred acres, lay around me within the belt of forest, and on the right extended, first, the stubble field, fifty or sixty acres in extent, and then the wide field of Indian corn not yet gathered in. The maize presents a somewhat curious appearance in the calm moonlight--an appearance, at least, to which we are unaccustomed in Europe, especially when it is ripe. It looks almost white, yet something tells you--I know not well what--that it is not snow which covers the land. Often is it so tall, that a man of full height could pass through it unperceived; but the spring this year had been backward, little rain had fallen, and the corn was considered stunted and deficient. Thus, when I had passed through that field, the long reed-like stalks, with their broad leaves, had not reached higher than my shoulder, and I could now plainly perceive a thick group of dark objects making its way towards the house, still at the distance of a quarter of a mile. All in external nature was very calm and still and pleasant; and the flat and somewhat monotonous scene acquired an aspect almost picturesque, from the accessories of light and shade, and the resplendent heaven above it. But there was that moving group of black objects, which, sometimes pausing for an instant, and always proceeding very slowly and cautiously, kept still advancing towards the house, and added a different sort of interest to the scene. While I was making my survey I continued to charge my gun, and endeavoured, to the best of my power, to calculate the number of the enemy. I could only make out twenty-four; and I do not think I was wrong by more than one or two on either side. In the meantime the boy stood beside me, apparently calm and tranquil, without saying a word. There was an heroic sort of quietude in his demeanour which struck me very much. I knew that through the whole of the south of the United States the idea of a revolt of the slaves is one of those fearful phantoms of the imagination which is present to the minds of all men, although, in the affairs of business, or the excitement of pleasure, they may, from custom, forget it, and take no notice of the shadow of Nemesis which is cast upon the festal board--the sword suspended by a hair, which hangs over the head even of the lord of the feast. They are like people inhabiting a volcanic region, who trim their vines, and sing and dance in their harvests, forgetting altogether the proximity of danger and death, till the first tremulous motion of the earth announces the coming earthquake, and then they start up confused and alarmed by the coming of events which they might have foreseen in the due course of nature. That boy's coolness and tranquillity, in the circumstances in which we were placed, struck me very much. None of us at that time could tell how all these things were to end: no one was aware how far the conspiracy had extended, or what preparations had been made to insure its success. All that we knew was, that the blacks were infinitely superior in number to the whites; that they had risen with merciless fury against their masters; and that they had not yet met with any decisive check: that every house they had attacked they had taken without difficulty, and massacred the inhabitants without consideration of age or sex. Such was our position; yet that boy stood there beside me as cool and quiet as if there was no risk or danger in the coming contest.

"Now, my good lad," I said, after I had taken my survey, "you and I are to defend this window, I suppose."

"I suppose so, sir," he said; "my father told me to stay here."

"Are you not a little nervous?" I asked, with a smile.

"Yes, sir," he answered frankly; "but I always do what father tells me."

"Well," I answered, "there is no great danger, and you are a good, brave fellow. I have seen a good many of these affairs; and it is such hearts as yours that always carry victory with them. Now, I am an old soldier and an officer, so you must obey orders. Go and get a pillow from the bed, and place it on the window-sill. Now, kneel down there; rest your gun quietly over; fix upon the man you intend to shoot, keeping him always under cover of the muzzle, and do not fire until I tell you. I'll bet you a dollar you'll bring him down."

"Won't you have a pillow, too?" asked the boy.

"No," I answered; "I intend to stand here, covered by this corner of the window-frame; but you had better whisper by a hint of what man you intend to fire at, that we may not both mark the same."

"I'll fire at the biggest," said the boy; "I am more sure to hit him."

"And I will take the little one," I answered. "We shall give a good account of both, depend upon it." There was no real levity in what I said; for I could not but feel, that whatever might be the lad's inherent courage, yet with his want of experience in such scenes of strife and bloodshed, there must be some awe, if not timidity. In the meantime Doctor Blunt passed along from room to room, seeing that all his little garrison were well placed, and doing his duty as commander-in-chief very creditably. At length he returned to us, before he took his own post at one of the windows, slapping his son on the shoulder, and saying,--

"Well, Simon, my lad, here you are, under the command of a gallant officer, who, I see, has taken care of you. Do your duty boldly, my son, and we will give these fellows a peppering."

"I will try, father," replied the boy, modestly, and Doctor Blunt continued looking out.

"Ay, they have come into the open ground. They have determined upon it, but I think we can match them."

"You had better, I think, reserve your fire, Doctor Blunt," I said. "If they should perceive us at the windows, as probably they will, let them fire at us first. If they make a rush to break into the lower story, they are lost with the small number they have; for we can pick them off at our ease, if we do it coolly, while they cannot touch us up here."

"Do you give the word, Sir Richard, will you?" said Doctor Blunt. "I will tell the people not to fire till you speak."

"Very well," I answered; "but let each mark his man as he comes up, and keep him constantly covered, that the first fire may be a telling one. Those who have double-barrelled guns had better reserve the second barrel, that they may keep the enemy employed while they are are re-loading."

"I understand, I understand," said my host. "I will go and tell them all; but you cannot expect very well-disciplined soldiers here, Sir Richard."

"We must do our best, my good sir," I answered; "and I have no doubt of the result. One of us is equal to five or six of them, when we are not taken asleep in our beds." Doctor Blunt moved away to give the orders I had suggested, and I again put my head out of the window. The body of insurgents was now not a hundred and fifty yards from the house; but I don't think they saw me, for that side of the building was completely in shadow. They advanced very cautiously, however, taking advantage of the trees of the peach-orchard, to cover their approach; and there was evidently some hesitation at its verge, before they came out in the clear moonlight. They might, indeed, be laying their plan of attack. At length one man came forth, about ten or twenty yards before the rest, and took a leisurely survey of the whole front of the house. I was greatly afraid that some of our party would fire; but all kept still. At length the negro returned to his companions, and then they marched forward in a long, straggling line; each man with his gun raised to his shoulder, covering the upper windows.

"Keep down!" I said to my young companion; "keep your head down, and let them fire. Then raise yourself, choose your man, and when I give the word, pull the trigger." I have always found it a very difficult thing to get men to reserve their fire. There is a sort of natural anxiety to have the first chance, which causes many a shot to be thrown away. There was no nervousness, however, upon the present occasion; and all remained profoundly still, while the insurgents advanced to within about thirty paces of the house. We could now see all the men distinctly; so much so as nearly to distinguish their features, though that is somewhat difficult with a negro, even in the daylight. They evidently saw us too, and our white faces made us a better mark; but, as I had expected, the having to fire upward disturbed their aim. When they were at the distance I have mentioned, the word "Halt!" was pronounced; and the whole line came to a stand. Then there seemed to be some little hesitation; but, after a moment some one shouted, "Fire!" And nine or ten guns went off right at the windows. The glass crashed and rattled above us in the upper part of the frame, and a bullet seemed to strike the wall just below where I was standing; but not a single shot took effect upon anybody in the house. I had a great mind to let them come a little nearer still, that we might be more sure of our aim; but I knew that every one was impatient round me; and, seeing a movement amongst the negroes, as if to make a rush upon the lower part of the house, I gave the word to fire. Every one was prepared; every one had selected his man, and all the guns went off almost at once. Never was such a scene as now ensued. Six or seven of the insurgents fell down at once; and then there was a general scamper. Away they went in every different direction--tumbling over their fallen companions--running against the trees of the orchard--throwing away their guns to fly the better; and showing every symptom of that panic terror which so generally accompanies want of discipline. From the boldness with which they had marched up to the house, and the deliberation with which they had fired, I had not thought that the affair would be so soon over; but they were now evidently routed beyond any chance of a rally; and I gave one tall, big fellow, who was running faster than any of the rest, the advantage of my second barrel. He stumbled and fell, but was up again in a moment, and away, though he must have been wounded. Several more shots were fired amongst the fugitives from the other windows. Running round to Doctor Blunt, I said--

"If we make a sally now, we may capture some of them." Three or four of the gentlemen followed me downstairs; and rushing out, we got into the orchard as fast as possible, amongst the trees of which, several of the insurgents were endeavouring to shelter themselves from the shots which had been coming after them from the windows; though they might have made a good fight of it still, had they not been so completely scared. But no resistance was offered. Three or four ran away across the fields as fast as they could go, when they saw white faces in the orchard; but we captured two of them and marched them up towards the house. On the spot where the negro line had been formed we found the rest of our party, with a lantern and a sort of link or flambeau, examining the fallen. Billy Byles was hauling up one of the wounded men, while Doctor Blunt and another gentleman were stooping down over a tall fellow, who seemed quite dead, and holding the link to his face as if they saw something very curious in it.

"The most curious head I ever beheld," said Doctor Blunt's companion. "Did you ever see such a development? The organ of combativeness enormously full, and destructiveness as big as my fist. I must have that head for my cabinet, doctor."

"Ah, Sir Richard, I see you have brought in a prisoner," said Doctor Blunt, raising his head as I came up with the man I had taken. "This is my friend, Doctor ----, the famous phrenologist."

"Did you ever see such an extraordinary head, Sir Richard?" said the enthusiastic professor of what was then almost a new science. "Why, it is all back; it has neither top nor front. The posterior portion must weigh ten times the anterior. You, sir, what's your name?" he continued, turning to my prisoner. "Do you know who this is?"

"That is Will, sir," answered the unfortunate man;--"that is the gentleman who said we were to kill all the babies."

"There, I told you so!" cried the doctor, rejoicing in the triumph of his art. "He could not help it. That organ of destructiveness did it all. That man should never have been suffered to go loose. Henceforth, if crimes are committed, it is the fault of society. We can always detect the propensity to mischief by the certain laws of phrenology, and our business is to guard against it. If we suffer men like that to go loose, the crimes they commit are chargeable to our own negligence." I was not inclined to stay longer to hear the worthy gentleman's dissertation; and, touching Doctor Blunt's arm, I said--

"We had better return to the house and secure these two men. I must also ask you to do me the great favour of lending me a horse to ride to the county town; for I cannot be satisfied till I see this Colonel Halliday."

"You had better postpone your journey till to-morrow morning," answered the doctor, walking with me towards the door. "Don't you think it will be dangerous to go alone at this time of night?"

"Oh, no," I replied. "These people will not rally; and you may be sure they brought up their whole force. If I am not mistaken, you may look upon the insurrection as at an end. They have met with a check which they will not soon recover; and your neighbours will have much to thank you for, Doctor Blunt."

"Well, sir," replied the doctor, evidently much gratified, "I trust we have done our duty; and if every one will do his duty in such circumstances, the state will have nothing to fear."

"Your gallant young son, sir, has done his duty too, nobly," I replied; "I am quite sure he brought down his man; he was as steady as an old soldier."

"I am delighted to hear you say so, Sir Richard," answered the father, doubtless with a proud heart. "He has been brought up to obey orders, without hesitation, and I trust he has a right--a hereditary right--to courage. His family has not produced a coward, sir, and I trust it never will; but you had better come in and finish your supper, Sir Richard, while they get a horse for you. Will it not be better to have one saddled for your man Zed likewise? He knows the roads more thoroughly than you do, I suspect, and might be of assistance to you in case of danger." I gladly embraced the offer and was not sorry, to say sooth, for some more food. Nor did I altogether refrain from Doctor Blunt's good wine; for I felt that night, more than I ever did in my life, those sensations which doubtless lead many a man to drunkenness--the need of something to keep up my spirits, to enable me to cast off the load of thought, and pursue my course amidst whatever painful circumstances might surround me. I did not drink much, it is true; for out of the bottle of Madeira, set by my side, several of my companions in the late affray came in and helped themselves very liberally. In fact, for the next half-hour, as may be well supposed, the house of Doctor Blunt presented a scene of excitement and confusion sufficient to banish everything like sober thought. Every one was talking; every one was moving about; every one was asking questions, and nobody answering them. Some were examining where the balls had struck; many were describing their own deeds, and telling how they had picked off their man: and certainly if all had been done which they asserted, a dozen negroes must have fallen instead of six. All were talking; some were laughing loudly; and, strange to say, even the captured and wounded negroes were joining in the merriment, almost as if they had been of the victorious, instead of the defeated, party. I saw one fellow sitting in the hall, just opposite the door, with a bullet through his shoulder, and his hands tied behind him, show his white teeth from one end of the range to the other, exclaiming, with a laugh,--

"I wish somebody would tie my hands afore instead of behind. My golly, how hot dat hole feel! I tink dey must shoot wid red-hot shot." At length it was announced that the horses were ready, and I rose to depart.

"What, going, Sir Richard!" exclaimed Billy Byles, coming in. "Hang it, you have stolen a march upon them. I shall go in to-night. Blunt, you had better march the prisoners in. There's no use of keeping them here all night. Hadn't you better wait for us, Sir Richard?"

"No, my good friend," I answered; "I cannot rest satisfied till I hear more of Miss Davenport." Billy Byles was of that sanguine and immovable disposition, which from one success infers that everything else must go right, and he answered,--

"Oh, she is quite safe, depend upon it." Although not an hour before, on hearing of the situation in which she had been left, he had exclaimed, "Poor Bessy!" in tones of melancholy augury, which still rang in my ears. I declined to delay my departure, however; and, shaking hands with young Blunt as I passed, I walked forward to the door, where the horses stood. Zed crept after me slowly, with much the air of an offending dog, who expects, as he follows his master's heels, to have a kick every minute, and keeps himself prepared to jump back and avoid the blow. Much shaking of hands took place on the steps of the house; but at length I mounted, and took my way on.

CHAPTER XXVII

It was as bright and beautiful a night as ever was seen; and the roads through the woods, flooded with waves of light and shade, were full of tranquil grandeur. In one spot, the eye could wander deep into the heart of the forest, guided by the moonbeams, as they rested here upon a piece of green turf, there upon a swelling mass of wild plants; here caught upon the bole of an old tree, there glistening amongst the reeds of plashy savannah. At another time, a deep, heavy mass of giant trees, mingled with evergreens, intercepted the rays, and cast a thick shadow over the path, only enlivened by the prospect of another gleam of brightness beyond. Silently I rode forward. A sudden and momentous strife and excitement had interrupted my thoughts and feelings in their natural current--dammed them up, as it were; but only to flow over again, with deeper, though somewhat stiller, waves. I need not say that all my thoughts were of Bessy Davenport. They were very anxious, very gloomy, very bitter. I blamed myself for having left her at all. I thought that if she had met with danger or death, I should never forgive myself. No language which I can find will convey any idea of the sensations I experienced--the internal shudder, as it were, the wringing of the very heart of my spirit, when my mind rested, even for a moment, on her possible, nay, her probable fate. It was in vain I tried to console myself by trying to think I had acted for the best. The homely but true and startling words of Billy Byles came back to my mind,--"D----n the best; it is always the worst thing a man can do;" and I was ready to pile curses upon my own head for having abandoned, even for a moment, the task of protecting the dear girl, with which Heaven seemed to have charged me. Censure on myself, however, made me feel inclined to be more lenient to others. Poor Zed, though I could not help feeling some bitterness still, had only done, according to his views and capacity, what I had done myself. He had acted for the best; and, softening towards him, I called him up to my side; for hitherto he had ridden two or three horse-lengths behind me.

"Tell me, Zed," I said, "and now, mind you tell me the truth, for I will forgive anything rather than falsehood."

"I will tell the truth if I can, master," answered Zed; "but sometimes, when I'm in a hurry, I can't tell de truth. The lies come so thick and fast, they get all the uppermost, and I have no time to put them down, and get the truth up from de bottom of de well, as men say."

"Well then, take time and do not hurry," I answered. "You say you saw Colonel Halliday in the wood. Was that true?"

"Oh, yes, indeed, master," he answered; "I saw him there, and six or seven men with him."

"Was he on horseback or on foot?" I asked.

"He had been on horseback," replied Zed; "but he left his horses in de path, and went in on foot, just where the two roads meet. I heard him swear he saw a large smoke, and he would know what it was. I did not let him see me, for he is a wild man, and was just as like to cut me and uncle Jack down as not, because we had black skins."

"Then he went right on towards the smoke?" I demanded.

"Yes, that he did," replied the man; "and he must have gone some way down, for his voice sounded quite small when he came out upon the road again, and he hallooed to the people to bring him down the horses."

"Then he did not find any of the negroes?" I asked.

"No, how could he?" answered Zed; "for they did not come up till he was gone. They saw him, I guess, and scattered to keep out of his way. But he came first, that's certain. I can't tell quite sure where he went, for I did not see him go; but he could not have been gone long before you came up." The man's words gave me great comfort; for it seemed certainly more than probable, that if he pursued the course Zed mentioned, he must have found Bessy and old Jenny where I had left them, and taken them away under his escort; although I could not understand how the former happened to have quitted the place without leaving something to indicate what had occurred. She knew--she could not but know--the deep anxiety I should feel; and Bessy Davenport's was not a heart, I thought, to look upon that anxiety lightly. However, still I was comforted. Hope and expectation revived; and as soon as we got upon the high road, I pushed my horse on rapidly towards Jerusalem. He went very slow, it seemed to me; and indeed he was not the very best-blooded animal that ever was mounted. But at length we came to a spot where the town was first visible in the daylight; and there Zed, who knew the whole country well, checked his horse, exclaiming--

"Gorra mighty, master! they have set the town a-fire." At first sight, it seemed so; for up above the little town, rose upon the sky a bright red glare which could be produced by no ordinary cause. I checked my horse, too, and contemplated the blaze for a moment or so; but I remarked that the glare was steadfast, not rising and falling, nor spreading from place to place; and that though some flicker and some rolls of smoke were visible, yet there was none of that rapid change or those thick curling clouds which always hang over a considerable conflagration. In fact, it was more like the glare which hangs over a large and well-lighted city, than that of a fire.

"We will go on, Zed, and see," I said; "I can't tell what this blaze is; the town is certainly not on fire."

"Very well, master," said Zed, without the slightest hesitation; and on we pushed at the same rate as before. As we came to the first houses of the little town, we could hear the loud murmur of many voices, proceeding from the central part of the place; and, riding on, we came upon a very strange and even picturesque scene. I have before described, I think, the little market-place of the town, which the good people of the country have thought fit to call Jerusalem, upon what grounds or pretences it is impossible to discover; for certainly neither in architecture nor construction, nor natural site, does it bear the slightest resemblance to the capital of the kingdom of Judah. However, when the Mount Ida of this country is a hillock, not much bigger than a man's knuckles, and Syracuse is completely an inland town, it becomes clear that the people had very little reference to the Old World in the names they have bestowed in the New. On one side of the square stood the inn, a wooden building of no great extent, with what is called the liberty-pole right in front. When I had been there before, the bright, burning sun had shone distinctly on the groups of farmers and gentlemen coming from the country on business, with their waggons, horses, and dogs. A different light now presented the place under a different aspect. A fire of pitch-pine logs was burning in the middle of the little space, at the distance of perhaps sixty yards from the inn; and close to the building itself were a number of torches, some in the hands of mulattoes or negroes, some fixed to stakes set in the ground, to posts, to rails, or anything to which they could be attached. By the red glare of the fire and of these torches could be seen the fronts of the various houses round; the windows crowded with faces, principally of women, in every sort of dress and undress; and numerous groups of men, scattered over the space below, all armed, many on horseback, talking, laughing, gesticulating, and, in some instances, swearing. In front of the right wing of the inn was a little body of cavalry, not very regularly drawn up in line, nor was every man upon his horse; but there they were about thirty or forty, stout, tall, powerful fellows, who would have put all the insurgents who had ever yet been mustered in Virginia to the rout in a minute. A group of officers, intermingled with a dozen or so of gentlemen, amongst whom I recognized my long-boned friend the sheriff, stood immediately before the door of the inn, all in vehement and eager discussion; while just above their heads was a sort of balcony, running along the whole front of the inn, crowded with ladies, some sitting and some standing. Tremendous was the confusion, great the noise, and terrible the glare; and every now and then a fresh movement and different arrangement of parties took place when a horseman or two would ride in, from this side or that; and from each of the groups several persons would detach themselves, and ride up to inquire what intelligence the new-comers brought. I myself was thus assailed as soon as I entered the marketplace.

"Which side do you come from, sir?" asked one.

"Have you seen anything of the niggers?" interrogated another.

"Did you see anything of Captain Jones's party?" demanded a third.

"Has any fresh house been attacked?" cried a fourth.

"One at a time, gentlemen, one at a time," I replied, "and I will answer you. Then you shall give me an answer to one question. I come from this side of Dr. Blunt's house. I have seen plenty of the negroes--all, I fancy, which they have in the field. I did not meet with Captain Jones's party; and the last house the negroes attacked, or will attack, I imagine, was Dr. Blunt's. And now, if you please----"

"What came of it? what came of it?" cried half a dozen voices, before I could propound my own question.

"They were repulsed with considerable loss," I replied. "Six were killed or severely wounded, two were taken prisoners, and the whole body was dispersed,--I suspect, never to meet in any force again."

"Hurra! hurra!" shouted the little crowd that had gathered round, and off they ran to spread the intelligence over the place. I took the liberty of catching one gentleman, however, by the arm, before he could get away, saying:--

"On my life, this is hardly fair, gentlemen. I have answered all your questions, and you do not stay to answer mine. May I ask if Colonel Halliday has been in the town lately?"

"Colonel Halliday?" cried the good man; "why, yes, he was here not half an hour ago with his party; he may be here now for aught I know."

"Had he a lady with him?" I demanded.

"Oh, yes, a whole drove of 'em," answered my companion, who seemed a bit of a wag. "Funniest sight you ever saw--half of them mounted on horseback in their night-shirts." Thus saying, he broke away from me, and joined the principal group before the inn-door. Towards it, also, I directed my horse; but the gentlemen composing it instantly moved forward in mass towards me as soon they heard the intelligence I brought, and I was surrounded in a moment by twelve or fifteen persons, and overwhelmed with innumerable questions at once. The sheriff alone was quiet and practical.

"Glad to see you, Sir Richard," he said; "perhaps you will give us a brief statement of what occurred at Dr. Blunt's; for if you answer all these questions, we shall have daylight upon us before we have done." As it was evident I should get no satisfaction myself till they were all satisfied, I thought it best to comply with the sheriff's suggestion; but in the meantime all the other groups began to draw near to hear the intelligence also; and I was soon surrounded, and even pressed upon, by at least two hundred people.

"Speak loud, speak loud!" cried one.

"Bring him a drink," said another. "Dare say the gentleman's thirsty."

"He had fighting enough to make him so," said Zed, who kept close to me, evidently in some alarm of the results of the general objections to his colour. I went on with my story, however, making it as brief but as clear as I could, and taking care to notice the gallantry of young Blunt, which called forth a sort of half cheer from the people. But they did not seem to care much about details, and were soon satisfied. Man by man they began to drop off, or broke up into parties to talk the matter over in their own little synods; and, springing from my horse, I took the sheriff's arm, saying,--

"I want to speak a word or two with you, Mr. Sheriff. Take my horse to the door of the inn, Zed--I suppose he will be safe. He is a very faithful fellow, and has saved my life."

"Oh, quite safe," answered the sheriff. "Don't you see we have as many blacks as whites here? This bad spirit is by no means general. Had it been so, we might have fared worse; though it has been bad enough, God knows, as it is." Zed led away my horse; and, being left nearly alone with the sheriff, I explained to him my anxiety about Bessy; told him the cause I had to suppose that she had been found in the wood by Colonel Halliday, and carried to some place of safety; and asked if he had seen that gentleman in the town.

"Oh, yes, he was here a little while ago," answered the sheriff. "He brought in several ladies with him, but I really did not notice who they were. He took them to the inn, I think, and you had better see if you can find Miss Davenport there."

CHAPTER XXVIII

I know no more anxious, more irritating, more painful occupation in the world than that of seeking (when we are apprehensive and doubtful of the fate of one we love) amongst a great, confused and pre-occupied crowd, for some traces of the lost one. It has been my fate twice in life to aid in the search for a strayed child; and the agony of the father communicated itself, in part at least, to me, and gave me the power of feeling a portion of all the torture which imagination inflicted upon him at that moment. Every one we speak to seems so selfish, so volatile, so obdurate, that we can hardly believe there is anything like feeling or sympathy in the human breast; when, perhaps, scanned accurately, our own sensations would be found to be selfish, and our own accusations return upon our own head. Who could tell, in that mixed crowd, what were the motives, what the feelings, what the doubt and dread, which created the sort of fierce anxiety in my heart? Who could see in my look, or detect in my voice, more than the most minute portion of that anxiety? Yet, I felt a very unreasonable degree of anger and irritation at the utter indifference of every one around me to all that was going on within my breast. I forced my way, however, onward towards the door of the inn; but before I reached it, a fresh little party entered in the town, and cut across my path, presenting that strange mixture of the ludicrous and the horrible, which is, perhaps, more dreadful than the purely tragic. Doctor Blunt, the whole of the party from his house, and two or three mounted dragoons, who had joined them somewhere on the way, were bringing the prisoners, now increased to three by the presence of one of the wounded men, who had recovered sufficiently to walk into the county capital. First came two or three horsemen, and some more armed men brought up the rear; but between the two bodies of whites marched the poor black fellows who had been taken, very much as they had appeared when they attacked the house, except that their muskets had been cast away. The first of the negroes (for they marched in single file) was the man whom I had captured myself, with a gay scarf over his shoulders, and a handsome regimental sword by his side, which I had not thought it worth while to take away. He carried something in his hands, which I could not distinguish clearly till he came into the blaze of the torches; and then, to my disgust and horror, I saw that it was the bloody head of one of his late companions--the very head which had so strongly excited the scientific enthusiasm of the phrenologist, who had doubtless cut it off, before he quitted the scene of strife, to place the skull as a specimen in his collection. The party halted directly opposite the inn door, and several of the officers, who were gathered together there, advanced to take a look at the prisoners. One of them seemed to recognize the man with the head, but that attracted his professional eye but little. The scarf and the sword were "matter more attractive;" and, giving a light touch to the hilt of the latter, he said,--

"Why, Nelson, where did you get this?" The negro instantly raised the swarthy head in his hands in the full torchlight, and replied,--

"This here gentleman gave it me last night." A loud burst of laughter, very horrible to hear, broke from the whole party round at the idea of the man's calling a dead negro's head "this here gentleman;" and I must say, the captive negroes themselves, with the certainty of being hanged within a few days after, joined in the laugh as heartily as any of the rest. I could not do so; and pushing my way through the throng, I entered the inn. The passage was crowded to suffocation; the bar, which lay on the right hand, was surrounded by a mob, two-thirds of whom were drunk, and the rest hardly sober; and before I had taken ten steps through the mass, I had been invited to drink at least as many times by persons I had never seen in my life before. I remarked that they did not seem at all pleased when their invitation was declined; but I was in no very polite mood, even if I had been at any time inclined to get drunk for the pleasure of strangers; and I made my way straight for the foot of a staircase, round the bottom of which the crowd was reeling to and fro, not quite so densely packed together. Four or five steps up, supported by two strapping mulatto wenches, was a stout, well-fattened white woman, whom I judged, by her dress, to be the mistress of the house. The moment I set my foot upon the stairs, however, she screamed at me in a tone calculated to drown all the din below.

"You can't go up, sir. The whole above-stairs is occupied by ladies; and as some of them have nought but their night-dresses on, they don't want no company."

"But, my good madam," I said, "I saw two or three gentlemen amongst the ladies in the balcony."

"That's nothing here nor there," answered the Amazon. "Them gentlemen have brought in friends, and have a right to stay with them."

"But I have a friend here, too," I answered, "and I want to see her. I will see her, too. I think you mistake me for some of those people who have been drinking at your bar; but there you are in error. My name is Sir Richard Conway, and----"

"Sir Richard this, or Sir Richard that!" cried the woman, "is no matter to me. You can't go up, so that's enough, and shouldn't if you were Lord Dunmore."

"I want to speak with Miss Davenport," I replied; "to hear of her safety, and to inquire if I can serve her in any way further."

"Miss Davenport!" cried the hostess, in a tone somewhat mollified. "Why, I didn't know that Bessy Davenport was here--have you seen her, Imoinda? Why, I thought she was killed in Stringer's house."

"That she certainly was not," I answered, hating the great, fat, coarse woman from the bottom of my heart; "she and I escaped from Mr. Stringer's house together--I am her near relation, you know."

"Oh, ay," cried the woman, still screaming at the top of her voice, in order to be heard above the din; "you are her English cousin who shot Bob Thornton. But you can't go up for all that." I felt the greatest possible inclination to take her by the back of the neck, and pitch her down amongst the mob below. But refraining with an ill grace, I said--

"I have every reason to believe that Miss Davenport was escorted here some short time ago by Colonel Halliday; but I am not sure of it, and I am determined to ascertain whether she is safe or not. So now, good woman, you shall either satisfy me on that point, or I will bring the sheriff to make you."

"Good woman!" cried the hostess, with her face all in a blaze. "You saucy coon! Why do you call me 'good woman?' My husband, the colonel, shall 'good woman' you. Do you think that you English have got the dominion in the land still? No, no! I think we taught you better, when we whipped you all through the country. 'Good woman,' indeed!"

"Why, surely, you would not have me call you *bad* woman, would you?" I retorted, a good deal irritated. "But I see, I must bring some one who will be able to persuade you better than I can." And descending the two or three stairs which I had mounted, I once more forced my way through the crowd in search of the sheriff. That gentleman, however, was no longer to be seen in any of the various groups immediately in front of the house. I just caught a glance of Billy Byles as I passed out of the inn; but he was speaking to some lady up in the balcony above, and I passed on without interrupting him. From one little knot of people to another I went; and perhaps at any other moment, with a disembarrassed mind, the strange medley of men of wealth and men of none; of men of education and men without; of men of refined habits and men of the coarsest manners; and the perfect familiarity which existed between them all--would have given occasion for much speculation in my mind as an Englishman. But I was too much occupied with the one predominant idea to think of anything else, and I exhausted nearly half an hour in searching for the sheriff in vain. I was just turning back to the inn, when some one called me.

"Sir Richard, Sir Richard," said a voice. And, looking round, I perceived Mr. Byles coming up from the side of the marketplace I had just left.

"I have been looking for you everywhere," he said. "Louisa Thornton wishes to speak to you. They are all here, except Mr. Henry Thornton himself. He determined, like Doctor Blunt, to stay in his own house and stand it out, with some friends he has got there. Mrs. Thornton is frightened out of her wits, and gone to bed, but Lou said she would remain in the balcony till I brought you." I explained to him briefly, as we walked along, the anxiety of my mind in regard to Bessy Davenport, and the obstinate refusal of the landlady to let me pass upstairs in search of her.

"Oh, the old jade!" said Billy Byles, "she's a perfect Turk. They should call *her* the colonel instead of her husband, who is as meek as Moses, poor man! She would not let me pass either, though I coaxed and bullied, and did all sorts of things. But it is about Bessy Davenport that Louisa wants to speak to you. She says she is certainly not in the inn." My heart sank again; but I hurried on, and soon stood under the place where Miss Thornton was leaning over the balcony.

"I wanted to tell you, Sir Richard," said Miss Thornton, after a few words of ordinary courtesy, "that Bessy is certainly not here. Where did you leave her?" I explained to her all that had occurred, and the reasons I had for supposing she might have been brought into the town by Colonel Halliday and his party.

"Perhaps she may be in some of the other houses," said Miss Thornton, "for they are all full; and everybody, all over the place, seems to be searching for some one lost in the confusion of this terrible day. But I hope and trust that no harm has happened to her, as you left old Jenny with her." While we had been speaking, a little crowd had gathered round Mr. Byles and myself; for I must remark that nobody in the United States appears to comprehend that any other person can have private business with which he has nothing to do; and you must lock your door very tight, if you would not have others come and listen to what you have to say. One of the gentlemen who was standing by here joined in our conversation saying,--

"Colonel Halliday, I am sorry to tell you, did not bring in Miss Davenport. I saw him just as he came in about an hour ago. He had with him two negroes, whom he had captured, and three young ladies, whom he had brought from houses along the road--Miss Corwin and the two Miss

Joneses; but I know Miss Davenport was not there, for I stopped and talked to them for a minute." Here at once was knocked away every frail prop and support on which I had built my hopes and expectations. Hope was indeed not destroyed; for hope is immortal, reaching to the grave and beyond the grave. Yet there was no resting-place for her footsteps; a light, pale and faint though not extinguished, flitted, wandering like an *ignis fatuus*, over a wild, an insecure ground, where there was no path to guide, no solid basis to support. Where was she? What had become of her? Who could tell? The glimmering light rested principally upon one point alone. No corpse had been found in the wood: no trace of the sanguinary acts which had left terrible witnesses behind them wherever they had been perpetrated. But a faint hope, though not so full of temporary distress, is, perhaps, more agitating, more engrossing than a painful certainty. Billy Byles and the gentleman who had just spoken continued to converse for some minutes, without my hearing or attending to anything that passed between them. I believe that Louisa Thornton spoke to me from the balcony above; but I fear I did not answer her. Standing with my eyes fixed on the ground, and my thoughts bitterly preoccupied, I saw, I heard nothing, and it was not till Mr. Byles touched my arm, saying,--"That is a good thought; let us try it," that I woke from this dreadful reverie.

"What is?" I asked; "I did not hear."

"Why," answered Billy Byles, "Captain Wilson proposes we should go down to the old block-house, erected in revolutionary times to defend the river, and where the prisoners are confined, and examine them as to what became of Miss Bessy. Those we took at Doctor Blunt's must be the same who passed over the ground where you left her; and the devils will tell at the first question, for they have all got a looseness of tongue which prevents them from having any concealments. That is the difference between an Irishman and a negro; the one, pretending to tell all, tells nothing, for fear he should hurt himself or his hundred-and-fiftieth cousin; the other tells everything, without caring whether he implicates his own life or that of a dozen more."

"Let us go," I cried, seizing upon the suggestion eagerly; for I was a drowning man, and a straw seemed some support. "Which is the way to this place?" Billy Byles hade Miss Thornton adieu in tones which implied that his suit had prospered, and then led me across the market-place towards the banks of the little river which flowed past the town. Here we came to a small stockaded house, which had served in former times to defend the stream, and before which two sentinels, with muskets on their shoulders, were sedately walking. Only another person was visible, who, though he attracted but little of my attention, seemed considerably to excite that of Billy Byles.

"Hang me," he said, "if I do not believe that is Colonel M----. What can he be doing there, down by the side of the river with a spade in his hand? Why, he has got a basket there too."

"Never mind," I answered; "we have something more important to think of." And advancing towards the block-house, not without turning his head several times, he demanded admission, which was immediately granted. We had no light but the moon; and the black faces of the handcuffed prisoners were not very easily distinguished, the one from the other.

"Which is Nelson?" demanded Billy Byles.

"I'se he," answered one of the men, advancing.

"Well now, Nel," said my companion, "we have got a question or two to ask you; and what you say, if you tell us the truth, shall not be used against you, but rather in your favour. But if you tell us lies, hang me if I don't cut your throat with my own hands."

"I tell de truth, Master Byles, be you sure of dat," answered the man in a bold tone. "Everybody knows what I have done, and here I am; no use of telling of lies now."

"Well, then, tell us exactly," answered Billy Byles, "all that happened after five o'clock this evening, till the time when you marched upon Doctor Blunt's house." I cannot follow the negro's jargon through the long account he gave of the events of those few hours. The substance was as follows:- -The party of Nat Turner, after having advanced towards Jerusalem, and having been met by a severe fire from a party of white men on the road, retreated in good order through the by-paths of the wood, known to few but themselves. When they came to the meeting of the two paths I have mentioned, they found they had been outflanked by a party of horse in pursuit. They saw well enough, he said, a smoke rising up in the wood, though they could not tell whether the fire had been lighted by their own people or by an enemy. Knowing, however, that smoke would attract the attention of the white men, they determined to leave it on their left, and to take shelter amongst the bushes in the thicker part of the wood, being certain that they could not outstrip their pursuers before they came to the open ground. Signals were agreed upon; Nat Turner, who, according to his account, was perfectly calm and confident, laid himself down at the foot of the tree where I had found him, and the rest concealed themselves in the thick bushes. There they lay till after I came up. Nelson stoutly denied having seen any woman in the whole course of their retreat. Nothing could make him swerve from this assertion. When, remembering the two tracks I had seen, the one to the right, the other to the left, at the thick laurel-brake, I asked if his party had not divided into two. This he denied, stating that they had pursued one undeviating course, and had merely scattered themselves round their leader, when they found a sure place of concealment. At length, I put the questions to him straightforwardly, whether he knew Miss Bessy Davenport? whether he had seen her during the preceding day? He answered he had known her ever since she was a child, and positively asserted that they had seen nothing of her.

"We hunted for her at Mr. Stringer's," he said, "for we had heard that she was there; and Will wanted to kill her, though Nat did not. But we could not find her, and we never saw her at all." After the pause of a moment or two, during which I and my companion remained silent, the man looked up in my face, saying,--

"I dare say, if you want to find her, master, some of old Miss Bab's servants can help you. Depend upon it, they know all about it." Here was both a renewal of hope, and some clue to guide me; but the light was faint, and the clue somewhat frail.

CHAPTER XXIX

I have hitherto adhered as strictly to what I did and saw myself, as if I were in a court of justice, and bound by the law of evidence; but you, who are at a distance, may, perhaps, require some further explanation, to enable you to comprehend clearly the state of things around me. I think Rumour ought to be represented, not only with a hundred tongues, but with a great magnifying-glass in her hand; and she did not fail to use it on the present occasion, although I have certainly seen events of less importance much more magnified before they got very far from the scene in which they were acted. Indeed, the principal excitement and exaggeration were in the neighbourhood of the spot itself, where the insurrection had taken place. Here everything was in confusion, if not amongst the military, amongst the inhabitants. No one seemed to know the number of the insurgents; whether there was one man or many; what direction they were taking, and whether there were ramifications of the conspiracy in other counties and states. Consequently, Jerusalem and the whole neighbourhood was in a state of the greatest alarm; and very dark and gloomy apprehensions were entertained, even by the best-informed and the calmest of the county authorities. Every one felt as if he were standing close to a powder magazine in which a slow match was burning; and I have no doubt that if the revolted negroes had gained any success, a considerable number more of the slaves would have risen, and a very formidable body of armed men would have been collected, although I by no means imagine that anything like a general revolt would have taken place. Indeed, the conduct of many of the negroes on this occasion showed the strongest attachment to their masters, and a firm determination to resist all temptations to join the insurgents. Throughout the whole country round, however, a feeling of alarm and uncertainty spread far and wide; but vigorous measures were immediately taken to crush the insurrection in the spot where it had originated, and to guard against its spreading farther. Bodies of troops and marines were instantly sent up from Norfolk and Fort Monroe. Detachments of volunteers and militia were despatched from Petersburg and Richmond, and abundance of arms and ammunition was collected and forwarded with all possible haste. The public journals again and again warned their readers against exaggerated reports and unnecessary alarm; but they aided a good deal to increase apprehension, by such reports as these,--

"That the insurgent negroes numbered about four or five hundred. That although repulsed in one or two skirmishes with the militia, they were retreating towards Colonel Allen's plantation, where they were likely to be greatly reinforced." Other reports said that they were falling back on the great Dismal Swamp, known to be the place of refuge already of a great number of fugitive slaves. And again, that they were all well armed, mounted, and supplied with ammunition. The statements of the number of white persons who had been slain, and the number who were missing, were also very much exaggerated, and carried into many bosoms the same anxiety and terror which agitated mine. Although the account given by the prisoners at the block-house certainly afforded some relief to my mind, and re-awakened hope, I could not shake off apprehension; and I would fain have set off that very hour to ascertain whether poor Bessy had really found a refuge amongst the old servants of Aunt Bab. I found that was impossible, however; and, after having met all my suggestions, by objections unanswerable, Billy Byles added,--

"Depend upon it, Sir Richard, there is nothing to be done by you to-night, but to get some food and some rest. With the first ray of light to-morrow morning I will be ready to set out with you, and to-night you shall share a little dog-hole of a room which I have secured for myself in the midst of all this scramble and confusion. As to food, that will be a more difficult matter; for I do not believe there are provisions enough in Jerusalem to feed one-half of the people here. Plenty of good whiskey is to be got, and bad brandy; but everything else, as far as I can learn, is exhausted. Come, first, let us go and see what our good friend the colonel is doing down there. I can't imagine what he can be about, poking away at the corner of the bridge by himself." Billy Byles was one of those men who were made for happiness, whose minds may perhaps be susceptible of strong impressions, but those impressions are merely temporary. Now I have heard it argued that men of this character suffer as much diminution of their pleasures as their pains. But I do not think so. In the first place, few will assert, I imagine, that in this world of trial the pleasures are at all equal to the pains; and, in the next place, I do not see that it is a necessary consequence of men being a little susceptible of a pang, that they should be little susceptible of an enjoyment. At least, at that moment, I envied him the facility with which he could cast away the thought of all the dreadful things which had been passing around us, and walk unconcernedly down to the river side to see what a gentleman had been doing in whom he had no particular interest.

The distance could not be above twenty or thirty yards. I remained where I was; but the moment after, he called out,--

"Hurrah! Treasure trove, treasure trove! Gentlemen both, I seize and impound you on behalf of the state, and of William Byles, Esq., of Dunmore, near the Cross Keys, and the county of Southampton, in the state of Virginia." And up he came, carrying in each hand a large, short-necked black bottle.

"What have you got there?" I asked.

"London porter, for a hundred dollars," answered Billy. "That fellow knows what good living is. Oh, he's as cute as a sea-gull, and I see how he has set to work, He has somehow got up some London porter, and finding victuals and drink rather scarce in this great city, and good friends plenty, who would help him through it, he has gone and hid it down there, in the corner under the sand, to come down and drink his own health when nobody is by. There are more bottles there. You had better go and get a bottle. London porter is meat and drink too." I declined, however, helping myself from another man's store without his permission; but Billy Byles only laughed at my scruples, and we returned into the heart of the village. There he introduced me into what he called his dog-hole, which was a neat little room enough, in a neat little house, belonging to a free mulatto and his wife--quadroons, I suppose I ought to call them, for the portion of dark blood seemed to be very small. They were all attention, and even affection, towards Mr. Byles, who informed me that they had been slaves of his father, but were made free at his death. The old man hurried to get a couple of glasses as soon as Billy exhibited the porter bottles; and while he was gone, my companion fell into an unwonted reverie, which was explained as soon as his coloured friend returned.

"Jacobus," he said, "there's something I want you to do for me, and you must do it cleverly--here, cut this wire over the cork. You know Miss Davenport, don't you; Miss Bessy Davenport?--there, take that fork, thrust it through the wire, and twist it round--well, she escaped from Mr. Stringer's house with this gentleman, my friend Sir Richard Conway; but somehow she got lost in the woods about six or seven o'clock this evening. Now, I want you--cut the string, there's a knife--now, I want you to go out and inquire everywhere, and of everybody--d----n it, you'll let all the porter jump out of the bottle. Pour it out quick into the two glasses. Sir Richard, your health.--You see, Jacobus, we must, and will find out, this very night, what has become of Miss Davenport, and you know quite well that every piece of news throughout the whole country gets tossed about from hand to hand amongst your people just like a ball amongst a pack of children; so you must go and find out if there's anybody in the whole place who can tell you where she is. Ask the people as if it were a great secret, promise them to tell nobody, and then come and tell us."

"I'll do my best, Master Billy," said the old man; "but you know there's been such confusion these last two days, that we are all straggled, and nobody has had any time to find out anything. You say she was lost about six or seven this evening?" Mr. Byles added all the information that was necessary, and his envoy departed, somewhat proud, I imagine, of his commission.

"He won't find out anything to-night," said Billy Byles, as soon as the man was gone; "for, most probably, nobody in the place knows anything about the matter. But he'll go and talk to all the coloured people, and then they'll all begin jabbering, and chattering, and inquiring. The question will go, heaven knows how, down all the high-roads and by-ways, and to-morrow we shall have a whole budget of intelligence. Halloo! that sounds like cannon coming in." And, going to the window, he added,--

"So it is, by Jove! Two brass pieces, and a squad of artillerymen. We'll pound them to-morrow, if they take the field. Let us come and see what is going on." I accompanied him to the door; but we had scarcely reached the threshold, when we were met by Mr. Henry Thornton, his fine, tall figure looking very imposing in the garb of a colonel of militia. He shook me warmly by the hand; but I could see that a good deal of grave anxiety was upon his countenance.

"I did not think of coming into town to-night," he said, "but I heard of your fight at Dr. Blunt's, and that the poor devils had been dispersed with great loss. One serious check is enough to discourage them altogether. I think we shall have no more of it; and, at all events, it is over for to-night. But what is this I hear about poor Bessy Davenport?" I related to him everything that had occurred, and watched his countenance eagerly as I did so, in order to divine, if possible, what were the conclusions at which his mind arrived. He looked very grave, especially when he found we had ascertained that Bessy had not been brought in by Colonel Halliday's party?

"Not that he is the man," said Mr. Thornton, after expressing some painful disappointment at the breaking down of that hope of her safety-

-"not that he is a man whom any of us would choose to act as her escort under ordinary circumstances. But he dare not--no, he dare not," added Mr. Thornton, somewhat sternly--"take any advantage of his position."

"Who is this Colonel Halliday?" I asked. "You all seem to have some doubt of him."

"Why, don't you know?" cried Billy Byles. "He was Bob Thornton's second in the duel with you."

"He acted in a very gentlemanly manner there," I said.

"Ay, that might be," answered Mr. Thornton. "But he's a wild, unscrupulous fellow, notwithstanding. He certainly was colleaguing with Robert Thornton when that worthy tried to cheat her out of her whole property. Perhaps you do not know that he proposed to marry her, when she was not sixteen, and we had afterwards every reason to believe that there was an understanding between him and Robert, that they should share the spoils between them.

"Bessy, however, settled the matter for herself; for she told him she would sooner marry a rattlesnake; and I do not think he has ever forgiven the disgust--ay, the disgust, that is the only word--which she expressed towards him. She was quite a girl then, and a wild girl too; and she spoke her mind more freely, perhaps, than she would have done, had she been older. There is no use of making enemies in this world, even of people we do not desire for friends." Mr. Thornton fell into a somewhat dark and gloomy reverie, and it may easily be imagined that my thoughts were not particularly pleasant. After a moment or two, however, he said,--

"Well, Sir Richard, it is now near one o'clock. You had better go to bed, and try to rest. I will do the same. We will both be up early to-morrow; and, after having taken counsel with our pillows, we may be able to devise some plan for tracing poor Bessy out." He was turning away, when suddenly he held out his hand to me in his frank, kindly way, saying,--

"Do not alarm yourself, my dear sir. I have no doubt our dear girl is safe. If she had met with any harm from these misguided people, her body would have been left where they murdered her. They have taken no pains to conceal their deeds. All I want to get rid of is this horrible feeling of uncertainty; though, indeed, we are in the same case with a hundred others in this town; for there is hardly a family that is not doubtful and anxious about some one of its members. I am not one to use the name of God on every occasion; but trust in Him is, in such circumstances, our best stay and only consolation." Thus saying, he left me; and his last words recalled to my mind the better and the surer sources of hope and comfort, which had been too much forgotten in the excitement and anxiety of the last few hours. A mattress and a blanket were brought in for me, to Mr. Byles's room; and though he, in his universal good humour, would fain have had me take his bed, I cast myself down upon my lowly couch, and resolutely tried to sleep. I had by no means recovered my full strength; I was weary and exhausted with the labours of the day and with want of food. Perhaps in such a state of fatigue, the glass of porter which I had taken had more effect than it otherwise would have produced; and though I was half angry with myself when I felt the leaden weight pressing down my eyelids, I was soon in a profound sleep. I do not believe, if an axe had been suspended over my head, or a pistol presented at my ear, I could have kept myself awake.

CHAPTER XXX

Though my sleep was dead, heavy, and dreamless, it lasted not long. I awoke with a sudden start and a sense of terrible apprehension. I am certain, indeed, that even when no visions perpetuate vaguely, during slumber, the thoughts which have occupied us waking, the sensations of the heart--if I may make such a distinction between heart and mind--persist, while all the ordinary faculties are steeped in oblivion, and knock at the doors of the brain till they awake us. I struck my repeater, and found it a quarter past three; and although I knew that in this latitude an hour or two of darkness had to intervene before the first dawn of day, I could find no more refuge in sleep. I lay there, and revolved the circumstances in which I was placed, and, as I imagined, all the probabilities--nay, even the possibilities--of the case. But I made no progress towards any conclusion. The prospect was as dark and dreary as ever! perhaps more so. At least it seemed so to me; for I know no more unpleasant hour to wake at, with feelings of apprehension on the mind, than three o'clock in the morning. It seems as if all the grizzly phantoms of imagination and dread gather thickly round our bed; and the dark sensation of that gloomy Nemesis, which hangs for ever brooding over human happiness, is felt more powerfully than at any other time. I struggled hard against it. I tried to put my trust in God. But there are moments when Faith and Hope seem darkened; when God's inspiring grace seems withdrawn; when the power of the prince of the air seems mighty over us in the darkness, and every image that can shake our trust is presented with appalling force.

"How many," I thought, "had the very night before risen from their knees to lay themselves down to rest with hope and faith in Him in whom I now strove to put my trust, and had never risen but to receive the death-blow of the murderer, or to weep over the ruin of every edifice of love. Oh, man! man! here lies our fault. Our hopes, our wishes, our faith, our trust, go not beyond this world. The dark chasm of the grave stops human thought and human feeling in their course, and we neither fully trust nor believe beyond." Such, at least, was the case with myself at that time. And the next hour and a half that passed, till the grey glimmer of the dawn began to appear, were amongst the most melancholy I ever endured in my life. Oh, Bessy! if you could have seen my heart then, you would have known more than words could ever convey. Before the sun was fully risen, Mr. Byles and I had quite a little levee around the door of our room. The first who appeared was Zed, who had found out where I had housed myself; and, coming with the first rays of dawn, had roused our worthy host and hostess from their short slumber. The second was good Mr. Jacobus himself, who reported that he had been able to learn very little, notwithstanding his utmost endeavours. All, in short, he had obtained was a vague rumour that Miss Davenport had been seen somewhere with old Jenny, Aunt Bab's cook; and that she would most probably be found with the other servants of the family at the sheriff's plantation, about seven or eight miles off. Next to him came Mr. Thornton, who had conducted his inquiries better, and had more reasonable suggestions to make than any of us. He cleared the room of the other two visitors; and then, seating himself in the only vacant corner, said,--

"I have been making inquiries this morning whether Halliday returned to the town last night. I find he has not been here since eight or nine o'clock, and I cannot discover where he has gone. This strikes me as somewhat strange; and I should propose, that as soon as they are awake and up, to inquire of the three young ladies whom he brought in, if they saw anything of Bessy and her companion. I dare say we shall be able to get speech of them presently; for people's minds have been too much agitated for much sleep to have hung over Jerusalem last night."

"In the meantime, however," I said, "I will ride over to the sheriff's quarters, and inquire if anything has been heard of the dear girl there."

"You had better wait till these young ladies have risen," rejoined Mr. Thornton. "They cannot be very long, I think; and they might give us information which would lead us in a totally different direction." I was too impatient to wait, and Billy Byles seconded me.

"Oh, they will sleep better now the daylight's come in," he said. "You won't have them up for these three hours; and by that time Sir Richard and I will be back again." A difficulty, however, occurred to me which I had not thought of before. I had no horses but those I had borrowed of Doctor Blunt for the purpose of riding into Jerusalem; and I did not think myself altogether justified in taking them any farther. The objection, however, was easily met by Billy Byles, who exclaimed,--

"Oh, there are lots of horses here, belonging to everybody and nobody. Come away over to the inn-stable, and you'll soon be able to provide yourself with a steed." I succeeded in doing so sooner than even he expected; for, on entering the stable, in the third stall to the left, what should I see but my own horse, which I had bought in Norfolk; and a little further on, that on which I had mounted Zed. Of course I had no hesitation in taking possession of my own property, though the ostler was inclined to make some opposition; but the word of Billy Byles was omnipotent with all who had to do with horse-flesh in that part of Virginia, and he declared he could swear to my horses amongst ten thousand. The ostler fairly owned that he did not know who had brought the beasts in, and the only further question was about saddles and bridles.

"Oh, take any one, take any one," said the ostler, with a grin; "we have been in such a state of confusion that nobody knows whether the saddle is on the right horse or not."

"Here's yem, master, here's yem," cried Zed, who had followed us into the stable; "but where mine is, Lord help us, I cannot tell. So I had better take the best I can find." These matters being at length arranged, we looked to the charging of our arms, and prepared to set out; but Zed approached my horse's side, asking what he was to do with Doctor Blunt's horses.

"Would you be afraid to take them back to Doctor Blunt's alone, Zed?" I asked.

"Oh dear, no, massa," he answered; "nobody hurt old Zed; and, besides, I think them fellers is had enough of it." I accordingly gave him money to pay for the animals' food, with orders to take them back to their master's house at once. Billy Byles and I set off at a rapid pace; but I could easily discover that my horse, although he had hardly been worked at all for the last two months, had been so hard ridden during the preceding four-and-twenty hours as to abate his strength and spirit considerably. Indeed, I afterwards found that he had been stolen by the insurgents from Mr. Stringer's house, on the night of the massacre, and had been used incessantly, without food, till the man who rode him was captured by a party of the militia. It was thus nearly an hour before we reached the lane which led down to the sheriff's plantation, upon or near which, we were told, aunt Bab's old servants were now quartered. We had not been able to find that tall and worthy functionary before we set out; and, consequently, we were without any specific information as to where the poor negroes were to be found. We rode direct towards the house, however; and, as we approached, saw a worthy gentleman--who might perhaps have some shade of colour in his blood, though very slight--quietly mounting a stout horse, of that round, compact form which generally betokens great powers of endurance.

"Here's the overseer," said Billy Byles. "We'll ask him where we can find the poor people." He accordingly rode up, and put his questions; and the good overseer, bowing civilly, said,--

"I will show you, gentlemen: they are at what we call the old quarters, two miles off, just upon the edge of the Swamp. Mr. ---- thought it would be better to place them there, as the cabins are comfortable and were vacant; and no one could get at them to steal them without crossing the plantation. I have put them," he added, "to a little task-work, just to give them something to do. But a regular account is kept of what they earn, which will be given in, when the courts decide to whom they belong." He looked at me as he spoke, as if understanding fully that I was one of the claimants; and I thought I recognized his face as one of those who had been with the party who pursued the kidnappers of these poor people, as far almost as the frontier of North Carolina.

"I suppose the negroes are very well content," I replied, "to remain here, and not go to New Orleans."

"That they are," answered the man, "and very much obliged to you, sir, for stopping them just when you did. I believe one-half of them would have died, if they had taken them away. They were born here and bred here, and have all been very happy here; and you'll find very few that like to quit Virginia, go where they may." I could not but smile at the man's patriotism; though, to say the truth, I did not much doubt he was right; for, as far as I had ever seen then, and have ever seen since, the existence of slavery--great as the evil is in every form--is so mitigated in that state, that I doubt not the slaves themselves would "rather bear the ills they have, than fly to others that they know not of."

"Pray," I asked, as we rode on, "when speaking of task-work, what do you consider as a fair day's task here?"

"That depends upon the nature of the work, sir," he answered. "But I can show you, as we go along, what we should consider a fair day's task in several different kinds of field labour." He did so; and I found that it was rather less than one-half of what an English labourer could perform easily in a day.

"Do you mean to say," I inquired, "that one of your hands cannot get through more than that in a day?"

"Oh dear, no, sir," he replied. "They can do twice as much in ordinary weather. Sometimes, it is dreadful hot to be sure; and then they can't do as much; but generally they have a good many hours to do what they like about their own place, if they are industrious--if not, to be still and sleep, as some of them do. Task-work, I think, is the best plan for them; the master is sure to get his work done; and, just as the hand is active and willing, he gets the advantage of it, which is an encouragement." There was something honest and straightforward about the man's manner and speech which pleased me;

and I remarked also, that the negroes whom he met upon the road showed him not only that respect which might proceed from fear of his authority, but a degree of affectionate familiarity, which could only be generated by kindness on his part. One big fellow, in a light cotton jacket, ran along by the side of his horse for a quarter of a mile, with his hand upon the mane, talking to him about things he wanted done; and the women laughed and showed their white teeth, while they bobbed a courtesy, as if they were glad, rather than afraid, to see him. Billy Byles, to whom all such matters of Virginia detail were too familiar to be of any interest, whistled absently as we walked along; and it was only when my questions turned towards the fate of Bessy Davenport that he woke up to some degree of attention.

"I have heard nothing of the young lady myself, sir," said the overseer; "but as for that matter, we'll soon get information. She is very much beloved about all this part of the country; and whoever these black devils hurt, I hardly think they would venture to hurt her."

"I fear you calculate too much upon their forbearance," I said. "Have you not heard how indiscriminate their rage has been?"

"O yes, sir," he replied; "we have heard a great deal about them, although we have been rather out of their way here. Some passed over the corner of the plantation, I hear, last night, on their way towards the Swamp; but they seemed to be flying in great haste, so the men say, and did not stop to talk with any one."

"They were too near the sheriff's quarters," said Billy Byles. "His people are all right and straight, are they not?"

"O yes, Mr. Byles," answered the overseer. "Not one of them stirred, or wanted to stir. I sat up all night; but I might just as well have gone to bed; for master is always just with them. He always will have his work done; but he requires no more than is fair. He never punishes a mistake, or even a folly, though he may reprimand it; but he punishes a fault, if he sees it was intentional, always a little within the law, and never till he has considered the matter full four-and-twenty hours. It is those who have been too hard with them, or too soft with them, who are likely to suffer whenever there is a rising." Thus talking, we rode along, partly through woods, partly through open fields, till we reached a spot, where, built round a little sort of amphitheatre, sloping downwards towards pleasant meadows or savannah, beyond which again appeared a wide extent of ragged forest-ground, with glimpses of gleaming water here and there, appeared thirty or forty very neat and tidy cabins. At the doors of several were groups of women and children; and a number of men, with various implements of husbandry in their hands, appeared just setting out to their labour. To a

European eye, accustomed to nothing but white faces, the sight of a number of negroes gathered together is a curious spectacle, to which people do not easily get accustomed. But very soon, other feelings, as we rode up, carried me away from the interest I felt in the spectacle of so many of what old Fuller calls, "God's images carved in ebony." The men rested at the sight of the overseer; the women rose; but, after a moment or two, some of them recognized me as aunt Bab's nephew, and as the man who had prevented them from being sold into another state. Great and loud was the excitement and the clamour. The word passed from mouth to mouth. The women and the men surrounded me; the little boys and girls tumbled head over heels; and though I do not think the Virginian negroes are very clamorous, a scene of din and excitement succeeded which made Billy Byles laugh, caused the overseer to smile, and prevented me, for some time, from explaining the object of my coming. At the first word, however, of probable danger to Bessy Davenport, everything was still. The capering and the singing and the laughing ceased; and the black, gleaming eyes were turned upon each other's faces, as if some terrible marvel had been told them.

"What! our missie?" cried an old woman at length, in a deep, horrified tone. "Our Bessy! Have they hurt her? Oh, I will tear out the hearts of them! But it can't be! They darn't." I explained to her and those around that all was in uncertainty--that Bessy and I had escaped from the house of Mr. Stringer; but I had lost her in the wood, and that she certainly was now missing. Another silence fell upon them all; and it was clear, from the astonishment with which the tidings had been received, that Bessy had not found shelter there. At length, one tall man, of about forty, stepped forward, and asked in an eager tone,--

"How was she dressed, massa? Had she anything white about her?"

"Yes," I answered; "she had a white shawl on, and a gown you might take for white, at a distance." The man mused, and spoke for a few moments in a low tone to a woman who had a baby in her arms. In the meanwhile, a lad of nineteen or twenty came forward, saying,--

"Didn't you tell us, sir, aunt Jenny was with her? Missus' cook that was." (I nodded my head.) "I'll find her; she is my aunt, massa, and been as good as a mother to me."

"We'll find them both," said the big man, turning round again. "We'll find them both, living or dead. Massa Overseer, no offence, sir, I hope, but we can't work to-day, because we must find Miss Bessy and aunt Jenny. You know you can trust us. We'll all be back before sun-down; but find them we must, and we will. I think I know where to look."

"Where, where?" I asked, eagerly.

"No matter, just yet," answered the man. "P'r'aps I'm mistaken, but we'll find her, massa, be you sure of that, if there's a living man left of us."

"Well," I answered, "any one who brings me intelligence to the town of where Miss Bessy is, between this hour and tomorrow morning, shall have a reward of a hundred dollars. I trust, sir, you have no objection," I said, turning to the overseer, "against these good people seeking for the young lady."

"None whatever," he replied. "I am quite certain they will all come back; for I don't think any of them has had anything to complain of during his whole life."

"Never, sir, till our old missus die," said the tall man; "and never since we came here, I will say. Robert Thornton's time was a different case. The dirty nigger! he ought to have the racket." He then turned to talk with his companions; and so eager were they all with the matter in hand, that they took very little further notice of us, and hardly seemed to perceive our departure. The overseer, it is true, remained with them, wishing us a civil good day, and though I gave all credit to their zeal, I was not sorry they should have some one to direct it aright, who had more extended experience than themselves.

"You are an extravagant fellow, Sir Richard," said Billy Byles, as we rode hack towards the town. "Your promise of the hundred dollars won't help the finding of poor Bessy a bit."

"I must leave no means or inducement untried," I said, in as calm and tranquil a tone as I could assume. "Miss Davenport, you see, was under my protection. I cannot help blaming myself for having left her at all; and every one will have just cause for censuring me severely if I neglect any means of discovering what has become of her." Billy Byles laughed aloud.

"My dear Sir Richard," he said, "I dare say you have got a thousand good reasons for your eagerness; but I divine one little one which you do not mention, and that is just the one which would make me hunt up Louisa Thornton in the same manner, if she were in the same predicament. Come along, here's a place where we can gallop; and though Jordan is a hard road to travel, the sooner we get back to Jerusalem the better."

CHAPTER XXXI

I could not help thinking, as we rode along, now through deep woods, now across small pieces of cultivated ground, what a favourable country this would be for a desultory guerilla sort of warfare; and I easily conceived how the Indians, in former days, had maintained their woody fastnesses against all the advantages of European discipline. Indeed, had the insurgents, on the present occasion, but known how to profit by the opportunities the country afforded--had they kept their hands from any indiscriminate massacre, and contented themselves with picking off their assailants from behind the screen which the forest afforded in every direction, they might, and certainly would, have been beaten at last, but they would have been much more successful in the beginning, and maintained the contest for a greater length of time. I did not feel at all sure that they would not have a shot at us from the denser parts of the forest, as we passed along through the narrow paths which we had to thread in order to reach the high road; and I kept my gun upon my knee, to give it back again in case of need. But the great highway to Suffolk was reached at length, and on we went in more security. A large, lumbering, heavy stage-coach passed us, with its tall springs and huge body, looking like a great solitary capon, and quite unlike the neat, compact, dashing vehicles which roll along with such tremendous speed over our smooth English roads. It stopped for a moment, to give time for the passengers and driver to ask us--"What news?" and then went on again, rolling and wallowing through the sand, and the ruts, and the holes, like a porpoise in a rough sea. About two miles farther on, just as we were coming to the opening of another road branching to the left, I heard a well-known voice exclaiming,--

"Hi, massa, hi!" Looking round, I saw Zed just starting up from a large log on which he had been sitting. He ran as quickly towards us as his crooked leg would admit; and, coming close to my horse, he said, in a low, mysterious, and important voice,--

"Got news of Miss Bessy, massa. Saw an ole woman in her cabin, half-way between Doctor Blunt's and Mr. Hiram Shield's; and she tell me that she saw four men and two women, a-horseback, pass by last night just as it was growing dark. They were all white men, and one was a white woman.

She says, she swears, she was Miss Bessy. T'other woman's face she could not see; but she says she was mighty fat, so that must be aunt Jenny."

"Which way did they take?" I demanded, though I did not exactly see why there should not be other fat women in the world besides aunt Jenny.

"Oh, they have gone to Jerusalem, of course," cried Billy Byles. "It was some of Halliday's party, depend upon it. Very likely they split into two; but they have all taken to Jerusalem, you may be sure of it. You see, in the crowd and confusion last night, no one could find anything, and the search for Bessy was like looking for a needle in a pottle of hay.

"Ole woman thinks they took t'other way," said Zed; "but you see, massa, her cabin just stand at de corner, where you can see no way at all; for they could turn either right or left when they got a hundred yards farther; and she only judge by the sound of the horses' feet."

"Oh, they've gone to Jerusalem," said Billy Byles. And turning to Zed, he added, "She was quite sure they were white men?"

"Oh, she swore by gorry dey was white men," answered Zed. "No doubt of dat."

"Then she is safe, at all events," answered Billy Byles; "and we had better make the best of our way on to town and seek for her. So that she hasn't fallen into the hands of these devils, we have no occasion to be afraid." Zed's intelligence certainly was a great relief to my mind; yet I was not entirely at my ease; for there were various points which seemed strange to me, and I could not feel satisfied till they were accounted for. Nevertheless, Billy Byles's plan seemed the only feasible one for the moment. Therefore, telling Zed to follow as fast as he could, I rode towards Jerusalem. We found the town somewhat more orderly and quiet than it had been on the preceding day, although it appeared that several parties of military had arrived during the night and that morning, and two pieces of artillery were planted in the square. Provisions had arrived likewise; and breakfast was going on with great zeal in the inn and the different houses which had given shelter to the fugitives. In the inn we found Mr. Thornton and all his family; but his first question showed me that he himself had obtained no satisfactory information.

"What news do you bring?" he said. "Do aunt Bab's people know anything of our poor girl?"

"Nothing whatever," I replied; "but we have since got some important intelligence." And I told him all we had heard from Zed.

"That is satisfactory, at all events," he said, with a brighter look. "We shall hear more soon, and most likely see her come trotting in in the course of the day. I dare say she has gone to some plantation where the people are on their guard, and feel secure. At all events, she is safe, and our worst fears are allayed." He then went on to inform me that he had spoken with the young ladies whom Colonel Halliday had brought in, and found that Bessy had certainly never been with them. He had brought them, however, Mr. Thornton said, from a house quite close to the high-road after having made a tour with his party through the woods in search of the insurgents. He had returned on his search, immediately after having lodged them in safety, and he might have met with Bessy either before or afterwards.

"The only strange thing is," continued Mr. Thornton, "that Halliday himself has never returned; but I trust he will appear very soon." Mrs. Thornton, who always was rather of a despondent disposition, here expressed a hope--which, with her, generally meant a dread of an exactly opposite event--that Colonel Halliday had not met with a superior party of the negroes, and been defeated. A friend of mine, who was somewhat of a susceptible and apprehensive character himself, but who took especial care never to express any gloomy forebodings, used to declare that he always eschewed, the society of what he called *dread-ful* people; "for when I am in a fright about anything myself," he said, "they are sure to drive me half mad with all sorts of possibilities." Now, though I do not intend to apply the term *dread-ful* to my excellent friend, Mrs. Thornton, yet I did wish she had spared me this suggestion. I had argued myself into believing that there was no doubt of Bessy's safety, although, of course, I could not be altogether easy till I saw her again; and though the phantom which Mrs. Thornton conjured up was not very tangible, it made me uncomfortable. If it was not probable, it was within the range of possibility; and upon it my mind rested with very unpleasant sensations.

"Pooh! nonsense, mamma!" said Louisa Thornton. "Mr. Halliday had too many men with him for anything like that. Did you not hear how they were all scattered and dispersed at Doctor Blunt's? In the meantime, Sir Richard is getting no breakfast and must be half starving."

"And so am I too," said Billy Byles; "but you don't care whether *I* starve or not, Miss Louisa."

"Oh, I have no fears about you," she answered. "You will never starve when there's anything to be got to eat. You had better make haste, however, and get down to the dining-room, for there is a famishing multitude round, which will leave not a morsel if you do not fight for it." What she said was literally true. The breakfast we got was very scanty, although Billy Byles did almost fight for it; but it served, at all events, to appease our hunger; and, what was perhaps of more consequence to me, to fill up some short space of time in which I had nothing else to do. Active exertion was indeed most necessary for me; but for the time, the opportunity was wanting. Zed had not yet returned to the town; and my horse was too tired, what with the morning's ride and the fatigue he had undergone during the preceding night and day, to go any farther without some repose. Nothing was to be done, then, but to wander about amongst the various groups in the town, to converse with those whom I knew, and to gather the scattered pieces of intelligence which were brought in from the country. All seemed agreed that the negroes had been completely dispersed the night before; that they had lost heart and hope; and that the insurrection was at an end. Several families who had taken refuge in the town moved back to their own dwellings, and some parties of the militia and volunteers marched out to return home. Still Colonel Halliday did not appear, and still no farther intelligence came of Bessy Davenport. Zed came in about two hours after Billy Byles and I reached the town, although the distance he had to walk was not more than four miles; but he assured me he had been making all sorts of inquiries, and I doubt not but what he said was true; for where is the negro who can pass another without stopping to ask him some question? After I had heard his excuse for the delay, I told him to get the horse he usually rode, ready for me, adding,--

"He must be rested by this time; and if Colonel Halliday doesn't come in in an hour, I shall go out to talk with this old woman, you mention, myself."

"You had better take me with you, massa," said Zed. "You'll not find out much by yourself. People will tell ole Zed when they won't tell you. But dere's dat free yellow man looking after you, I think, where you sleep last night." I looked round in the direction to which his eyes were turned, and saw good old Jacobus standing at a little distance, apparently waiting respectfully till my conversation with Zed was over.

"What is it, Jacobus?" I said, approaching him. "Have you anything to tell me?"

"Yes, sir," said the man, speaking in a low and mysterious tone. "There's a boy on the bridge wants to see you. He won't come into the town, for he seems afraid of the soldiers and the cannon; but he says he has a message for you." I turned hastily away, and walked towards the bridge. There were two or three people at the nearer end, but no one was upon it except a man driving a cart, and a young boy of perhaps thirteen years old, who was mounted upon the rail and swinging himself backwards and forwards over the water. He was as black as ebony; and I had no recollection of having seen him before. But he grinned from ear to car as I came up, evidently recognizing me; and, dismounting from his rail, he ran forward, saying,--

"Hercules say, mas'r, he got news already ob Miss Bessy. You don't leave de town till you hear from him again."

"And who is Hercules, my good friend?" I asked.

"Oh, our Hercules," answered the lad, with a look of wonder at my ignorance. "De great big nigger. You saw he dis mornin'."

"And has he got intelligence already?" I inquired. "He must have been very quick. It is hardly four hours since I saw him."

"Ah, dis nigger run all de way," cried the boy, "right troo de woods-- neber stop for noting."

"Then you must need something, my good boy," I replied. "Come into the town with me, and I'll see if I can get you some breakfast."

"O no, mas'r," answered the boy. "Had good drink out there," and he pointed to the river. "But mind you now, you wait till Hercules come. He can want you in a minute, he say. He am very fierce about someting, and get half de nigger together and went away again, so soon he sent me off." I tried to get some further information from the boy, but it was in vain. He evidently knew nothing more than the message with which he had been charged; and giving him some pieces of silver for his trouble, with which he seemed mightily delighted, I let him go. On returning to the inn, I found the dining-hall occupied by a party of gentlemen arranging their plans for a very melancholy duty. This was to divide the district in which the massacre had taken place into sections, and in parties of sufficient force, to visit the houses which had suffered, in order to take the necessary steps to dispose decently of the bodies of the victims. A good-looking military man was in the chair, with a calm and intelligent countenance. I found afterwards it was General Eppes, the commandant of the district. He was just addressing a few words of advice and exhortation to those who were about to set out.

"I believe, gentlemen," he said, "that all danger may be considered over. The insurrection may be said to be at an end, though several of the leaders have escaped as yet. I would advise you, however, to go well armed, and five or six in a body, lest you should fall in with any scattered party of these unfortunate people. I would beseech you, however, should you meet with any of them, to be calm, and to forbear from anything like violence or cruelty. Let them be brought in to await the action of the law; but do not permit indignation and anger to move you to acts as barbarous as their own. You may think it strange, and perhaps improper, that I should address such advice to you at all; but I have just received intelligence of a most brutal outrage committed upon some unoffending negroes by persons who should know better. My good friend, the sheriff, has just set out to inquire into the whole matter, and I trust will bring the offenders to punishment. For it is dangerous and intolerable, on an occasion like this, when the restoration of tranquillity depends as much upon justice and forbearance as upon courage and activity, that the peaceable and well-disposed should be treated like the malcontent and the guilty, especially," he added, in a very marked tone, "where private malevolence may be suspected as the motive for a cruel and unjustifiable act. This is all I wish to say; but I think it is worth your attention, for I know that many who hear me must set forth with feelings highly irritated, which will be naturally increased by the sad spectacles they will have to witness." His tone was calm, firm, and dignified, and he was listened to with evident attention and respect. Some, indeed, wished that he would give farther explanations in regard to the particular case of outrage to which he had alluded. But he replied, after a moment's thought,--

"Gentlemen, my information is vague, and I do not like to give circulation to rumours affecting the character and conduct of any gentleman in the neighbourhood. We have had too many rumours already, and, until the particulars are well ascertained, I shall say no more. The matter is in the hands of the sheriff, whose energy and activity you all know, and it will be thoroughly investigated." The meeting then began to break up, organizing itself into different parties to perform the mournful duty they had undertaken. Each selected its particular little district to act in, and each chose a leader for itself to direct its proceedings. This spirit of organization is one of the most peculiar and serviceable traits of the American character. In other countries, a mob is a mob; every one strives for the lead; every one tries to cram his own opinion down the throats of others. But no sooner do a number of Americans meet for any purpose whatsoever, than the first thing they do is to organize; they choose their leaders and their officers, and thus, very often, the most disorderly acts are performed in the most orderly manner. This is one of the ancient characteristics of the Anglo-Saxons, showing itself amongst their remote descendants. Our pagan, piratical, barbarous, bloodthirsty ancestors, had no sooner taken possession of Great Britain, than they devised, and carried out, one of the most beautiful systems of organization ever conceived; and if both Englishmen and Americans have, as I am afraid is the case, inherited some of the piratical propensities of our worthy forefathers, they have come in for their share of the better qualities also. Mr. Henry Thornton was placed at the head of one party, Billy Byles of another, and I think about seven little bodies of men were formed to visit the different houses where massacres had been committed. I was asked by Mr. Thornton to join his party; but I explained to him that

I wished to remain in the town till Colonel Halliday made his appearance, and I besought him, if he obtained any intelligence of Bessy, to let me know at once.

"Halliday's absence is very strange," said Mr. Thornton; "but let me advise you, Sir Richard, if I may do so without seeming impertinent, to deal with him calmly when he does come in. There are various circumstances which may make him irritable in regard to any matter where Bessy is concerned, and I think we have had pistols and bullets enough for some time to come." Thus closed our conversation, and when the various parties had set out on their way, I betook myself to the open space before the inn, not alone to be ready for whatever might occur, but to dissipate my impatience, as it were, in a way that could not be annoying to others. I ought, perhaps, in politeness, to have gone to sit with Mrs. Thornton and her daughters in the balcony; but I felt that I was not fit for society, and that my company could not be very desirable to any one in the mood which was then upon me.

CHAPTER XXXII

About half an hour had passed, during which I had walked up and down, exchanging a few words, from time to time, with different gentlemen in the street, when I saw a negro-lad coming at a quick pace from the side of the bridge. I thought I recollected his face, though I have always found it very difficult to distinguish one of his race from another, by the features, when there is no mixture of the white. I accordingly advanced to meet him, and saw at once that it was of me he was in search.

"Come along as quick as possible, mas'r," he said, "you is wanted down dar very much. Mas'r sheriff gone down; but you wanted too. I met mas'r sheriff on the road. Poor Hercules and two other is shot. Dey tink him die, and he want to see you."

"Shot!" I exclaimed. "Good Heaven! by whom?" The boy had been speaking low; but he now dropped his voice to a whisper, while he replied--

"Mas'r William Thornton, and his son Bob, and dat Irish driver." I paused to ask no further questions; but called to Zed to bring out the horses as fast as possible, which he did with more than his usual alacrity. My own beast still looked very tired, and stood with his head drooping. I determined therefore to take the horse that Zed usually rode, and to go alone, although my good servant, who always had a sort of protecting air with him, as if he thought that, as a white man and an Englishman, I was not at all fit to take care of myself in Virginia, urged me strongly to take him with me. I rode away without him, however; proceeding slowly, till I was beyond the town, with the negro-lad walking by my side. But we had hardly passed the bridge when he said,--

"You know de way, don't you, mas'r?" I nodded my head, and he added--"You had better get on den, fear poor Ercles die first. Dis nigger come after." I marked the road too well to miss it; and putting my horse into as quick a pace as possible, I hurried forward till I reached the turning which went down by the sheriff's plantations. Rapid riding is rather favourable to rapid thought; but I had very few data on which to base conclusions in the present case. This event, which the boy had communicated to me, was evidently the outrage to which General Eppes had alluded shortly before; but I puzzled myself in vain to assign some motive for such an act on the part of Robert Thornton. Could it be mere malice because the slaves had been taken out of his hands; I could not believe in such brutality. Yet what other inducement could he have? It was all in vain; and, turning through the woods, I was soon near the sheriff's house. I found no one there, however, except some women and children, who told me that their master had gone down to the old quarters. One woman was crying bitterly, and I asked her if poor Hercules was dead. She said she believed not; but every one said he would die. No further information could I get; for the poor creatures seemed ignorant of everything except that some of their friends, perhaps relations, had been dangerously hurt. On I went then as fast as possible, till I reached the group of cabins which I have before described. Round the door of one of them the greater part of the negroes seemed to have collected; and thither I rode, judging at once that the wounded man lay there. A boy sprang, forward to hold my horse. Another whispered as I dismounted,--

"Doctor's wid him, sir." But I went in notwithstanding; and there, upon the lowly, pallet-bed, saw extended the large frame of the negro I had beheld in the morning, full of life and energy, but now apparently reduced to almost infant weakness. Bending over him with what I suppose was a pair of forceps plunged into a wound in his right side, was Doctor Christy, the surgeon who had attended me when suffering from a much lighter wound. The poor negro's eyes were closed, and he did not open them till the ball was extracted; but when he did, and they fell upon me, he raised himself a little on his elbow, as if about to speak.

"There! lie still, my good fellow, lie still," said the surgeon. "We have got the bullet out; keep quiet and all will go well."

"I want to speak with that gentleman--I *must* speak with him, though I die. I'se going to die anyhow, I know dat, and I will speak with him when I can."

"I hope he is likely to recover, Mr. Christy," I said advancing.

"I hope so," answered the surgeon, in a somewhat doubtful tone. "But he must keep quiet, and not speak much; for I am not sure that the lower edge of the lung has not been touched." While he spoke, he was busily engaged in putting on compresses and bandages; but the negro eagerly beckoned me towards him, and judging that he would not remain quiet till he had said what he wished to say, I walked up and bent down my head, telling him to speak slowly and calmly.

"Miss Bessy was dere, I'se sure," said the poor man. "Bob Thornton never shoot us for asking after her, if she warn't. She mayn't be dere now, for I dar say he send her away, 'case she saw all he do."

"Then was it Robert Thornton himself who shot you?" I asked. "I thought he was still too ill to move."

"Ay, but he shot me himself," said the negro. "He came to de window in his dressing-gown, and leaned de gun on de chair. Ole Bill and de two Irishmen shot de others; but *he* shot me. But hark'ee, mas'r, if you and sheriff don't find Miss Bessy, go right across de Swamp. He got de ole house dere--right across, mind, straight east. You find her dere, I tink. Dat's anoder State. He won't keep her in Virginny after what he hab done."

"I cannot really let this go on," said Doctor Christy. "The poor man's life depends upon his being quiet."

"Well, good-bye, Hercules," I said. "I will see you tomorrow."

"Ah, you bring me word dat Miss Bessy found all safe," answered the wounded man. "Dat do me more good nor anything." I drew the surgeon towards the door, round which the other negroes had remained all the time in perfect silence, and asked him in a low tone if it would not be better to have the man's deposition taken down, as he evidently believed himself to be dying.

"What's the use of his deposition?" asked the surgeon drily. "Don't you know a negro can't testify against a white man? His voice will be quite as powerful in the grave as when he is living. But I think he will do well. These negroes always think they will die when anything is the matter." No good could be done by staying; and deeper interest called me away.

"Can any of you show me the way to Mr. William Thornton's house?" I asked, speaking generally to the little crowd without.

"Here's de nigger who can," said an active young negro springing forward. "We'll soon catch up de sheriff. He not long gone. I can run all de way. I wish I hab a gun," he continued, looking at the one which was strapped across my shoulders. "I shoot Bob Thornton wid all my heart."

"Well, come along," I said, with feelings too much akin to his own to reprove him for his sanguinary wishes. "Take the shortest way, and never mind wide paths or narrow; we'll force our way through." On he bounded like a deer, without care of brambles or thorns, of rough places or swamps; and, to say truth, though he was on foot, and I was on horseback, I had a good deal of difficulty to keep up with him. The way was rather long; and the by-paths he took did not strike a wider road, for at least five miles; but when we had gained the more open way, we almost immediately found ourselves in the presence of the sheriff, with a considerable party of white men, and two or three blacks. Amongst the rest, I instantly recognized Robert Thornton, very pale, but apparently quite convalescent. There was an elder man, whom I took to be his father, from the strong personal resemblance, though the latter was thin, fox-faced, and eager-looking, with that peculiar, quick, and hungry aspect which I have never seen except in men who have spent a life and employed all their energies in a fruitless pursuit of wealth by cunning and dirty means--a look of shrewd activity, rendered almost fierce by disappointment. Behind, with handcuffs on them, were the two Irishmen whom I remembered well to have seen with Robert Thornton when he was attempting to carry off aunt Bab's servants. The rest were men whom I did not know. The moment the sheriff perceived me, he drew up his horse, and said,--

"I am sorry to tell you, Sir Richard, Miss Davenport is certainly not there, although we had every reason to believe that she was. I had not, indeed, time to pursue my inquiries as far as I could wish; for my other duties call me to Jerusalem as fast as possible. But I searched every room and every cabin round the house; and, whether she has been there or not, she is not there now."

"You will take notice, Mr. Sheriff," cried Robert Thornton, before I could say anything in reply, "that I again protest against this proceeding as altogether illegal and unwarranted; and I give you notice, I shall undoubtedly bring an action against you for false imprisonment, which you know quite well will lie."

"You will do as you are advised, Mr. Thornton," replied the sheriff, coolly. "The district is in an exceptional state just now, and the presumptions are very strong against you. But, as I said before, my mind is perfectly made up as to my course. You have not often known me abandon my determinations; and I shall not suffer any of you four gentlemen to depart till you have given sufficient bail to meet any charge which may be preferred against you."

"Why, you have not even a pretence, sir," said the elder Mr. Thornton. "Nothing but the idle tattle of a parcel of niggers." The sheriff smiled sarcastically.

"You forget," he said, "we may yet have some curious testimony from Colonel Halliday, and various gentlemen of his party; and, moreover," he continued, more slowly and emphatically, "some testimony, which, though it is not present, and may not even be in this State at the present moment, may become available hereafter. At all events, I will take my chance of what is upon the cards, and please God, I will carry you to Jerusalem this night." I could see that the countenances of Robert Thornton and his father both fell considerably at some parts of the sheriff's reply, which they understood better than I did, and they did not attempt to make any further opposition.

"Sir Richard," said the sheriff, beckoning me a little aside, "you had better return with us. You will not find the lady there; and, without guides and some force, I don't think you will be able to do anything to-night."

"I will go on at all events," I answered. "I have got some hints from that poor fellow whom they have wounded, which I want to follow up at once. I shall probably be back to-night, or at latest, to-morrow."

"Well take care what you do," he replied. "Remember you are not in your own country. But I shall be round in the direction which I suppose you are taking early to-morrow; and, if there should be any difficulty, may be able to give you assistance, though I think this man's creatures will be completely cowed when they find he is apprehended. Indeed, that Irishman there on the left, is going to turn State's evidence, or I am very much mistaken. I would go with you; but I have a great deal to do to-night. Mind what you do in the Swamp; for people have got in there who have never got out again. Now, gentlemen, we will go forward, if you please. Mr. Thornton, you will have the goodness to cease your communications with that man. I wish him to give his evidence unprompted; and as it is a matter which may affect his own life and the lives of two or three others, he had better be permitted to speak freely. I suppose you are aware this district is under martial law at present."

"Then your functions are suspended," said Robert Thornton, sharply.

"Excuse me, sir," said the sheriff. "I am acting under due authority; and, at all events, might makes right in the present instance, as you will find." Thus saying, he rode on; and as Robert Thornton passed me, though his tongue said nothing, his look said a great deal. Poor Hercules had told me to go straight east across the Swamp, if I did not find dear Bessy at Mr. William Thornton's house; and the sheriff assured me she was not there: so that I was inclined at first to leave the house, which was now in sight on my right, along a path which seemed long beaten. On second thought, however, I determined to go up to the house and make further inquiries; not that I doubted the sheriff, or had the vanity to attribute to myself superior acumen; but I have often remarked that where one man of intelligence has been unable to obtain information, or get a clue to some secret, a second man, perhaps inferior to himself, will stumble, by accident, upon the very thing that is wanted. In fact, there are two sides to every hedge; one man takes one, and another man takes the other; and where the form is, there the hare will be. At the door of Mr. Thornton's house, stood two or three negro women and one man. Springing from my horse without hesitation, I gave the rein to my companion, and walked up to them in a familiar manner. They seemed a dull, sullen, heavy set of people, indeed the lowest specimens of the negro race I had yet met with. Yet the conduct and the character of the master must have been that which had brutalized them, for they were exactly of the same race as all the rest round about; and, indeed, most of them seemed to have some portion of white blood in their veins.

"How long is it since Miss Davenport went?" I said, taking out my watch.

"I don't know anything about her," answered the man, in a surly tone.

"I didn't ask you, my good friend," I said; "I asked the woman who attended upon her. You were the girl," I continued, picking out a young woman of two-and-twenty, who looked cleaner, and was more neatly dressed than the rest. "You are the girl who waited upon her last night, are not you?" She hesitated and stammered in her reply, and seemed a good deal confused by the directness of my assertion. At length, however, she blurted forth,--

"Don't know what you are talking about, mas'r." In the meanwhile, the man had walked slowly away, as if he had had enough of my questions; and, turning to an old woman who was one of the party, I said,--

"At all events, goody, you can tell me where aunt Jenny is--Mrs. Bab Thornton's cook. She is my servant now, you know, and I don't want her ill-used or neglected."

"I don't know nothing of nobody, mas'r," replied the old woman. "But I do know we'se got to obey orders; and if we stands here talking to strangers about mas'r's 'fairs, we'se likely to get flogged."

"Neither Mr. Thornton nor his son will ever flog you again," I answered; "for they have both gone to prison for what they did here this morning."

"Can't tell, don't know, mas'r," answered the old woman. And she beat a retreat into the house, followed by another, somewhat younger than herself. The youngest of the party, however, stood her ground; and, after a quick glance round, apparently to see that no one was watching, she gave a rapid movement of her thumb, over her shoulder towards the wood, which, on the eastern side, came within two hundred yards of the house. My eye followed her gesture, which certainly was not the exact direction I had intended to take; and, as I could perceive no horse-path, I looked, I suppose, a little puzzled.

"You go down dere quick," said the girl, in a whisper; "follow de track, you find it." Then raising her voice aloud, she said, evidently intending her words for the ears of others,--

"Can't tell you anything, mas'r. Don't know; so no use your waiting." Beckoning the lad to follow with my horse, I crossed the field in the direction she had pointed out, guided by a narrow, and not very distinct, track of footsteps, which, however, widened out and became more like a beaten path as we approached the wood. There two or three other little paths converged; and I found I could pass on horseback easily enough. How far I had to go, I know not; nor what might be likely to occur on the way. But, after some consideration and some doubt, I determined to send back my companion, and proceed on my journey alone. As soon as we were completely out of sight of the house, I took the rein from him, saying,--

"I will not take you any farther, my good boy. I think you had better find some other way back, so that they may not see, from the house, that you have left me."

"Oh, I do dat easily, mas'r," answered the lad; "go down de edge of de Swamp and round."

"First, tell me," I said, "where does this road lead?"

"Ole Billy Thornton's ole house," answered the youth.

"But this is not, I think, the road that poor Hercules intended me to take?" I added, interrogatively.

"Dar say he meant the waggon-road; but it is all de same," replied the lad. "Dey both come out close together, and dat ar gal jog her turn dis way. I see her, dough she were mighty quick." And he laughed with the peculiar laugh of his people.

"Then I cannot miss my way to the old place," I observed.

"Oh, dear, no," answered the boy; "only just follow de track; keep always de biggest; and when you ride 'cross de savannah, look where him very green. Don't you go dere, for he's very deep dere. But keep where him brown and bushy, and where you see ox or horse feet." His directions were very good, as I found afterwards; although I will confess that I had no idea at the time of the sort of place I was venturing into, called, and not without reason, "The Great Dismal Swamp." I am told that in the spring of the year, nothing can be more deceitfully beautiful than the aspect which it puts on. The whole ground, even in the most plashy places, is covered with flowers.

The trees are literally robed and loaded with the yellow jasmine, the trumpet honey-suckle, and other climbing plants. The cedars and junipers mingle their darker colours with the light-green foliage of the spring; and the very snakes as they glide across the path, or curl among the branches, look as if they were masses of living gems. In the height of summer, or the beginning of autumn, the scene is very different. Still, however, there is something grand about it from its very gloom. A profound sense of loneliness came upon me as I rode on. I don't know what it was, or how to account for the feeling, but the sensation produced by the aspect of these woods was different from that of any other forest scenery through which I had passed in Virginia. Where patches of woodland, very often of considerable extent, had been scattered amongst the cultivated ground, one always felt that one should soon reach free air and human associations again; but here, it seemed as if one were at the end of man's domain--as if the ground one trod upon never had been, never could be, cultivated; that there was a bar, and a proscription, and a curse against it--that one was proceeding away from civilization, and tending towards nothing. The first half-mile was through dense, deep forest, with tall, thin trees, rising up so close together that they evidently had not room to glow; each struggling with his fellow, as, in too densely a crowded population, every man stinted his neighbour in his own struggle for life. Then came a track, where I know not what catastrophe seemed to have terminated this overcrowded contention. For three or four square miles, the scene was one of desolation and decay. Fallen trees, stunted bushes, low junipers, plashy pools, thickets of laurel and ivy, silver gleams of small ponds, scanty lines of savannah--here, a dried-up patch of black mud, cracked into deep fissures; there, an undrainable spot, where the horse sank above his knees at every step in slimy ooze; now, a tangled brake, where a hundred men might have concealed themselves; and now, a swampy piece, from the long grass of which a tall white bird would spring up and soar away,--such were the objects that presented themselves on every side; and when viewed from the rather more elevated ground, by which the track was approached, showed like a wild and dismal moor with here and there a clump of tall trees rising above the rest of the expanse, and a deep, lowering belt of forest in the distance, girding it in on every side. On I rode, however, my horse sometimes stumbling over the thorn-trees, sometimes sinking almost to his girths in the deep, black mud. The sun declining in the sky, and the gloomy aspect of everything round me, sank into my heart, and depressed my spirits. Oh, how closely allied in this mysterious state of being is the material and the moral--how susceptible is even the soul itself of the influences poured in upon it through the channels of the external senses! The memories of all that had been taking place during the last two days seemed to combine themselves with the gloomy features of the scene around me. Hope diminished, apprehension increased. Imagination triumphed over reason; and I felt as if I were going on towards sorrow and disappointment and misfortunes. Such gloomy fits have sometimes possessed me before; but it is man's privilege and his duty to triumph over them; and whenever I feel the shadow of the cloud, I try to nerve my heart to resist, and to call up faith and trust to support mere human resolution.

"There is a special providence in the fall of a sparrow." "Not a hair of our head falls to the ground unnumbered." And if so, God is with us. Onward!

CHAPTER XXXIII

The sun was approaching his hour of setting; and the scene, lately so dreary and desolate, was now resplendent with colours which defy all description. It was not merely the purple and gold with which, in the weakness of language, we are forced to designate the hues, which neither pen nor pencil can bring before the mind, but it was the sparkling vividness, the transparent splendour of those colours--making them as spirit compared to mere matter--which spread an atmosphere-like enchantment over the scene, changing its rude features, brightening its dull heaviness, glorifying its gloom, and giving startling variety to its monotony. It was like the wonderful power of imagination, seizing upon the most incongruous materials, and harmonizing them in the life-like light that streams from itself. The mind, still subject, like the skin of the cameleon, to the aspect of things round it, took a brighter tone from the changes of the sky. Suddenly, however, I heard, as it seemed to me, at some little distance, a voice calling. At first, I was hardly certain whether it was not the cry of some wild bird; but presently I distinguished clearly the tones of a human voice; and, reining in my jaded horse, I turned round and looked in the direction from which it seemed to proceed. Running my eye over the ground, I could perceive nothing for a moment or two; but there were so many stumps and bushes and broken trees, that a hundred men might have been near me in that dim and scattered light without my perceiving their proximity. Still, however, the voice called, and I thought I could distinguish the word, "Mas'r." Cautiously I turned my horse amongst the bushes, and rode on towards the spot from which the sound seemed to come; and I soon began to discern the outline of a figure sitting at the foot of a tall, conical cypress-tree, almost assuming the form of one of the beautiful cypresses of Eastern Europe, and perched upon a little knoll, rising above the rest of the Swamp. It was not Bessy's figure; but, with no light satisfaction as I drew near to her and more near, I made out the heavy outline of good aunt Jenny. No words can express the good woman's joy and satisfaction when she saw me; and my own was little less, for I knew that I should now have a clue, and that some light, at least, would be thrown upon the mystery which had kept my mind for so many hours in a state of terror and anxiety. Poor Jenny, however, was weak and exhausted--to such a degree even, that she could hardly speak in answer to my questions; and the first consideration was how to revive her failing strength. At the distance which I supposed we were from any human habitation, no food, of course, was to be procured: night was coming on fast, and there seemed no prospect but of her dying there actually of starvation; till suddenly I remembered the hunting-flask of brandy which I had brought from the house of the hapless Mr. Travis, and of which I had never thought since. It was still in the pocket of my jacket, and it proved indeed a most seasonable relief to the poor woman, who soon recovered sufficiently to be able to tell me, vaguely and confusedly, that some twenty minutes after I had left her and Bessy in the wood, a party of white men, headed by Colonel Halliday, had forced their way through the bushes and hurried them away, offering to lodge them securely in Jerusalem. At Bessy's request, the leader promised, she said, to leave two men on the spot to give me warning when I returned; and poor Jenny declared that she heard him herself give the order to that effect. When they reached the path, however, they found more men and horses there; and the party separated into two divisions. Everything was in confusion, the good woman said; and before they were well aware of what was happening, she and Miss Davenport were riding away with one division, while Colonel Halliday took another direction with the other. It was not till they had gone some hundred yards that either Bessy or herself perceived that old William Thornton was with their party. I need not enter into more details, as I shall have to speak of them more fully hereafter, and as the good woman's account was very confused; I learned, however, from her that Bessy and herself had been detained at Mr. Thornton's house all night, but kept separate from each other; that she, at least, had had no food, and that she had seen a party of three or four of aunt Bab's negroes who came to the house, civilly inquiring if Miss Davenport was there, fired at from the windows without the slightest provocation. Immediately after that, Bessy had been placed upon horseback against her will and carried away.

"They turned me out as soon as she was gone," said aunt Jenny, "without even a cup of cold water; but I knew very well where they took her, and so I came on after my darling. But you see I got faint, master, and thought I should die for want here in the Swamp.

"But what did they take her away for, Jenny?" I inquired. "Why did they not let her remain where she was?"

"Why she see'd them shoot poor 'Ercles and the other two," replied the old woman; "and they knew she would witness against them; so they got her out of de State, and will keep her till it's all blown over. Dat's de reason, I am sure."

"Then why did they not send you away, too?" I asked.

"'Cause I'm a coloured woman, and my oath worth nothing," answered aunt Jenny.

"But if they have taken her into another State, how shall we ever find her?" I exclaimed, almost in despair.

"Oh, she close by--not two miles off," she answered. "Why we are in Nort Carolina now."

"Well, take a little more brandy, aunty," I said. "I will lift you on my horse, and we will go on, if you can show me the best way, for it is beginning to grow darkish." She would fain have walked, declaring that she was quite able, and that the brandy had done her "a mighty power of good." But I would have my own way, and we made our road forward just as the last glowing spot of the sun's disk sank below the horizon. He left a bright and beautiful twilight behind him, however, and we had no difficulty in finding our way onward, the road soon after beginning to rise out of the swamp into the firmer ground beyond.

CHAPTER XXXIV

Though it might be called night when we came in view of a house which Mr. William Thornton had formerly occupied, and which his people still called the old place, or the old quarters, everything around was distinctly visible by the pale, whitish light, which often in this part of the world lingers long in the sky after the sun is down. It was a desolate-looking scene, in which everything spoke of neglect and decay. In the fields, which had been once cultivated, and probably exhausted, young self-sown pine-plants might be seen springing up wherever the ground was not too thickly covered with weeds. Fences there were none, except some fragments round a kitchen garden at the side of the house, which seemed the only spot still cultivated. The house itself, though not actually tumbling down, was sadly dilapidated. Some of the rooms had not even the window-frames in them, and in several others the glass was gone or broken. I never could make out how it is that an uninhabited house always gets its windows broken. Can it be that the persecution which always dogs misery, extends itself to inanimate objects, and that the same spirit which leads a dog to bark at a beggar on no other pretext but his rags, leads the hand of mischief to hurry on ruin wherever it sees it commenced? I marched straight up to the front door, and aunt Jenny slipped quietly off the horse, while I tried the door, and knocked with my knuckles on finding it locked. The head of an old negro, covered with white wool, was speedily put out of a window above, and I was saluted with the words, spoken rather sharply,--

"What you want, mas'r? Can't get in dere."

"I want a night's lodging, and something to eat," I answered boldly. "I have travelled a long way, and can't go farther. Come down, and open the door."

"Can't, mas'r," answered the man, with a low chuckle. "Got the rheumatiz very bad. My ole ooman out, and she got de key." That the man was lying there could be no doubt, and I determined to get into the house by some means, whatever might be the risk. I looked round to see if there was any window near enough to the ground for me to force it open, and then, for the first time, perceived that good aunt Jenny had disappeared. The next minute I heard the sound of steps, running down the stairs inside of the house, and a voice calling out,--

"D----n you! What you doing dere? Let dat door alone. I teach you to come in here, you ole debil!" But aunt Jenny was too quick for him. I heard the key turn in the lock, and, putting my shoulder to the door, I pushed it open, when a scene presented itself which would have made me laugh at any other time. My rheumatic friend from above, who had once been a tall and powerful man, had got aunt Jenny by the throat, and, with the expression of a demon, seemed bent upon strangling her, while she, with not the sweetest expression either, was belabouring his head and face with the large key which she had withdrawn from the door as soon as she had unlocked it. I soon settled the strife, however, by taking hold of the man's collar, and throwing him back to the farther end of the hall.

"Ha! ha!" cried aunt Jenny, laughing, yet panting from the struggle. "I know de way in. He not keep me here two months for nothing, arter missus die. Why, old Sambo, arn't you 'shamed of yourself?"

"I'se an old man," said the negro, again advancing towards me. "And I'se a nigger; but I can tell you, mas'r, dere will be udders here very soon, not so old, not so black as I be."

"Who may they be?" I asked quietly.

"Why, mas'r Thornton," answered the man; "and de udders who he left here, but who is just step out."

"As to Mr. Thornton and his son," I answered, "you are not likely to see them again for some time, as they are both in prison for what they have done to-day. As to any others that Mr. Thornton left, I will settle with them when they come in again."

"Prison!" ejaculated the man. "Prison! You don't say mas'r Thornton in prison?"

"Yes," I answered, assuming a very potential air; "and whether I send you to prison or not will a good deal depend upon your behaviour. Go, take my horse to the stable, and give him some oats and hay."

"Lor' bless 'ee, mas'r, I got no oats and hay," answered the man.

"Then give him some corn," I replied, in a peremptory tone. "I shall come down presently and see that he eats it. Be quick; do what I tell you. Return here quickly, for I want to speak more with you." The man seemed to hesitate for a moment; but negroes, unless they are greatly excited, are swayed by a commanding tone. After twice pausing on his way to the door, he went out, took the horse, and led it away towards the back of the house.

"Now, Jenny," I said, "make the best of your time. Get some food, see who is in the lower part of the house, and come back and join me speedily, for I have got to search for Miss Bessy."

"Let's look for her first, mas'r Conway," answered Jenny, eagerly. "I get on now. Dat brandy make me quite strong."

"Let us search the lower part first," I replied. Passing from room to room, through the dilapidated house, we came to the kitchen, or sort of out-house, where we found two old women, seated by a large open fireplace, and apparently concerning themselves but little as to what took place in their neighbourhood. They seemed, indeed, withered up, and hardened by neglect and solitude, and hardly took any notice of us, except looking over their shoulders, till I ordered one of them to get some food for my companion, when she mechanically rose, and, opening a cupboard fixed to the wall, produced some salt fish and coarse bread. Jenny, however, was too eager in pursuit of her young lady to waste her time in eating; and, taking some of the food in her hand, she followed me up the creaking stairs to a large window at the top, on the sill of which old Samuel had apparently been seated when we arrived. The house was not a very large one, and the doors of several of the rooms were open, showing a scene of utter desolation within; but as darkness increased every moment, I thought it better to try what effect my voice would have in discovering whether Bessy was there or not; and I called as loudly as I could,--

"Bessy, dear Bessy, are you here?"

"Here! here!" answered a voice from the end of the corridor. Springing forward, I found a door, locked, but without the key in it.

"Are you there?" ejaculated I.

"Yes, yes," answered that sweet, never-to-be-forgotten voice. "Is that you, dear Richard?"

"Stand back from the door, love, and I will drive it in," I exclaimed. And putting my foot against the balustrade of the stairs, and my shoulder against the old, dilapidated door, I speedily forced the lock from the wood-work, and fell almost headlong into the room. # The windows looked to the eastward, so that it was darker within than without; and I could just see a woman's figure at the other side near the windows. But Bessy saw me better; and in another moment she was in my arms, and weeping on my bosom. I am afraid I kissed her very often, and very freely; but, in that moment, all restraint was broken down. She and I both felt that she was mine; and her lips answered mine, I am sure of it. Old Jenny hugged her in turn, though she was very discreet not to interrupt us too soon. But there was no time to be lost; and as soon as we had somewhat recovered ourselves, I said,--

"Now, dearest Bessy, what is to be done? You know the state of affairs here better than we do. Robert Thornton and his father have been apprehended by the sheriff, and I find only one old negro man here and two women. Is it safe to stay here till to-morrow morning?"

"There is another, younger man somewhere about," she answered; "but I should think they would not venture upon any violence, especially when they know their masters are in prison. Besides, you are well armed, are not you?"

"I have this double-barrelled gun and one pistol," I replied. "You had one, love, and Jenny here had one."

"Ah, dey took mine from me," cried Jenny, who was munching away as hard as she could at the handful of bread and herring she had brought from the kitchen; "dey got dat from me 'fore I knew what dey was doing."

"I have got the one you gave me, safe," said Bessy; "and, indeed, to have it was a great comfort to me; for I did not know what might happen next; and I am afraid I felt as if I could have shot any of them."

"I tell you what to do," cried Jenny; "better not stop here. We are in Nort Carolina here. Let's get back, just to de State line. In Virginny we shall be safer, and know what we are doing."

"But, my good woman," I answered, "this dear girl can't remain in the Swamp all night; and if we were to try to get back to the sheriff's plantation, a thousand to one we should be lost in the night, and she might perish."

"Ay, ay," answered the old girl, with a conceited nod of her head. "Leave all dat to aunt Jenny. Why, dere dat nice cabin, Habakkuk built for hisself just upon de line, arter Miss Bab's death. Don't you know, Missie Bessy? All of felled logs. There you be quite comferable, and I cook for you."

"But where will you get anything to cook, Jenny?" asked Bessy, with a laugh. "I have fared but poorly since I have been here."

"Oh, I see plenty in de kitchen," said Jenny. "I look about me--two or tree dozen eggs, and butter, and tree gallon loaves. We take what we can find. If dey carry us away, dey must feed us. When once we are dere we are quite safe; for dere be two good large room; and dey could never get old Habakkuk out." After some consultation with Bessy, I judged that it was better to follow the old woman's advice. We could not tell how many of Mr. William Thornton's people were near us. We had no reason to believe that our good friend, the sheriff, would venture to come over the Virginian line to our assistance; and it was quite possible that Mr. Thornton and his son might get bail that night, and be upon us early on the following morning. It was evident, too, that they had already gone so far in a daring and lawless course, that no slight considerations would stop them; and in that old and dilapidated house, which seemed to have only two rooms tenantable, there was no possibility of making a good defence against violence from superior numbers. I believe Bessy's evident anxiety to get away from the place as speedily as possible contributed not a little to fix my determination; and it was at length settled that, after allowing a little time for my horse to feed, we should set out for the hut which Jenny mentioned, and to which she professed to know the way perfectly, night or day. Before we came fully to this determination, we heard the voice of the old negro speaking to the woman below; and he twice came to the foot of the stairs with a lighted pine-knot in his hand, and looked up; but he immediately retreated to the kitchen. As soon as our resolution was taken, I unslung the gun from my shoulders, and, leading the way down, proceeded at once to the kitchen, to carry the war, if war it must be, into the enemy's territory. I thought it very likely that the party might, by this time, be reinforced; but I was mistaken. No one was there but the old man and the two old women, and they seemed inclined to be more civil. They all moved out of the way as we advanced towards the fireplace, of which, although it was a very warm night, I made my little party take possession, as a good strategetic position; and, knowing the advantage of acting on the offensive, I said to the old man,--

"How dare you to be art and part in depriving a free white young lady of her liberty?" I then told him I had a great mind to tie his hands behind his back, and carry him into Virginia.

"I am told there is another man here," I added; "where is he? Call him up to me. I am determined to punish you all."

"He not here, mas'r," said the old man, in a subdued tone. "He am gone over to see what de row over dere. Dey tell him, him cousin shot. I only do what I'se told. It's mas'r's fault, not mine. He tell me keep Miss Bessy here, and not let her see nobody, no account whatebber. What can I do, poor nigger man?"

"Your master cannot make you do an illegal thing," I answered. "But come, bring out whatever you have got to eat: we are all hungry."

"I see arter that," cried aunt Jenny, who seemed quite at home in the kitchen. "Now, Venus, where you put de milk?" Venus, who was as unlike her Grecian namesake as could well be conceived, declared the cows were not milked; adding,--

"That black nigger Jack had gone away across de Swamp, and forget 'em." But Jenny, who could play termagant when the occasion required it, drove out the old man to milk the cows himself. Our meal was certainly unwillingly given; but the grudging did not detract from its savour to very hungry people; and I must say, we made perfectly free with Mr. Thornton's house, without any remorse of conscience. After we had supped, Aunt Jenny gathered together whatever she could find of an edible quality, helped herself to a basket, and piled upon the top, besides a candle or two, a number of knotty pitch-pine pieces, which often, in this part of the country, served the purpose of torches.

"Now, come along, Sam'l," she said; "I'se not going to let you 'bide here, plotting. I hope you fed de horses well, for we'se a long way to go, to-night, and 'praps mayn't get to de sheriff's afore to-morrow morning. Dat's why I'm taking all these purvisions; and if Mas'r Thornton say I stole 'em, you tell 'im Sir Richard Conway will pay for 'em when he send in his bill." The old man grumbled; but she drove him out before us, to the stable, where we found my own horse, and that which had carried Bessy thither. There was also a mule in the stable, which I had a strong inclination to borrow, for the purpose of mounting old Jenny; but the good woman declined the honour, saying she had rather walk; she didn't like "'orseback," it made her "uncomferable." With some little trouble, we got everything in order, and set out; the moon, though not yet above the trees, afforded us light sufficient. We went very slowly, and more than once I turned my head to make sure that the old negro was not following to watch us. Jenny seemed to divine my suspicion, and, at length, said, with a laugh,--

"Don't you be afraid, mas'r. He'll not come after we. He's a lazy old debbil, as cross as two sticks; but he would not walk ten steps to save his own soul, if he could help it. I know him long time, and was two months in de house wid him. Oh! and he tell such big lies too. He go and say to Mas'r Thornton, you came wid ten men and took away Miss Bessy, and he couldn't help it; and he'll give all their names too, jist as if he see 'em wid his own eyes."

"Those are lies which can do us no possible harm, Jenny," I answered; "for if these two Thorntons were by any chance to get bailed out to-night, they would not like to pursue us, if they thought we had a large party." Bessy was very silent as we rode along, and doubtless was tired and exhausted; but we had good reason to thank Heaven for the hardy education she had received from Aunt Bab; for one half of what she had gone through during the last two days would have killed any ordinary Virginia girl. After having ridden on for about twenty minutes, we passed a very large tree standing nearly alone, and Aunt Jenny said in an oracular tone,--

"Nort Carolina line. Now we'se in Virginny. Tank God for dat!" Here she turned away to the left, keeping, I supposed, along the boundary line of the two states; and, in little more than a quarter of an hour, we came to an open space just upon the edge of the Swamp land, where, though the moon had now risen, and I looked round on every side, I could perceive nothing at all like the cabin she had mentioned. She trudged on sturdily, however, for a hundred yards further, and then turned round the edge of a little clump of bushes which had hitherto concealed, completely, a low hut, formed of logs, roughly hewn square with the axe, and placed one upon the top of the other, to form the walls. It seemed well thatched with branches and reeds, and had two windows, or rather apertures, and a door, giving it somewhat the appearance of the houses made out of a cat's head, which we draw to amuse children.

"Ah! here it is!" cried Aunt Jenny. "Dis is de place, mas'r, where ole Habakkuk live for a long time, 'cause he would not be under Mas'r Thornton, when ole missus die. Mas'r Thornton could never find him out; and we, none of us, never say a word. De ole man build it all himself wid his own hands. A mighty smart man he were, and made himself quite comferable here. I guess his ole bedstead here still; so dat you and Miss Bessy can lie down and rest." By this time we had arrived at the door--and Jenny was about to open it, when I suggested that it might be better to have some light before we went in, if she had the means of procuring any.

"O dear, yes," said Jenny. "I brought away de flint and steel. You give me drop of gunpowder, mas'r, on de wick of dis candle, and we'll soon have a light." I did as she desired; and, after lifting Bessy from her horse, I took the candle, which by this time was lighted, and went into the cabin. I must say it had a much less desolate appearance than the house of Mr. Thornton. The old man who constructed it must have had no little skill, taste, and perseverance. He had divided it into two rooms; patched up all the crevices between the logs with moss and mud; formed two shutters for the windows, and a tight-fitting door; and had, apparently with his own hands, constructed from the branches of the trees, and the fallen logs in the neighbourhood, four seats and a table in the outer room, and a bedstead, somewhat in the shape of a knife-tray, in the inner one. Though so near the Swamp, there was no appearance of damp about the hut; and I heartily rejoiced, notwithstanding all its roughness, that Bessy would have such a place of shelter for the night. She and Aunt Jenny had by this time, followed me in; and, seating the dear girl in one of the rude chairs, I pushed back the hair from her forehead, gazing in her face to see what change all the fatigues and annoyances she had undergone had made in her. She looked pale and fatigued certainly, but not ill; and comprehending my anxiety, she took my hand gently in hers, saying,--

"Oh, I shall do very well, dear Richard. A few days' rest and quiet is all I want; and then I shall be as well and saucy again as ever. But you had better look to the horses for fear they should ran away." They had had too much work lately for that, and were still standing with drooping heads at the door of the hut when I went out. Taking off the saddles and bridles, I easily contrived to hamper their feet with the stirrup-leathers; and then, leaving them to provide for themselves during the night, I returned into the cabin and closed the door. It had, unfortunately, no lock, bolt, or bar; but I had already made up my mind to sit up and watch, so that the want of fastenings did not so much matter. In the meantime Aunt Jenny had been bustling about, and had really given an air of some comfort to the place. She had gathered some fragments of wood which lay about the door; had lighted a little fire on the broad, flat stone which served for a hearth; had fixed the candle into a hole in the table which had previously served for a candlestick; and had fastened one of the pine-knots against the wall, adding more light to the interior, though accompanied by a strong, but, to my mind, aromatic smell, from the burning of the resin. Seating myself beside Bessy, I took her hand in mine, saying,--

"One more night, dearest, one more uncomfortable night, and then I trust all our troublous hours will have passed, and the memories of them will be but like a distressing dream. Had you not better go and lie down to obtain some sleep? We can easily get some leaves and dry reeds to make up a tolerable couch."

"You had better, Missie Bessy," said old Jenny. "Dere going to be storm to-night. Better get asleep before de tunder comes, and den you sleep it troo."

"You go and sleep with her, Jenny," I said; "you must be tired out too, poor woman! I will stay here and watch till morning. Then I will wake you, and you shall get us some breakfast before we set out."

"Indeed I am not the least sleepy," said Bessy, with a smile. "Do you know, Richard, so dull and insensible have I been--or perhaps I should say, so benumbed by all that has occurred--that this morning after they brought me to that old house, and I found I could not get out, I fell sound asleep, and must have been still asleep when you arrived. I will sit up and watch with you for an hour or two; but Jenny had better go and sleep, for I am sure she must need it."

"Well, p'raps I do," answered the good woman. "Then you call me by-and-by, and come and sleep yourself, my darling; but let's set off, whatsoever, by daylight." Jenny was somewhat more particular in regard to her bed than most people of her colour. Going forth to the edge of the swamp once or twice, she brought in several bundles of dry rushes, shaking her head each time she returned, and saying,--

"Goin' to storm very soon. Great a'mighty big clouds coming up; hope de water not come in." At length all her preparations were complete; and retiring into the little inner cell with a lighted pine-knot in her hand, she closed the door between, and left Bessy and myself alone. I drew my chair close to her, and I think I may be forgiven for putting my arm round her and making her pillow her head upon my bosom as she had done two nights before. I might also be forgiven for pressing my lips upon hers, and drawing her somewhat closely to my heart. At least *she* forgave me, and that was all I cared about. I told her how anxious I had been, how terrified, when I found she was gone from the spot in which I had left her; what a night and day of agitation and alarm I had undergone; and how I longed to hear all that had befallen her from her own sweet lips.

"Oh, I will tell you all," said Bessy. "I wish I could call it a 'Midsummer Night's Dream,' dear Richard; but it has been too terribly real for that. However, it will wile away half an hour of the night; and so you shall hear it."

CHAPTER XXXV

You remember, when you left me, I promised, if anything should make me quit the spot, to strew some pieces of paper or fragments of my handkerchief upon the ground as I went, to give you some indication of the way I had taken. For about a quarter of an hour--it could not be more (though it seemed to me more at the time)--all was quiet and still; and I and Jenny and the girl Minerva sat and talked, listening every now and then for your return. At length one of the other mulatto women came from the place where they had lighted a fire, to say that their cooking was ready; and, seeing me and Jenny, asked us to come and partake. We declined, however; and Minerva went away and left us. But a minute or two had passed, when we heard a distant noise of horses' feet; and then the sound of people talking loud not far off. I started up and prepared to fly, but Jenny's sharp ears had distinguished the voices better than I had, and she said,--

"Those are white men's tongues!" I listened, and convinced myself she was right; and after a good deal of conversation had gone on, apparently between the new comers and the mulatto women, we saw seven or eight while men coming up, guided by the girl Minerva. They were headed by a person whom I knew, though I cannot say I ever much liked him, and would rather perhaps have had any other escort. On this occasion, however, he behaved quietly and like a gentleman, telling me that his party would convey me to a place of safety: that they had several spare horses with them and women's saddles; but that, as it was growing late, it would be necessary for me to come with him directly. I informed him, in return, that you had gone to see if the way were clear to Jerusalem, and that I did not think I ought to go, till you came back. He said he could not wait that time, as he had several other young ladies to take up at different houses on the road; but that he must insist upon my not remaining there exposed to danger from any of the lawless ruffians who were roaming about; at the same time, to satisfy me that you would have information of my departure and safety, he said he would leave one or two of his men on the spot. I heard him give the order myself, and I do believe he was at this time acting in good faith, though he did not behave rightly afterwards. If I acted wrongly, dear Richard, forgive me; though I have hardly forgiven myself since, knowing and feeling what you must have suffered. Is not that a vain speech, Richard? But you see how I count upon your love, and I don't mind your seeing it.

Well, I was satisfied that you would soon know, and your mind be put at ease; and I and Jenny went with Colonel Halliday and his party to the path on the right, where we found all the horses and half a dozen more men. Once there, we were mounted immediately; but the men continued on foot talking together for some minutes, arguing, it seemed to me, upon some arrangements. At length they jumped on their horses; and Halliday, and five of the men, rode off in one direction while the rest pushed to the right, taking me and Jenny with them. We had not gone a quarter of a mile, when who should ride up to my side from behind, but old William Thornton, Robert's father. "Well, cousin Bessy," he said, "we will take good care of you. We will put you in a place of safety. What a lucky thing, you escaped out of Beavors! Why they have murdered all the rest."

"I understood Colonel Halliday, he was going to take me to Jerusalem;" I replied; "and this is quite a contrary direction, Mr. Thornton."

"Oh, you mistook him," replied the old man; "you can't get to Jerusalem nor he either. The road is in possession of the niggers. There's full four hundred of 'em." At first, Richard, I was frightened, and thought of you, and how you would get through. But the next moment, something in my own breast, told me the statement was all false. I knew the man. I knew what a knave he was, and what efforts he had made to get me into his hands when I was a child; then a selfish fear, a fear for myself took possession of me. I was now in his power. I doubted not the people who were with him were all his own creatures; and, after a minute or two of wild consideration, confused and inconsequent enough, I thought it would be best to let him take me where he would, believing that in this country of law, he dare not use any violence or do me any injury. At all events, I had got the pistol you had given me, and at that moment, I looked upon it as a treasure indeed. Well, he carried me to his own house, and took me there to a nice room enough, where he said he would send me up some supper. He was exceedingly polite and civil all the time, and excused himself for not taking me into the parlour, because his son Robert was there, who was not quite recovered. Presently a negro girl brought me some lights; for by this time it was quite dark. Then came some supper, and some wine, of which I partook heartily, confess; for I was weak and faint, and I felt the necessity of some adventitious courage. My supper was hardly over when William Thornton and his son both came in. The old man carried some papers in his hand; and the son, after speaking a few civil words, sat himself down right between me and the door.

"Well, Cousin Bessy," said the father, "I dare say, after all your fatigue and fright, you will sleep well to-night. You are quite safe here; for we have got three white men in the house, Irishmen, who will shoot down any one I order them to destroy; so you need not be in the least alarmed."

"I am not alarmed at all," I answered; though I am afraid, Richard, it was a great fib. "Don't you know, Mr. Thornton, it takes a great deal to alarm me?" The old man looked a little confounded at my reply; but he said,--

"Well, well, we will soon leave you to go to sleep; only there are some old accounts and things between you and me, Cousin Bessy, in regard to matters that occurred when I had the management of your property, which I think we had better settle now. I only just want you to sign these receipts and acquittances. They are all right, as you can see. Give me down the ink; here's a pen." Robert Thornton brought the ink from the mantel-piece, and his father put the papers before me. I did not pay much attention to them; but I just caught in one part, some words which I think were, "For, and in consideration, of the sum of thirty thousand dollars, the receipt of which is hereby acknowledged." I pushed them away at once to the other side of the table, saying,--

"Mr. Thornton, I will sign no papers whatever except in the presence of Mr. Hubbard, and Mr. Henry Thornton; and if these papers are fair and right, I cannot understand your pressing them upon me at such a moment, and in such circumstances."

"The reason of their being pressed upon you, Miss Davenport," said Robert Thornton, with one of his cold sneers, "and the reason why I shall insist upon their being signed at once, lies in the very circumstances to which you do not choose to allude; namely, that you are about to be married to a man whose father deprived you of your father, and who himself nearly deprived me of life. Unless these are signed before your marriage, difficulties must and will arise which I am determined----"

"Stay, stay, Bessy!" I cried, interrupting her narrative; "let me hear that again."

"Not now, Richard, not now," she said, eagerly. "He alluded to your father, Sir Richard Conway; but the very allusion drove me half wild; and I am afraid that I showed myself such a dragon that you would never wish to marry me, if you had seen me then." I took up the papers, and tore them into a thousand pieces, and then said, with as big a look as I could put on--I can hardly think of it without smiling--"Leave the room, sirs! and do not venture to come back again!" The old man got up and drew back; but the younger kept his chair, saying coldly,--

"The papers are soon re-written; and, though sorry to prevent you from sleeping, we shall bring them back in about a quarter of an hour."

"Then mark me, Mr. Robert Thornton," I answered, taking out the pistol; "the first man who attempts to intrude into this room again, I will shoot before his foot crosses the threshold, and these fragments will show the reason why. Leave the room, sirs, instantly." They *did* leave the room-- the elder gentleman with a considerable degree of trepidation. But, my dear Richard, I was a mere bully all the time; and although, I am sure, I looked twice as tall as I really am, and talked twice as loud as I ever did in my life before, I was frightened out of my wits all the time. The next unpleasant thing was to hear them lock the door; but, thank Heaven, there was a great bolt in the inside; and if they kept *me* in, I was determined to keep *them* out, or I believed that help must come soon, as too many people knew that I was there for concealment to be long kept up. I need not tell you all the little incidents of that night. I would let nobody into the room but the servant-girl, and made quite sure that only one step had come up the stairs, before I would open the door to her. But the discomforts of that evening were nothing to the horrors of the next morning. What the hour was, I do not know; for my watch was left behind at poor Mr. Stringer's; but I suppose it must have been about nine or ten o'clock; when, seated behind the blind at the open window, I saw five or six negro-men coming up towards the house. When they came near, I recognized several of them at once as poor Aunt Bab's servants, and I saw a great tall man, whom I knew very well, come forward and knock at the door, after which he retreated five or six steps from the house; and I heard old William Thornton's voice speaking to him out of a window on the same floor as the room in which I was.

"Go away, go away this instant," cried the old man; "go away, or I'll shoot you. Not one of you ruffians shall get into my house. Here, Pat Macrea, bring me my gun, and get your own. Bob, Bob," he continued, calling across the passage; "here are a whole heap of the Beavors niggers come to rescue her."

"Fire into them--fire into them!" cried my worthy Cousin Robert, with an oath. "You can say you thought they came to attack the house. I'll be with you in a minute." You may judge how terrified I was, Richard; but, putting my head out, I saw old Mr. Thornton and one of his Irishmen leaning forth from two of the windows with guns in their hands. Just at the same moment, poor Hercules exclaimed,--

"For Heaven's sake, don't shoot us, Mas'r Thornton! We only want to speak with Miss Bessy."

"Go along!" cried the old man. "She's not here, I tell you."

"Why I see her there now," cried the negro. At the same moment, Robert Thornton came to the window, crying,--

"March off, you scoundrels!" Then, adding something in a low voice to his father, he put a gun to his shoulder.

"For shame, Mr. Thornton--for shame!" I cried, as loud as I could speak. But it had no effect. All the guns went off almost together, and three of the poor negroes fell. Two started up again immediately; but poor Hercules remained upon the ground till the rest carried him off. I thought I should have fainted; and the dreadful deed they had done seemed to have awed and terrified the other people in the house. I heard them talking loudly and eagerly; and, from fragments of their conversation which I caught, I easily comprehended that what terrified them most was the fact of my having witnessed their proceedings.

"Oh, the old devil can do no harm," said Robert Thornton. "She's a nigger and a slave, and can't testify. As to this girl, you must send her across the line, and keep her there till the matter is settled. The court sits next Thursday week."

"But how shall we get her to go?" asked old Mr. Thornton.

"I will make her go, or serve her the same," said Robert Thornton, bitterly. "Here, Pat," continued he, "you and Dan won't be afraid to follow me into the girl's room, though she has got a pistol. I will go in first, and she can but shoot one of us."

"Afraid! not a bit," answered the man. "We'll soon master her, whatever devil there may be in her. But you won't hurt her, Master Thornton; I can't see a woman hurt." All this conversation was carried on very close to my door; and I will own, Richard, I was completely cowed.

"Mr. Thornton," I cried; "Mr. Thornton--speak to me through the door. I know what you are afraid of, and what you want; and I am willing to go peaceably where you wish me; for I do not want to have a cousin's blood upon my head."

"Well, undraw the bolt, then," said Robert Thornton, "and let us come in."

"No, no," I answered, "I will make my conditions. Nobody shall come in, and nobody shall touch me. Bring the horses round before the house, and I will come down the stairs quietly and mount, if you will promise that nobody shall come within two yards of me. Do you all promise?"

"Yes," answered Robert Thornton, "nobody wants to come near you, Miss Bessy, or to do you any harm."

"Very well," I answered; "I will trust to your promise. But mind, if any one comes near, I will shoot him as sure as my name is Davenport; and the consequences be upon your own heads. Now bring round the horses and keep away from the door." Three horses were brought round almost immediately, and some one came and unlocked the door. I heard him go down stairs again, and then, opening the door, I went down with the pistol in my hand. I tried not to shake, Richard; and I don't think any of them saw how terrified I was; for I heard the old man say when I got out before the house,--

"What a devil she is!" He little knew how my heart was sinking at that moment. As I approached the side of the horse on which the woman's saddle had been put, Robert Thornton offered to help me; but I was still afraid he would get the pistol from me, and I told him to stand off. Without farther parley, we set out as soon as I had mounted, one negro man going on horseback before, and another following closely. None of the white men accompanied us; but I heard old Mr. Thornton giving as strict directions to the man who followed, as if I were to be imprisoned for some criminal offence. He ended by saying,--

"Now, mind, if she gets away, I will cut you to pieces; so see to it." In this manner I was brought over to the house where you found me, and there locked in that miserable room by the old man Samuel, and another younger negro whom I have not seen since.

"And now, dear Richard," said Bessy, having finished her story, "don't you think me a terrible termagant? When I think of all I said and did, I feel almost ashamed of myself, and I dare say, hereafter, I shall blush whenever I think of it."

"Why, dearest Bessy," I answered, drawing her closer to me, "what could you do? The gentlest hearts are not always those most devoid of spirit."

"But have you not sometimes thought mine a cold heart, Richard?" asked Bessy; "so cold as to give you pain without cause. Oh, you know not when I have given you pain what agony I have inflicted on myself!" Closer and closer I drew her to my bosom; kiss after kiss I pressed upon her lips, till she became almost frightened, and exclaimed,--

"O Richard, remember, nothing is changed!"

"Yes, dearest," I answered, "everything is changed. One little word you have spoken insures that you shall never have need, or fancy you have need, to inflict pain upon me or yourself again." I was going on, but such an awful clap of thunder burst over our heads, that she started from my arms like a guilty thing, and event after event came fast to stay further explanation.

CHAPTER XXXVI

There was but a momentary pause. We had not, occupied as we had been with each other, seen the flash which preceded or accompanied the thunder; but before I could persuade Bessy to sit down by me again, a blaze, gleaming through every crack and cranny of the hut, dazzled our eyes, succeeded by a peal, breaking just over head, as if mountains had fallen, which, echoed and re-echoed round by the forest, exceeded, in deafening roar, anything I had ever heard, even in the Indian ocean. Then came the rushing sound of the descending rain, first pattering heavily on the thatch, and then sounding with one continuous noise, like that of a waterfall. The frail covering above us could not withstand the flood, and here and there the water began to drop on the floor, especially near the walls. The space around the table, indeed, remained free; but, fearing that our poor brown companion in the adjoining room might suffer before she was aware--for negroes will sleep through anything--I ventured to look in. Jenny had heard no thunder, nor had the lightning passed before her eyes with any effect. She slept as soundly as if there was no war of elements, nor any other dangers nigh. But the thatch over that room had been more solidly constructed, and the rain had not penetrated. Satisfied on that score, I returned to the other room, and again seated myself beside Bessy, placing my gun and a pistol on the table, where I could see that they did not get wet. I had not returned a moment too soon, for I had no time to utter a word before the door of the hut was pushed sharply open, and a dark form presented itself at the aperture. On the first impulse, I snatched up the gun, and, pointing it at the doorway, exclaimed, "Stand!" while Bessy cowered down in her chair with a look of terror, but did not speak or move from her seat.

"Stand!" I exclaimed again, seeing the man take a step forward, "Stand, or I fire! What do you want?"

"Shelter--food," answered the negro. "Fire, if you like! It matters little." As he spoke, I perceived by the dim light that the intruder was the leader of the sanguinary band who had crushed out so many a happy hearth, and made so many a household desolate.

"Keep back for a moment," he said, turning to some one without. Then, confronting me again, he added, "I am starving, and so are those with me.

God's storms are raging through the forest. Will you give me some food? Will you allow me and mine to take shelter here till the deluge has passed over? On my life, no harm shall happen to you; if not, fire, and you will find you have killed the only one who could protect you."

"Will you swear by the God whom you adore, and who you fancy has guided you," I asked, "that neither you nor your companions will offer any violence, and that you will quit the hut the moment the storm is ended--nay, that you will not move forward from that side of the cabin while you are here?"

"I swear!" he answered. "But you, too, must promise that you will not betray me." I thought for an instant; but the consideration of Bessy's safety prevailed over every other, and I promised.

"Who is in the other room?" he asked, seeing a light gleaming through a chink in the door.

"Only one other person," I answered, "who is under my command. You are quite secure if you keep your oath. If you do not, I have three lives, at least, at my disposal."

"I have sworn by the Almighty," said the man, in a tone almost of indignation. Then, turning to the door again, he exclaimed, "Come in!" Two other negroes instantly appeared from behind him, and as all three were armed, the odds against me, in case of strife, were somewhat serious. I had trusted, however, to my own conception of the man's character, for, although every sort of abuse had been piled upon him by all ranks and classes in the county town, and though certainly his deeds, during the last days, had been of the most remorseless and brutal nature, yet I had come to a conclusion which nothing could shake, that superstitious fanaticism was at the bottom of all his actions--good and evil. Nor had I any cause to change my opinion from his conduct towards me. He pledged himself by the Being whom he madly believed to be his prompter and guide in all his wickedness; and I rightly believed he would keep his word. He himself and both his companions looked gaunt, exhausted, and famished; and I am convinced that had I refused them the boon of food and shelter which they required in their desperate condition, they would not only have taken it, but the lives of all within the hut.

"There, in that basket, is the only food I have to give you," I said. "Take it and share it amongst you. We have not been well supplied ourselves; but you want it more than we do." One of the men was starting forward to seize the basket; but Nat Turner put him sternly back, saying,--

"I have promised that you should not go a step forward from that side of the cabin. By your permission, sir, I will take the food, for we do want it indeed."

"Leave us some, leave us some," cried a voice behind me; and, turning round, I beheld old Jenny, who, though she had slept through the thunder, had woke up, it would seem, at the sound of human voices.

"I was well nigh starved to death to-day by that old Thornton, and I don't want to die o' hunger to-morrow, nor see you nor Missie Bessy either, Mas'r Conway." A grim sort of smile came over Nat Turner's dark countenance as he threw the pine-knots out of the basket on the floor, and helped his companions with his own hands to the coarse bread and raw salt fish which lay beneath. He took a small portion himself also, but less than he gave them; and, looking first at me, and then at Bessy, he said,--

"You have found, I fancy, that white men can be as hard and cruel as negroes--but without the same cause." As he spoke, he rolled his eyes in his head with a fierce, almost insane look; and then added abruptly,--

"This cabin was built by an old negro as a place of refuge from the brutality of one of your white men. We break forth for a moment when we can bear no longer, destroy, kill, murder, if you like; but has any one of us inflicted as much misery, done as much harm, as that man in the course of his long life? If we had done rightly, he would have been the first sacrifice to the God of vengeance. We should have chosen our victims equitably; and perhaps it is for this that the Almighty favour is withdrawn from us; but the time may come when it will be restored."

"Ah, Nat, Nat," said Jenny, "I did not think you would have done such terrible things as you have done--you, who always seemed kind and good, and to be a God-fearing man."

"Woman, I did God's bidding!" answered Nat Turner, with a sharp, angry look; "and I will do it still, but more wisely." He then fell into a fit of deep thought, fixing his eyes upon the floor, and remaining on his feet, though his two companions had seated themselves on the ground. Every two or three minutes the lightning continued to flash, and the thunder to roar, and the rain still poured down in torrents.

"I wish, dearest Bessy," I said, in a low voice, "you would go into the other room and rest. This man will keep his word with us. There is no danger."

"I will stay by your side, Richard," she answered in a whisper; "this is my place." A long pause ensued; and certainly curious sensations arose-- sensations not very pleasant, when I reflected that before me were three men whose hands, within the last eight-and-forty hours, had been steeped in the blood of nearly eighty human beings, most of them women and children. At length, Nat Turner broke silence, saying abruptly, and in a gloomy tone,--

"What was that you told me about the sign I saw in the sun--an eclipse you called it?" I gave him the same explanation I had done before, telling him that it was a mere natural phenomenon, which occurred at periods easy to be calculated, in consequence of the regular movements of the planets.

"Can I have been mistaken?" he muttered between his teeth. "No, no!" he added in a louder tone; "the sun shall be turned into darkness, and the moon into blood, before the great and terrible day of the Lord! It was the sign, it was the sign! The vision and the prophecy cannot be mistaken. I saw him stand on my right side with a rod in his hand, and he pointed to the sky, and he told me to be up and doing. It shall be fulfilled even yet. But the wheat must first be winnowed from the chaff, and the tares rooted out, that it be the work of the husbandman. What though there be few left, others shall rise up. Hands more meet hearts more firm, to do the mighty and terrible work of the Lord." His two companions fixed their eyes on his face, evidently regarding him as one inspired; and I watched with no slight anxiety, knowing well that one can never calculate what turn superstition may take. But he fell quietly into another reverie, which lasted nearly half an hour, and his mood seemed to be soothed by his own reflections. I fancy the truth was, that irritating doubts had suggested themselves as to the truth of his fancied revelations; but that now, by his own arguments, he had satisfied his own mind again, and that his heart felt lighter in consequence. The storm, though very severe, was brief. Before Nat Turner brought his meditations to a close, the thunder grew fainter, and followed, at a long distance, the flash of the lightning. The rain no longer pattered on the thatch; and the negro, looking up, said, though in what connection, I could not discover,--

"Was not the moon very red when she rose to-night?"

"She was red enough last night," answered aunt Jenny, "and I dare she was redder to-night. But I did not look at she, Nat. She was as red as blood last night 'bout this time."

"Ay, ay!" replied the man in a satisfied tone. Then, after a few minutes' silence, he added--"It has done raining, I think, and I will keep my word." He opened the door of the hut and looked out, and we could see gleams of the moon's light flitting over the Swamp as she struggled with the parting clouds. After gazing forth, for a minute or two, he returned, and approached the side of the table, saying,--

"I want you to give me some gunpowder, Sir Richard Conway. Mine is almost out."

"Not if it were to save my life, and all that is most dear to me," I answered. "Not one grain. I have given you food and shelter, but I will not give you the means to injure others."

"So be it," he replied, quietly. "God, mayhap, will give what you refuse." And calmly throwing the damp powder out of the pans of his guns, which had nothing but flint-locks, he primed the weapons again, and made his two companions bring their guns to him to undergo the same process. He then shook the flask at his ear, saying.--

"One more charge a-piece, and before that is out, we must find more. Now, boys, leave the cabin." They seemed to obey his lightest word; and when they were gone, he turned to me, saying--"I do not thank you, for I have as much right here as you have, as much right possibly to the food. But I will keep my word with you--I will keep my vow and more. You may sleep in quiet and peace. I shall be near, and no one shall molest you. Goodnight! We may meet again, when I shall not ask you for anything, or you refuse me." And he left the cabin, drawing to the door after him.

CHAPTER XXXVII

"Now, dearest Bessy," I said, as soon as the man was gone, "you had better go into the other room and lie down to rest. Take Jenny with you, and I will remain here. That man will keep his word with us, depend upon it, and we shall see no more of them. But, as a precaution, I will push this table against the door, so that no one can take us by surprise."

"But you want sleep yourself, Richard," she said.

"I will get some in this corner, where it is dry," I answered. And, after some persuasion, she left me. Did I sleep? Oh, no. Not only the necessity of watching to guard against any intrusion kept me awake, but I had pleasant--nay, joyful--thoughts to dwell upon. I had discovered a secret, at least I thought so, upon which all my future happiness depended; and the happy reveries which followed might well occupy the two or three hours which remained of night. At the end of that time I could perceive a faint greyish light, glimmering through the chinks of the rude shutters; and I thought I might as well reconnoitre the ground without. I did not feel sure that the negroes had quitted the neighbourhood; and though I was inclined to believe that, after what had passed, they would offer us no violence, even if we encountered them; yet there is so much uncertainty and even treachery in the character of all barbarous people that ever I have seen, that I did not like to risk taking Bessy from the shelter of the hut till I was sure the man had gone. Partly removing the shutter, so as to leave perhaps half a hand's breadth for sight, I gazed out upon the wild and desolate scene presented by the Swamp, which looked more wild and desolate than ever, in that dull and unconfirmed light. All was still and quiet; and no moving object met my eye for a moment or two, till I saw the grass agitated slightly, not a couple of steps from the front of the hut. An instant after, a huge rattlesnake dragged himself sluggishly out of the long, dry grass, and crawled lazily towards a little knoll where the light fell most strongly. He seemed as if he were going out to take his morning's walk before his human enemies came abroad. The next instant I beheld one of those beautiful creatures called the king-snake, not half the size of the other, dash out in his checkered coat of jet-black and ivory-white, and dart at the great sluggish reptile. A desperate fight ensued. They coiled one with the other; they bit, they struck at each other with their heads; and I could hardly imagine that the great rattlesnake could not easily destroy his little antagonist. But I was mistaken. At the end of three minutes, the rattlesnake lay writhing on the ground in the agonies of death, and the king-snake, apparently uninjured, glided round and round several times, evidently calculating whether there was any possibility of swallowing him. That was impossible, however, from the relative size of the two creatures; and, contented with his victory, the brilliant little conqueror glided away.

"How happy it would be," I thought, "if, in the world of human life, the reptiles thus destroyed each other--ay, and so they do sometimes." I knew not how soon I should see my fancy verified. While I was thus pondering, I thought I heard a faint and distant sound; but it seemed to me as if, mingled in the noise, were tones of the human voice, and the footfalls of several horses. Before the hut, as I have said, and hiding it, but only partially hiding it, as I found afterwards, from one of the paths across the Swamp, was a clump of bushes, with a tall pyramidal cedar or two rising up in the midst. I dare say, in the confusion of objects, the trees, the bushes, the green and yellow leaves, the fallen trunks, cast in every wild variety of attitude; the plashy ground, and here and there a higher piece of sandy bank with gray and yellow surfaces, thousands of people might pass along that way without a suspicion that any cabin was near. Still it was not fully concealed; and afterwards, when I passed along that very path, knowing where it lay, I could clearly distinguish the lines of the little gable with its thatch. I listened eagerly, and the sounds grew more and more distinct--horses' feet beating hard and fast, and people talking. A minute after I could discern the party through the branches--three white men on horseback, and a stout young negro. They were bidden again; but in another moment I saw them more distinctly, and I recognized Robert Thornton and his father. The other white man's appearance was somewhat familiar to me, but I could not remember where I had seen him before. It was that of the man, Matthew Leary, who had accompanied Robert Thornton when first I encountered him, and whom Billy Byles had described "as a man who would sell his own father, if he could find any man to buy him." They passed on behind the clump of bushes, right in front; and, thinking them gone, I was turning to wake Bessy, in order that we might find the horses, which I could perceive nowhere in the neighbourhood, and then proceed across the Swamp as fast as possible. Suddenly, however, I was stopped by the sound of voices again quite near. I put my eye to the chink, which I had nearly closed; and, somewhat to my consternation, beheld the whole party before the hut.

"Why, I told you so!" cried old Mr. Thornton. "It is a cabin by ----. Who the devil built it here, I wonder?"

"Well, come along, come along, father!" cried Robert Thornton, in an impatient and even angry tone; "if you dawdle on in this way, we shall miss our mark entirely. You can come back and see all about this when we have got her off. I tell you, if they catch hold of her, and bring her back, we are ruined." He muttered something about an old fool; and his tender father called somebody a d--d jackanapes. But the old man seemed habitually under the control of his worthy son, and he rode on in the end, though apparently very unwillingly. As they passed onward, a negro drew partly out from amongst the bushes, with a gun in his hand, which he raised for a moment to his shoulder, but then let it drop again, as if he doubted his distance or his aim. The next moment he glided back quietly into the bushes, and disappeared entirely. I continued to watch for a minute or two; and once I thought I saw a dark face appear as if gazing out in the direction which Mr. Thornton's party had taken; but it was seen only for an instant, and I turned to think what had best be done. The question became, what was the greatest risk? Mr. Thornton, I judged, was very likely to return as soon as he found that Bessy was liberated; but, whatever violence he might venture to indulge in towards the comparatively unprotected negroes, I felt assured that he would hesitate a good deal before he would enter into a struggle which he knew must be carried to extremity with white people. On the other hand, Nat Turner and his companions had bound themselves by no very extensive engagement. They had promised us security during that night; but they might well look upon the bond as extending no further; and, moreover, the great moral power of responsibility was taken from them. They had dared and incurred the utmost penalty that human laws could pronounce; no mercy shown towards us could atone for their past inconceivable guilt; no fresh murder, no fresh barbarity could add one iota to the punishment which they were certain of receiving in this world. If they were not watching for our coming forth, why did they remain hiding there in the bushes just opposite the hut? I could not but suspect, also, that, hampered as I had left them, the horses could not have got out of sight without having been removed. Added to these thoughts came the considerations, that if we went out from the hut we could be attacked on any side, unaided by any or either party; but that as long as we remained within it, I could defend the door with very little difficulty against a more numerous force than I had yet seen; and, in addition, I thought that it was more than probable the sheriff, when he found, on returning to his own house, that neither I nor Bessy had returned, would scour the country along the state-line, and, perhaps, even pass it in search of us. Bessy still slept soundly, to all appearance; and at length, after much hesitation, I determined not to rouse her. I employed, the time in sawing out, with the old saw which lay in the corner, several stout pins and bolts to fasten the door. For this purpose I took part of the table, and in a short time I made the entrance secure. The shutters of the windows ran in grooves, and the woodwork, both of them and of the door, was almost an inch and a half thick; which, though penetrable by a musket-ball, was sufficient to deaden the shot greatly. There were no apertures at the back of the house: the square aperture which served for a window, commanded the only approach; and, satisfied that my little castle was fortified as far as possible, I waited, watching to see if the negroes would quit the covert, though I had some apprehension that they might make their exit on the opposite side. I had hardly resumed my post at the window a minute, when Bessy crept up to my side. The noise of the axe and the saw had awakened her; and I had to tell her all that had occurred, and to go over with her all the reasonings which induced me to remain where we were. She seemed to have an unquestioning faith in my decisions; and while I tightly fastened up the window in the other room where she had been sleeping, she kept watch in the first room, never moving from the spot where I had placed her.

"Nothing has moved," she said, as I rejoined her; "not a twig has quivered, not a rain-drop has fallen from a leaf."

"Then probably the men remain there still," I answered; "for I suspect they have horses with them, and the batch of bushes is too narrow for any large body to move out unperceived."

"I do not think," observed Bessy, after meditating for a moment or two, "that there is any fear of violence from Mr. Thornton or his party. Robert is a coward, I am sure. He may bolster himself up to some degree of determination when he is forced to it by fear of the world; and he may do terrible and cruel acts where poor negroes or women are concerned. But he is always more or less cowed, as I have seen, when he is opposed to a free man, and more especially to a gentleman. He does not seem to know how to act; and, in his hesitation, he gets alarmed."

"I agree with you," I replied; "for although in the unfortunate affair between himself and me he did not actually show want of nerve, I could plainly perceive he would a great deal rather have avoided fighting, had it been possible. But see! there is something moving in the bushes." It certainly was so, and the movement was towards the side at which we were standing, but nobody issued forth; and after waiting for a few minutes more, sharing in my watch, Bessy left me to call old Jenny, who had slept uninterruptedly through all that had taken place. The good old cook set to work at once to light a fire again; and I did not think it worth while to prevent her, for the negroes already knew that we were there; and if Mr. Thornton came at all, it would be to search the place, so that the treacherous signal of the smoke could do us no harm. Indeed, in the present instance, it did us much good. Our breakfast was destined to be very scanty. Bread, there was very little. The fish was all consumed; and some eggs, which aunt Jenny roasted in the ashes, were all that remained of the more solid fare. Worst of all, we had no water; and I perceived, with no light apprehension, that if our enemies could not take us by storm, they might soon starve us out by a blockade. We took it by turns to watch and to eat, making old Jenny breakfast first; but she had not assumed her post at the window for three minutes, when she exclaimed,--

"Here dey comin', mas'r--here dey comin'!" Starting up, I ran to her side. I instantly saw the party, and distinguished who they were. Mr. William Thornton and his son had visited the old place, as they called it; found that I had taken Miss Davenport away, fixed at once upon the cabin they had seen in the wood, and pursued us thither. They had dismounted at some little distance, had given the horses to the negro-boy, and were approaching towards the hut on foot, when I saw them. I placed on the table the powder and the slugs, and the two pistols ready loaded.

"Bessy," I said, "can you load rapidly, as soon as I have fired, in case of need?"

"Yes, yes," she answered, "I have seen it done often. I am sure I can do it."

"Then you stand between me and the table, Jenny," I said, "and hand the weapons to and fro. As soon as I have fired, if I should have occasion to fire, give me another weapon. One man here," I added, with a smile to encourage them, "is equal to five or six without." I then pushed back the shutter a little more, leaned the muzzle of the gun upon the sill, and looked out, careless of further concealment. Mr. Thornton's party, that is to say, the three white men, had stopped at the distance of about one hundred and fifty yards from the cabin, apparently to consult. But a moment after they turned to march forward again, and their eyes instantly fell upon me at the window.

CHAPTER XXXVIII

I remained perfectly still and silent at the window of the hut, with my eyes steadily fixed upon the other party, believing that some embarrassment would be felt by all of them in regard to their next step, if I gave them no excuse for violence. I have often remarked that the most daring and unscrupulous men prefer provoking a quarrel step by step, to plunging into a conflict at once. I was not mistaken in this instance. Mr. Thornton and his son both stopped again when they saw me, and their consultation was renewed. They soon settled their plan, however, and did the best thing they could to attain their object, and throw the onus upon me. Without speaking one word, they advanced in a body towards the door of the cabin, and had come within twelve or fourteen paces of it, when, finding that action was absolutely necessary, I exclaimed,--

"Stand back, gentlemen. Do not advance any further."

"And why should we stand back, Sir Richard?" asked Robert Thornton, in a wonderfully calm tone.

"Simply, because if you advance a step further, I will shoot you," I replied with equal coolness.

"Upon what pretence, sir?" asked the elder Mr. Thornton, holding his son back. "We know that you are rather fond of shooting; but you generally contrive some excuse for it. Do you remember, sir, that you are in a civilized country? that the cabin in which you are is my property? and that I simply require to enter what I may call my own house?"

"It is not yours, ole tief," cried Jenny from behind. "It's not on your land, nor of your building."

"Sir," I replied, "I am quite aware of what I am about. The cabin may be yours, or may not, for aught I know; but of this I am assured, namely, that you and your son, and that worthy with the red hair, are now in the prosecution of an unlawful enterprise--"

"To wit?" said Robert Thornton, with a sneer.

"To wit, then," I rejoined, "the abduction of a witness to a homicide committed by you yesterday morning, for the purpose of screening yourselves from punishment in due course of law. Your consultations were overheard; your motives are all known; and the execution of your plan in part susceptible of proof. You now come here with superior force to take that witness from Virginian soil and my protection. Consequently, I feel myself justified in shooting you down one by one; and I will do it if you advance one step further in execution of your designs. You know me, Mr. Robert Thornton!"

"But, sir, we do not entertain any such designs," cried old Mr. Thornton, his face growing redder than before, though it was rubicund enough at all times.

"I judge of your present motives and intentions by your past conduct, sir," I answered; "by your conduct yesterday, and the motives for that conduct expressed in the hearing of a competent witness. Therefore--stand back, I say!" The latter words were uttered in a louder tone than the rest; and, as I spoke, I raised the gun to my shoulder; for the Irishman, seemingly tired of the discussion, had taken a step forward. Old Mr. Thornton pulled him hastily back, not liking, I suppose, to bring a shot into their party, the especial direction of which he did not feel sure of.

"This is too bad!" he cried. "By ---- this is too bad!" And he and his son entered into a low conference again. It was suddenly broken off, however, almost as soon as it had commenced, by some sounds which I did not hear.

"Run round those bushes, Mat," cried Robert Thornton to the Irishman, "and see what horses those are coming up. Don't let them see you--don't let them see you." The other obeyed, hurrying round the clump in which the negroes were concealed; and father and son were soon deep in a whispered and hasty consultation, with their faces still towards the hut, and their backs towards the bushes. My eyes continued fixed upon them for a moment or two; but then some sound--I know not what--made me raise them. The shrubs which lay behind them, at not twenty yards' distance, were agitated as if by some large body passing amongst the branches; and the next instant, no less than four negroes drew out from the bushes with a stealthy, quiet step. The two first had each a gun raised to the shoulder, and pointed towards Mr. Thornton and his son, as if the men sought to approach nearer to their victims, but were prepared to fire as soon as they saw the slightest movement. The other two negroes were also armed; but they were at a somewhat greater distance, leading two or three horses through a gap amongst the brakes, where the beasts' feet would not make so much noise. Though both father and son well deserved whatever fate they might meet, I could not bear to see two human beings shot down like wild brutes; and, by impulse, rather than anything else, I shouted,--

"Take care! take care!" And both started and turned round. At their very first motion there was a flash and a report; and Robert Thornton fell forward on his face. His father staggered; and then ran towards his horses, seemingly to shelter himself behind them; but the young negro who was holding them, apparently terrified at what had occurred, cast the reins loose, and ran away as fast as he could go. In the meantime, Nat Turner, who was standing in front of the shrubs, followed the flying man with his second barrel as deliberately as a sportsman follows a bird on the wing. Before he got near any of the horses, the trigger was drawn, and, with a wild cry of pain, the old man fell upon his knees, and then sank gradually down. At the same moment Matthew Leary came running round, with evident fear in his face, exclaiming,--

"It's the sheriff! it's the sheriff, with a large party." The moment he saw his two masters on the ground, he stopped short, like one thunder-struck, without uttering a word, and glanced his eye towards the cabin; but a shot from one of the negroes, who were leading up the horses, knocked his hat off, and soon showed him whence the murderous volley had come.

"Bring them up quick! bring them up quick!" cried Nat Turner, waving to the other men. He had evidently heard the announcement of the sheriff's approach, and he and two of his companions were mounted in a few seconds. The fourth seemed to have no horse, but ran to catch one of those which had brought Mr. Thornton's party thither. This caused a little delay; and before they could escape, the sheriff's party, consisting of nine or ten persons, appeared, some on one side of the little copse, and some on the other.

"Now," I thought, "these blood-thirsty fellows are caught at last." But I was, in some degree, mistaken; and I could not help admiring the presence of mind and ability displayed by Nat Turner in that perilous moment. The approaching party, attracted by the report of the guns, had come up at speed, and in some dismay; nor were they, it would seem, at all prepared to meet with any of the revolted negroes there. In an instant, Nat Turner seemed to perceive where they were weakest and most scattered, as well as where he could soonest reach the difficult ground of the Swamp; and, clubbing his gun, he dashed at that point, calling to the others to follow. He had to pass Matthew Leary as he went; and the man attempted to catch his rein; but one blow from the stock of the gun brought the Irishman to the ground; and, had his skull been originally constructed in any other country than Ireland or Africa, he never would have risen again. It did not interrupt the negro for a moment in his course. A tall farmer tried to stop him likewise, but he was struck from his horse in a moment. The other negroes followed through the gap he had made in the line of the white men, and the three first burst clear through. The fourth was captured on the spot.

"Follow, follow quick!" cried the sheriff. "Take them, alive or dead." But Nat Turner and his companions galloped on, and scattered as soon as they got into more open ground. Pistol shots were fired after them; but on they went, plunging through the morasses, leaping the fallen trees, and taking advantage of every obstruction in the ground to distance their pursuers. One even had the hardihood to turn and fire upon a man who was chasing him; for one of the sheriff's party returned shortly afterwards with a pretty severe wound in his shoulder. In the meantime, I had unfastened the door of the cabin, and joined the sheriff and the four or five gentlemen who remained with him: Bessy, and old Aunt Jenny, also, came to the door, and one of those confused scenes of inquiry and explanation took place, which it is hardly possible to describe.

"Why, how is this?" inquired the sheriff, in his dry, laconic way, as soon as he saw us. "All sorts of birds gathered together! Miss Davenport, I am glad to see you safe at last. Your uncle Henry, with Billy Byles, has gone on to seek you across the line; but here is matter we must look to at once. Here, you fellow, you Leary----"

"Don't call me a fellow, sir," said Leary, in an insolent tone. "I am a free American citizen, and as good as you any day." The sheriff's lip curled with a contemptuous smile.

"I should not like to be as bad as you, Master Leary," he said, "for I know I should have the penitentiary very often in my thoughts; but is your master here, dead or living?"

"I know nothing about him, and he's no master of mine," answered Leary; "but I'll just turn him over and see." In the meantime, the sheriff and most of the other gentlemen had dismounted, and we all surrounded the body of Robert Thornton, who lay perfectly still with his face on the ground. Mathew Leary turned him over; and we then saw a large pool of blood which had flowed from a wound in his chest, through which the bullet had passed out. It was on the left side, and there could be little doubt the shot had gone right through his heart. His career of wickedness was over. "His account was closed," as a quaint old writer has it; "every item transferred from the day-book to the ledger; the balance struck, and the whole to be settled at the great day of reckoning." This is one of those cases of retributive justice which come from time to time to convince all who are convinceable of the moral government of God; while the numerous exceptions form a strong argument--used potently by Voltaire--in favour of the immortality of the soul, the punishment of vice, and reward of virtue hereafter on that great day when every man shall be judged according to his doings. Robert Thornton and his father had set out in life well-to-do in worldly circumstances: had deliberately cast from them the restraints of justice and honour, of religious and of moral principle; had gone on trusting to subtlety and fraud, in despite of repeated failures and reiterated warnings; had hardened themselves against the very reproofs of the results of their own actions, till they had deprived themselves of character and honour, of means and resources--till the very necessity of their condition drove them from bad to worse, while the hedged-in way of disgrace and ruin grew narrower and more inevitable at every step they took. And, at last, one of the two had fallen in a disgraceful scheme to cover one outrage by another.

"Here, leave him there," said the sheriff, after we had gazed a moment upon the pale and inanimate features. "Nothing can be done for him. Who is the other lying out there?"

"That is Mr. William Thornton," answered Matthew Leary; "but what's become of the black boy, I can't tell; unless he's gone off with the other niggers. The old man's as dead as a door nail, I'll bet; for his blood was so near the skin, that the least hole would let it all run out."

"Hold your tongue, sir," said the sheriff; "this is no time for joking."

"Devil a bit am I joking," answered Mat Leary, "as the priest said to us the other day, when he told us we were all going to hell, and no mistake. I think he was right too." The sheriff moved sternly away, and, with the rest of the party, approached the spot where Mr. William Thornton lay. The wounded man was lying on his side as he had slipped down, rather than fallen; and, when his face was visible, it was clear that, though badly hurt, he was neither dead nor in a dying condition. He said not a word to any one, though he must have known many of those present; but he gazed silently in our faces, with a clear, undimmed eye, as I have often seen a wounded bird. The first shot which had been fired at him seemed to have grazed his shoulder; but the second had inflicted a much more serious wound in his hip, and he was bleeding profusely.

"We had better carry you to the cabin, and try to staunch the blood," said the sheriff, bending down over him; "we can remove you to your own house afterwards." The old man made no answer; and some of the party took him up as gently as they could, and carried him between them to the hut, at the door of which still stood Bessy, with a very pale face. As they went, they could not help passing the body of Robert Thornton, and inadvertently took that side towards which the old man's eyes were turned; but he gazed composedly at the corpse, without a word or an inquiry; and, indeed, I could not perceive the slightest change of countenance. If human attachments had been lost either in the selfishness of pain or the apathy of age, human resentments were not extinguished. They laid him on the table, and I whispered a few words to Bessy, who had shown so much skill in stopping the bleeding of my arm. She gave a slight shudder, but answered at once.

"Certainly, Richard--I forgot--I did not think of it; but I have been terrified and shocked. I will try directly;" and approaching the table, she said, "Let me try, gentlemen; I have had to do this before. Mr. Thornton, I think I can soon staunch the blood."' The old man suddenly raised himself with a start upon his elbow, exclaiming, with the look of a demon,--

"Get hence, girl! You have been the ruin of me and mine. We have never seen you, spoken to you, thought of you, I do believe, without some evil happening to us. Touch me not! Your very name has been a plague to us."

"And well it might, Billy Thornton," said a bluff old gentleman, who had come with the sheriff, "for you would never let any who bore it alone. You began all the mischief, and your son continued it. Who egged on the quarrel between poor Davenport, her father, and Richard Conway, when Conway wanted no quarrel at all? Who stopped the letter of explanation, and got Davenport killed, and was, more or less, the cause of Conway being drowned?"

"Hush! hush!" said the sheriff. "This is no time or place for recriminations. We must do the best we can to stop the bleeding ourselves, as he refuses the kind aid of hands that would do it better. Sir Richard, you had better take Miss Bessy away out of the cabin, and get her some water; she looks faint. Send off one of the men to the Thornton old place, and bid them bring down a mattress and a cart. You had better let Mr. Henry Thornton and Billy Byles know you are here, and then ride away with them to my house; it is the nearest, and, though but an old bachelor's residence, you will find a dear old maid there--my sister--who will make it comfortable to you, and cheer this young lady. Come, Miss Bessy, do not look so sad. All will go well, yet; and we who stand here living this day, without having lost our nearest and dearest, have much to thank God for."

"We have, indeed!" said Bessy; "and from my heart I do thank God." I led her quietly out, and turning away from the spot where several of the party were still gathered round the dead body of Robert Thornton, I seated her on a little rise at the other end of the cottage, and then proceeded to express the sheriff's wishes to some people before the hut. I hardly liked to leave her, even for a moment, for I had a sort of superstitious feeling upon me, after all that had occurred, that if I lost sight of her again I should never behold her more. Two men on horseback set out at once for the old place, as it was called, and, returning to Bessy's side, I strove to cheer her, and to lead her mind away from all the terrible and distressing events which had been crowded into so marvellously short a space of time. Indeed it was extraordinary how three days, in the midst of one year, could have crowded into themselves in the midst of a peaceful and happy country so many and terrible facts as occurred during the three principal days of the Southampton massacre. We were allowed but very little time for anything like tranquil conversation, however. First, came back one of the men who had gone in pursuit of Nat Turner and his companions, and then another. Dismounting from his horse, the first sauntered up to us, interrupting my conversation with Bessy, by saying,--

"There's no use trying to catch him. That man has got the devil in him, I do believe, and has got away into places where I wouldn't take my horse Maggie, for all the niggers that ever run. Isn't she a pretty creature? Have you got any horses like that in England? I guess not." The next who came up was the poor fellow who got hurt in the pursuit, and he gave me and Bessy occupation for some time in bandaging his wound, though it did not seem a very severe one. This operation was not quite over, when the sheriff came out of the cabin and joined us. He was looking stern, and somewhat irritated.

"That old man," he said, "seems to have been taken possession of by Satan. He abuses everybody and everything, and will make his wound prove mortal, if he doesn't mind, by his own bitter irritability. What changes circumstances do produce in men! I remember him, not many years ago, one of the most jovial and good-humoured sort of persons I ever saw--always cunning and ready to take advantage, it is true, but still he did it all so good-humouredly, that one was inclined to laugh rather than be angry."

"Don't you think," I asked, "that circumstances may have brought out the real character of the man, which cunning had concealed? We have a saying that the devil is good-humoured when he is pleased. I have seen more than once a man who carried on very artful schemes under an appearance, of careless jollity, turn out fierce, malicious, and vindictive, when those schemes were finally frustrated."

"Perhaps you are right," answered the sheriff. "I have heard that he would occasionally do a malevolent thing in former years. But here comes our friend Henry Thornton, I think--this man's very opposite in every respect. That is his head approaching at such a rate over the bushes of the swamp, isn't it? Well, my dear young lady, how do you feel now?"

"Somewhat calmer," answered Bessy, quietly; "but I shall not be better, my good friend, till I have had two good things."

"And what are those?" asked the sheriff.

"A good sleep and a good cry," answered Bessy. "I have had the current of so many tears choked up during the last three days, that I feel they must flow over soon."

"Well," answered the sheriff, with a good-humoured sort of smile, "a good sleep and a safe one, I trust, you will soon have; but as to a good cry, I can't help thinking a good mint julep would be better. I wish to Heaven I had one to give you, or to drink myself, either, for I am pretty weary and very thirsty."

CHAPTER XXXIX

As the sheriff spoke, Mr. Henry Thornton, Billy Byles, and another gentleman, whose face seemed familiar to me, rode up towards the cabin, but checked their horses suddenly as they came upon the body of Robert Thornton, which was still lying where he had fallen. They had evidently not received full intelligence of what had occurred: for surprise, as well as horror, was in the expression of their faces. All three sprang to the ground and gazed at the corpse for a moment in silence, while I and the sheriff advanced towards them.

"Why this is a terrible consummation!" said Mr. Henry Thornton, shaking me warmly by the hand. "How did this happen?"

"Nat Turner's work again," said the sheriff, before I could reply; "and the worst of it is, he has escaped us once more. He made his way through, and got into the swamp in spite of all we could do, though we came upon him before the smoke was out of his gun. Old William Thornton is hard hit too, but he is still living, and would live, if he were to keep himself quiet, and not curse, and swear, and abuse everybody."

"I suppose I must be content then," said the stranger, who had some up with the other two gentlemen; "for I was just going to call this unfortunate fellow to an account, as I find he has brought suspicion and discredit upon me, and my back is not sufficiently broad to bear all that people are inclined to pile upon it already."

"Well, well," said Billy Byles, "there is no use of talking any more about that, Halliday. All has been explained, and will be explained; and there lies Bob Thornton, the maker of all the mischief in the county, not likely to make any more mischief now, I fancy."

"Sir Richard Conway does not recollect me, I presume," said Colonel Halliday, speaking in a somewhat stiff and formal manner.

"I did not at first, Colonel Halliday," I replied; "but I do now, and am glad to see you."

"So am I to see you," he answered; "for I have much wished to explain to you that these two men, though friends of mine from my youth up, were neither aided nor countenanced by me in their late conduct towards Miss Davenport. They, and two or three others who were with them, promised me faithfully to see her safe to Jerusalem, while I went on to rescue some other young ladies from a somewhat dangerous position. Perhaps I ought not to have trusted to their word; for, I am sorry to say, I had known it violated before; but I had no suspicion at the time of anything like unfair play, and I gave orders to two men to wait to let you know where Miss Davenport was. They, however, were frightened away by the arrival of the negroes. I hope this explanation will be satisfactory to you, sir; but, if it is not, all I can say is, I am ready."

"Hush! hush! nonsense!" said Mr. Henry Thornton. And I immediately replied,--

"It is perfectly satisfactory, Colonel Halliday, though it was unnecessary. Miss Davenport has already done you full justice; and I easily attributed the conduct which has been pursued to the right parties, and to the true motives."

"Well, that is all right," said Billy Byles, in his easy, unconcerned way. "It is as well to get things over one by one; and now that is settled, what is to be done with this poor fellow's corpse, Mr. Sheriff? It cannot remain lying here, you know. Had we not better take it up to the old place?"

"We cannot carry it out of the state," replied the sheriff. "It will be better to put it out of sight amongst these bushes, till the cart I have sent for comes down to take the old man up to the house. We can then remove it to the cabin, and let it await the coroner's inquest there. In the meantime, Mr. Thornton, will it not be better for you and Sir Richard to ride over with Miss Bessy to my house? You will find my sister there, who will take care of the young lady; and if I might advise, she would not go further to-day, for she must be worn out with all she has gone through; and, indeed, she looks tired to death."

"A very good plan," answered Mr. Thornton; "and, at all events, we will wait at your house till you return, Mr. Sheriff." An alteration of plan, however, was forced upon us. The horses which had brought me and Bessy thither were not found for half-an-hour, having hobbled away three-quarters of a mile into the swamp. And when they were found and brought back, they had to be saddled for our journey. By this time, the cart which had been sent for had arrived, with a mattress stretched in the bottom. Old Mr. Thornton was carefully removed from the cabin and placed in the vehicle; and though a good deal reduced by loss of blood, he still seemed in a highly irritable and excited condition, cursing the men who moved him, for the pain they could not avoid inflicting. Three of the men who were present volunteered to accompany him to the old house; and the sheriff, after having given directions for sending for a surgeon, prepared with all the rest to set off together across the marsh.

"Where's old Jenny?" cried the sheriff as we were about to go, "where's old Jenny? We must not go without her. She is really a good creature, and tended that unhappy man quite kindly, notwithstanding all his abuse."

"Here I am, mas'r," cried Jenny, coming out of the hut. "You go 'long, I'll come after. Nobody hurt me, and I want to lay out Mas'r Robert."

"No, no, Jenny, come along," said the sheriff. "Let him alone; the coroner must see him just as he is. One of you lads catch that horse--or the other one there; I suppose they belong to William Thornton; but we must press one to carry the old woman."

"No, no, I rather walk," said Jenny eagerly. "I'se not ride a horseback. It bumps me shocking; I'se too fat. If Miss Bessy and Mas'r Richard stay beside me, I'll walk along wid dem." Mr. Thornton and several others, however, determined to bear us company, and to keep at a walking pace across the swamp; but we took a spare horse along with us in case Jenny, as I knew would happen, should get tired out before we reached the sheriff's house. I could have been well pleased if old Aunt Jenny's own plan had been followed, for I longed for a quiet talk with dear Bessy; and the good old lady would have afforded no interruption to our conversation. With Mr. Thornton, however, talking to us the whole way, inquiring into all that had occurred, and giving us little pieces of intelligence in return--with Billy Byles whistling one air upon our right, and a young farmer humming another behind us, anything like private conversation between the dear girl and myself was of course totally out of the question. Perhaps it was better as it was; for Bessy was certainly not in a condition to bear any more agitation; and I, like most other men, might not have been quite as considerate as I ought, had the opportunity been afforded to me. Our journey was, of course, very slow; but it afforded an opportunity to Mr. Thornton to tell us all that had occurred since I had quitted the county-town. The insurrection, he said, was now considered completely at an end; the troops were returning to their several stations, and but a small body remained at Jerusalem, more to act as police in apprehending the fugitive malefactors, than to guard against any renewal of violence. Just as he was setting out, he asked us to conduct Mrs. Thornton and his family back to their own home, the sheriff having come in, bringing William Thornton and his son as prisoners. The outrage they had committed upon the poor unoffending negroes excited the greatest indignation of the town. General Eppes had published a vigorous proclamation on the subject, warning the people to abstain from such barbarous acts; and it was with the greatest difficulty they could obtain bail for their appearance. They maintained sturdily that they knew not what had become of Miss Davenport; and though they admitted that Colonel Halliday had placed her under their charge, they declared she had quitted their house that morning, and they knew nothing more. A consultation ensued between Mr. Thornton and the sheriff, immediately after they had given bail and left the town. The suspicions of both fixed at once upon the place to which they had sent poor Bessy, and they arranged together to raise a large party and pursue the search for her, even into North-Carolina. They met early in the morning at the sheriff's house; and, somewhat to the surprise both of Mr. Thornton and Billy Byles, they found Colonel Halliday of the party. That gentleman, Mr. Thornton went on to say, on returning from a long reconnoitering expedition, had been exceedingly irritated to find that Mr. William Thornton had broken his word with him, and that suspicions had been excited against himself, both in me and others, in regard to Bessy's disappearance.

"So angry was he," continued Mr. Thornton, "that I thought it necessary to exact a promise from him, before we suffered him to go with us, that he would not proceed to any act of violence against Robert Thornton, if we met with him; for he asserted, what was very true, that Robert ruled his father completely." Almost all that occurred after they set out we already knew; for we had learned from the sheriff that neither he nor any of his party had the slightest idea that there was a cabin in the neighbourhood of the road they passed; and that it was only the sight of Matthew Leary watching them, and the report of two or three guns, which had brought them up to the spot where William Thornton and his son had fallen.

"I, Byles, and Halliday," resumed Mr. Thornton, "here quitted the sheriff and the rest about a mile from the spot where we afterwards found you, and rode on to the old place, which Mr. William Thornton and his son had quitted but a few minutes before. An old negro, called Samuel, on Halliday assuring him he would skin him alive if he did not tell us the truth, informed us that you had been there the night before, with five or six men, and carried Bessy away with you. His two masters, he said, had gone to look for you; but it was with the greatest difficulty that we got him to admit that one of the old women about the place knew of a small hut, which had been built upon the line, and had watched you go in that direction. We forced her to give some explanation where the place lay; and soon after, passing the sheriff's men on the road, got further directions.

"When we saw the body of Robert Thornton lying dead on the ground, we very naturally concluded, my dear Sir Richard, that a conflict had taken place, and you had shot him. I am indeed glad that it was not so, for this has been a sad business altogether."

"It has indeed," said Bessy Davenport; "the saddest week that Virginia has ever known."

"Well, my love, we must submit to what God appoints," responded Mr. Thornton. "And the first thing you have to do, Madam Bessy, is to take care of yourself, for you are looking quite haggard and old, and you will never get a husband if you don't put on better looks than that." Bessy gazed quietly up in my face, and a faint smile played about her lips; but Mr. Henry Thornton went on without noticing it, saying,--

"You must come home to-morrow, Bessy; and, under your good aunt's nursing, you will soon get as plump as a little partridge again."

"There, don't you take dat road, Mas'r Thornton," cried aunt Jenny, who was toiling along after us. "T'other is not quarter of a mile out of de way, and I do want to see what's become of poor 'Ercles."

"Well bethought, aunty," said Mr. Thornton; "you are a good, kind old woman; but really we must contrive to get you upon the horse, or we shall not reach home to-night. I must get to my own house this evening, Jenny, or the mistress will think we were all lost together." Poor Jenny, who was really tired by this time, was, with some difficulty, seated upon the inconvenient saddle; and though, in compassion to her, we did not perform our cavalry evolutions at very quick time, we certainly proceeded more rapidly than when she was on foot. At the end of about an hour's march after Jenny was mounted, we reached the dwelling of Mr. William Thornton; and here we found another very curious exemplification of how rapidly news flies amongst the negro race in this country. We knew of no one who had crossed the Swamp in that direction but ourselves, since the fatal events had occurred at the State-line, for the sheriff had taken the other road; yet the negroes were now gathered together round the door of Mr. Thornton's house, evidently agitated by some strong feelings.

"Look at those poor people," I said, addressing Mr. Henry Thornton; "is it possible any rumour of what has befallen their master can have reached them?"

"More than probable," answered my friend; "there is no accounting for the rapid spread of intelligence amongst the negroes. I have been sometimes really tempted to think that a bird of the air has carried the tidings. See, here comes one of them to ask us some question." As he spoke, the girl who the day before had given me the only indication I could obtain of the direction in which Bessy had been taken, ran up as we were passing at a little distance from the house, and inquired, in a tremulous sort of tone,--

"Oh, can it be true, Mas'r Henry, that dere hab been a fight out dere, and people killed?"

"No fight, my poor girl," answered Mr. Thornton; "but I am sorry to tell you, Nat Turner and his gang have been at more mischief, and your master has suffered." The girl wrung her hands, and then said, in a low voice,--

"And Mas'r Robert?"

"One has been killed, and the other badly wounded," replied Mr. Thornton. "You will, doubtless, hear more about it soon, and learn more accurate particulars than I can give you. Who told you anything of a serious nature had happened?" On that point, however, as usual, we could obtain no satisfaction. One negro--and several had now gathered round-- had heard it from another, also present, and he from a third, till it made a complete circle, and then went round again. It was evident that some or all were lying; and, giving the question up, Mr. Thornton inquired if they knew anything of the state of poor Hercules.

"He war very bad dis morning," said one of the men; and the girl shook her head and looked sad.

"Let us go on, uncle Henry," said Bessy. "I must see the poor fellow myself. It was in trying to serve me he was injured; and I must see him."

"Well, Bessy, I will not try to stop you," said her uncle; "although, my dear child, I much fear you are over-exerting yourself, and must suffer for all this. Let us go on, however."

CHAPTER XL

When we approached the little semicircle of huts which I have described before, and in which poor Aunt Bab's negroes were lodged, there appeared no crowd round any of the doors, such as I had seen there on a preceding visit. On the contrary, all was now still and silent; and I could not but fear that the wounded man was dead. Mr. Thornton, however, judged better.

"Oh, no!" he answered, when I expressed my apprehension; "they are most likely out in the field. If he were dead, you would hear noise enough. It is only with people educated to control their feelings that grief is silent. With these poor childlike creatures it is always noisy. But there is a horse's head between two of the huts. Perhaps Christy is with him." So it proved. The good surgeon was there, seated on a little stool by the poor man's side, with his fingers on the pulse, and his eyes half closed, almost as if he were dosing. A woman and a child were also in the cabin, standing at a little distance behind the surgeon. Though she was the man's wife, she was quite a young creature--almost a child herself--and she looked quite bewildered with grief and apprehension. We had opened the door without Doctor Christy moving or unclosing his eyes; but the moment Bessy Davenport entered, he started and looked up.

"I knew it!" he cried. "I felt it in the poor devil's pulse. Miss Bessy, you have no right to make any one's pulse gallop so, has she, Sir Richard? Squire, your very humble servant. You have all come just in the nick of time, for I want help here. All the people are out in the field, and this poor girl is hardly able to help herself."

"Oh, dear Miss Bessy, I'se so glad to see you, and with your own people too," cried the poor man. "You'se very good to come and see poor Ercles."

"Hush!" said the doctor, "not a word, if you would have me save your life."

"Oh, I knows I'se going to die any how, Mas'r Christy," said the man.

"You shall die if you talk, and I won't try to save you," answered the doctor.

"How hot his hand is!" said Bessy, who had gone up and taken the gigantic black hand in hers.

"Yes," said the doctor, oracularly; "he has had great irritation all night, and is now somewhat low. But I have made up my mind to two things, since I have been sitting here, in the hope that some sensible person would come to help me. The first is, that no vital organ has been touched, though, as so often happens in wounds, all sorts of mortal places lay in the way. The second is, that two balls were in the gun, fired so near that they did not spread at all, and that one of them is still in the wound."

"I feel it burning here, close to my back, mas'r," said Hercules,

"I dare say you do," answered the doctor; "nothing else could produce the symptoms which I perceive. Now, I must get that ball out; and I want some one to hold his right arm down while I operate; for yesterday he *would* move it. The poor fellow could not help it indeed--it was involuntary when he felt the pain."

"Can I do it?" asked Bessy, in a low timid tone.

"No, I thank you, Miss Davenport," replied the doctor, with a quaint smile. "When I have a robin to operate upon, I will ask you to hold it, but not Goliath of Gath. Sir Richard, perhaps, or Mr. Thornton, will hold the arm; and we will reserve for you an easier task. Here, Miss Bessy, take the second bottle out of that little black-leather case there, and put about a teaspoonful in some water. Then stand here, while I seek for the ball; and give him the draught if you think he is likely to faint. We must guard against fatal syncope. Now, Hercules, if you are quite quiet, you shall have relief in a minute or two; and if you keep quiet you shall get well. Why, old Jenny, I did not see you. You can hold the hartshorn-and-water." "No, I will do it, Doctor Christy," said Bessy. "I never have shrunk, and never wish to shrink, from that which is needful to help a fellow-creature."

"I know you don't," answered the surgeon; and, baring his arm, he proceeded to place his patient in the proper position, and remove the bandages from the wound. Bessy turned her eyes away at first, and I could see her lip quiver a little with agitation; but I would not interfere; and Mr. Thornton, who was watching her face also, walked round and stood behind her, evidently believing that *she* might faint sooner than the patient. The moment the operation began, however, she fixed her eyes upon the poor negro's face, and seemed to watch for any change. At the end of a minute or two (for the operation was a somewhat long one), she suddenly put the little cup to the man's lips, saying--

"Drink some of this, Hercules." He drank; and, almost at the same moment, Doctor Christy exclaimed,--

"I have got it! I have got it fast."

"Oh, that is comfortable! Oh, that is cool!" cried the poor fellow, as the surgeon drew out the forceps, with the ball in their gripe.

"Ay, and you will do well now, Hercules," said the surgeon. "That fellow must have been a bloody-minded scoundrel, to put two balls in the gun. You will do well now, I tell you."

"Dar say I shall, Mas'r Christy," answered the negro; "I feels quite easy like, and I do think I could fall asleep if Missy Bessy would but sing just a little bit. Many a time I'se stood to hear you a' singing under the window at old Beavors."

"That I will, Hercules, if it can do you any good," answered Bessy. And, sitting down on the little stool, with a voice that trembled, but was yet exquisitely sweet, she sung the negro song I have mentioned before--

"The shocking of the corn."

The poor man's young wife crept round, as she sang, and, kneeling at her feet, gently kissed her hand: the negro's eyes closed drowsily, opened, and closed again, in the sleep of exhaustion and relief; and Bessy, suffering her voice gradually to die away, closed the song at the end of the third stanza. The surgeon wiped something like a tear from his eye, and we all stole quietly out of the cabin.

"Well, I do think you are an angel, after all," said the good doctor, addressing Bessy, when we were in the open air.

"Hush, doctor, hush!" answered she almost sadly. "I never felt myself more completely mortal than at this moment--more weak--more worthless."

"Well, then, what is perhaps better than an angel," added the enthusiastic old gentleman, "you are the best specimen of a right, true-hearted Virginia girl. God bless them all! I never could get one of them to marry me; but it was not my fault, and their good luck."

"But tell us about the other men," said Mr. Thornton. "I heard there were three wounded."

"Oh, mere flesh wounds," answered the surgeon; "they will get well without much doctoring, when negroes or labourers are in the scrape. They are very serious, of course," he added with a comical smile, "when rich gentlemen and baronets from foreign lands are under our hands. With *them*, the cases are all very peculiar; and we get as much credit and as many fees out of them as we can. I have no patience, however," he continued, "with this Robert Thornton, for putting two bullets in his gun, to shoot a poor negro. I am sorry I helped to cure the bloody-minded scoundrel, and I shall tell him so the next time I see him."

"You will never see him more, Doctor Christy," replied Mr. Henry Thornton. "He was shot dead this morning, by Nat Turner, near the State-line." The good surgeon actually gasped with surprise; but he soon recovered his facetious mood; for sometimes doctors, like undertakers, become so habituated and familiar with death, that they can joke with the "lean abhorred monster," as if he were a boon companion.

"Nat Turner! again Nat Turner!" he cried. "Why, this fellow is ubiquitous. But I suppose his killing Bob Thornton will be a good thing for him; for, though a jury may condemn him for his other murders, of course the governor will pardon him in reward for this. I am sorry for the old man, however; he won't know what to do without his son. By his help, he had got three-quarters of the way to the dogs already; and now he will have no one to show him the remainder."

"He will find it easily enough," said Mr. Thornton, drily. And, mounting our horses again, we were about to ride on to the house of the sheriff, when Bessy perceived that old Jenny was not with us. On inquiry, we found that she had remained in the cabin; and when the surgeon beckoned her out, she approached Mr. Thornton's horse, saying,--

"Please, Mas'r Henry, I think I'll stay here, if you'se no objection."

"What for, Jenny?" asked Mr. Thornton; "are you too tired to go on?"

"No, dat's not it at all," answered the good woman; "but I wants to help Pheme to nurse poor Ercles. You see, Mas'r Henry, Pheme's no more nor a child in such matters; and she don't know how to nurse her husband at all. So I'd better stay."

"A capital good thought, auntie," said the surgeon; "you and I have nursed many a one through a bad illness before, and you're a handy old girl."

"Then," said Jenny, "we are close by ole Will's house, and that er hoss belongs to him. So, if you just take him off the hook, he'll go way home."

"I'll see to that," said Doctor Christy. "You ride on to the sheriff," added he, addressing Mr. Thornton, Bessy, and myself, "and leave me and Jenny to manage the sick man, and the well horse, too." The sheriff's habitation was different from any Virginian house I had seen, both in site and appearance. It was a low, cottage-looking structure, extending over a considerable space of ground, with its pleasant verandah all round it, and not seated, as usual, upon the very edge of the cleared part of the plantation, but still sheltered by the original wood. It was raised upon a little knoll in the forest, perhaps two hundred yards wide, and that space only had been cleared in the vicinity of the house. It looked dry and comfortable, yet cool and shady, with the large trees devoid of underwood, forming a sort of grove all around it, and giving it much the aspect of an English forest-lodge. The sheriff himself came out to receive us as we rode up, followed by his sister, of whom he had spoken; the very reverse of himself in many respects; for, whereas he was fully six feet, two or three, in height, she was very diminutive in stature, and certainly made up for the sheriff's occasional taciturnity by her own good-humoured volubility of tongue. In her dress she was a perfect model for elderly ladies in a state of single blessedness. It was the perfection of trim neatness, from the beautiful little white apron to the small Quaker-looking cap. No superfluous ribbon--no gaudy colour--no fantastic ornament was there; but she put me in mind of some of those neat little brown birds, which are generally the sweetest songsters. We were all welcomed heartily; and a good deal of hospitable bustle took place to make arrangements for getting some more becoming clothes for Bessy and myself; the little old lady justly remarking that we looked more like fugitives from the penitentiary than anything else. Mr. Thornton, however, speedily set her anxieties on that score at rest.

"I will just stay to take some dinner with you," he said, "and then ride on to my own house. As soon as I get there, I will send over some of my people, Bessy's maid, and her own clothes; for these she has evidently stolen somewhere. I took the liberty, Sir Richard, of bringing your man Zed over to my house; and as I had the melancholy task yesterday of making all the sad arrangements at Beavors, I and Zed brought away your baggage from the room you occupied there. Perhaps I had better send poor Zed over with such articles of apparel, et c[ae]tera, as his taste and judgment may select. He will then have the opportunity of assuring himself, with his own eyes, that you are safe and well, for the poor man went about all yesterday evening mourning after you, with a voice as melancholy as a whip-poor-will."

"But, my dear sir," I answered, "you take it for granted that I am going to stay here when I have not even been asked."

"Oh that's of course," cried the sheriff. "Nobody thinks of asking his friends in this country; they always come when they like, and the invitation is understood."

"Pray do stay, Richard," said Bessy, laying her head on my arm. "I have a great deal to talk to you about to-morrow; for I am so tired, and feel so weak, that I shall go to bed soon this evening--do stay."

"Assuredly," I replied. "I was only putting on a little mock-modesty about the invitation, Bessy."

"Well, well, go and wash your hands and faces," cried the sheriff. "We shall allow you time for no other toilet; for you have lingered so long on the road, that I fear the dinner has spoiled, and I hear certain sounds issuing from the back of the house, which indicate that fried chickens are on their way to the dining room. Listen, and you will presently hear a terrible crash, announcing that a large dish has fallen in the stone passage, and that Ham has tumbled out of the ark--a daily occurrence in Virginian houses, Sir Richard."

"No, brother Harrisson, I do declare," cried the sister. "It never happened in this house. Come away, Bessy, he's a libeller. Come away, Sir Richard, and I will show you both your rooms, quite snug, side by side."

"With a chink in the wall, like Pyramis and Thisbe's?" asked the sheriff, with a funny smile. Bessy shook her finger at him with the rose bright in her cheek; and then we both followed his sister to two very neat little rooms, which looked charmingly comfortable and tidy, after the strange, wild scenes in which some of our nights had lately been passed. When I returned to the parlour, I found Mr. Thornton and the sheriff in somewhat eager conference.

"We shall need you over at my house, and perhaps, at Jerusalem to-morrow," said Mr. Thornton, as I entered. "We would not, it is true, break up so pleasant an arrangement as Bessy has made for you; but business must be attended to, Sir Richard."

"What, in *Virginia?*" I asked with a smile, remembering his own description of the business habits of the people. "However, my dear sir, I will not promise to be over before two o'clock, for Bessy and I have really a great deal to talk of. She is my devisee, you know, Mr. Sheriff; and, of course, our business is very important--though I have some suspicion, my good friend," I continued, turning to Mr. Thornton, "that the clever arrangement we made for conveying all my right, title, interest, et c[ae]tera, to one Bessy Davenport, spinster, will have to be remodelled."

"We shall see," answered Mr. Thornton, quite gravely.

"At all events, our business is important," I urged.

"Not half so important as that which waits us in the next room," cried the sheriff impatiently, "if these two women would but come. Now, I'll answer for it, that excellent sister of mine is making our dear little friend give her a true, full, and particular account of all that has occurred to her during the last week; totally forgetting those fried chickens we were talking of. Jack," he shouted aloud from the door, "go and throw down a large china dish at your mistress's door, to let her know that dinner is ready. Mind you break it all to pieces with a good smash."

"Brother, brother, I am coming," cried his sister, who, of course, had heard the whole. "Don't be so foolish; the man might misunderstand you. Come, Bessy, my love, these voracious men are ravenous for their dinner." I must acknowledge that I certainly was ravenous for mine. Poor Bessy had every right to be hungry also; for we had not tasted any food since the preceding night. It is, indeed, wonderful, how agitation, alarm, or the eager activity of the mind, exercised in any way, will stay the cravings of appetite; and, at all events, it is not till a certain point is reached that hunger is at all felt when we are earnestly and vigorously employed. Oh, those two strange twins of Leda, mind and body, the godlike and the earthly! Though the one may rise when the other sets, the power of the one can always dominate over the other. In fear for her china dishes, the lady of the house very speedily entered the parlour, followed by Bessy, and we were soon seated at a comfortable and well-supplied country table, where everything that farm, garden, stream, and woodland could supply, was found in abundance. Nor to our appetites, purified by fasting, did anything seem over-cooked or under-cooked, although the sheriff, with less than his usual tact, decried some of the dishes as being too much done.

"Well, my good friend," rejoined Mr. Thornton, "we have only to apologize to your sister, by saying we have spoiled her dinner by deviating a little from the straight road on our errand of charity. We went to see that great, big fellow, Hercules, who was shot by Robert Thornton yesterday morning; and when once there, Doctor Christy kept us to aid in all sorts of operations."

"How is he, how is he?" asked the sheriff. "Had I thought of it, I would have passed that way myself; but I have so many matters jostling each other in my mind just now, that one half of them escape notice or remembrance in the crowd."

"The man, I hope, is likely to do well," observed Mr. Thornton. "The good doctor extracted a second ball just now; but I think Bessy was the best doctor of the two, for she sang him to sleep, though he had not been able to close an eye for the last twenty-four hours. It was not the best compliment to your song, my dear niece, to fall asleep over it; but I dare say it will do him a great deal of good."

"It was the best compliment I could wish him to pay me," replied Bessy; "for it was that at which the song was aimed. But you gentlemen, my good uncle, often think that we women are seeking for compliments when nothing is less in our thoughts. Besides, I would never think of seeking one in your presence, being sure that you would spoil it before it reached me." In such conversation, with the agreeable accessories of eating and drinking, and the pleasant, soporific sort of consciousness of being once more in a comfortable chair in a comfortable house, and safe amidst all the charming little luxuries of civilized life, three-quarters of an hour passed away very quietly, and then Mr. Henry Thornton rose to depart. I walked by the side of his horse for some way along the road, pretending to myself to desire much to know what were the matters of business which he wished to discuss with me the next day; but, in reality, much more anxious to ascertain what was the cause of a certain gravity which had tinged his manner, when I had vaguely hinted at the possibility of Bessy Davenport becoming my wife. He did not easily take my hints; but, at length, I came so nearly to the plain question, that he could neither mistake, nor affect to mistake, my meaning.

"The truth is, my friend," he said, "Bessy believes that there are insuperable obstacles; and depend upon it, she does not think so without cause. She is very tenacious in her resolutions; but she always believes, at least, that they are founded on good motives and sound reasons; for, lively and playful as her manner is, I know nobody who is at heart less of a coquette than Bessy Davenport. Before deciding in this instance, she put several questions to me by letter; in answer to which I was obliged to tell her the truth, although she did not conceal from me, that the reply which I was forced to make might greatly affect her own happiness."

"Would there be any objection to your telling me the question she put to you?" I asked.

"I think that would be hardly fair, my dear young friend," answered my companion. "But it seems you are to have a conference to-morrow, and then, doubtless, all will be explained to you by herself. All I can say is, I wish you success with all my heart; and I trust that the various scenes you have lately gone through together, and the vast services and kindnesses you have rendered her, will be found to outweigh all objections. Yet I will tell you fairly, Sir Richard, that I entertain considerable apprehensions--and I grieve to entertain them--in regard to the result to her own health, whether she marries you, or whether she does not."

"What you say puts all my conjectures at sea again," I replied; "for you, at least, must be well informed as to the events of preceding years; and I fondly fancied, up to this moment, that she had made a great mistake, which I could easily rectify. However, I would rather hear the whole facts from her lips, than from any other's; and, as she has already promised to leave the decision to me, I assure you. Mr. Thornton, I will try to decide as may be most for *her* happiness, rather than for my own."

"Do so, do so, I beseech you, Sir Richard," replied Mr. Thornton. "To break such a heart as hers, would be worse than a murder; it would be a sacrilege." There we parted; and walking back to the sheriff's house, I found Bessy still in the parlour with himself and his sister, although, by this time, it was growing dark.

"I have stayed to wish you good night, Richard," she said: "but I must really go to bed now, for I am fairly worn out. When shall our conference be? to-morrow, Richard? Before breakfast, had it not better be? You know my early hours, and I can never sleep after five if I try."

"I will be down before then," I answered; "and we will make a regular appointment to meet here, dear Bessy, if we do not shock too much our kind host and hostess."

"O no, do as you like," cried the sheriff; "you are beyond my competence." Bessy had spoken perfectly calmly and quietly throughout, with not the slightest trace of doubt or agitation. And when she had wished the sheriff and his sister good night, I walked with her to the door, and into the passage.

"I wish I could be as calm as you are, Bessy," I said, with a sigh. She looked up in my face, and put her hand upon mine, gazing at me with an earnest, steadfast gaze.

"I am calm, Richard," she answered, "because the decision of my fate and of him whom I love best on earth is entirely in his own hands, and because I have such faith and trust in his judgment, that I have almost taught myself to believe his decision will satisfy my conscience whatever pre-conceived opinions I might now entertain. But let us not enter on it now. Let us decide all to-morrow. Good night, dear Richard, good night!"

"Stay a moment," I said, holding her hand. "I have got something in trust for you here. These papers were found upon your table at Beavors by Nat Turner, and he gave them to me. Believe me, dear Bessy, when I tell you, that although I knew they contained a clue to all the painful mystery, which, within the last week or so, has made our intercourse one of doubt and anxiety instead of joy and hope, I have not read one word."

"Oh, you might have read them," she said; "but never mind; you shall read them to-morrow, and then tell me what I am to do. You are the lord of my fate, and I will obey you as--as my----"

"Husband," I added, hope springing up anew. "I must have one kiss before we part, after such scenes. If to-morrow I find I am wrong in taking it, I will give it back again." She gave it readily, murmuring,--

"Oh, Richard, if such are your bargains, I know already how you will decide." Then, freeing herself from my arms, she ran away, and left me. At the end of little more than an hour, Zed and Julia, Bessy's maid, made their appearance, with a quantity of goods and chattels, sufficient to half-fill the cart in which they came. Soon after their arrival, I, too, went to bed, and only feared that, in the unwonted softness of my couch, I might oversleep myself on the the following morning.

CHAPTER XLI

What it was that woke me, I know not. It certainly was not the lark, for there is no such heavenly benison of dawn on this side of the Atlantic. It might, indeed, be a crowd of those large birds of the swallow tribe which they call here the bee-martins, who had congregated round the windows, daring each other to wanton, purposeless flights. But I think it was something within, rather than without--some of those strange, silent operations, amidst which the mind still lives and acts when apparently dead in sleep--some of the heart's sentinels calling the watches of the night. I was to rise to meet Bessy in the early morning, and I did not lie awake to count the hours; I was too weary for that. I slept, and slept soundly, the allotted time; and then I woke, as if a voice had said, "Arise!" The day was yet unconfirmed; the hues of the east were still russet, rather than red; but, as I dressed myself, the rose and the gold must have grown stronger in the sky, for many a magic hue poured varying through the pathways amongst the trunks of the old trees, and, streaming across the turf that covered the little rise on which the house stood, seemed to spread a many-coloured carpet before the windows. I took some pains in my toilet, but I was in the parlour and at the window some time before five o'clock struck. I amused myself with gazing forth, and the quiet, pleasant scene, with the sun at length, "*perfundens omnia luce*," sank into, and refreshed the spirit. But that spirit was all the time busy with other things. It was like thinking in the midst of music--one of the sweetest things I know in life when the heart is at ease--when we feel that harmony, are harmonized by it, and yet lose not one thread of the golden web we are weaving. There was a certain degree of waywardness in my mood, which, perhaps, that morning-scene encouraged, though I know not whence it originally sprung--a feeling of power, which I was inclined to sport with. May I own it? I experienced, I fancy, some of the sensations of the despot, when he remembers how much happiness or misery hung upon his will. Could it be that the treacherous heart was too conscious of the power Bessy had given me to decide her fate and mine for both? No, no, I will not believe it; and, at all events, if I was inclined, as I have said, to sport with the power, I was not inclined to abuse it. But, somehow, during the calm, refreshing sleep of the preceding night, confidence had returned; and I felt as if something was ever whispering in my ear that there could be no possible circumstance in the past or the present which could place a barrier between me and her I loved. Bessy did not keep me long waiting; for she was by my side before the clock had finished striking; and, oh, she looked very lovely, though her cheek was paler than usual, and her eyes somewhat languid. The eyelashes looked longer and darker than ever, the iris more full, though more shaded by the drooping lid. The beautiful, dark, silky hair was perhaps not arranged with all the trim care of former days; but the wavy lines were more plainly seen, making, as some old poet called it, "traps for sunbeams." I could see that she had made up her mind to her fate during the night--that she had prejudged my decision--or else felt that, after all that had passed, we could not be separated; for when she gave me her hand, she held up her lips to me also for the morning kiss, as if she would have said,--"I know how it must be." Bessy had got the packet of letters in her hand; and I was leading her to the sofa, but she stopped me, saying,--

"Let us go out amongst the trees, dear Richard. You know what a wild, fanciful girl I am; and when I have to encounter anything that is likely to agitate me, I would rather have breathing-room in the free air, and trees, and flowers, and birds around me, in preference to tables and chairs."

"And do you think anything will agitate you this morning, love?" I asked, somewhat maliciously, I am afraid.

"Oh, yes," she answered. "How can it be otherwise? although I know quite well, Richard, how you will decide, and what you will say, and I will abide by my promise; yet the very talking of such things must agitate me much."

"I do not think you know what I will say, dearest," I replied, walking by her side towards the door. "I may have much more to say than you can even guess; but let us go out; I prefer the free air, too, my beloved. Under the clear sky, one feels in the presence of a purer power; and with the great trust you have placed in me, I should wish to deal as if the eye of God were visibly fixed on me the whole time." We went forth together, passed across the little open space, and wandered on a short distance into the wood to a spot where we could see the cleared part of the plantation without being quite hidden from the house. We there seated ourselves in the shade, though a ray of the early sun stole through between the trunks of the old giants, and crossed with a gleam of golden light Bessy's tiny foot and delicate ankle. She laid the bundle of old letters upon my knee, and was apparently about to speak of them; but I forestalled her, taking her dear hand in mine, and holding it there.

"Bessy," I said, "these have been four eventful days--ay, and four eventful months to both you and me."

"They have, indeed!" she answered with a sigh.

"Have you remarked," I continued, "how fortune has seemed to take a pleasure in binding our fates together link after link in a chain that cannot be broken? How, from the first, event after event drew us nearer and nearer to each other, as if to sport with all your cold resolves, and with my unreasonable expectation?"

"It would seem so, truly," she answered, gazing down on the grass in thought.

"Let us recapitulate, my beloved," I said, "before we go farther. Here, to begin with myself, in man's true egotistical spirit, as you would have said not long ago,--I came to this country, without ever dreaming that I should find any one to excite anything in my heart beyond a passing feeling of admiration. I had made no resolves; but I had gone through many years and scenes, without ever seeing a woman I could wish to make my wife-- without seeing any one to love, in short."

"And to fall in love, at length, with a wild Virginian girl, quite unworthy of you!" said Bessy, looking up with one of her old bright smiles.

"Nay," I answered, "to find a treasure where I least expected it. But let us go on----"

"Ay, but you have not added, dear Richard," she said, still smiling, "that you did not think it at all a treasure when you found it first."

"Perhaps I did not recognize its full value," I replied; "but I soon found it out when I came to see it nearer."

"I do not wonder that you saw nothing worth caring for in me at first," rejoined Bessy. "If you had hated me, and despised me, I could not blame you; for when I think of my sauciness and folly that night and the next morning, I feel even now quite ashamed of myself. But there is some excuse to be made for a wild, somewhat spoiled girl, Richard, who has never known love, or what it means, or what it is like. She says and does a thousand things that she would never think of if she had a grain more experience. But now tell me, when was it you began first to judge a little more favourably of me? for all this has grown upon us so imperceptibly, that I do not really know where it began."

"It began on my part," I answered, "that morning when we first rode over to Beavors--when you and I went to look at the pictures in the dining-room together. Then Bessy let me get a little peep at her heart, and that was quite enough, dear girl. I was more than half in love with you, Bessy, when we mounted our horses to return after the storm. It was high time that I should be so, Bessy; for I do not think if there had not been something more buoyant in my breast than mere humanity, we should ever have got out of that river."

"I am afraid, Richard," said Bessy, "that by that time there was something more buoyant, as you call it, in my bosom, too. I don't mind telling you now, but all that afternoon, at Beavors, I had been feeling very strangely about you, and could not be half so saucy as I wished. I do not think I should have cared much about being drowned before I knew you; but then I did not like the thought of it at all."

"Well, love," I answered, "that adventure was the first of those links between us, which I am now recapitulating--danger of the most desperate kind shared together."

"Ay," cried Bessy, eagerly, "and benefits conferred--life saved--bold and noble daring to save it--O Richard, how could I ever think of making you unhappy after that?"

"Assuredly, it bound us very closely together," I answered "No two people, after having experienced such sensations of interest and anxiety for each other, could ever feel towards each other as they did before."

"It was very soon 'Richard and Bessy' after that," she answered, thoughtfully. Then, raising her eyes to mine, with one of her sunny smiles, she added--"And I fancy in our own hearts it was 'dear Richard' and 'dear Bessy.'"

"It certainly was in mine, dear girl," I replied; "but there were other ties to be added, Bessy: the interest you showed in me--your anxiety about me, before the duel with Robert Thornton, and your gentle care and tendance afterwards; but, more than all, your frank kindness, and the courage of your tenderness, were never to be forgotten by me. Bessy, I do not think, if nothing else had happened to link us still more closely together, we could ever have made up our minds to part. But more, much more, has happened since then--how much within the last three days! Our flight together from a terrible fate----"

"Your saving me from death a second time," she added.

"The strange, close intimacy into which we were thrown during our long wanderings--intimacy such as, perhaps, never before existed between two unmarried persons."

"And which you used so nobly," she added. "Oh, Richard, if there were nothing else but your generous, delicate kindness during that night and day--kindness which, while I loved you as a wife, made me trust and rely upon you as a brother--were there nothing but that, I should, I believe, feel myself justified in overleaping barriers which would be insurmountable in other circumstances, and casting away all consideration but of what is due to you."

"But my happiness must not be alone consulted," I replied. "Whatever we do must be for your happiness also. Dear Bessy, you have lain and slept in these arms; your head has been pillowed on this bosom; your heart has beat fondly against mine. Now tell me, would you withdraw yourself from that resting-place?"

"Oh, no, no, no!" she cried; "never, never! I can never have any other upon earth." And, leaning her head upon my bosom again, she wept.

"And will you be perfectly happy here?" I said, putting my arm around her.

"There," she said, raising her head with a start, but without answering my question--"there, you need not read those papers, Richard. It needs no further consideration. I am yours, willingly, readily--without a doubt. Give me the letters. I will throw them away; and, with them, I will try to cast off all memory of what they contain. But you must promise me one thing, Richard. If, in after times, when I am your wife, you should see some shade of sadness come upon me, a slight and temporary gloom, as if a cloud were passing across a summer's sky, you must not for a moment think that Bessy regrets what she has done--that there is even a shade of repentance, or, as I once called it, remorse, for you have opened my eyes. I see what is right to be done, and I will do it, both for your happiness and for my own. A memory, however, of what these pages contain may, perhaps, from time to time, come back and sadden me, whether I will or not. But it is well that it should be so--that there should be some little thing to take away from the very sweetness of the cup. Were it not for that, I should be too, too happy. Life would be too bright, and I should hardly know how to bear it. Give me the papers, Richard. We will think of them no more."

"May I not read them?" I asked.

"Yes, if you will," she answered; "though I see no use in it. They may make *you* sad too; and my course is now completely decided, If you still wish it, this hand is yours, and nothing but death shall take it from you. It can serve no good purpose to read those sad words." I drew her very close to me, and kissed her cheek, saying,--

"It may serve a very good purpose, Bessy. If I am not mistaken, it will enable me, I do believe, to remove from your mind an error, which, as you have said, might grow into a sad memory, might overshadow our mutual happiness as we stood together at the altar, and often come like a dark cloud over the brightness of our future fate."

"Indeed!" she exclaimed, with a doubting and bewildered look; "I do not see how that can be, Richard."

"May I read, Bessy?" I again asked.

"Assuredly," she answered; "do, if you wish it. But there is only one which it is needful for you to read, and that is not very long. It is here." And turning the papers over rapidly, she pointed to one, which had the post-mark, I think, 'Yorktown.' She then put her hand over her eyes, as if resolved not to see the letters any more; and, still leaning her head on my shoulder, remained silent while I read. The letter ran as follows; for having it by me as I write, I may as well copy it as it stands:

"My Dear Madam,--Mr. Winthorp brought me your letter of inquiry yesterday, and also one from Mr. Hubbard. But it was late at night before I received them; and though I notified the sheriff and the magistrates immediately, it was considered too late to do anything that night. Alas, that I should say it! it was too late altogether.

"Early this morning--one of the saddest mornings I have ever seen--I went out to the village; and, upon inquiry, found that the constable and a *posse* had gone out in one direction, while there was reason to believe that Colonel Davenport had gone in another; that is to say, down towards the bank of the river, so as to have the means at hand for either party to escape out of the State. I rode whither these hints directed me as fast as I could, though, God help me! I had no power or right to interfere. Had I possessed either, I was too late, however; for the matter was all finished and over, and the deed was done before I arrived in the meadow.

"It is very sad to have to tell you that, of two dear friends, I found one dead, and the other almost in a state of distraction. Davenport had been killed at the first fire, and *Sir* Richard Conway was nearly insane at the act which he had committed. Tearing his hair and wringing his hands, he sometimes walked up and down the field, and sometimes stopped to gaze upon the dead body, crying out that he had killed his best friend, his brother, the man he most esteemed on earth. In fact, he spoke very hard words of himself, but still harder of another, who shall be nameless, but whom he accused of having nursed up a jest into a quarrel, and a quarrel into a murder; and who, he said, had suppressed a letter offering every explanation on his part which an honourable man could give.

"The man he spoke of was there upon the field present; but he kept out of his way, and being a near connection of yours, though I believe you are 'scarce cater-cousins,' I think it better not to allude to him more particularly, although all the people present, who were in numbers quite unbefitting the occasion, laid much blame to his charge, and I had some fear that violence would be shown to him.

"Davenport was dead, and there was no help for it; but Conway's grief seemed to touch them much, and when a report spread that the justices were coming, they hurried your brother down as fast as possible to a boat which was in readiness, whether he would or no, and one of them got in with two sailors to steer him over to the eastern shore of Maryland.

"I trust, my dear madam, that you will communicate these sad facts as gently as possible to her who has the deepest and the saddest interest in them, unless, indeed, Rumour, who has a thousand wings as well as a thousand tongues, has carried to her the tidings before this reaches you.

"I may add, and I do it reluctantly, although I tell you fairly I give no credit whatever to the report--for whenever anything sad and disastrous occurs it is sure to give rise to a thousand vague whispers of other calamities--that a rumour has reached this place, since the fatal event of the morning, that a boat has been capsized in the bay, having four persons on board, all of whom were lost; and credulous people will have it that this was the boat which was carrying your brother. However, you may make your mind quite easy on this score; such a thing occurs very rarely in the Chesapeake, and I dare say the whole tale is a fabrication. Yet I cannot but condole with you very sincerely upon the terrible disaster which has actually occurred. That is sufficient, without anything more, to strike you with profound grief; for to see such near connection falling by each other's hand, to the disruption of all family ties and kindred associations, is, indeed, very terrible, although I am inclined to think that neither Davenport nor Conway were so much to blame as those who pretended to act as their friends.

"Believe me to be, my dear madam, with sincere sympathy and respect, your faithful friend and servant,

"Agar Harcourt."

"*Postscriptum*--I am truly grieved to inform you that the rumour of a boat having been lost proves to be too true. Do not alarm yourself yet. We have no particulars; but simply that about ten o'clock this morning a small boat was seen crowding sail across the bay, when by some sudden accident, no one knows what, she was seen to capsize at a great distance from shore. No assistance could be rendered; for all the vessels which saw her were far distant, and a gale was blowing at the time. Let us hope for the best, however, and put our trust in God."

I read the letter attentively. I scrutinized--I examined every word. There was no doubt it was a genuine letter, from some gentleman I had never heard of, to good aunt Bab. Yet there was something wrong. There must be some mistake. The post-mark was there--the address was written in the same hand as the letter itself; but there was some mistake or some fraud about it. At length I turned to the docket, written in a neat, round, legal-like hand, and in very fresh ink; and it gave me the clue. This Mr. Agar Harcourt, who had written the letter, was evidently intimately acquainted with all the parties, and could not have made a mistake. The letter expressed what he believed to be true, and there was no probability of his believing anything that was not true. Yet there was a falsehood somewhere. The docket, however, read thus,--

"Letter, from the Rev. Agar Harcourt to Mrs. Barbara Thornton in regard to the death of Colonel Edward Davenport by the hands of Sir Richard Conway, baronet, father of the present Sir Richard Conway, now serving in the ---- regiment of dragoons in the Presidency of Bombay." I could easily conceive how such a letter, so designated, must have affected my dear Bessy when first she saw it. What feelings of terror and anguish, and hesitation, must have been produced in her mind when she learned to believe that she was about to give herself, heart and mind, and soul and body, to the son of one who had slain her own father. My mind, though not light, was relieved; for I knew that, by other proofs, I could show her the error easily; yet I wished to prove it to her from the letter itself, to show her the villany which had been perpetrated, and which I knew that letter, if thoroughly and properly analyzed and scanned, must display in some part. I accordingly turned to the very beginning again, and read it once more, examining every word. In the meantime, Bessy removed her hand from her eyes, weary of waiting for my long examination. She fixed them on my face, however, and not upon the letter, and at length she said, in a low and timid tone,--

"Well, Richard, was not that enough to shake and terrify, and almost drive me mad?"

"It was, my love," I answered, pressing her closely to me, "and I grieve that a scoundrel should have had the power to inflict upon you such pain. You shall suffer no more on this account, Bessy; but let me go on and examine this paper more closely."

"Oh, it is certainly Mr. Harcourt's handwriting," replied Bessy. "There are several more of his letters there, and I have got two or three others. I know his writing quite well."

"I doubt it not," I answered; "yet there is a falsehood somewhere. Let me examine farther, dear girl." I read the first page, and part of the second, and then something struck my eye which made me pause.

"Look here," dearest, I said. "This docket on the back tells you that this is a letter describing the death of Colonel Davenport--your father, I presume--by the hands of Sir Richard Conway, whom it points out as *my* father. The docket purports to have been written when I was serving with a regiment in the presidency of Bombay. That is eight years ago, Bessy; for I exchanged almost immediately after that period, when I was merely a cornet, into a regiment in Bengal. Yet the ink seems to me exceedingly fresh. I suspect that it has not been upon the paper more than ten days. But now mark another thing. Look here at this line; you see it stands thus: 'Davenport had been killed at the first fire, and----' The line is almost full if you end with that word '*and*;' but crowded in at the end of the line is the small word 'Sir,' and then, in the next line, come the words, 'Richard Conway.' If you will remark closely the handwriting and the ink of that small word, 'Sir,' you will perceive that the one is different and the other bluer than those employed in the letter."

"I see, I see!" cried Bessy, eagerly. "It *is* different; but what object could be attained by adding that word?"

"To bear out the docket that was written by Robert Thornton," I answered, "and to snap the love and the engagement between us like a withered twig, by making you believe that my father had killed your father, and the parricidal drops would stain the hand which you clasped in mine at the altar. Then you did believe it, Bessy?"

"I did, indeed," she answered. "But where you have twice saved my life, Richard, where you have risked your own to do it--where you have been so kind, so noble, so generous, surely, surely, the barrier is broken down, the stain wiped out, and my father himself may look down and bless us. Oh, do not gaze at me so! Tell me--tell me what you mean! What do your looks mean? Is it not so? Is not this letter true?"

"No, no, no! Bessy," I answered. "With the interpretation put upon it, and that small word, 'Sir,' added, it is not true! My father, Sir *Henry* Conway, was never in America in his life; though my uncle, Major Richard Conway, was. My father died only thirteen years ago. My uncle, Richard Conway, was drowned in Chesapeake Buy, some nineteen or twenty years ago. Richard Conway was the youngest son, and never inherited the baronetcy. That word '*Sir*' was introduced solely to make you believe he was my father. Cast all feelings of doubt and hesitation from your mind, my beloved. My uncle, it is true, may have killed your father for aught I know; for I never heard of the fact till now: but, believe me, my father was as innocent of your father's blood as I am; and I have every reason to believe, from what I have heard this day, that my uncle would have been as innocent also, if it had not been for the base and treacherous conduct of old William Thornton, who was your father's second, and who would not suffer an honourable explanation to take place.

"And now, my beloved Bessy, have I not kept my word with you? Have I not extracted from this letter--which was meant to poison your peace, to divide you from a man who truly loved you, or to render your union with him a wretched one--the antidote to its own venomous insinuations?" Bessy did not answer. Some minutes before, while I was clearing away cloud after cloud from her mind, and she had hidden her face upon my bosom, I thought that I felt her heart beating violently; but now she was quite silent and still--so still that, for a moment, I thought she had fainted. I raised her head gently, and saw that the tears were flowing fast from her eyes. She wiped them away hastily; and through the drops beamed a bright smile, telling me they were not drops of sorrow. She hid her face again; but I heard her murmur,--

"They have come at last, Richard--they have come at last, and will bring relief--do not wish me to check them: they are full of joy and comfort."

"Then weep on, dearest," I said; "and may you never shed any but such tears as these." Gradually she grew more composed, and looked up, saying,--

"Oh, this is a happy hour! It is like the clearing away of dark mist; not alone giving back sunshine to the spot where we stand, but opening out bright prospects all around us."

"Then I may tell your uncle that you are mine without doubt or hesitation?" I asked.

"Yours, joyfully, gladly," she answered. "Richard, if ever you thought me a coquette, you shall not think me so now; for you shall find me as ready to own my love as I was formerly to declare I never could love. How you ever came to love me, I cannot tell; but I know right well how I came to love you, and I should hate and despise myself if I did not."

"I came to love you very easily, dear Bessy," I answered. "It was simply, as I told you one day, I found you out."

"And I did not believe you," she replied; "but no wonder, for then I had not found myself out. But there is one thing that puzzles me still, which is, why--for what cause, or on what motive, Mr. William Thornton has so persecuted me and mine. I can easily believe that Robert was moved only by the desire for money, and the habit of fraud; for all the country knows what he was; but as for his father, I have heard people say, who knew him in his youth, that he was a gay, thoughtless, open-hearted man, who spent all he had, and more, with profusion, rather than liberality; yet even at the time of my poor father's death, it would seem he had the same bad feelings towards us, though he concealed them."

"It is indeed strange," I replied, remembering the extraordinary vehemence of hatred the old man had displayed towards Bessy herself. "There may be some mystery in the business; but it were as well not to inquire into it too far, dear Bessy. Let us be content that we have frustrated all their schemes against us, without prying into their motives. There is, they say, a skeleton in every house; and we may as well not open the closet door. Something puzzles me also," I added; "but that is of no very fearful nature. It is this: that your uncle Henry did not know all the circumstances of this sad affair between your father and my uncle; for only yesterday he seemed to think you had good grounds for refusing to unite your fate with mine."

"I do not think he knows anything but what I wrote to him," replied Bessy. "At the time the duel was fought, he must have been in Europe; for about that time he travelled with my aunt for three years; and the subject has been carefully avoided ever since. Even dear aunt Bab never gave us any particulars. One day, indeed, when warning me not to fall in love with a duellist, she told me my poor father had been killed in a duel. But that was the only allusion to the facts I ever heard till I received these letters. Even Mr. William Thornton, when he used to come to see me often, 'on business,' as he said, never even approached the subject."

"It must have been a painful--a dreadful one to him," I answered. "I do not wonder he abstained."

"Bessy, Bessy!" cried the voice of our good old maiden hostess. "Sir Richard, if you have had your chat out, will you come in to breakfast? We have a guest here who knows you." Bessy and I would both have dispensed, I believe, with the breakfast and the guest; for that morning, as a Persian poet says, in speaking of the conversation of happy lovers, we had certainly "fed on roses," and we desired no company but our own. However, we were forced to go; and, after Bessy had made me assure her that her eyes did not look very red, we returned to the house.

CHAPTER XLII

The sheriff was standing with his sister at the door, and his first unceremonious exclamation was,--

"Why, Bessy, my young friend, you look as if you had been crying."

"If I have been crying, they have not been unhappy tears, Mr. Sheriff," answered Bessy; "and you know happy tears are out of your jurisdiction. You have plenty to do with unhappy ones, I have no doubt."

"Go along for a saucy girl," said the sheriff, laughing; "wash your eyes, and then come to breakfast; for we have a great critic of female beauty here, and you may miss a chance, you know, if you don't look your best."

"I'm not in the market," answered Bessy, running into the house.

"And who is your guest, Mr. Sheriff?" I inquired. "You say he is a friend of mine, which saves my question from impertinence."

"Oh, we have no secrets in Virginia," answered the sheriff. "This is Mr. Wheatley, of Norfolk. He says, as we have been cutting each other's throats here, he has just come up to see all his dead friends; for, as I dare say you have found out, Wheatley must have his jest, even on the most serious subject. But here he comes." While the sheriff had been speaking, his sister had retired to the breakfast-room, and Mr. Wheatley joined us, as brisk, as gay, and as composed as ever.

"Ah, Sir Richard," he said, "how are you? You have had some shooting affairs lately on a grander scale than when I last saw you. But I dare say this is nothing to India, where you make a battle of Rajpoots for your afternoon's amusement, and shoot a score or two of rajahs before breakfast; to say nothing of a sultan or two as a big head of game." I laughed, saying, that of course such sport as we had lately had was rather flat after the amusements he mentioned. Then, turning to the sheriff, I remarked,--

"What a beautifully organized country this is, Mr. Sheriff, where, on going and demanding the assistance of a public officer, instead of a long bill of costs, we get a good breakfast, a hearty welcome, a towel, and some cold water."

"Oh, the bill will come by-and-by," said the sheriff.

"By way of desert?" asked Mr. Wheatley. "Well, if it does, we must try to swallow and digest it."

"But, if there be no secret, what is it all about, Mr. Wheatley?" asked the sheriff.

"Oh, no secret at all," replied my Norfolk friend. "One of those matters of business which occur every day--a gentleman, who owes to me and my Boston partners certain banks of ducats, as that funny old fellow, Shakspeare, would call them, which he neglected to pay; he promised them the day before yesterday morning, on the nail, in the city of Portsmouth, at the hour of the arrival of the stage; but neither he nor the dollars ever appeared. I had warned him that this was the last time--it was about the fiftieth--that he should break his promise, and I pointed out to him that though habits of intimacy and some kindness shown to me, a long time ago, when he was a man of about forty, and I a youth of twenty-two or twenty-three, had induced me to forbear, notwithstanding the after-conduct which had severed our friendship; yet, as there were other persons concerned, who had befriended him, at my request, I was now bound to see them paid."

"But who is he--who is he?" asked the sheriff.

"Oh, your neighbour, Mr. William Thornton," replied Mr. Wheatley. "He told me he was to receive thirty thousand dollars this week, and would pay them over immediately; but he was like Hope, that told the flattering tale, which turned out untrue."

"He has had his hands somewhat too full of business lately," replied the sheriff gravely.

"Yes, my dear sir," answered Mr. Wheatley. "I dare say there has been a little bustle in the country; but I cannot allow the sports and pastimes of a number of coloured gentlemen to interfere with regular commercial transactions."

"You are not aware, my good friend," replied the sheriff, "that this unfortunate gentleman was, himself, severely wounded yesterday, and his son shot dead on the spot, by some of the revolted negroes. These are the latest victims of Nat Turner's insurrection. I trust they will also be the last." Mr. Wheatley looked aghast.

"Poor devil!" he exclaimed. "Of his son I know nothing; but of himself I saw very much in my young days, when this Robert was a boy."

"I trust, under the circumstances, Mr. Wheatley," said the sheriff, "that you will not judge it right to disturb this unfortunate man on his death-bed."

"I must see that the property is some way adequately secured," said Mr. Wheatley, gravely, after a moment's thought. "For myself, I should not care, sheriff. I could make up my mind to lose the fifteen thousand dollars, which is my share of the business; but there is another gentleman concerned, who never knew him, and is greatly irritated at his conduct."

"He has been very unfortunate, you know," urged the sheriff.

"Nay, sir, nay," replied Mr. Wheatley, drawing himself up with a sterner look than I ever thought his face could assume. "Unfortunate, truly, in being destitute alike of principle, and honour, and generosity; but in nothing else. The base and scandalous transaction which broke off my intimacy with him was the beginning of what you call his misfortunes."

"I do not understand what you allude to," answered the sheriff. "What did he do?"

"No matter, no matter," answered Mr. Wheatley. "I cannot enter into particulars; but he grossly and grievously insulted an excellent lady, the wife of his dearest friend, while her husband was absent on a sporting trip. It was within my hearing, though he did not know I was near. That was enough to sicken me of him; but when I afterwards found that he contrived to slay Uriah the Hittite with the sword of the Philistines, then Sir ----. But here come the ladies to announce breakfast, I do hope; for that is a much pleasanter thing to discuss than what we are discussing.--Miss Davenport, I kiss your shoe-strings."

"Mr. Wheatley, I never wear shoe-strings," answered Bessy.

"Then may your shadow never be less!" rejoined Mr. Wheatley.

"God grant it!" cried Bessy; "for it is little enough already." And we all laughed and went in to breakfast. It is wonderful how the human mind recovers from the most severe shocks. There is an elasticity, a buoyancy, about it which no one knows or believes, till he has remarked closely what I may call the evenings of the terrible days of human life. Some dreadful event has happened--some ghastly, sweeping desolation--something which has shaken all hearts with anxiety, or chilled them with fear. A few hours have passed: the event is over, the deed done, the consequences ascertained; the whole thing is fixed, firm, and certain, beyond all recall; and though a certain portion of sad remembrance, a mourning spirit, if I may so call it, remains like a cloud, yet every now and then the corruscation of a smile or a jest enlivens the gloom; the tears dry up in the re-awakening sunshine, and shade by shade the fragments of the cloud depart. To call our little breakfast-party gay, would be to apply a wrong epithet. Yet it was not altogether uncheerful--far more cheerful than might be expected by those who consider nothing but the dreadful scenes gone before. They very naturally leave out of consideration all the bright reaction which takes place in the human heart when it finds itself suddenly freed from the weight of dread and horror and anxiety for the next moment; when security and peace are restored, and the spirit springs up, and rejoices in the removal of evils and terrors which once clouded the prospect all around. In the moral as in the physical world, nature re-acts against oppression. Look at the thunder-storm, with its heavy clouds and its darkened sky, the flash, the roar, and the deluge; and then see the clouds rolled away, and the blue sky smiling above, and the sun shining in his splendour, and every drop upon the blades of grass sending back, like diamonds, the cheerful rays he casts upon them. It is true, that, as we sat round the table, it was not all brightness. Moments of sombre thought would fall upon us; impressions of great calamities past; recollections of things that never were to be more; and the shadows which the experience of danger and sorrow ever projects upon the future. Still, these were but the shadows of the fragments of past clouds, and the sunlight of the relieved mind shone out bright between. After breakfast, Mr. Wheatley, and the sheriff, and myself walked quietly out into the porch, to re-discuss the subject which had been broken off an hour before. The kindness of the worthy magistrate's heart was strongly evinced in this instance.

"I have no great love for William Thornton," he said; "I never have had; still it is a sad thing to see writs, or executions, or foreclosures, put in force against a man lying in a dangerous, if not a dying, state, from a severe wound. Now, I think you have said, Mr. Wheatley, that you did not mind for your own share in the business, if you could secure your partner."

"Rather a hard case, sheriff," replied Mr. Wheatley, with one of his short laughs. "I have breakfasted since, and have, of course, grown hard-hearted. Nothing like an empty stomach for tenderness towards anything, except broiled fowls or cold lamb. However, I won't go back from what I said. If he can secure Mr. Griswold, I will take my chance out of the sweepings."

"I have no doubt," said the sheriff, "that Miss Davenport will advance the money to repay your friend."

"No! no!" cried Mr. Wheatley, with a burst of eager feeling which I had not expected from him. "She shall not do it--I will not take it from her. He insulted and outraged her mother; he brought on the death of her father to conceal what he had done; he was, more or less, the murderer of the one and of the other, for grief killed *her*, and the pistol killed *him*; and the daughter shall not be called upon, with my consent, to save him from the consequences of his own folly or his own faults."

"Well, Mr. Wheatley," I said, interposing before the sheriff could reply. "Another means, perhaps, may be found. Suppose I advance the money, and place myself in the position of your friend, who originally lent it."

"Oh, that is quite a different case," said Mr. Wheatley. "If you choose to do such a thing, I have nothing to say against it. Every man to his taste. Some love helping scoundrels; some prefer to help honest men. The first was rather a passion of mine, some years ago; but I have got over it, and the latter is more to my taste now."

"Still," I replied, "for particular reasons of my own, I should like Miss Davenport, in the first instance, to offer this loan to her relation--merely, I will confess, to see what will occur in consequence. The advance shall be mine in the end; but I should like to obtain her permission to make the offer from her."

"Ha! ha! ha!" cried Mr. Wheatley. "Pray arrange your little embroglios as you like for me. She will consent, of course; knowing on whose pocket the loss will fall at length, whether *you* advance the money or she does. But go and ask her--go and ask her; and then I think we will ride over, Mr. Sheriff, to Bill Thornton's plantation, and see what is the real state of affairs."

"Very well," replied the sheriff; "but, remember, till you produce all formal processes, I take neither officers nor *posse* with me, and I must be back in a couple of hours." I did not detain the gentleman long. I found Bessy in the parlour, and her consent was given at once.

"It will not hurt us, Richard, if we lose it," she said. "We shall have enough for happiness, I dare say."

"Oh, quite," I answered. "But now I am going over to see this unfortunate man, and I trust my dear girl will spend the time till I come back in pondering upon the happiness which her affection confers upon one who loves her with his whole heart. If I know my Bessy rightly, she feels no greater pleasure than in making others happy."

"I wonder if it is to be so through all my life," said Bessy. "Every one has spoiled me--parents, friends, relations. And now comes a husband to do it more than all! Richard, Richard, I really must find some occasion to quarrel with you, that you may not make me altogether a spoiled child. There, go away now, and tell the poor man I am ready to do anything I can for him. I wonder that Mr. Wheatley can be so unkind as to ask him for payment of debts, when he is in such a condition." When I rejoined the two gentlemen in the porch, I found that an alteration of plans had taken place. The sheriff had recollected some business he had to transact in another quarter; and it was agreed that I and Mr. Wheatley should ride across the Swamp to the place where Mr. William Thornton lay.

"I shall tell Harry Thornton that you won't be back till two or three," said the sheriff; "and, as I know he has some business to transact with you, I will try and get him and all his party to come over here, and dine and sleep: four or five girls, and four or five lovers, and four or five elderly people, and talking, and music, and flirting----a fine way of transacting business, truly; but it is the Virginian mode, and so let it pass. I will order the horses, Sir Richard; you go and get on your boots." I now proceeded to my room, where I found Zed, after his own breakfast, arranging all my dressing-articles and apparel in the most inconceivable derangement. It would not only have puzzled [OE]dipus, but the Sphynx herself, to discover where any single article was; and yet he was as proud as a peacock of the whole. Poor Zed seemed quite thunderstruck, however, when I told him to get me a pair of boots and another coat.

"Lor a masey!" he cried; "what, going away again? Why, I haven't seen you, mas'r, for such a long time; and I thot you were going to tell me all about it. Well, at all events, you had better take me wid you, for you never comes to no good when I isn't there."

"I dare say that is all very true, Zed," I replied; "but I think this morning I must go by myself, or rather with Mr. Wheatley only, for I have a good deal to say to him as we ride along."

"Lor, mas'r, what does dat sinnify?" asked the persisting negro. "I shan't int'rupt you." But I remained firm; and in a few minutes Mr. Wheatley and I were upon the road. I have never been fond of long prefaces to anything; and I was hardly out of sight of the house, when I dashed at the subject which was uppermost in my thoughts.

"You accidentally came upon a topic before breakfast," I said, "which bears strongly upon some questions which had been puzzling Miss Davenport and myself this morning a good deal. Now I wish, Mr. Wheatley, that you would give me some further information in regard to this Mr. William Thornton, and his connection with Colonel Davenport. You were in the high road to do so when we were summoned to breakfast."

"Oh, no; I had said all I intended to say," replied Mr. Wheatley, with what I may call an unwilling look; "though I should fancy, Sir Richard," he added, "*you* had not said all you intended to say this morning before breakfast; for you and Miss Bessy were so deep in conversation that you did not even see me when I arrived; and that conversation seemed to promise wide extension." I was not to be led away from my point, however; and I answered,--

"We were talking of the very question to which I have just now alluded. Yesterday morning, Bessy and I had a very strange proof of old William Thornton's personal hatred towards her. He would not even allow her to stanch the bleeding of his wound; and used language not only fierce, but indecorous. We were wondering, when summoned to breakfast, what could be the motive of the persecution he has shown her through life; and it was, in some degree, to test the extent of this virulent antipathy that I desired she should offer the money rather than myself. I should not be surprised if he were to refuse it at her hands."

"I think it very likely," replied Mr. Wheatley; "but tell me how you and she happened to be so near when the old man was shot?"

"I will tell you all about it," I answered, "if you will give me the explanations I wish in return."

"Well, well," he replied, "it is a subject I neither like to think of, nor to talk about. Indeed, I may call a considerable portion surmise; for, although I am as much morally convinced of the inferences I draw from the facts, I know, as well as that I am alive, there are many of them for which I have no proof. However, we are now going to see this unhappy old man. There is no knowing that he may not himself tell you all, for his moods are very curious, and the fear of death may act strongly upon him. But if he does not do so, *I* will. And now let me hear how you and Miss Davenport have passed through all these terrible scenes. All that I could learn about you, by the way, was that you and the lady had escaped from poor Stringer's house, and had been wandering alone in the woods ever since--no very unpleasant pilgrimage, I should think--ha! ha! ha!" And there his laugh stopped short, as usual.

"It was, of course, by no means unpleasant," I replied, "when once I could convince myself she was safe, Mr. Wheatley. But our adventures were numerous; and it was not till I and Mr. Henry Thornton brought our sweet young friend to this house last night, that I could be at all satisfied she was secure." I then went on to relate briefly all that had happened to us, from the time that old Zed ran into my room to warn me of our danger, till our arrival at the sheriff's on the preceding evening. Mr. Wheatley seemed to take a great deal of interest in the whole matter, and expressed much indignation at Mr. William Thornton's conduct. At that part of my narrative, where I spoke of the father and son wishing to force Bessy to sign some papers, while they held her in a sort of duress, he exclaimed,--

"That was to pay the thirty thousand dollars, depend upon it. If we could find the fragments of those papers she tore up, I would bet you a

thousand dollars to a ten-cent piece we should find some gross fraud--
the admission of some debt, or some promise to pay, or something of that
kind, all wrapped up nicely in legal-like phrases, and guarded, and double
guarded, by allusions to former transactions in order to make a piece of
roguery seem fair and honest. But I can tell you one thing, Sir Richard--this
does not look well for the ultimate payment of my money, and I certainly
do not intend to shuffle off a bad debt upon you or Miss Davenport either. If
we find there is any tangible property sufficient to guard you against much
risk, I shall be very willing that you advance the fifteen thousand dollars to
pay off Griswold, for he is becoming impatient and irritable; but it is clear to
me these men must have been desperately pushed to have had recourse to
such means; although, to say truth, from all I hear, Robert Thornton always
preferred the rashest and most violent paths of roguery, to the quiet and
peaceful ones."

CHAPTER XLIII

I had concluded that the wounded man still lay at the house on the other side of the Swamp, to which he had first been carried; and had it not been for an accident, we should have had a long ride for no purpose. Just as we approached what they called the new place, my horse began to go lame; and seeing an old negro standing at the door, I beckoned to him to come and take out the stone which I was sure had got jammed into the beast's hoof. The old man name up at a slow pace; and, as he approached, to my surprise, I found it was that very remarkable person, Uncle Jack. Between him and me, the stone was soon removed, and I happened to ask him, just as I was re-mounting, what he was doing there.

"I am waiting to see Mr. Thornton again, sir," he said; "Mr. William Thornton. His son Robert, you know, is dead."

"Do you mean to say the old man has been brought over here?" I exclaimed.

"Yes, sir; he would be brought over last night, in spite of all remonstrance, and I fear he has killed himself thereby," was Uncle Jack's answer. I called to Mr. Wheatley, who had ridden on, and beckoned him back; and while he was returning, I proceeded to ask Uncle Jack what he meant by saying that he was waiting to see Mr. Thornton again.

"Why you see, sir," answered the old negro-preacher, "I knew the gentleman whom you call the old man, when he was quite a little boy; and much used I to talk to him at that time, so that even when he had grown up to be a lad and did things which I hope God will forgive, I had much influence over him--very much for a poor ignorant negro to have over a well-educated white man. He would listen to *me* when he would listen to nobody else; and, more or less, has done so all his life. So I came here as soon as I heard what had happened. I found him very rash and raving last night; but this morning he is down, sir--down, down, very low indeed--down in mind, and body, and heart; but it is by the blessing of God it is so, for I trust yet to bring his mind into a better frame to meet his Maker; and you know, sir, we must never despair, after the thief on the cross. This morning he listened to me quite willingly; and seemed to take comfort when I told him of mercy and pardon. Last night, he would not hear at all, but cursed and blasphemed till I was glad to get away." The concatenation of a black teacher and a white neophyte had probably not occurred since the days of the apostles; still I was very glad to avail myself of any circumstances which would enable me to obtain light in a matter where the whole feelings of my own heart and that of another were so deeply interested. There are some cases in the world were we know no compromise--where, for the sake of our own peace, we must know all, see all distinctly--really--as it is, lest there be, somewhere in the dark outskirts and corners of the den of circumstances, some incubus which may swell and grow, and oppress the heart till it crushes us to death. Such seemed the case with me. I determined to know all, if it could be known--I determined that there should be no dark and cloudy spot, no storm upon the edge of the sky, the course and nature of which I did not know; and, although the future, the dark predestined future, no man can truly divine--the past, upon which the seal of destiny was set, the true, irrevocable past, might well be scanned, till the real gold of truth should be separated from the dross of doubt and falsehood.

"We want much," I said, addressing the old negro, "to see Mr. William Thornton upon business of great importance--business which has even reference to the hour of death, and which must not be postponed. Indeed, this gentleman *must* see Mr. Thornton in order to spare him greater discomfort at this sad and perilous moment. I may have more personal views; but at the same time, my good friend, I cannot help thinking that he who parts from this world with a free confession of his errors in it, and some expression of regret, sets forth for the wide future with more comfort and more hope."

"Assuredly," replied the negro; "and I will try to bring him to receive you as tranquilly and as willingly as may be. But I cannot answer for success; perhaps he may refuse--perhaps you may have to force your way to him whether he desires it or not, as I had last night; but at all events, I will do my best. Wait here, and I will return to you presently. He was somewhat drowsy when I left him; and I was glad to give him a little repose; for the words which I had read to him from the Great Teacher had tortured him like the first effect of a strong medicine for the cure of a terrible disease." The old man paused; and, after a moment or two of silent thought, went back into the house, telling some of his dark brethren to take care of our horses. We followed him into one of the lower rooms; and the contrast was certainly very sad between the aspect of his dwelling and that of his cousin Mr. Henry Thornton. They had set out in life very nearly equal in fortune--perhaps, of the two, William Thornton was the more wealthy; yet the one had surrounded himself with family ties: had lived in comfort, if not in splendour, had done right and justice to all men; had preserved a high and unspotted name; and, in moderation, had continued in peace and competence. Probably his household presented no difference from the state in which it existed twenty years before; he had sought for nothing higher, he had fallen no lower. On the contrary, in the house wherein we now stood, we could trace the footsteps of dishonest ambition, disappointment, and decay. It was the latter stage, indeed, which was altogether visible. Misery and dilapidation--neglect, and the consequences of neglect, made their abiding place in this dwelling. Yet, every here and there, were slight indications of the steps by which the consummation had been arrived at--a velvet sofa worn through to the sacking--a rich carpet trodden out to the warp--window-frames long unpainted, with the glass rattling in the shrunken wood-work--many a pane cracked and not repaired--chairs broken and unserviceable--tables wanting castors, and leaning, like cripples, on one side--everything, in short, which could display the careless apathy of minds either occupied by eager schemes for the future, or crushed by the disappointment of the past. In that melancholy parlour the black preacher left us, saying,--

"I will go up to him again and see what progress I can make. He is in the room just above; and if I stamp with my foot, it is to show that you had better come up to the door, where I will give you some sign when you shall come in. It is better that you should present yourselves quietly, than run the risk of rousing him into one of his fits of fury, when nothing on earth is to be done with him." Thus saying, he left us; and Mr. Wheatley and I remained a quarter of an hour or more very nearly in silence. He was more impatient than I was, for I think he is naturally of a more irritable disposition. He would sit for a few minutes, and then rise and walk about the room. Then he would open the window-blinds and look out; and then he would sit upon another chair and listen. We could hear, during the greater part of the time, a murmur of low voices; but it was impossible to distinguish who was speaking. At length, Mr. Wheatley, with his whole patience exhausted, jumped up, exclaiming,--

"Come, we had better go up and see what is taking place. We may be kept here all day; and you have business, and so have I, to attend to." Without waiting for reply or assent, he opened the door, went out, and mounted the staircase; but at the top we heard the murmur of voices from a room on the left; and putting my hand upon his arm, I stopped him just as he was about to enter.

"Stay a moment," I said. "It is cruel to intrude upon a dying man. That voice sounds very differently now."

"Pooh! that is the old preacher's voice," said Mr. Wheatley, pushing the door partly open. But he paused immediately; for the scene within had a simple solemnity in it which affected even him. There lay old William Thornton, stretched upon a faded bed, with his head turned partly away from us, but with the long, whitish hair, uncombed and rough, scattered on the pillow. Kneeling at the other side of the bed was the good old man, Uncle Jack. A book was open before him, and he was reading aloud that sublime chapter in the Gospel wherein the Saviour teaches his disciples how to pray. His voice was fine, and, notwithstanding his great age, unbroken; and there was a peculiar tone of loving confidence in it as he read the only perfect prayer, that was very touching. He laid particular emphasis on the words,--"*Forgive us our trespasses, as we forgive them that trespass against us.*" But when he stopped, Mr. Thornton remarked, in a very feeble voice,--

"Well, it is very fine; I always thought so; yet I don't half understand it, old man. Let us hear what you make of it."

"I doubt, master, that I am competent to make much of it, where you, so much better taught, do not understand it," answered Uncle Jack.

"I don't know," said the dying man. "You have thought of nothing but such things, and I have thought of them too little, perhaps."

"Well, I will try," said the negro. "You see, sir, there is no piece of writing that I know of in which every word has so much meaning. It first begins by teaching us what God is."

"I don't see that," said Mr. Thornton. "But go on--go on."

"It tells us that He is a Father to those who pray unto Him sincerely--One who has the feelin? and affection of a parent--not alone the Being who created us, but who still regards us as His children, however wayward and sinful--who is as ready to be reconciled to us as a Father to an erring child, and to give us all good things as a Father gives good gifts unto his children. Oh, what a tender idea it gives us of our God, when we are taught by His own word to address Him as our Father! But then it shows us His greatness also--His majesty and power. It is not an earthly Father whom we address, who may not be able to give us what we seek--who may have no power to protect, no means of comforting or blessing us; but our Father which is in Heaven. That does not mean here or there--in this place or that; but above all, ruling all, upon the throne of His majesty and His power, in the centre of, and throughout all His universe, in the Heaven of His own glory and love.

"Well may the prayer go on, '*Hallowed be thy name!*' Let His great name always be sacred; but, above all, let it be hallowed when it is written, '*Our Father which art in Heaven!*'

"'*Thy kingdom come!*' are the next words."

"Ay, that I do not understand," said Mr. Thornton, faintly. "Why should people pray to die when they want to live? I could never understand that."

"It is no prayer for death, sir," said the old negro teacher. "Our Saviour has said,--'*The kingdom of God is within you!*' and it may either be a prayer that the holy and happy kingdom of God be established with all its peace in our own hearts, or that it be established in its purity and unity throughout the whole world. '*Thy will be done!*' are the succeeding words; and these teach, first, that resignation to the will of God which is one of the purest forms of His worship--a humble acknowledgment of His wisdom, and mercy, and love; and a profession of our full faith, and trust, and confidence in Him; and secondly, taken with the words that follow, *how* we ought to do God's will ourselves, and how we ought to wish all others to do it, '*in earth as it is in Heaven!*' not slowly, not grudgingly, not doubtingly; but with joy and alacrity, and full faith and trust--as it is performed spontaneously by the holy angels." Mr. Thornton moved impatiently in his bed; and the old man, as if afraid that he would interrupt him, proceeded more rapidly.

"The prayer then goes on to say, '*Give us this day our daily bread!*' That means, I think, the complete provision of God's mercy--all that is needful for us during that day, as well for the body as the soul--the bread that sustains the flesh, and the bread of life itself--all, in short, that we want and require--"

"Well, that is sensible," said the wounded man, in a somewhat stronger voice. "It is a very fine prayer; I don't deny it."

"You can't think, sir, what a comfort it would be to you if you could but make up your mind to repeat it."

"I think I can repeat it," said Mr. Thornton. "I am sure my mother made me say it so often when I was young, that I can't have forgotten it--though that is a long time ago. Let me see." And he began the prayer, murmuring in a low, but still articulate voice. He proceeded very fluently till he came to the words, "*Forgive us our trespasses, as we forgive them that trespass against us.*" There he paused, and muttered something between his teeth.

"Those are the most important words of all," said the old negro, earnestly. "Upon these words hang the only hope of being forgiven. Oh, Mr. Thornton, do say them. If ever you have done anything to offend God--if you have ever done anything to injure man--if you have any cause to fear the judgment hereafter, and which of us has not?--if there be one act in your whole life which you could wish to blot out--forgive, if you would be forgiven."

"Davenport!" ejaculated Mr. Thornton, in a wandering tone, "Davenport! He did not trespass against me; but his wife did. She spat at me--she called me villain, and scoundrel--said she would tell her husband all. I recollect how he looked when he died. She could not have told him, Uncle Jack, for there was no time; yet he looked very much as if he thought I had done something. It was a bitter, reproachful sort of look. But I say, uncle, do you think that we are obliged to forgive those who have never trespassed against us as well as those who have? That's the question." The man's mind was evidently beginning to wander, and Mr. Wheatley entered the room without further ceremony.

"Ah, doctor," cried the wounded man, turning round in the bed as soon as he heard a step; but when his eyes fell upon Mr. Wheatley, a strange and fearful change came upon his countenance. When he first turned it, it was not only as usual, red from long habits of somewhat excessive drinking, but apparently flushed with fever. When he beheld Mr. Wheatley, however, the colour changed in a moment to a cadaverous white, with here and there a bluish spot; neither did it resume its former hue: the effect was permanent, and he remained looking more like a dead man than a living one. Wheatley saw the change which had taken place; and, advancing to his bed-side, he spoke kindly to him, and in a cheerful tone.

"Ah, Mr. Thornton," he said, "I am sorry to see you ill. I came over to inquire after you, and try if we could not settle that little matter between you and me amicably."

"Who is that man?" said Mr. Thornton, glaring at me, as I stood a little behind my friend. "I have seen him before. It can't be Richard Conway come out of the Chesapeake--he is very like him."

"No, no," said Mr. Wheatley. "He's been dead near twenty years."

"Ay," said Mr. Thornton, gloomily, "he's rotten enough by this time."

"Just try to gather your thoughts together," said Mr. Wheatley; "and see if we can't arrange this matter about the thirty thousand dollars quietly. I think we can; for as to my share of the matter, I can wait; and as for Griswold's, I have a proposal to make to you."

"Uncle Jack," said Mr. Thornton, in a low voice, "give me a tumbler full of whisky--make haste, man, I feel faint. There's the bottle by the bed-side." With evident reluctance, the old negro found out the spirit, and the dying man drank it off at a draught. It seemed to revive him a little, but it made no change in his colour.

"A proposal!" he said, in a stronger voice. "What proposal? I cant pay you the first cent. I have been disappointed in the money I expected; that's the long and the short of it. As to the estate, you can't touch that; for that's settled upon Robert long ago." He had forgotten that his son was dead; but it seemed suddenly to flash upon his recollection, for he paused and put his hand to his head, stammering forth,--

"I forgot, I forgot. A proposal! what proposal?"

"Why this, and I think it a very kind one," said Mr. Wheatley. "A young lady--a very good and generous young lady--offers to advance you the sum necessary to pay off your debt to Mr. Griswold. For my part, I shall not trouble you, in the situation in which you now are; but he, depend upon it, will have no hesitation in taking everything he can take, if the money is not paid by noon to-morrow. You had, therefore, better accept this lady's proposal at once."

"Who is she?" asked Mr. Thornton. "Give me some more whisky, Jack. I feel--I don't know what I feel. Who is she, Wheatley?"

"None other than Miss Davenport," replied Mr. Wheatley. A spasm like that of death came over the sick man's face.

"I won't have it--I won't take it--I won't have to thank Bessy Davenport for a cent," he cried in a voice preternaturally loud. "Give me the whisky, you old black villain--give me the whisky."

"Oh, Master Thornton," said Uncle Jack, "forgive, if you would be forgiven! Don't you know, don't you feel, that you are dying? That you are going before that God to whom you were just now trying to say, 'Forgive us our trespasses, as we forgive them that trespass against us.' Does not poor Bessy Davenport forgive you? And should you keep up rancour towards her? Oh, take her offer, sir, and follow her example before you die."

"Dying," said the old man feebly. "Am I dying? I do believe I am. Give me the whisky, Jack. I can't die yet--I am not yet ready. Oh God, give me a little time to think!" The old negro looked across to somebody who had just come in and stood behind me. It was Doctor Christy, who said:--

"Give it to him; it can neither do good nor harm; but it may keep him up for half-an-hour or so, if there's business to be done. You see," he continued, speaking to me in a lower tone, as I turned towards him, "there is the Hippocratical visage. No escaping from that!"

"Am I dying?" asked Mr. Thornton, as soon as he had drunk the whisky; "am I dying, doctor?"

"Yes, sir, you are," replied the surgeon, almost sternly.

"How long?" asked the other, in a sad and a subdued tone.

"Long enough to show repentance if you will," answered Doctor Christy. "Long enough to make your will, if it is not a very long one."

"The will be d----d," said the old man, in his usual phraseology, which he could not abandon even at that awful moment. "Everything is in confusion. I have no time for that."

"Oh, sir," said Uncle Jack, "let me pray----"

"Hush!" said the dying man. "You told me I was to forgive--but forgiveness is nothing, unless I redress--did Bessy Davenport really make that offer?" he continued, looking at Mr. Wheatley.

"She did," replied the other.

"Here, get me the keys out of my pocket. There, take this one," he continued, as soon as he had got them. "Now open that cupboard door, that mahogany cupboard in the corner. On the shelf you will find a tortoise-shell casket, I think they call it.--Have you got it?"

"I haven't opened the door yet," said Mr. Wheatley. "Yes, here it is."

"Bring it here then, and the key that lies beside it. Heaven! how my head swims. There, take that to Bessy Davenport. Tell her I sent it to her with my dying hands. Tell her I am sorry for all I have done--very sorry; that I have often been sorry, but that I would not let myself think so. There, take it. She will find in it what puts all questions about Aunt Bab's property at an end. Now, doctor, tell me, upon your soul, am I dying? Can nothing be done to save me? If you could extract the ball?"

"It would be no use," answered the surgeon. "It has got in amongst the bones of the hip-joint, and your face shows me at once that mortification has set in. There was a chance yesterday, if you would but have been quiet, and abstained from drinking: to-day there is none."

"Well, then, all of you leave me to die like an old fox in his hole," said Mr. Thornton. "Stay, stay, Uncle Jack. You turn to, and see what you can do for my soul. We won't think of the body any more. There! Go the rest of you. I don't want to hear you talk any more. My time is but short, and I must do what I can with it."

CHAPTER XLIV

"And so goes out a bad life," said Mr. Wheatley, as we mounted our horses and rode away. "It has been compared to the end of a tallow-candle by somebody, I don't know who--in fact, I never can recollect who it is that has written anything. I can remember the thought; but I cannot recollect the words, nor trace 'back to it's cloud that lightning of the mind.' Well, it is strange to see how men misuse opportunities. This fellow, this Thornton here, set out in life with the very brightest prospects; friends, fortune, relations of commanding influence, talents, education--everything but conduct."

"And principle," I interposed.

"Ay, and principle," said Mr. Wheatley, musing very deeply. "I have come to that conclusion myself, Sir Richard. At one time, I doubted it; for often, when I acted honestly--by accident, of course by accident--ha! ha! ha!--I was diabolically cheated. I was not successful. Principle did nothing for me; I saw the rogue triumphant, the honest man vanquished. I perceived that in worldly wisdom I had acted like a child, and I said to myself, 'Conduct is fate.' But since has come the question, What is conduct? and I am inclined to believe that, in the end, here, even here, honesty is the best policy, principle is the surest guide, and, like the mariner who steers his bark by the compass and the star, though we may look ahead for the breakers or the reefs, the permanent guides to our course are aloft." Sublime truth was clad in his homely language, and we were both silent for several minutes.

"I wonder what the deuce is in this box?" said Mr. Wheatley, holding up the little casket he had received. "I should like very much to open it and see; but I think, after what we have just been talking about, it wouldn't do. I should feel my fingers shake, and you would turn away your head and blush. Yet we could find many a plausible reason. We might wish to save Miss Davenport some unnecessary shock--we might fear that the old man was playing some trick upon her--there might be a loaded pistol, with cunningly-contrived machinery, ready within to shoot the person who opens the box. In short, Sir Richard, was ever act committed, so base and mean, which could not find a pretext to justify it, good and valid in a court of law? Now that old man there is going to judgment, granting himself a poor, miserable sinner, and giving me this box, and thinking that the confession and the reparation are quite sufficient to close the great account and strike a fair balance in the everlasting day-book." We rode on till within a quarter of a mile of the sheriff's house, without meeting any one; but there we saw Mr. Henry Thornton and the worthy magistrate himself riding towards us. "I was coming after you, Sir Richard," said the former, as he rode up. "Mr. Hubbard is at my house waiting for you, and we are sadly afraid, do what we can, the escheat will pass. Robert Thornton has so hedged his father in with one legal technicality and another, that we almost fear good aunt Bab's will will be declared null and void; for the real and personal estate are so mixed up in her devise to you, that it is hardly possible to separate them; and if the will is declared null, even those poor slaves will fall into the hands of others."

"They shall be free, notwithstanding," I answered.

"Stay, stay, all of you," said Mr. Wheatley. "I have got here upon my saddle-bow, Mr. Thornton, Pandora's box, out of which I hope all the miseries of human life have long ago escaped, leaving nothing but pleasant hope sleeping at the bottom."

"What do you mean?" asked Mr. Thornton, almost impatiently. "I do not understand."

"Simply," I said, "that Mr. William Thornton is dying--probably dead by this time. When he discovered how near he was to his end, some degree of remorse seemed to seize upon him, and he gave Mr. Wheatley that little case to deliver to our dear Bessy, with an intimation that it would set all right."

"Then we had better carry it to *our dear Bessy* at once," said Mr. Thornton with a gay smile. "From your sweet terms, Sir Richard, and from Bessy's radiant face when I saw her just now, I conclude you are a successful kidnapper, and I don't know whether to wish you joy or to cut your throat; for when you take Bessy Davenport away from amongst us, you deprive our little district of half its sunshine."

"It is but right and just, my good friend," I answered, "that the rest of the world should have some portion of the same rays; and, believe me, even were there not many bonds of kindness, friendship, and affection between my heart and many a heart here, the spot where I had met Bessy Davenport would always be dear to me, and I should visit it often to revive memories so deeply interesting."

"Pooh, pooh!" ejaculated the bluff sheriff. "When you get her across the Atlantic, you wont bring her back again in a hurry; but we can't help it; and, whatever may happen, foul fall the man who would impede Bessy's happiness for an hour." By this time we had nearly reached the sheriff's house, and it needed some hallooing, being about the middle of the day, to bring any one to take our horses. When, at length, we entered the house, neither of the ladies were to be seen; but the curiosity of the whole party was raised too high for any forbearance, and the sheriff went whistling and calling along the passages without any reverence for the mid-day sleep, so often taken by the ladies in Virginia. At length, his sister and Bessy joined us; the box was placed before the latter, and the circumstances in which it had been sent were explained.

"Will you give me a chair, Richard?" said Bessy, calmly. "I have too frequently found unpleasant things in Mr. Thornton's communications to open them without fear and agitation." She unclosed the case, when she was seated, with a hand which trembled a good deal. At the top were a number of jewels and trinkets wrapped up in silver paper, some of them of considerable value; but none of us cared to regard them much, for there were some papers to be seen below. The first of these that Bessy took out was the only one of any real importance, and it was conceived in the following words:--

"Codicil.--Whereas, my will, already declared, signed, sealed and published, on the ---- day of ---- in the year of grace, 1829, was drawn up by persons in whom I have not full and entire confidence; and, whereas, I have been lately admonished and advised, that certain clauses and provisions of that will are contrary to the laws of this state of Virginia, and may void, nullify, and render of no effect, the whole of the said will or certain parts thereof; now this is to declare, and I do hereby declare accordingly, that it is my intention that the said will shall have effect in all those clauses, provisions, bequests, demises, appointments, and all and every other particular whatsoever, which shall be consonant to, lawful and permitted by, the laws, customs, and statutes of this state of Virginia, and in no other case whatsoever; and that should it appear after my decease that any provision or bequest of my said will, dated as aforesaid, is contrary to the said laws, statutes, or customs, or any of them; then I desire and intend that any benefit, property, right, or inheritance, which might accrue, be taken or possessed by the person or persons to whom the same was, by the said will, devised, had the said provisions or bequests been lawful, shall be absolutely vested in and conveyed by my executors, named in the said will, to my dear niece, Elizabeth Davenport, to have and to hold, to her, and to her heirs, executors, administrators, and assigns, in as pure, free, and perfect right as if no other bequest or devise whatever had been made in the said will, to which these presents are a codicil; and, especially, should it be found by my executors in the said will appointed, that in regard of real estate, no alien can, within the limits of the State of Virginia, hold lands in fee simple, either by demise or of inheritance, and that, consequently, my dear nephew, Richard Conway, commonly called Sir Richard Conway, Baronet, is incapable of holding the real estate bequeathed to him by me in my said will, and that the same is liable to be escheated to the State, or else claimed by certain persons on pretence of kin to whom I do not wish the said real estate to descend, then I leave and bequeath the said real estate, previously devised to Richard Conway, to my aforesaid niece, Elizabeth Davenport, and revoke, recal, annul, and disallow the bequest previously made to the said Richard Conway."

The codicil was duly signed and witnessed, and Mr. Henry Thornton waved his hand in the air, exclaiming:--

"That settles the whole affair. There can no longer be either lawsuits or roguery, unless you two young people choose to go to law with each other, which I do not think particularly likely."

"Richard, will you go to law with me?" asked Bessy, smiling.

"Decidedly, dearest," I answered, in a low tone. "I shall bring a suit before yourself, for yourself, and even press the court for a speedy decision." She coloured a little and said;--

"Hush! You must be good and patient--unless," she added, with a light laugh, "something of very great importance requires your presence in England imperatively."

"Business of the greatest importance calls me there," I answered, following her to the door, towards which she had been retreating; "no less, dear Bessy, than the best happiness life can bestow."

"Now, I could almost tell you to go and settle that important business and then return to seek me," answered Bessy. "But I will not coquet with you, dear Richard. You have long been the arbiter of my fate. You are so still, and I will go with you where and when you like. But you must forgive me if all this agitates me a good deal. For any young girl to commit her whole happiness to another, is no slight trial; but in my case both the confidence and the trial are still more, for I leave all other friends, the scenes of my youth, my very habits of thought, and my native land, to go with you afar. But I have no doubt, no hesitation, no fear. You are now all to me, and I am now yours altogether." A tear, crushed between the long dark lashes, fell like diamond sparks upon her cheek; but I found means to bruit away; and, before I left her, the day was named. Oh that I could have you, too, with me, my dear sister, when that day arrives, were it but to make this dear girl feel that in giving herself to me she only leaves old friends to find others to whom she will be as dear; and to assure her that in a new land, and a strange home, she will not be received as a stranger. Mary, my quiet spirit, you must not smile at your brother's enthusiasm, wherever it may appear in these pages; for I intend you to own that if I have been long in choosing, I have chosen well, and chosen one whom you can, from your heart, call sister.